THE LOOT

0 ℓ 55⁻2/
0 330

Also by Craig Schaefer

The Daniel Faust Series

The Long Way Down
Redemption Song
The Living End
A Plain-Dealing Villain
The Killing Floor Blues
The Castle Doctrine
Double or Nothing
The Neon Boneyard

The Revanche Cycle

Winter's Reach
The Instruments of Control
Terms of Surrender
Queen of the Night

The Harmony Black Series

Harmony Black
Red Knight Falling
Glass Predator
Cold Spectrum

The Wisdom's Grave Trilogy

Sworn to the Night
Detonation Boulevard
Bring the Fire

THE
LOOT

CRAIG
SCHAEFER

THOMAS & MERCER

Text copyright © 2019 by Craig Schaefer
All rights reserved.

Published by Thomas & Mercer, Seattle

www.apub.com

Amazon, the Amazon logo, and Thomas & Mercer are trademarks of Amazon.com, Inc., or its affiliates.

ISBN-13: 9781542042697
ISBN-10: 1542042690

Cover design by Kaitlin Kall

Printed in the United States of America

THE LOOT

ONE

Between Logan International Airport and Spencer, Massachusetts, most of it on an old warhorse of a Greyhound bus that stank of diesel and midsummer sweat, three people eyed her olive fatigues and thanked Charlie McCabe for her service. The last was a little boy, couldn't have been older than five, who dutifully recited the words he'd been taught while his parents looked on with expectant pride from two rows down. The adults who said it got a polite and perfunctory "You're welcome." The child, she was more patient with.

"Do you want to be a soldier when you grow up?" she asked him.

He stared at his shoes. "I dunno."

"It's not for everybody," she said.

Charlie was never sure what to say when strangers thanked her. She had a vague suspicion, more often than not, that the person offering thanks was doing so out of some reflexive and imagined duty. Like she was an object on a pedestal, a symbol, not just a person who had volunteered for a tough job. Still, they meant well, and that was enough to buy a smile even if it didn't always reach her eyes.

She'd gone halfway across the world to do a job. Now it was eight years later, she was eight years older, the job was done, and the future yawned out ahead of her like a storm front rolling over a gray and endless plain. Big and empty, no signposts to mark her way. She'd become a creature of regimen, discipline, structure. Now she had absolute freedom, same as any other civilian, and no idea what to do with it.

She decided to go home. It was just a place she knew.

The bus dropped her off at the edge of nowhere. A cab took her all the way to the middle, carving a winding path through the hilly Massachusetts countryside. Big woolly elms shrouded the road, and October Glory maples spread their scarlet boughs, red as pomegranates under a darkening sky. It had been ten minutes since they'd left the highway and another ten since they'd seen any other cars on this stretch of road.

The cabbie nodded up at the gray clouds. "They say we might get a nor'easter."

"Wrong time of year," Charlie said.

He glanced at her in the rearview. He took in her neatly pressed cammies, the wispy blonde bangs poking out from under the brim of her cap.

"Nothing happens when it's supposed to anymore. Rains when it should snow, snows when it oughta rain, hot when it's supposed to be cold. Y'know what I think? The weather got weird when we started messing with the crops. The bees eat that GMO stuff; they get all confused. It's the, what do you call it, the butterfly effect." He took another look at her. "Thanks for your service."

"Uh-huh." She stared out the window.

He dropped her off on the outskirts of Spencer, on a one-house dirt road at the bottom of a tall forested hill. A crude dugout ran along the base of the hill like a World War I trench, built to catch rainfall instead of bodies. She stood at the end of a stubby gravel driveway with her olive duffel bag heavy on her left shoulder. A humid summer breeze kissed her tanned cheek, carrying the smells of cedar and fresh-cut grass. She breathed it in.

Charlie hadn't seen her father in three years.

The loose gravel crunched under her boots. Up ahead, the door-knob rattled, and the front door swung wide. She braced herself for her father's face, not sure what she'd see in his eyes. He had company, instead, letting themselves out. Two men she didn't recognize, not locals. Boston men, with scornful eyes and jackets too heavy for the summer wind. One wore a knit cap, and his red and puffy face bore a hairline scar along the stubble of his jaw. He was built like a steel piston, short and squat and hard. His partner was all gristle, tall and lumpy, like life had chewed on him for a while before spitting him back out again.

The man with the scar stared Charlie up and down, lingering longer than he had to. "Ma'am," he politely said, only meeting her eyes in passing. The other didn't say a thing, ghosting past her on the way to their car. They'd parked at the driveway's edge, arriving in a sleek black Mercedes E-Class. They left the same way. Charlie watched them drive off, her brow furrowed, until their car was a purring phantom on the dirt road's horizon. She turned back to the house.

Her father's ranch house was a mirror of the man who lived inside. It had been new once, young, proud. Now the weathered eaves were sagging, stoop shouldered, and the ivory plastic siding had faded to dirty gray. The only other car in the driveway was her dad's beater, a '93 Ford pickup with an Easter-egg pastel paint job and a back bumper held on by spools of knotted twine.

She studied the truck. She studied the house. She stalled until she couldn't pretend she wasn't stalling.

Charlie rang the bell. No answer, but she could hear footsteps shuffling around inside and the muffled blare of the television set. She pushed the button again.

The door groaned open. "I *told* you people—" the man behind the door snapped. Then he saw her face and froze like a kid caught stealing from a cookie jar. "Oh. Charlie."

"Hey, Dad."

It had been three years since her last visit stateside, but it felt more like thirty. Her father had a greasy paunch, sunken eyes, a head with more brow wrinkles than hair. He squinted at her like he'd just woken up and wasn't sure if he was still dreaming.

"Didn't know you were on leave."

She turned her ankle, boot toe rubbing on the welcome mat. "I'm, uh, not. I'm out."

"Out-out? For good?"

She lifted one hand in an awkward wave. "Charlene McCabe, newly minted civilian."

He fell silent, not sure what to say to that. Then, "How long are you gonna be around this time?"

"Just a few days," she said. "While I get my feet back under me. Look, I don't want to impose—I mean, I can go to a motel—"

He stepped aside and nodded her in. "Guest room's still yours."

He shut the door behind her, sealing her in the dusty mustiness of the ranch house's living room. She could barely see the space for all the ghosts. There was the line of pictures on the flagstone mantel, vacation photos of her, her father, her mother, one smiling and still-breathing family. Another picture of her mother, framed in an oval of brass, stood propped up on the end table next to her dad's recliner chair. Dad kept the drapes half-pulled and the lights down low, abandoning the day's potential for a tired, empty twilight.

"Who were those men?" she asked.

He sagged into his recliner. He had a tremor in his hand as he scooped up an open can of Bud Light.

"Salesmen," he said.

"What were they selling?"

"Don't know," he said. "I wasn't buying."

She let the lie drift to the floor between them, where it nestled on the shabby rug, untouched.

"I'm gonna unpack," she said.

He answered with the remote control, taking aim at the television and firing. The crowd roared for a touchdown pass.

Charlie's room—the "guest room," they'd dubbed it after she'd left home, though nothing had changed and they never had guests—was a time capsule. The dresser was occasionally dusted, the hardwood floor was occasionally swept, but it was like she'd never left. Her old clothes still lined the dresser drawers, and a scattering of outfits hung in the half-open closet, draped in plastic dry cleaners' sheaths.

She tossed her duffel onto the single bed. Then she stared at herself in the mirror and took her cap off, running fingers through her short sandy-blonde hair. The cap went on the dresser, transformed from a piece of uniform to a memento in the space of a breath.

It wasn't like she didn't have civvy clothes, most of them rolled up and filling space in her bag. She just wanted . . . she wasn't sure what she wanted. She'd done the exit interviews, the mandatory counseling, all the programs and regs intended to ease her transition back into the civilian world. It still didn't feel real, not until she took her cammies off one last time.

She hadn't been expecting fireworks and a parade, but Charlie had always thought her moment of homecoming would be bigger than this, somehow. Instead, she just rummaged through the closet until she found something she liked—a well-worn chambray blouse and a sturdy pair of khaki cargo pants—and got changed. It was just another day. She traded her boots for dusty white sneakers. Her old clothes landed in the laundry hamper. Her boots went in the closet, neatly lined up against the baseboard.

"All right," she told her reflection. "I can make this work."

She stood on the edge of the living room. Her father didn't look at her, lost in the television's glow. She couldn't stop seeing the faces of the men on her father's doorstep. They weren't salesmen.

"Dad? If . . . if you were having trouble with anything, with anybody, you'd tell me, right?"

"Mm-hmm." He sipped his beer. "So. When you got discharged, they do anything for you? Help you find a job or something?"

She held up her phone. Not sure why. He wasn't even looking at her. "I have to go talk to some people. I've got interviews. I'm gonna go outside, see if I can get a cab out here or a Lyft or something."

"Take the truck," he said. "Keys are in the bowl on the kitchen counter. There's a spare set of house keys on the ring too."

"Are you sure?"

He shrugged. "I'm not going anywhere. Stop at the packie on your way home, pick me up some Bud? I'm running low."

"Sure," she said. "Anything else? You need food, groceries?"

"I got food."

Charlie glanced through the open archway into the kitchen. Pizza boxes, smeared with cold grease, formed a leaning tower beside a sink filled with unwashed dishes.

"Sure, Dad. Thanks."

She scooped up the keys, cold and hard against her hand, and left.

The truck seat's springs groaned under her, jutting against the sun-bleached vinyl bench, and the door rattled like it might fall off. Rust flakes showered down onto the gravel drive. She held her breath, said a prayer, and cranked the engine. It coughed to life on the third try. The truck lurched backward, out onto the dirt road, and jolted her hard against the seat belt as she shifted into drive.

Charlie sat there a moment, out on the open road with the truck wheezing, as she realized she didn't have anywhere to go.

That wasn't true, though. She needed cash, and she needed to find out what kind of trouble had been hanging out on her father's doorstep while she'd been gone. She thought back to her CO's advice, the last thing he'd said to her before she'd gotten onto the plane.

"Don't get slow, McCabe. Don't get lazy. I'm gonna check on your ass next time I'm stateside, and you'd better believe you'll catch ten shades of hell if I think you got lazy."

"Yes, sir," she'd said, holding his steel gaze.

"I want you to remember something: no matter what they tell you, you might stop wearing the uniform, but you never stop being a soldier. And a soldier needs a mission."

"Sir?" she'd said.

"This mission is over," he'd told her. "Go find a new one. Dismissed."

Two

The Crab Walk wasn't anyone's idea of paradise, not even for the handful of regular barflies who dutifully bellied up by noon and stayed around until half past closing time. It was just an all-American back-roads dive bar, a low-slung shack where the eaves were draped with boat netting and petrified starfish. The vintage Seeburg jukebox was stocked with seventies classic rock, a rotation that never changed and never would, and the humid air smelled like stale beer and oversalted peanuts.

It was already dark when Charlie's pickup rumbled into the parking lot, finding an open spot at the end of a row of beaters and rust buckets. As she jumped down onto the asphalt, Charlie cast a gimlet eye at a shiny new Escalade straddling a pair of parking spots, one of them marked as a handicapped space. Definitely not a regular. She saw that someone had already done the sacred duty of scraping a key along the paint on the driver's side door. She nodded in approval at the display of street justice and pushed through the tavern doors like a gunfighter.

Lynyrd Skynyrd blared on the jukebox, and a well-worn cue cracked against the break, sending colored balls scattering across the scuffed green felt of the Crab Walk's single pool table. Half the chairs were full—half was a good night for this place—and nobody gave her a second glance as she made her way over to the bar. Nobody but the bartender, who nearly dropped a plastic pitcher of beer when he caught a glimpse of her face under the dim electric light. He slapped the pitcher down and waved her over.

"Ho-lee—*fuck*," Dutch shouted over the music. "Charlie Mac, in the flesh."

"Alive and kicking," she said.

Dutch stood six feet five in his steel-toed boots and wore every hard year on his deep-lined face. He sported muscles like iron cables under his gray tank top, faded tattoos standing out on his weathered skin: a snarling devil dog on one bicep and a globe, anchor, and eagle on the other. He came out from around the bar and swept her into a bone crusher of a bear hug.

"How long you back for, anyway?"

"How long's forever?" she asked.

He stared at her with new eyes. Nodding, slow.

"You're out, huh?"

"Just like you taught me." Charlie steepled her fingers and narrowed her eyes. "I entered the suck. I embraced the suck. I allowed the suck to pass through me and became one with it."

He put a fatherly hand on her shoulder. "And now, you have transcended the suck. Well done, my Padawan apprentice."

Dutch turned and snapped his fingers at a barfly perched on the closest stool.

"Hey, Lester. Make way for a homecoming vet, huh?"

The barfly gestured at his pint glass. "I ain't done."

"I ain't asking. Take it over to the cheap seats."

He cleared off. Charlie slid onto the stool while Dutch stepped back behind the bar.

"Beer me," Charlie said. "Something homegrown. I haven't had anything local since . . ."

She trailed off, counting the days, and he picked up the slack. "Three years, two months, and change. And put your damn wallet away—you know the house rules. You don't pay the night before you ship out; you don't pay the night you come home."

"All others pay cash at all times," she recited. He gave an approving nod and reached under the bar. A peal of crowing, drunken laughter rang out over the guitar riffs of "Sweet Home Alabama." Charlie glanced over her shoulder. College kids, townies with trust funds, crowded around a table and compared credit cards. She'd identified the occupants of the double-parked Escalade.

"Tourists," Dutch muttered. He popped the cap on a bottle of Mean Old Tom and slid the stout her way. "Here, this'll put hair on your chest. So what are you doing back *here*? I mean, what'd they do, give you a plane ticket and kick you to the curb?"

Charlie tossed back a swig, half smiling and half wincing at the bitter taste. "Nah, the army's really good about that. I had to do this career-counseling track, all this postmilitary planning. They actually had job fairs. Like, at the base, civvies coming around to pass out business cards and brochures."

"Didn't see anything you liked?"

"Sure. I got a job in Biloxi. Entry-level paralegal working for a lawyer's office."

"When do you start?"

"Today," Charlie said. She tilted back the bottle.

"This ain't Biloxi."

"Nope," she said. "And I'm not some ambulance chaser's secretary either. I almost went. Almost. And I was standing there in the airport stateside, about to make my connecting flight, and I just . . . didn't. I changed up my ticket and came home. I was like . . . who do I even know in Mississippi? Is this what I want? To start my life over in some town I've never been in, in a career I don't care anything about?"

"So what do you want?" he asked her.

"Figuring out that I wasn't going to Biloxi—that was step one of my cunning plan for reintegrating into society. This is step two, which is the part I'm a little hung up on. I figured I'd come home for a few days, try to get my head sorted out."

"Good a plan as any."

One of the college kids shouted over from his table. "Hey! Barkeep! Can we get another round over here?"

"In a second," Dutch called back. He lowered his voice and rolled his eyes. "'Barkeep,' Jesus. 'Prithee, yon sirrah, thank thee for gracing my humble tavern.' So . . . let's draw up a plan of attack. What's your real hang-up here? Moving to a strange city or working behind a desk?"

"Can I say both? Mostly the desk. If I can get used to Afghanistan, I can get used to Biloxi." She frowned. "Three weeks ago I was crouched at the side of a road, at the edge of a province whose name I couldn't even pronounce, sweating buckets inside an eighty-pound bomb suit. I was crouching over this IED, some Frankenstein contraption one of the local assholes built from a pressure cooker, rusty carburetor parts, and some leaking explosive glop that was probably brewed from fermented goat shit. And dealing with that, making it safe, was my job. For the better part of a decade, that was my job. Now I'm supposed to . . . what? Pretend none of it happened? Like I can sit in a lawyer's office and answer phones all day, like a normal person?"

"Nobody said it'd be easy. But look, you've got help, if you reach for it. It was a different time when I came home. A different war. People weren't lining up at the airport to thank us for serving, you know?" Dutch gave her a close look. "It's easy to land the wrong way when you come home. Easy to hit the skids. I did, and it took me a long-ass time to claw my way back to standing upright. I don't want to see you making my mistakes. You're smarter than that."

An AC/DC song revved up on the jukebox. One of the trust fund kids shouted over the music. "Hey, Grandpa! Can we get another round or what? Paying customers over here!"

Dutch sighed and reached for a pint glass.

"Excuse me one second," he said. "I gotta spit in another round of beer."

"Don't do anything on my account."

"Won't be. Just my general sense of decorum. One more thing to noodle over: Are you home because it feels like the right place to be, or are you home because you've got unfinished business to take care of?"

He left her alone with her thoughts and the music and her bottle of stout. She tapped her bottle against the sticky, varnished bar in time to the beat until Dutch came back around again.

"Last time I saw you," he said, "was at the funeral."

"I know."

"You were out the next day."

"They needed me back," she said.

"They didn't need you that bad."

She shifted gears. "Does my dad still come around?"

Dutch shook his head. "He did; then he didn't so much; then not at all. I ain't seen him in a year, maybe. He either quit drinking or does his drinking at home."

Charlie held up two fingers. "Door number two. Bonus question: You hear if he's into anything he shouldn't be?"

Dutch's unkempt eyebrows knitted tight. "Such as?"

"Such as a couple of guys from the city, guys with scars and scuffed-up knuckles, paying him a social call."

His eyes darted to one side and took in the faces around them. Just a quick, furtive check as he reached down and came up with another two bottles of stout. He opened one for her, one for him.

"Treat this like a top-priority intel briefing," he said.

"Secondhand, out of date, and probably wrong?"

"There you go. You know your dad always had a thing for the sports book."

Charlie frowned. "He's gambling again?"

"Someone said that someone said he is. You know how it is. Small towns. Anyway, unconfirmed word is he got in a little too deep."

"He's retired and living on his factory pension," Charlie said. "How deep could he possibly get?"

"Deep as his bookie *lets* him get. And before you ask, no, I got no idea who he's placing bets with. Point is your houseguests are probably debt collectors. They didn't hurt him, did they?"

Charlie shook her head. "No, he wasn't bruised. He just looks . . . he looks tired, Dutch."

"He's been through a lot."

He was kind enough not to add the word *alone*. He didn't have to. She heard it, loud and clear.

"I'll do a little digging," she said. "Sort it out. Meantime, I've gotta find a source of ready income, or this is my last beer for a while. Also, you know, I need to pay for food and a roof over my head. That too."

"You ever think about security work?" he asked.

"What, like a mall cop?"

"No, like bodyguard work. I know a guy in town, Jake Esposito; he runs an outfit called Boston Asset Protection. It's piecework, contract jobs whenever he needs extra hands, but the pay is decent, and he likes hiring veterans. Not out of the goodness of his heart either. He wants to work with professionals who can follow orders and get shit done. The job requires a certain temperament, you know? Gotta be able to simmer down a situation before it boils over, but also be ready to get rough if and when you have to. Half diplomat, half boxer."

"Sounds like my old job."

Dutch flashed a yellowed smile. "Don't it, though? It ain't a desk at least. Sound like something you might be interested in?"

Charlie eyed her bottle and smiled.

"Yeah, what the hell. Could be fun."

Their bottles clinked. Dutch rummaged in an old Rolodex, tugged out a half-wrinkled card on faded cream paper, and passed it over. The card had an address in Copley Square in stark black type.

"I'll call him and let him know I'm vouching for you. So make me proud, kid. Go on over tomorrow; he'll put you through your paces."

"Thanks, Dutch. Thanks for giving me a shot."

He tossed back a swig of beer and ran the back of his hand across his whiskers.

"Hell, I'm not *giving* you anything. Impressing the man, that's on you. Just stay sharp. Jake's . . . got his eccentricities, is all I can say. He doesn't hire brain-dead gorillas in suits, either; tough only goes so far in that line of work. He's looking for folks with at least as much wit as they've got muscle."

"What's he going to do," Charlie asked, "make me solve math problems?"

He regarded her with a faint, impish gleam in his eye.

"Just stay sharp, kid."

THREE

Charlie's father was asleep by the time she puttered into the driveway. The pickup gave a last melodramatic cough as she turned the key. Her dad was in his recliner, legs up, television tuned to a home-shopping channel. She turned off the TV and doused the lamp. He snored through it all. She lugged a case of Bud Light into the kitchen and stashed it in the fridge before padding up the hall to her old bedroom.

She stowed everything from her duffel bag, sorting her dresser's top drawer neat and tight. Socks and underwear in razor-straight rows, shirts folded, a life in compressed order. She took down linens from the hall closet and made the bed tight enough to bounce a quarter off the fitted sheet. Good enough. Then she stripped down, slipped under the covers, and tried to sleep.

Tried to.

Maybe it was the house; maybe it was all the changes; maybe it was just too damn quiet. The silence of the countryside was an oppressive, heavy thing. She expected engines, aircraft, the machinery of a military base in constant motion. All she got was the trilling drone of crickets outside her window and a tidal wave of bad memories to see her through to the dawn.

Charlie finally found a few hours of shut-eye. Then the first rays of dawn speared into her eyes and forced her out of bed. She groaned, rolled out from under the covers, waking up as her feet touched down. She pulled on a pair of gray sweats and went for a run.

Two miles up the road, two miles back, her trainers pounding the muddy roadside as she fought her way up a towering hill. It was a cool morning, and a light fog drifted through the trees like strings of gossamer smoke. Charlie hated running. She hated it right up until she hit the wall of endurance and burst through, feeling the endorphins flood her body, a chemical high that mingled with the burning in her lungs and the ache in every muscle. Tomorrow she'd hate it all over again. This was her before-coffee, before-conscious-thought routine, had been for years whenever she was at liberty to do it. She couldn't argue with the results; running had kept her fast and lean, good traits for a soldier standing five feet two.

Her father was awake by the time she got back. He ate cold leftover pizza off a paper plate, silent in the glow of the television screen.

"I have to go into town," she said. "Got a job interview."

"Take the truck," he told her.

Boston traffic was a full-contact sport. The city was an hour east, a straight shot down the I-90 corridor, and it didn't take long before Charlie's knuckles turned white on the steering wheel. The striped lines on the pothole-riddled pavement were more suggestions than rules, and trucks strong-armed each other to fight for exit lanes off both sides of the road. Charlie took exit 22, got off on Stuart, and cruised through the streets of Boston's Back Bay as she hunted down the address on the rumpled business card.

She realized, as she slowly rolled through a sluggish intersection, that she was still in Afghanistan.

Her eyes were in ten places at once but perfectly focused everywhere they landed. The trash can by the roadside. The man with his head ducked against the wind, walking too close to the curb. Every open window, every rooftop perch that might hide a sniper. Consciously, she knew she was home. She wasn't taking point in a convoy, watching for IEDs and suicide bombers; she was driving her father's battered pickup truck and going for a job interview. She was safe now. Deep in the marrow of her bones, though, in the training and habits she'd internalized for the better part of a decade, she couldn't accept that. Her mind and body had been taught to survive in a land that wanted her dead. She couldn't turn it off like a light switch.

She wondered if she ever would.

Charlie found the address on Newbury. She wasn't sure what she'd been expecting; the idea of a security company conjured thoughts of reinforced doors and fences topped with concertina wire. Instead, the corporate offices of Boston Asset Protection sat snug along a row of placid storefronts, two doors over from a clothing boutique and a cozy-looking coffeehouse called the Thinking Cup. She found a spot to park a few streets down. She paused, checking her face in the rearview mirror, and brushed her bangs to one side. She'd done the best she could to dress up for the interview; she'd found a wool blazer the color of charcoal and a nice pair of slacks in her old closet, still sheathed in plastic from the last time they'd been dry-cleaned. She wasn't sure how a prospective bodyguard was supposed to look, so she'd opted for "professional, but not too dressy." Something to show she cared about her appearance but wasn't afraid to get her hands dirty. She'd gone for a clean pair of running shoes instead of heels, in case the interview got physical; she wasn't looking to jog another couple of miles, not with the sun up and the muggy summer heat on the rise, but she'd jump a literal hurdle or two if it'd prove she was the right woman for the job.

Just inside the front door, she saw the room exactly how her training had taught her to study a new and strange place: in slices and snapshots, a string of hard data fed straight to her brain stem. Lobby, storm-gray walls, ten feet by fifteen feet. Three exits: closed doors left and right of a curved wood desk the color of beach sand, and the glass door at her back. One other person. Late forties, frizzy black hair, and plastic-rimmed cat-eye glasses, sitting behind the desk. The air smelled like warm potpourri. As Charlie walked in, the receptionist flipped her nameplate facedown, laying it flat on the desk. Then she hid her hands behind the wood.

Charlie glanced at the flat nameplate, then at the receptionist. The woman smiled at her in silent expectation. No explanation for the bizarre gesture, but somehow Charlie felt she was intended to notice it. Like the woman wanted to throw her off a step and see what she'd do before they'd said so much as hello. She decided to leave the bait alone.

"I'm Charlene McCabe," she said. "I've got an appointment with Mr. Esposito."

"Let's see," she said, running her finger down a notepad. "Yep, gotcha right here, sweetie. *Jake!*"

Charlie winced at the sudden shout. A box on the receptionist's desk clicked, and a man's tired voice echoed over the speaker grille.

"Sofia, please, for the love of God, use the intercom. I bought it for a reason."

Sofia cupped her hands to the sides of her mouth and shouted at the closed door on the left. "Loud and clear, boss! Can I send her in?"

A long-suffering sigh gusted over the speaker. "Please. And maybe put a fresh pot of coffee on? Don't . . . don't feel you need to reply. Just do it. Thank you."

Sofia adjusted her glasses and smiled sweetly across the desk. "You can go right in, honey."

The office behind the door was as bare bones as the man behind the desk. Jake Esposito had a bland, agreeable face and short, slicked-back hair, and he moved with meager economy. Every gesture reserved, every expression muted. He shook hands like a robot trying to pass for human, a steel grip but hesitant, like he was afraid he might crush Charlie's hand by accident. His desk was sparsely populated, just an intercom box, a phone, and an accountant's lamp. A filing cabinet and a slender bookshelf rounded out the furniture, the rest just a span of empty presidential-blue carpet and pristine walls. Jake gestured to a solitary chair opposite his, and they both took a seat.

"Dutch says you're good people," he told her, his voice measured and tinged with a Latin accent. "He doesn't give recommendations lightly, and I don't take them lightly. He said you just got out of the service?"

"Yes, sir. Army, honorable discharge. I can provide paperwork—"

He held up two fingers, cutting her off. "First thing, call me Jake. I haven't been 'sir' in a long-ass time, and I plan to keep it that way. Second, I trust Dutch more than I trust paper. He said you were a specialist."

"Yes, si—" She paused, catching herself. "Yes. I was an 89D, explosive ordnance disposal."

"Things that go boom in the night. Dangerous work. What made you pick that for an MOS?"

Charlie stared down at the desk. A light caught her eye, soft and amber, glowing on the intercom box.

"I was into electronics as a kid. Crystal radios, circuit boards . . . I guess I was sort of a nerd before it was cool to be one. So I had the baseline skills. Meant they didn't have to train me up from scratch."

"I'm fully qualified to shovel horse manure," he said. "Doesn't mean I want to volunteer for the job. There are safer and easier ways to get through a tour."

Charlie looked for a way to explain it. "I've never been much for 'safe and easy.' I'm stubborn that way. And my first week in-country . . . I saw what an IED can do, up close and personal."

Jake leaned back in his chair. He seemed to read her like the open pages of a book, written in a familiar language. "You lost somebody."

"Nobody I knew. It was this Podunk village, a few klicks outside the ruins of Chakari. Some kids were playing soccer, and . . ." She shook her head. "The thing about bombs is they don't discriminate. You have to aim a gun, aim a missile. You can't bury a bullet in the sand and kill somebody a week, a month, a year later with it. And it wasn't like the Taliban gave a damn: if they weren't trying to terrorize the locals into supporting them, they were punishing them for saying no. Those people didn't deserve that shit. They didn't deserve to live in fear; nobody does. So I figured I'd try to help 'em out a little. Least I could do, right?"

"I'd argue you could have done a lot less," Jake said. "So I imagine that's pretty detail-oriented work."

Charlie tapped her index finger against the side of her head. "When I wasn't in the field, I was training for the next time out. My CO always said that the detail you miss is the one that kills you. The enemy was always getting trickier, craftier. Each bomb was a puzzle. No prize for second place."

She was thinking about details. The light on the intercom. The bare desk, the bare walls, not even a ghost of a hole where any art used to hang. Nothing that said anybody actually worked here.

She remembered Dutch's sly warning to stay sharp.

Cataloging the room, breaking it down into slices of data, she shot a look at the bookshelf. Neat, short rows of business-management manuals, like the set dressing for an office comedy, and not a single one of them had a creased spine or a rumple. They might as well have been wrapped in plastic. Two shelves down, a small photograph stood in an oval frame. It depicted Jake and Sofia, smiling arm in arm, lifting coconut cocktails in some tropical paradise. The picture wasn't the detail that jumped out at her. It was the position of the frame.

It was tilted so that the photo was at her eye level, facing her seat. Not facing him like she would have expected. The memento was for her benefit, not Jake's.

Jake pushed his chair back and rose to his feet. "Excuse me, I'm going to see if that coffee is ready. Can I offer you a cup?"

"I'm good, thanks."

She wasn't good. As he left her alone, shutting the door behind him, Charlie rose and padded across the office carpet. She knew this wasn't normal interview behavior—tossing your prospective boss's office for clues was a good way to lose any hope of landing the job if she got caught in the act—but this wasn't a normal interview. She kept one eye on the door, her heart pounding, as she gently, slowly slid open the top drawer of the filing cabinet.

Empty. So was the second drawer. So was the third. She heard muffled voices behind the office door. Charlie shut the bottom cabinet, wincing as it closed with a metallic clunk, and checked the desk drawers.

Nothing but dust bunnies.

Jake's voice got a little louder behind the door, a little closer. Charlie darted around the desk and dropped back into her chair just as the door swung wide.

Jake walked back in with a steaming mug in his hand, white letters on blue reading **#1 BOSS**. While he took his seat, Charlie assembled the details in her head like she was solving a Rubik's Cube. She spun and twisted the facts until they all lined up just right.

"So," he said, "let's move on."

Charlie felt the dice in her hand, ready to roll. She was about to make a gamble, a big one, and if she was wrong she'd be out on the sidewalk and still unemployed in thirty seconds. Her gut told her she wasn't wrong, and trusting her gut had kept her alive.

"Let's," she said, "but shouldn't Sofia be in here with us?"

He studied her, cagey. "Should she?"

"Sure. After all, it's her company. She's not the receptionist. She's the boss, and you work for her. Which has to be a little grating, considering she's your sister."

Four

Jake didn't answer, not right away. He let the silence hang in the aftermath of Charlie's accusation, just long enough to curdle. She knew what he was doing; he was giving her a chance to walk it back, to swallow her words. She declined and held her ground.

"Not bad. Not bad at all." He lifted his mug in a wry salute and sipped his drink. "Also, I make the coffee. Sofia's coffee tastes like dishwater."

Sofia's voice—amused, confident, and completely devoid of her ditzy-receptionist routine—echoed over the intercom.

"I heard that," she said. "Hire the girl, Jake."

"Not yet, not yet." He gazed across the desk at Charlie. His eyes were bright, looking more animated than they had since she'd first arrived. "Walk me through it."

"Okay. I knew something was up when I first walked in. Sofia flipped her nameplate down before I could read it. I'm not sure if I was supposed to see her do it or not; I'm leaning toward yes, considering the placement of the picture." Charlie pointed to the framed photo on the bookshelf. "I was meant to spot that, at least, if I was observant enough. Side by side, the family resemblance is striking. Not enough to prove anything, but I got to thinking: Why wouldn't Sofia want me to see her nameplate? Well, maybe she didn't want me to see that her name is Sofia Esposito."

Jake steepled his fingers. "Go on."

"This office is a prop. Those books haven't been opened, ever, and your filing cabinets and your desk drawers are all empty. Nobody works here."

"You searched my office?" His eyebrows lifted.

"Damn right I did," she told him. "Something was off about this place from the jump. I wasn't just going to go along for the ride and pretend nothing was wrong. Another thing my CO always told me: If you don't have the intel you need, you go and *get* the intel. Never walk into a room or a situation without your eyes wide open. Now, the intercom light was on, meaning that Sofia was listening in throughout the entire interview. And considering you made a point of calling the intercom to her attention—and to mine, indirectly—it's not like you wouldn't have noticed. So she was eavesdropping with your knowledge and permission."

"All right," he said. "Bring it on home."

"You were running the interview, but it's Sofia's call. As to the reason for all the weirdness, I can't say, but considering I was clearly intended to catch at least some of it, I can only assume this was some kind of test."

Sofia's voice crackled over the speaker again. "Hire the girl, Jake. This one might be a keeper."

He cracked a smile. "You're half-right, but the half that counts. Sofia and I are partners. We inherited the company from our dad, fifty-fifty. Thing is, I'm not much of a desk jockey, and she graduated from Wharton with an MBA, summa cum laude—"

"So I handle the business end," Sofia chimed in, "while Jake is in charge of field operations. And you're right: nobody works here. We use this office for meetings. Our real HQ is up in Cambridge. Functional, but off the beaten path and just a little too shabby for impressing the clientele. My dear, beloved brother also uses this place for messing with people's heads from time to time. It's his hobby."

"So this was . . . what, exactly?" Charlie asked.

"Your interview," Jake said. "The purpose of this exercise was to test your detail skills and, just as importantly, see how you reacted in an unfamiliar, possibly dangerous situation. If you hadn't noticed anything was off about this place, or worse, if you did notice but decided not to say or do anything about it, I'd be politely thanking you right about now and showing you the door. Charlene . . . can I call you Charlene?"

"I go by Charlie," she said.

"Charlie. Do you know the length of the average assassination attempt?"

She shook her head. "Not long, I'd guess."

"Five seconds. There've been studies on this. Five seconds, from start to finish. And at the end of those five seconds, there's usually a fresh body on the floor. The assassin or the target. But just like at the poker table, people have tells. Spotting those tells, those little giveaways that let you know trouble is coming, can save a client's life."

"Half noticing, half doing something about it," Sofia added. "Most people freeze up in a crisis situation. They turtle and hope somebody else will take care of the problem."

"You didn't." Jake's smile grew. "You searched my office. I *love* that. Usually when I pull this bit, the best I can hope for is a verbal confrontation. You actually went digging for more facts before you laid your cards on the table. Anyway, you've got the right background and the right attitude; everything else can come with experience. I'd like to give you a test."

"Another test?" she said.

"An on-the-job kind of test. We've been hired for a corporate event tomorrow night, and I'm shorthanded. Party security, basically a milk run, nothing too exciting, but it'd be a perfect chance to try you out. See if you fit the job, and if the job fits you."

"Tomorrow?" Charlie blinked. "Don't I need, like, training and certification—"

"Security *companies* have to be certified in Massachusetts," Sofia said over the intercom. "Employees just need a five-thousand-dollar surety bond, which . . . hold on, typing . . . you will have, in about twenty minutes. I assume you haven't committed any felonies or crimes of moral turpitude?"

"Not to my knowledge."

"Well, you're still young. There's plenty of time."

"What about a gun?" Charlie asked.

"Eventually, yes," Jake said, "but not for tomorrow night. Our people generally only carry firearms at the client's request or if I think a situation looks dicey. Otherwise, I prefer less-than-lethal weapons—less potential legal liability if things go off the rails. Do you have an LTC?"

"I had a license to carry before I shipped out, but it has to be expired by now."

"Get your paper reupped and let me know. We reimburse on firearm purchases."

"To a *reasonable degree*," Sofia said. The sudden sharpness in her voice, and the pained look on Jake's face, told Charlie that someone had abused that privilege recently. Possibly Jake.

"We'll talk about that later," he said. "Realistically, most of our clients don't need protection from anything but the paparazzi. We're there to sell an image. On that note, dress code: any given event might be classified as formal or informal, and *informal* still means the sharper end of business casual. You're not just representing the company; you're representing our client. Regardless of the dress code, always wear shoes you can move in. Assume you'll be on your feet for at least an eight-hour stretch at a time, maybe longer."

"And tomorrow night?" she asked.

"Informal. What you're wearing is fine. Always wear a blazer or a suit jacket: whether you're carrying a weapon or not, you should look like you *might* be. We like to keep the bad guys guessing."

"Any chance of a company car?" Charlie asked, picturing her dad's pickup in a high-speed chase.

"Sure," Jake said, "but there's only one, and it's mine. I'll tell you up front: this isn't a high-paying career. Yeah, it's better than uniformed security, but you won't be living the lifestyle of the rich and famous."

"I'm used to sleeping on cots and eating MREs while people try to kill me on a regular basis. Three square meals and a little spending cash in my pocket, I'm a happy woman."

"That's what I love to see," Jake said. "Low expectations. I mean, an adventurous can-do spirit. Combined with low expectations."

Sofia cleared her throat. "We do offer health insurance after your three-month probationary period. Also, a 401(k) plan, nonmatching."

"Come on out to our place in Cambridge tomorrow morning," Jake said. "Ten a.m. sharp. We'll get you set up, introduce you around, and you can sit in on the briefing. After that, I'm going to pair you up with one of our veteran operators; tomorrow night your job is to shadow him, learn, and do what he does. Think you can handle that?"

Charlie smiled. This felt all right. Better than a desk job in Biloxi.

"I can definitely handle that."

Charlie went shopping. She told herself it was just common sense: she was going to need more outfits for work, after all. And she'd earned a little retail therapy. Tapping into her savings just this once couldn't hurt, especially since she was about to have a steady income again. There was still the matter of passing her "test" tomorrow night, but she had a good feeling.

For the first time since leaving the service, she had a good feeling about life in general. Nothing to the job but to show up, do her very best, and prove what she was capable of. Same thing she'd been doing for years.

Wandering the racks of a discount outlet, Charlie chose her new professional wardrobe with an eye for utility. Blacks, beiges, subdued colors that worked in combination, and nothing that would make her stand out in a crowd. Slacks she could run in, breezy blazers that could cover a shoulder holster without looking lumpy. She ran her thumb over fabric, checking its weight, testing seams; whatever she bought was going to have to last a while.

She came in under budget. *One little treat*, she told herself. She cradled her bags in the crook of her arm while she lingered in a sunglass kiosk. Bodyguards on TV and in the movies always had imposing sunglasses. A clerk watched her move from pair to pair as she checked her reflection in a narrow mirror.

"What are you looking for?" the clerk asked her.

"Something stylish, classic, with an understated 'don't mess with me' kind of vibe."

He handed her a pair of jet-black sunglasses.

"Wayfarers," he said. "You definitely want Wayfarers."

The look worked for her. She bundled her bags into the pickup truck, whispered a prayer as she cranked the engine, and shouldered her way into early-afternoon traffic. It was normally an hour's ride back to Spencer, and a sluggish clump of traffic bumped it to a ninety-minute crawl. The drive gave her time to get her priorities in line.

Step one, she thought, *ace this test and get the job. Step two, get a truck with an engine that doesn't cough like a ninety-year-old chain-smoker.*

Step three was getting out from under her father's roof. Her heart sank, just a little, as the pickup puttered into the driveway. Beyond the front door was gloom and dust, television and empty beer cans, and a past that didn't have a place for her anymore. The space between her and her father didn't feel like a gap. It was more like an invisible wall studded with razor blades; she wanted to reach out and try to touch him, but she knew it would hurt. She wasn't sure if he wanted to reach out to her, too, or if he just wasn't interested. They existed just as they had the last time they'd seen each other, three years ago at her mother's funeral: trapped in a state of polite neutrality.

At least she had a story to tell. Maybe it'd spark an actual conversation. Worth a shot. Charlie turned the keys in the front door, stepped into the gloomy, half-lit living room, and froze.

The pictures lining the mantel were down on the floor, glass shattered, frames twisted. The shards of a broken lamp decorated the grungy rug. Her father was slumped back in his recliner. One eye stared blankly at the ceiling; the other was buried under a ziplock bag filled with ice cubes.

"Dad!" She ran to his chair, crouching down at his side. "Let me see. What happened to you?"

She pried his fingers back. He had a hell of a shiner, his left eye puffy and dark. He yanked his head to one side, away from her, and pushed the bag of ice back into place.

"Nothing. It's fine."

"It is *not* fine," she told him. "What happened?"

"Fell down. Hit my head on the counter."

"Bull. Shit." She pointed at the wreckage. "You fell and accidentally trashed the pictures on the mantel and broke a lamp on the far side of the room on your way down? That's some skilled falling. You could go on the road with an act like that."

He squeezed his good eye shut. "I'm taking care of it, Charlie. It's not your business."

"I am *making* it my business," she said. "Now tell me what really happened."

—

28

FIVE

Charlie loomed over her father, hands on her hips, making it clear she wasn't going to budge until he told her the truth. He sighed his surrender.

"I . . . owe some people," he said. "I'm a little behind, that's all."

She remembered what Dutch had told her, the rumors about her father's debts.

"You started gambling again."

"Just a little," he said. "Here and there, you know? I was on a hot streak. Real hot. Then I got cold, so I was trying to . . . you know, get back again."

"How much do you owe?" she asked.

"I was so close I could taste it. Then that goddamn Bruins game, against the Senators. Who sends a center out on the ice with a bum knee? That coach oughta be drawn and quartered—"

"*Dad*," she said. "How much?"

He sagged in the recliner.

"Twenty," he said.

Charlie squinted at him. "Thousand?"

He gave a tiny nod.

"Twenty thousand dollars," she said.

"I was *up*, all right? I was fifteen up. I've never been fifteen up in my life. At that point, I mean, it's like you're playing with the casino's money; you can't lose."

"Casinos don't send people around to punch your lights out when you don't pay up. Who's your bookie?"

"I don't want you involved," he said. "This is my problem to deal with, not yours."

She threw her hands in the air. She paced into the kitchen and bit back every single word she wanted to scream at him. Breathing deep, counting to five, then to ten. Then she realized she could count to a million, and it wouldn't make her any less furious.

"I'm involved, okay? I'm not going to stand by and do nothing."

"Why not? That's about what I'd expect."

She froze in the kitchen archway.

"Meaning?"

"You know exactly what I mean," he said.

"No. I don't. Explain it to me."

"Your mother was dying."

"I was in Afghanistan."

"You could have come home," he said. "I looked it up, compassionate leave—"

"I was *fighting* a *war*."

"So was I!" he shouted, lurching upright and shooting a glare at her with his good eye.

Then he fell back into the recliner and stared up at the ceiling.

"So was I," he said, his voice soft and crumbling around the edges. "And you weren't here."

Leaden silence hung between them. Charlie folded her arms across her chest, tight. There was a more immediate problem to solve here. She was at her best when she had a problem to solve, something to fix. Guilt could wait. It always did.

"I want the name of your bookie."

"These are dangerous people, Charlie."

"I just spent eight years surrounded by dangerous people," she told him. "Some of them were trying to kill me. Some of them were on my side. And I learned from all of them. Best teachers I ever had."

"What do you think you're gonna do, huh? You go stirring up trouble, what are you gonna accomplish? You'll just make things worse."

"Give me a name."

He stared at the ceiling. She stared at him and waited. Eventually he broke.

"Jimmy Lassiter," he said. "He runs his book out of a tap house called Deano's, over in Charlestown."

"Thank you," Charlie said.

He didn't reply. She eyed the shattered ruins of the lamp on the carpet. Then she opened the hall closet and went rummaging for a dustpan and a broom.

Her father wasn't going to clean up. She'd have to do it for him.

Deano's felt like it might have been classy, once, but the owners had either stopped caring or just given up along the way. The brass railing of the nearly empty bar was grimy with fingerprints, and the mirror behind the rows of bottom-shelf booze hadn't been dusted in a dog's age. Sickly ferns dangling from wicker planters wilted like the hopes and dreams of the handful of drunks who called this place home. The sun was setting outside, sizzling in the midsummer sky, and the dirty gold light through the plate glass windows turned the narrow bar into a muggy, murky cavern.

Charlie didn't know what the bookie looked like, but she knew the two men loitering in the back of the bar. Her father's unwanted visitors. The squat, piston-built man with the scar along his jaw looked her way and elbow nudged his buddy. The other man, tall and lumpy and vulture eyed, stared her down as she strode toward them.

They were standing guard over the last booth on the end, a seat with one occupant. He was massive, almost as wide as he was tall, poured into the padded vinyl booth and filling it out like his gut was made of liquid. He had a bib tucked into the neck of his tailored shirt, diamond links glimmering in his folded french cuffs, and a twenty-four-ounce slab of porterhouse steak laid out in front of him.

"Jimmy Lassiter?" she asked.

"Maybe," he said, his Boston accent tinged with more than a trace of native Ireland. He looked her up and down. "Who's askin'?"

"Charlie McCabe. I'm Harry McCabe's daughter."

Jimmy's eyes gleamed. He wagged his steak knife at her and smiled.

"Huh, didn't know he had a kid. You here to make good on what he owes me?"

"I'm here with a question."

She turned to his two thugs and glanced between them.

"I want to know who blacked up my dad's eye."

The tall one stepped up, getting into her space. He had over a foot of height on her, and at least forty pounds. He flashed a broken-toothed smirk.

"Maybe it was me," he said.

She nodded, took a step back, and pulled in her body language. Showing him she knew she was out of her league. His smile got bigger, hungrier.

Then she threw a hard right hook, twisting her hips as she put her entire body into the punch, and smashed her fist into his eye. She grabbed his wrist with one hand and his shoulder with the other, spinning him around, and kicked the back of his knee. He buckled and went down. The side of his face smashed against the table, and she yanked on his arm, wrenching it behind his back. His buddy got behind her. She heard a pistol's hammer cock and felt the kiss of cold metal against the back of her head.

"Whoa, whoa." Jimmy laughed, holding up his open hands. "Grillo, do *not* shoot this bird. We don't shit where we eat, right? C'mon. No need for the steel. Let's be gentlemen."

The man with the scar—Grillo, she assumed—pressed the muzzle of his gun harder against her skull. "Let him go," he seethed through gritted teeth.

Charlie gave the other thug's arm one last good yank—not breaking it, just showing him how easy it would have been—and unclenched her grip. She stepped back. So did Grillo, but he kept the pistol, a cheap, janky revolver with walnut grips, loose in his hand. The bartender gave them an uneasy look, but he didn't pick up the phone. Jimmy might not have been the owner, but it was clear who ran this place. The tall man glowered at her as he stood up straight. He clamped a hand to his eye and sulked.

"Goddamn, Reyburn." Jimmy snickered and sawed off a hunk of steak, popping it between his wormy lips. He talked while he chewed. "You just got *jacked*, son. What hurts more, your face or your pride?"

Reyburn stared at the floor and grumbled something Charlie couldn't quite make out. Jimmy looked her way, seeing her with fresh eyes.

"And you. Feisty, I'll give you that."

"I'll give her more than that," Grillo muttered. He glared daggers at her, his gun hand twitching.

"Leave her be," Jimmy said. "She's defending her old man. I respect that. Reminds me of when I was back in short pants. This kid on the playground, Fergus Brogan, biggest kid in the whole damn school, he called my old man a faggot. Now, I knew I was gonna get my ass kicked, but I still had to make him answer for it. It's what you do. That's what family is."

Reyburn looked thankful for any chance to change the subject. "Did he? Kick your ass?"

"Sure." Jimmy chewed on another hunk of steak. "He put me in the infirmary. Course, once I got out, I waited for him on the way to school with a bike chain in my fist and jumped him in an alley. I took one of his eyes out, broke his spine, and put him in a wheelchair for life. I still send him a card every year on the day it happened, to commemorate the anniversary, just so he doesn't forget who did it to him. And in every card, I write the same thing: *This didn't have to happen to you. You chose this fate.*"

He looked back to Charlie, thoughtful now.

"We all choose our fates. Now, you traded a shiner for a shiner. That seems fair to me. Like you've done your familial duty. No more could be expected of you by any reasonable person. So now would be a real good time for a smart-looking lass like you to walk away."

Adrenaline surged through Charlie's veins, and her heart pounded a jackhammer beat against her rib cage. That old familiar rush of sudden violence and the aftermath. She kept her breathing as slow and steady as she could manage and pressed her hands to her sides to keep them from trembling. He was right. She'd just had a gun to the back of her head, and her situation could swing from bad to terminal in the blink of an eye if Jimmy's patience ran out.

Still, she held her ground.

"Nobody touches my father," she said. "I want that understood."

Jimmy reached for a bottle of A.1. He spanked the bottom of the bottle, drowning the rest of his porterhouse in a torrent of glistening sauce.

"Your father owes me a lot of money."

"And he'll pay it," Charlie said. "Every cent he owes you. Fair is fair. But nobody lays a hand on him. And you don't take any more bets from him either."

Jimmy shook his head at the steak. "The latter is not an issue. Man owes me twenty g's; he's cut off until such time as I see the money."

"And after," Charlie said. "He's done placing bets with you. For good. If he calls, you don't pick up the phone."

"I don't think you understand just how patient I've been with him up until now. Plus, you need to appreciate the greater issues in play. The dynamics of this little cottage industry I'm proud to represent."

"Do tell," Charlie said.

Jimmy speared a chunk of steak with his fork. He waved it like a conductor's baton while he spoke. Driblets of sauce rained down on the plate like blood spatter.

"My professional reputation is in question," he told her. "People watch; people hear things. Now, I let a guy skate forever on a twenty-grand debt? I look weak. And when I look weak, that's when the wolves start circling, looking for their shot at taking me down. Hell, you think your old man is my only customer? I got two hundred names in my little black book, and half of 'em owe me. Now, they hear about me going soft on a fellow gambler, they're *all* gonna stop paying me, and then where would I be?"

"Looking for an honest job?" she said.

Jimmy snorted. He leaned over and poked Reyburn in the side.

"You believe the mouth on this lass? *Honest job.*"

"Regular fuckin' comedian," Reyburn said, still cupping a hand over his eye. "Oughta try doing stand-up."

Jimmy's smile vanished as he locked eyes with Charlie.

"It's not about your old man. I'm protecting my name and my livelihood here. I feel for you; I really do. This isn't personal. But the best I can do for him is ten days. Ten days from today. And if I don't have twenty thousand dollars in my hand, cash, at the end of those ten days, he pays the interest with a kneecap. If I don't have it at the end of the next week, he pays with his other kneecap. And then we have to start getting creative."

Six

Charlie felt her father's burden weighing her down, like Jimmy Lassiter had just strapped a giant hourglass made of lead to her shoulders. Ten days of sand, slipping away grain by grain.

"Ten days," she echoed, as if making sure she'd heard him right.

"Best I can do," Jimmy said. "And that, you're only getting because I like you. Now, far be it from me to tell anyone how to live their life, but may I be so bold as to offer a suggestion?"

"I'm listening."

"Don't help him. Don't save him from himself. All you're doing is delaying the inevitable." He poked his fork at her. "You don't want to hear this, but you need to face the facts. Your father is a bum."

"He has a problem," Charlie said. "An addiction. But he can get better. He used to *be* better—"

"Uh-huh. Until he wasn't anymore." Jimmy pointed at his face. "You got eyes like mine. See, my dad, his love was the bottle. Same beast wearing a different mask. I bet you missed a few meals as a kid because your old man gambled away the grocery cash. Ever find yourself out of doors because he pissed away the rent one too many times?"

She didn't answer. He nodded, gave her a smug smile, and sawed at his steak.

"Sure you did. Don't even have to say it: I've walked the same road as you, my new friend. You need to learn what I learned. People don't change. And when you've got someone in your life who's bound and determined to drag themself down and take you with them, all you can do is walk away. Blood or no, don't be any man's collateral damage, and never fight another man's war for him. That's no way to live."

"People can change," she said. The words came out more vehemently than she wanted. For a moment, she wasn't sure whom she was trying harder to convince.

"People," Jimmy said, "act according to their natures, and nothing changes the nature of a man. I'm sure you know that old story, the frog and the scorpion?"

"Frog and the what?" Grillo asked. He still stared at Charlie like he was imagining her head on a spike, but the gun in his hand stayed pointed at the dirty linoleum. Jimmy rolled his eyes.

"Frog and the scorpion, ya ignoramus. Scorpion asks the frog, 'Hey, can you take me across this river? I promise I won't sting you.' They get halfway across, an' he stings him."

Grillo frowned. "What'd he do that for?"

"See, that's what the *frog* said. And as they're both going down, drowning in the river, the scorpion tells him, 'Mate, I'm a scorpion. The fuck did you expect me to do?'" Jimmy turned back to Charlie. "Your old man is determined to drown. He's aching for it. And it don't matter if you find the money and pay his debt this time around. It don't matter if I never cover his action again. Because this town is *full* of scorpions, and he'll go knocking on doors until he finds one. You seem like you've got a good head on your shoulders. Do yourself a mighty big favor and use it. Don't drown with him and don't drown for him."

"I'll get the money," Charlie said.

She knew, even as she said it, that she might as well have promised to walk on water. The odds were about equal.

"We all have to follow our nature." Jimmy held her gaze for a moment. "I think we're done here, don't you?"

Jimmy watched her leave. She looked like she had something else to say, and she was smart enough not to say it. Not respectful, not scared either. Smart.

"You shoulda let me pop her," Reyburn said.

Jimmy studied the hunk of steak on his fork.

"And by now you should know better than to tell me what I should and shouldn't do." He popped the steak between his glistening lips and talked between chews. "Got no reason to end the lass. Not yet."

"I got a reason," he said, cupping his hand over his eye.

"You got a life lesson," Jimmy said. "Leave it at that."

Grillo hovered behind his partner. "Why are we wasting our time? She can't get that kind of money, not in ten days. You know she can't do it."

Jimmy swallowed his bite. He dabbed a sauce-stained napkin at the corners of his mouth, set it down, and folded his hands.

"Life lessons all around, then."

SEVEN

The moon was up by the time Charlie came home, gleaming and gritty in the azure midsummer sky. She slapped a mosquito off her arm as her key jangled in the lock. The television was silent, and her father's bedroom door was closed. She wasn't sure if he'd gone to bed early because he was tired or because he didn't want to face her when she came back from talking to his bookie. Empty cans of Bud lined the kitchen counter; he'd been plowing through the case she'd bought the day before, pounding them down like it was his full-time job.

She went to bed too.

Sleep was a losing battle. She tossed and turned, flipping her pillow to find the cool side once her cheek had warmed it up, tossing off her top blanket, then pulling it back on again. Everything was too hot or too cold, too scratchy, too stiff. Normally, none of that would even register with her; she'd spent nearly a decade roughing it.

Seething in silent frustration, she realized it wasn't the bed keeping her awake. It was the quiet. The soft chorus of crickets trilling outside her moonlit window had no power to lull her off to dreamland. She needed engines and boot steps . . . the buzz of a world in constant movement.

She needed to tire herself out. Charlie tossed the sheets aside, rolled out of bed, and tugged on clean sweats and her running shoes. She let herself out as quietly as she could. Then she stretched for a minute, bending deep and feeling her calves burn as her fingertips brushed her toes. She hit the open road.

She jogged along desolate country lanes, no particular place to go, just a gray smudge under the shadowed canopy of leaves. Up ahead, amber eyes flashed in the dark. A doe, touching one timid hoof to the dusty road, turned and sprinted into the underbrush. Charlie slowed down to catch her breath. She watched the leaves rustle in the doe's panicked wake.

For all the weight on her mind, she ran without thinking much at all. Her father's debt, her new job, all the challenges ahead of her—all swallowed by the cool night wind and the mingled pain and pleasure of the run. Charlie didn't have any particular destination in mind, but she wasn't surprised when she ended her one-woman race at the darkened facade of the Crab Walk. It was just past closing time, and Dutch had shepherded the last lonely drunk from the desolate gravel parking lot. She burst across an imaginary finish line and slowed to a stumbling, achy walk.

Charlie heard cans rattling around back. The wind turned her sweat-soaked clothes to ice. Breathing deep, she rounded the side of the bar. Dutch was taking out the trash, tossing overstuffed Hefty bags into a dumpster. He glanced her way.

"Heard you pounding the pavement from a quarter mile away. What, your old man's truck finally die for good?"

"Fresh air and exercise," Charlie panted.

"Overrated and *highly* overrated."

"Couldn't sleep."

"Too quiet," Dutch said.

He studied the angles of her face like he was looking in a mirror. Behind him, mosquitoes buzzed around a hard white light, set in a cage above the bar's back door. Dutch jerked his thumb over his shoulder.

"C'mon in," he said. "Keep me company while I clean up."

She gazed across the dark, lonely taproom and bellied up to the empty bar. Dutch slid a bottle of beer along the lacquered wood, grabbed one for himself, and tossed back a swig.

"When I came back," he said, "I ended up in New York City. This was *old* New York, back before Times Square went Disney. I was squatting in this one-room shit box right next to a train line. The noise from the tracks helped. If I'd landed here first, out in the sticks, I'd have gone crazier than I did."

"Do you ever get used to it?"

"You ought to be in Boston," he said. "Get some city around you. Living out here is like being a turtle without a shell."

Charlie contemplated her beer.

"Can't leave yet."

"Jake called me. Said you aced the job interview. He says you've got moxie, whatever the hell that is."

"My tryout is tomorrow," she said. She glanced at the clock on the wall. Its short, stubby hand pushed past three a.m. "Well, later today."

"You got this." Dutch wiped the bar down, swirling the smudges around with a faded blue terry cloth. "Most of their jobs are in town. Make sense for you to live closer."

She looked away from the clock. Their eyes met.

"Can't leave yet."

Dutch's weathered brow furrowed, just a little.

"How bad?" he asked.

"Twenty thousand."

He let out a long, low whistle.

"Don't suppose he has it," Dutch said.

"Don't suppose he does."

"Who's got his marker?"

"Jimmy Lassiter," Charlie said.

Dutch went back to wiping down the bar.

"*Auribus teneo lupum*," he said.

41

Charlie stared at him over the mouth of her bottle. "Meaning?"

"It's Latin. It means 'holding a wolf by its ears.'" He set the cloth down and curled his hands in front of him, pantomiming. "You hold on, you're screwed. You let go, you're screwed."

"Damned if I do, damned if I don't?"

"Pretty much wolf chow all around. Lassiter's nobody to mess with. He's connected up to the eyeballs."

"Not looking to mess with him," she said. "Not looking for anybody to mess with my dad either."

"Might not be your decision. And Harry made his choices."

Charlie drank her beer.

"I couldn't deal with it, you know?" she said.

"At least you're not lying to yourself about it."

He left the *anymore* unspoken, but she heard it clear as a bell.

"I don't know how many times Mom almost left, when I was a kid. Bags packed, car warming up in the driveway. Christmas morning, I was eight or nine—that's the one I remember most. She'd given him some money to buy me presents the week before."

"Hell of a way to learn the truth about Santa Claus."

The memory was distant enough, the hurt scabbed over, that poking it just put a bitter smile on Charlie's lips.

"The front door's open, cold wind and snow blowing in; he's literally down on his knees pulling at her arm while she's walking out, begging her. Telling her how he was two hundred up, how he was going to make this the best Christmas ever, until he went bust. Wasn't his fault. Never was."

"She didn't leave, though," Dutch said.

"We were back by dinnertime. Longest we were ever gone."

Charlie studied her bottle of beer.

"I left, though."

"Harry made his choices." Dutch picked up a tray of cut limes and scraped them into a garbage can. "He's the only one who can. And only you can make yours. That's how this works."

"You said Lassiter's connected." Charlie watched him across the bar. "You used to be too."

He glanced up at her. "You looking to earn that twenty?"

"You used to hear things. You'd get wind of, you know, odd jobs."

"That was never the kind of work you wanted."

"That wasn't the kind of work you wanted to *let* me do," she said. "Still isn't."

"I was just thinking," she said. "I mean, I'm not looking to get any blood on my hands, but if you knew something, if you knew anyone looking for skilled help—"

"You don't make twenty g's without getting your hands bloody," Dutch told her. "Nobody pays that kind of money for a victimless crime. Forget it, Charlie. That road's not yours to walk."

They fell into a restless silence.

"Does it ever get easier?" she asked him. "Sleeping."

"You know what we say about ex-Marines?"

"What's that?"

"There's no such thing," Dutch said. "Once a Marine, you're a Marine for life. Don't matter if you're in or out; don't matter if you still wear the uniform or not. Once you're in, you're in. Now, part of that's a pride thing. Corps is big on pride. Comes from being the service that does the *hard* work, you know, as opposed to certain people who joined the army so they could take a nice, easy ride on our coattails."

Charlie lifted her bottle and cracked a tired smile. "Soon as I'm done drinking, you know where you can stick this, right?"

He chuckled. "Point is there's a deeper meaning. It comes home with you. Everything comes home with you. Get enough mileage on your tires, yeah, you can kinda feel like a civilian, maybe. Sometimes. But late at night, when the world goes quiet, and you're all alone inside your head . . . that's when the memories come back and you know the cold, hard truth. You're always gonna be a soldier, Charlie. You're in for life."

"Hooah," she said softly. She tossed back the last swallow of beer.

"And you got a new job," he said. "Which I recommended you for. So don't show up to your first day of work half-asleep and make me look like an asshole. C'mon, I'll give you a ride back."

"Thanks, Dutch. For everything."

He grabbed his keys and led the way to the back door.

"You oughta move into town, Charlie. Get some city around you."

EIGHT

The headquarters of Boston Asset Protection—the real HQ, not the show office in town—was a big industrial box out in Cambridge. Out of the way and nondescript, at the end of a corporate park filled with identical big industrial boxes. Most of the park looked like warehouse space. Charlie idled at the edge of the parking lot, listening to the pickup's engine rattle as a line of semitrailers pulled out and aimed their snub noses for the highway on-ramp.

Jake met her at the front door and squeezed her hand in a firm, confident grip. Even his first handshake yesterday had been a calculated lie. She matched his style.

"C'mon in," he said. "The place isn't much to look at—we go for function over form around here—but it's home."

A small lobby waited beyond the tinted glass doors, and she saw what he meant. The reception desk and a small clutter of mismatched chairs looked like they'd come from a hotel-furniture sale, and not from the same hotel. The walls were unadorned white, the floor bare concrete. The drywall was down on the left-hand side, exposing bare wooden ribs and bundles of colored wiring.

"We're also in the middle of some renovations," he said. "We've been in the middle of renovations since 2015, though, so . . ."

The receptionist—the real receptionist this time, a woman in her early twenties with cornrows and sharp brown eyes—was busy with a phone call. She tucked the receiver between her shoulder and neck as Jake and Charlie walked by, handing out a bundle of yellow sticky notes. Jake took them with a nod of thanks.

"Amenities: We've got a conference room, armory, break room, a small gym"—he leafed through his messages, leading the way down an unadorned eggshell-white hallway—"big room with modular walls we use for training scenarios and ops planning. Got a soundproof firing range, but keep that to yourself."

Charlie tilted her head at him. "Why's that?"

"We're not zoned for it, and it isn't exactly legal. And I keep a few weapons on site for training purposes that you're not technically allowed to own in this state. But you seem cool, and I think I can trust you not to narc on me. You're not a cop, right, Charlie? You know that if you're a cop, you have to tell me so, or it's entrapment."

She almost missed a step. "I—I don't think that's really how the law works . . ."

Charlie paused, catching the faint twitch at the corner of Jake's mouth.

"You're messing with me right now, aren't you?"

"I am *absolutely* messing with you right now. About the cop thing, I mean. The firing range is real, highly illegal, and please keep it a secret."

"The firing range does not exist," said the woman poking her head through a doorway just up ahead. "Also we totally don't have an after-hours betting pool. There is no gambling happening in this establishment."

The new arrival had a swagger in her footwork as she stepped into the hallway. She squared her hips in a gunfighter's stance and took Charlie's measure. Her dark complexion had traces of Spanish and Italian blood, and she wore her jet-black hair in a functional ponytail that brushed the sharp neckline of her blazer. Charlie quietly studied her square-toed shoes, her sturdy belt—*Not ex-military*, she thought. *Ex-cop.* She took Charlie's hand in a rock-firm grip.

"Dominica Da Costa. Call me Dom. Handy tip to remember about Jake, here: if his mouth is moving, he's probably full of crap. Get used to it."

"I'm also your boss," he told her, still faintly smiling. "Just pointing that out, not for nothing."

"That's funny," Dom said. "You say that, yet it's Sofia's signature on all my paychecks."

"Keep it up, see who gets assigned to parking lot detail tonight. I hear the forecast is calling for rain."

Dom put on a face of mock dismay and rested her hand on Charlie's shoulder, instantly familiar. Charlie didn't mind. She felt at home in the banter, the same kind of friendly ball busting she got from her squad back—

—*back home*, she thought for a heartbeat, before her brain course corrected.

"I'm sorry," Dom said, "I believe protocol and tradition dictate that the shit jobs go to the new fish, until such time as they've paid their dues."

"I'm pairing Charlie here up with Beckett tonight."

"Does he know that?" Dom asked.

"He will when I tell him. Sofia ready with the briefing?"

Dom gestured to the door at her back. "Waiting on you, boss."

Jake led the way into a dimly lit box of bare drywall, where more hotel-surplus chairs formed ragged lines facing a tripod-mounted projection screen. A folding table in the back sported a Sunbeam coffee maker and pylons of disposable cups, next to an overflowing plastic garbage can. Twelve or so people were milling around, drinking black coffee. They conversed in low voices while Sofia hunched over a laptop computer. Charlie took the crowd in. Jackets, polished but well-worn shoes: quiet professionals dressed for a quiet, professional job. Mostly men. She spotted only one other woman in the bunch beside Dom,

Sofia, and herself. Jake's sister looked up, pushed her cat-eye bifocals higher on her nose, and gave a quick wave across the room.

"We ready?" she called out.

"We ready." Jake shut the conference room door. "Let's get this show on the road."

The crowd broke up, the operatives finding places and scraping chairs across the concrete floor. Dom dropped into a seat in the back row. She saved the one next to her and waved Charlie over. Sofia tapped a few keys on her laptop, and the projection screen lit up with a corporate logo: a mountain of gray iron under a sky lined with silver clouds.

"Ladies and gents," Sofia said, "this evening's job is a one-night stand. We'll be providing protection at a corporate banquet to be held at the Stark House, in collaboration with hotel security. The client is one Mr. Sean Ellis, the current president of Deep Country. Deep Country is a privately owned mining company with holdings in Kentucky, West Virginia, and Wyoming."

A hand went up in the middle of the room. Sofia gave a nod.

"Same company that lost that mine in Rockhouse last month?" the operative asked.

"Bingo, give that man a gold star." Sofia adjusted her glasses. "See, kids? Reading is good for you. For those who aren't up on current events, I'll make a long and tragic story short. Mine? Goes boom. Miners? Thirty dead. Safety standards? Nonexistent, as it turns out. Too early for a verdict, but it looks like the executives were lining their own pockets by skimping on the regulations. And so, in one fell swoop, Deep Country has gone from a nonentity to one of the most hated companies in America."

Charlie leaned closer to Dom, frowning. She murmured, "And we're protecting these people?"

Dom let out a faint snicker and whispered back, "Get used to it. Perfect angels who say their prayers at night usually don't need to hire bodyguards. We mostly work for scumbags, minor celebrities, and the occasional minor-celebrity scumbag."

"This is the company's annual employee-appreciation banquet," Sofia continued. "We're being asked to provide coverage for the entire event, but our primary is Sean Ellis. As the public face of the company, he's become a target for everyone who has an ax to grind with Deep Country, especially after a, dare I say it, *spectacularly* stupid interview where he blamed the accident on the dead foreman. Continuing a rich tradition of our clients creating their own worst problems."

Another hand went up. "What about Boston PD?"

Sofia shook her head. "The police have strongly advised Deep Country to *not* rent out a public venue, at least until the heat in the press dies down. Ellis is . . . say it with me, kids—"

"*Creating his own worst problems,*" chorused half the room in a play-fully tired drone.

"Suffice to say, the cops aren't happy, and they're not sticking their necks out either. Expect minimal presence unless we call them in ourselves. On the plus side, I had a lovely conversation with the head of hotel security. Off the record, he's less than thrilled about his boss's decision to rent the venue to Deep Country, his staff is anxious, and they're glad to have us there. They're willing to let us take point and follow our lead tonight."

"A rare and wonderful thing," Dom murmured in Charlie's ear. "Security guards can be a pain in the ass to deal with. We meet a lot of mall-cop Napoleons."

"As far as threats go," Sofia said, "if you could put emails in buckets, I'd say they were getting buckets. A lot of noise and very little signal: they've forwarded the most dangerous-sounding letters to the FBI, but I'm not convinced Deep Country's staff knows what they're looking at, and the *real* wackos could be slipping past in the clutter. I talked to the feebs in the local office, and they've got a few credible threats. That said, they passed the leads on to Boston PD, and the PD isn't inclined to share with us. They're mysteriously not returning my phone calls."

"They're hoping Da Costa ends up as collateral damage," said the first man who'd raised his hand.

Dom's eyes flashed with genuine anger, and she lurched forward in her chair. "Hey, screw you, Malloy—"

Jake held up his hands, getting between them as he paced up the center aisle. "People, people, please. Focus up, huh?"

Dom sat back and folded her arms tight across her chest, glowering. Jake moved to stand at his sister's side.

"Secondhand, we've also got confirmed threats coming out of Rockhouse and neighboring towns in every direction," Jake said. "Lots of surviving loved ones, lots of angry families. Otherwise we're dry on intel. No names or mug shots to match up with the death threats. As always, assume the worst. It's a thirteen-hour drive from Kentucky to Boston. That said, anyone willing to murder Sean Ellis in the middle of a banquet is probably willing to drive thirteen hours to do it."

A stack of paper stood beside Sofia's laptop, printed-out packets stapled in the corner like a homework assignment. Jake held up one of the packets and fanned it out.

"In addition to the hotel floor plans and duty zones, we've got bios on the company's entire board of directors. Memorize faces and names; they'll all be in attendance tonight. Bear in mind that Sean Ellis is our primary: he hired us personally, and he's expecting star treatment all the way. This is our first job for Deep Country, and they aren't going to get *more* popular anytime soon, so there could be a lot more work in it for us if we shine tonight."

He craned his neck, meeting Charlie's eyes from across the room, and pointed her way.

"Before I get into duty assignments and the nitty-gritty, yes, we have a new face in the ranks. This is Charlie McCabe, she comes highly recommended, and tonight's her shakedown cruise, so treat her right.

Everybody come on up, grab a packet, and I'll be seeing each of you for some one on one."

As the room shuffled to its feet, clumping toward the front table, Charlie gave Dom a sidelong glance. The other woman was still sitting frozen, her face a mask of stone fury.

"You okay?" she asked.

"Fine," Dom snapped. "Excuse me. Need to have a word with somebody."

Charlie watched her stomp off. Dom waded through the crowd, corralling the towheaded man she'd called Malloy. He stepped back, wide eyed, as she jabbed a rapid-fire finger against his chest. Under the buzz of conversation, Charlie strained to hear her.

"Told you," Dom said, "you keep my name out of your damn mouth—"

The rest was swallowed by the room, a dozen voices bouncing off the drywall at once. Movement caught her eye. Jake was waving her over.

"Charlie," he said, "c'mere. Want to introduce you to somebody. You're about to graduate to the big leagues."

NINE

Charlie didn't know about the big leagues, but the *big* part definitely checked out. The man standing placidly at Jake's side was a monolith of muscle in a tailored jet-black suit, the razor-sharp fabric just a few shades darker than his skin. He was groomed to perfection, his scalp so smooth she couldn't tell if he was naturally bald or shaved it without missing a single bit of stubble, and the sculpted V of a thin goatee framed his generous mouth. He had a philosopher's eyes, taking in the world around him with quiet contemplation.

"Charlie," Jake said, "meet Beckett. He's been with me since we opened our doors. Our MVP, and the best guy you could ever hope to learn from."

Her small hand disappeared inside of his. He had a gentle, firm grip and looked her intently in the eye as they shook.

"Beckett," Charlie echoed. "That a first name or a last name?"

"Never seen a reason to be particular. People should go by whatever name fits 'em best. Take you, for instance. You do look like a Charlie, but I'm betting that's not the name on your birth certificate. You're a Charlotte or . . ." Beckett tilted his head, studying her. "No. Charlene."

Jake put his hand on Charlie's shoulder. "What she is, tonight, is your understudy. I want you to show her the ropes, teach her the ground rules. At the end of the night, you tell me if you think she can hack it."

Beckett's deep eyes didn't leave Charlie's face for a moment. "She moves like ex-military. You military, Charlie?"

"Army. EOD."

"Explosives," Jake said with an eager glint in his eyes. "Like that movie, *The Hurt Locker*."

Charlie winced. "That movie was, um . . . well . . ."

Jake had prodded a sore spot, but she wasn't sure how much leeway she had with her new boss. Beckett filled in the blank for her.

"Bullshit," he said.

Charlie sighed and nodded. "Pretty much. Fun to watch, but anybody who pulled cowboy stunts like that in my unit would've been *out* of my unit in a New York minute. EOD is careful work. Detail work."

"So you've got an eye for detail, and you can follow orders," Beckett said. "That about right?"

"I like to think those are my two best skills," she said.

"Then you and me are going to get along just fine."

"Tonight, I want you to be like a . . . a duckling," Jake told her. "You know how they imprint on whoever they see and follow along? Beckett's your mama duck."

"Your gift for analogies," Beckett said serenely, "never fails to underwhelm."

"You're welcome," Jake said.

Beckett nodded at Charlie. "C'mon, Little Duck. We need to get you sorted before the festivities. Get you a proper ID card and suchlike. Let's go talk to the boss."

"Hello," Jake said, waving a hand. "Boss. Right here."

Beckett's only reply was a deep chuckle. He led Charlie across the cluttered conference room. Midway through the milling crowd of operatives, most of them studying their packets and comparing notes, Charlie glanced over her shoulder.

"He gets that a lot, doesn't he?"

Craig Schaefer

Beckett favored her with a thin smile. "Don't be fooled. Jake plays the clown, but that man's got a mind like a steel trap. Loyal as all hell too. Most of us don't stick around for the sky-high benefits and luxurious work environment. We respect Sofia, but we *follow* Jake."

"While I'm learning the lay of the land," Charlie said, dropping her voice to a murmur, "what's the deal between Dom and that guy? Malloy?"

Beckett's smile drooped at the edges, and his eyes went bitter.

"You know anything about the French Foreign Legion?"

"Only the name," she said.

"They got this tradition. It's a tradition Jake and Sofia like, and I'm fond of it myself. See, when you join up, your loyalty is to the Legion and your fellow legionnaires. *La Légion est notre Patrie*: 'The Legion is our fatherland.' Whoever you were before you signed on, whatever you did, it's all in the past. Supposed to stay dead and buried."

Charlie nodded, catching his gist. "Supposed to be."

"Some fools always feel compelled to bring a shovel to the party. Just stay out of that whole mess. If Dom wants to tell you, she'll tell you on her own time."

"And Malloy?"

"I won't partner up with Malloy," he said, "and neither will you."

Her first day on the job was more of an entry-level college course than a James Bond adventure. Charlie sat for a photo, passport style, that Sofia ran through her printer and turned into an official-looking Boston Asset Protection ID card in a smooth black vinyl case with a lanyard. Next up was memorizing the briefing packet. She reached for the top copy on the dwindling stack. Beckett stopped her.

"Not that one. Sofia printed one up special, just for you."

Charlie took the stapled pages, still warm to the touch. It didn't take long for her to figure out what was missing: the plan. She had the bare-bones layout of the hotel, data on the staff, and the contract, but

54

while her new coworkers were going over routes and schedules, she stared down at a blank map.

"We start with the basics," Beckett told her. "Have a seat and take a good long look at what you've got there."

Beckett left her to study in the corner of the briefing room. He popped in to check on her twenty minutes later.

"Books closed," he said and waited for her to shut the stack of stapled pages. "The Stark House hotel has how many entrances?"

She closed her eyes and conjured up an image of the hotel floor plan.

"There's the front entrance. Valet parking, two side-by-side revolving doors plus two handicapped-accessible doorways, all glass. Employee and service entrance on the east face of the building, ground level. HVAC service access, also east facing. There's a second service entrance for the banquet and meeting rooms: it's north facing, connecting to a stairwell and leading into the Kennedy Ballroom." She paused, certain she was missing something. "Wait. The hotel restaurant, Revel: they've got their own loading and employee entryway, isolated from the rest of the hotel, but someone could pass through the kitchen and get in that way."

He bobbed his head slow, his expression inscrutable. "You sure you got all of 'em?"

"Pretty sure."

"No windows in this hotel, huh?"

He walked away. She sagged in the stiff-backed, hotel-remainder chair and went back to studying. Of course an assailant could get in through a window: any rookie could have seen that, *should* have seen that. She doubled down and got back to work.

Beckett stepped out into the hallway.

Dom was absorbed in her phone. She didn't look up, but she sensed his arrival all the same. "And the survey says?"

"Answer hazy, ask again later."

She lowered her phone. "That's not *Family Feud*; that's a Magic 8-Ball."

"All I got on me. Right now, I'd give it a fifty-fifty. Jake talked her up to me last night, and I like her bona fides."

"But," Dom said.

"She needs to figure out this isn't the kind of job where you take your tests sitting at a school desk. I'm hoping her instincts kick in and she shows me what she's really bringing to the table. If she does, you'll see her at the banquet tonight."

"And if not?"

"Then you won't," Beckett said.

Twenty minutes later, Charlie felt Beckett looming over her. She looked up, swallowed by his shadow.

"Pop quiz," he said. "How many hotel employees will be on site during the event?"

That was harder than the last question. She worked through it one department at a time.

"The Stark isn't a big hotel. Six on valet parking, five front desk staff . . . seven security, housekeeping will be sent home prior to the event start time, and catering is being handled by a private company vetted by Deep Country."

"Who vetted the hotel employees?"

"Head of hotel security."

"So we've got two unknown quantities, catering and hotel staff, and the vetting was done out of house. You okay with that?"

She wasn't, but she had to assume it was par for the course. "We have to assume they did their due diligence."

"How many of these external employees were hired in the last couple of weeks? As in, *after* Deep Country announced the plans and location for this banquet?"

Charlie froze. She thought back through the dossier. It wasn't there. And it should have been. She should have questioned it.

"I . . . don't know. I don't have that information; it's not listed here."

He gave the tiniest shake of his head.

"You going to trust your life on somebody else's spotty intel?" He paused. "You going to trust *my* life on it? Hmm."

Charlie deflated in her chair as he walked away.

She almost walked away too. She expected growing pains, getting into a new line of work, but this felt like playing hopscotch in a mine-field. She felt like a failure right out of the gate, like she didn't have any business being here. Maybe it'd be better to quit before she embarrassed herself any worse. It wasn't like this back in—

She froze in midthought. Her fingertips brushed the glossy page, tracing a map and a missing plan of attack. That was her entire problem. She was treating this like a new career, trying to come at it with fresh eyes, but Jake and Sofia hadn't hired her for her raw potential. They'd hired her for the job she already knew how to do. A job she was damn good at.

For a man of his size, Beckett could move like a ghost when he wanted to. His sonorous voice drifted over her left shoulder. "Presume we're being stationed on front door detail. List the main points of threat."

"The doors are south facing. Angles of approach from the pedestrian sidewalk, east and west. There's an alley one hundred yards east that can conceal an assailant or a small vehicle. Across the street . . ." In her head, she was back in Afghanistan. Remembering a hundred street sweeps, running point on patrol, watching the windows for the glint of a rifle scope. The stripped-down packet in her hands didn't say one word about what was waiting on the opposite side of Tremont Street.

Charlie stood up, digging in her pockets for her father's truck keys. "I'll be back."

Beckett studied her, curious. "We ain't done here. You still got work to do."

She held up the packet.

"*This*," she said, "isn't good enough. I never trusted my people's lives to somebody else's intelligence, and I'm not going to start now. I need eyes on. Firsthand intel."

The big man broke into a toothy, pearly smile.

"Goddamn, I was hoping you'd say that. I was *starting* to get worried. C'mon, I'll ride shotgun."

Ten minutes later he was drumming his fingers on the passenger's side armrest and squinting at the pickup's rust-spotted hood. The engine coughed like it knew it was being watched.

"You gain points for initiative," he said. "You lose points for style. Not as many. Just a few."

Eyes shadowed behind her new sunglasses, Charlie glanced into the side mirror and shifted lanes.

"It's only temporary."

"In the sense that we could both die when this thing spontaneously combusts," Beckett said. "Jake says you're living out in the sticks."

"Spencer, yeah. It's only temporary."

"Careful," he said. "Too many 'just temporary' situations can add up to living in a rut real quick."

She glanced at him. "I can't be in a rut. I just got here."

"Just saying."

The Stark House was an icon of downtown Boston, a vintage monolith in shades of beige and stormy gray, with iron fixtures and window frames dating to the mid-1800s. As they rolled past in syrup-thick traffic, Charlie studied the overhanging marquee out front, the glass doors that looked in on a vast, red-carpeted lobby. Her gaze flicked to the far side of the street. University buildings sprawled beside a small public park. The tallest campus building was five stories with more facing windows than she wanted to count. The park had tree cover and thick, wild bushes: pretty to look at, and a sniper's paradise.

"Back at HQ," Beckett said, "that was just a warm-up. School is now in session. Give me your assessment of the entire security plan from the ground up."

Charlie shook her head. "But I don't *have* the plan. You gave me a blank packet."

"Correct. You're a blank, too, far as I'm concerned. So I need to know how much of this job you've already got down, and how much I'm going to have to teach you. Need to know if you can be taught. So here's your first real challenge: I want you to come up with your own plan. Right here, right now. Pretend you're the brand-new head of security and tell me how you'd handle tonight's event."

He tore his gaze from the hotel facade and looked her in the eye.

"Your answer *will* be graded."

TEN

Charlie pursed her lips as she circled the block, looking for a place to park. She thought back over the packet she'd been handed. The bare-bones intel she had, and the gulf that was missing, obvious as an ink spill.

"You want me to come up with a security plan, my first night on the job, with no formal training as a bodyguard."

Beckett wore a poker face carved from basalt. "Too tough for you?"

"I didn't say that."

"Back at HQ," he said, "you told me you never trusted the lives of your people to spotty intel. Your people. So you were, in fact, entrusted with the lives of soldiers under your direct authority. Am I understanding that correctly?"

"I was an E-5," she said. "A sergeant. So . . . yeah. I wasn't top dog or anything, but I had my responsibilities."

"What were you more concerned about? The safety of your people, or making the brass happy?"

"My people," Charlie said, no hesitation in her voice. "Making the brass happy wasn't even an afterthought. Which is probably why I never made E-6, but I wasn't trying that hard either. Didn't want to promote myself out of a job."

"And here we are. Out in the field, because you knew you needed more intel than I gave you, and you decided to go get it." Beckett shrugged. "And yet you say you don't have any training."

"That was my gut talking."

"Rules and regulations, I can teach. A reliable gut, intuition and instincts, perception, brains—those I can't. So show me what you've got."

She pulled into a parking garage a block from the hotel. The side window fought her, gears grinding as it chunked its way down, and she leaned out to pluck a peach-colored ticket from a dispensing machine. The automated security bar lifted up, and she rolled on in.

Charlie nosed the pickup into an open bay. She killed the ignition. The engine sputtered and died in the concrete gloom.

"Going off what I've already seen," Charlie said, "renting this place was stupid, a total amateur-hour mistake on Deep Country's part, and there's a good chance somebody's going to get killed tonight. They need to cancel the event. Follow me. I want to show you something."

Beckett didn't say a word as he trailed her up the street. A hot wind ruffled Charlie's short-cropped hair and blew back the tails of her blazer. She felt beadlets of sweat along her spine turning to ice as she strode toward the hotel's front entrance. A semicircle drive ran under the overhanging marquee, merging in from Tremont Street on one side and out on the other. Bellhops scurried to load and unload luggage from a short line of cars.

"For starters," Charlie said, pointing to the university buildings across the street, "this is a shooting gallery waiting to happen. That's a college campus. Most likely minimal security, easy to get access to after hours for a determined-enough bad guy, and a shooter could pick their choice of perches. We've got zero control of the situation."

"So . . . you're saying we should station a couple of watchers," Beckett said. His voice was carefully even, noncommittal.

"Not good enough. Look at this driveway." Charlie paced the length of the drive, stopping midway down. "Maybe six cars will fit, end to end. Everybody else has their ass hanging out on Tremont while the valets race to keep up. Fine for everyday use, but a major event means a major traffic problem. And that leaves our VIPs sitting stock still in cars along the street for forty-five minutes to an hour, easy. Maybe longer. These are paper pushers who . . . before Deep Country shat the bed on the national news . . . had no reason to worry for their safety, so I'm guessing not even one in twenty of them has bulletproof glass or any kind of vehicle reinforcement. Give me two assassins and a motorcycle—one to drive, one to ride and shoot—and I could wipe out the entire board of directors before they even set foot in the hotel."

A couple of midwestern tourists gave her a worried look as they clambered out of their minivan. Charlie didn't care. Her mind was racing, back in her natural element as she drew mental lines and angles of fire. Back in the sandbox, planning a convoy, measuring every risk she saw and sniffing out the ones she didn't. Beckett stood like a statue, taking it all in.

"For that matter," she said, "let's talk about the valet parking. They move the vehicles to the garage we just parked in. Did you see any on-site security? I spotted cameras, but no idea if anybody's watching the feeds. So what's stopping somebody from getting into that garage and wiring up some explosives with a remote detonator, then blowing them all at once as the VIPs leave the event? Again, total elimination, minimal risk. What's the point of focusing on protecting the *inside* of the hotel, when ninety-five percent of the danger is *outside*? Either we need a security presence in the garage—our people, because I don't see any reason to trust theirs—or we need another way of handling the traffic situation."

Beckett didn't answer right away. She searched his face like a poker player hunting for a tell, no idea how far off the map she'd wandered. He might as well have been wearing a ski mask, for all the clues his expression gave her.

"Okay," he said.

"Okay?"

"You just told me all the problems you saw. That's half the job. Other half's fixing them. It's a bad venue, lots of danger spots, but the job is the job, and they aren't going to cancel the event, so this is the battlefield we have to fight on. Give me a plan."

Charlie pursed her lips. She stared at the revolving doors, thinking back to the floor plan in her briefing packet.

"First off, let's focus on the client. Jake said that our number one priority is keeping this Sean Ellis guy safe. The rest of his board is priority two. Ellis is the one getting death threats, by name. Now, the other guests, they're way lower on the totem pole. A motivated assassin is going to want the biggest fish they can catch, right?"

"Go on."

"There's an employees-only lot around the side of the building," Charlie said. "According to the map, it's isolated by a private alleyway and a security gate. Minimal exposure. It was built to keep the staff's cars out of sight and give them access to their jobs, not to look pretty, which has the added benefit of making it a hard target for a sniper. We bring Sean and his board in that way and station constant coverage on their vehicles to keep them from being tampered with during the event. That entrance connects to a staff-only stairwell and opens onto the Kennedy Ballroom. We can have the VIPs in place, at the banquet, before a single guest even passes through the lobby."

"Still listening," Beckett said. "And the other guests?"

Charlie looked up and down the valet drive, then to the revolving doors and the cavernous lobby beyond.

"Nothing we can do about the traffic jam on the street, but that's okay. Our big concern here isn't the safety of the guests; it's making sure nobody with bad intentions slips through pretending to *be* a guest. We can make it easier by setting up three queues inside the lobby proper and cordoning it all off—velvet ropes, maybe, like at a nightclub. Three two-person teams checking the list and invitations, six sets of eyes on everybody coming in. We can process them faster that way and be safer at the same time, as opposed to the current plan, which has just two people standing outside the doors and checking all the invitations one at a time."

"Huh," Beckett said. His expression was still a maddening cipher. "Anything else?"

"One thing. Revel, the in-house restaurant: it's got a service entrance through the kitchens, and that's exactly how I'd try to penetrate security if I was a bad guy. We should put somebody in the kitchen just to keep an eye on the door with a staff list, making sure only real employees get in."

Beckett rubbed his chin. He scrutinized her, looking her up and down, and nodded.

"Good catch on that one. I actually missed that in my first write-up, and Jake caught it. Just goes to show, even pros slip up now and again."

She saw something in Beckett's eyes. The faintest, slyest hint of a smile.

"So you're saying . . . ," she started, uncertain.

"I'm saying your plan is pretty damn close to the real deal. Using the employee lot and bringing the VIPs through the Kennedy Ballroom? Nailed it."

"So what now?"

"Now you get a shot at the real thing," Beckett said. "Keep it together, you might have a job at the end of the night." He glanced at his watch, a square of polished brass on a thick leather strap. "Makes my job a lot easier. We got some time before the festivities begin. I'm thinking about brain food. You like sushi?"

Charlie blinked. "I . . . guess? I mean, I haven't had a lot of it."

"There's this place two blocks up; the chef's an old buddy of mine. C'mon, I'm buying."

Eleven

Charlie and Beckett sat side by side at the end of a sushi bar. The restaurant was the size of a shoebox, done up in warm and buttery wood. The two white-garbed chefs behind the bar raised their hands and shouted a greeting to Beckett as they walked in the door, and he responded with a burst of rapid-fire Japanese. Charlie's eyes bounced like a ping-pong ball between him and one of the chefs, not understanding a word, as they took their stools.

"Spent a few years overseas," he told her by way of explanation. "Wouldn't call myself fluent, but I know enough to get by."

She wasn't sure about that. She knew the cadence when someone tried to speak a language they were only half-familiar with—like her own grasp of Pashto, picked up in bits and pieces during her time in Afghanistan—and Beckett didn't have any of that uneasy, stumbling hesitance. Still, she didn't press for details.

"You going to think I'm sexist if I order for both of us?" he asked her.

She stared at the laminated menu, a bewildering array of colorful fish slabs on rice, and shook her head.

"I'll think you're saving me from making a terrible decision," she said.

Beckett chuckled. "Nah. You can't go wrong with good sushi, no matter what you pick. But there's a difference between not going wrong and going very right."

After another burst of back-and-forth Japanese, the chef set to work in front of them. Charlie couldn't miss a flicker-fast glance in her direction and something that sounded like a question on his lips, then a faint smile at Beckett's answer. Ignoring whatever they'd said about her, her attention jumped to the chef's gleaming knife. He worked quick, with surgical precision, building ornate sculptures of rice and fish in perfectly measured proportions.

"Jake told me you've been with the company since the beginning," Charlie said.

"Day one," Beckett said. "First in, probably last out."

"Where were you before that?"

"Elsewhere," he said. She waited for him to elaborate. He didn't.

Her lunch settled before her on a squat-legged wooden tray. The colorful array nestled in rows alongside a small mound of green paste and thin-sliced strips of pink ginger. Beckett plucked a piece of ginger from his tray with his chopsticks, his big hands moving as delicately as a dancer's, and popped it between his teeth.

"Gari is a palate cleanser," he told her. He pointed the tip of a chopstick at her tray toward a translucent slab bound by seaweed to a bed of rice. "Good rule of thumb is to start with the lightest-color sashimi and make your way to the darker, heartier flavors."

Charlie didn't see any reason to doubt his wisdom on this. As she reached toward the first piece, her chopsticks extended in an uncertain hand, he subtly shook his head at her.

"Use your fingers," he murmured. "Chopsticks are for ginger and wasabi. You know about wasabi?"

"I know I ate too much of it once. Like brain freeze from ice cream, times a million."

"See, I was almost going to let you find out the hard way," he said with a grin, "but mind games are more Jake's bag. I like to keep things simple and uncomplicated."

The raw fish burst between her teeth in a flood of flavor, the tangy meat buoyed by the undercurrents of starchy rice and vinegar. Charlie blinked, wide eyed.

"This is . . . *really* good."

"Told you," Beckett said.

Some people used a shared meal as a vehicle for conversation. Beckett wasn't one of them. He didn't ask her any questions, and he didn't seem inclined to answer hers. They fell into a comfortable silence, enjoying the food, watching the chefs move down the line and practice their art as the lunchtime crowd filtered in.

Charlie finished the last bite, chewing thoughtfully. She felt just right: not hungry, not too full, energized for the challenge to come. Beckett took another glance at his watch.

"And that's sushi done right," he told her. "So, ready to get to work?"

"Let's do this."

Back at the hotel, the rest of Jake's operatives were filtering in. She spotted a couple of them at the check-in desk, another talking to the valet staff by the front doors. Jake himself, wearing a three-piece suit and looking like a corporate tycoon, strode across the cavernous lobby alongside a man in a red jacket and a name tag. They conversed in low voices. The lobby—a span of mahogany and marble under a vintage crystal chandelier—took on a hum of excitement. Anticipation and nervousness hovered in the air like a psychic miasma, and Charlie took slow, deep breaths to stop it from infecting her. It was just like being back in the field: the coolest heads were the most likely to come home intact at the end of watch.

"Rules to live by," Beckett said, leading her a few feet down a side corridor. They camped out there, right at the lobby's edge. "Rule number one, and I cannot stress how important this is: we are private citizens."

"As opposed to?" she asked.

"We aren't soldiers; we aren't cops. In any situation involving a violent altercation with another member of the public, that's exactly what the law treats it as: two Joe Taxpayers going at it. Maybe you'll be found justified in a court of law; maybe you won't, but the bottom line is we've got no special powers or privileges."

"So don't punch out any paparazzi," Charlie said.

Beckett snapped his fingers at her. "You get it. When an asset-protection specialist lands in hot water, nine times out of ten it's because they forgot their boundaries. That said, sometimes serving the client means sidestepping those boundaries a little bit. Every situation is fluid; it's on you to judge the problem and make the right call. On the plus side, there's a little trick you can use. Hold on—I'll show you."

He stood at the lobby's edge, eyes narrowed as he peered across the threshold at the milling tourists and staff.

"What am I supposed to be watching for?"

"Wait for it," he said.

A weary-looking traveler trudged their way, lugging a battered rolling carry-on case. Beckett had an ID card like the one Sofia had printed up for her that morning: crisp and laminated, featuring his unsmiling mug shot, in a professional-looking vinyl sheath. As the man approached the side hall, Beckett stepped up and stood in his path. He brandished the ID like a badge.

"Sorry, sir. Security. We've got this area closed off. I'm going to need you to go around."

The tourist's eyes went wide. "Oh, sure. Sorry."

As he backed off, Beckett gave him a firm but genial nod. "Thank you, sir. Have a nice day."

Beckett turned to Charlie, looking content, and lowered his voice. "You see that?"

"He even apologized."

"Yeah, that happens a lot." He flicked his ID card. "Legally, this card doesn't mean shit. He could have walked right around me if he felt like it. And if I laid hands on the man, that's me up on assault charges. I had no power over him whatsoever."

"He didn't know that," Charlie said.

"He did not. Which meant I had *absolute* power over him. That little trick I mentioned? It's called human nature. Ninety-nine percent of people out there are inherently submissive to authority. It's how we evolved. Buncha pack animals, looking for a leader."

"So if you present yourself as that leader . . ."

"Bingo. Look at the cops. A uniform and a gun help, sure, but know what they teach you at police academy? Assertiveness. You've gotta have the right tone of voice, the right posture, the right look in your eye, all to sell one very clear message: that you *will* be obeyed, and you will *not* be fucked with. A real pro can make an arrest in street clothes, with no badge and his hands empty."

Charlie tilted her head a little, listening closely. "You used to be a cop?"

"Nope."

As the afternoon stretched on, they made preparations for the banquet. Charlie helped shuffle tables around in the ballroom, arranged chairs, and laid out crisp cream name cards according to a tattered list some harried-looking caterer shoved into her hands.

She and Beckett stood at opposite sides of a table big enough to seat twelve. She lifted with her knees, heaving upward and lugging it ten feet to the right. "Didn't think party planning was part of our job," she grunted.

"Our job's whatever the client says it is. One time I was part of a security detail for this big pop star. One long month of walking her poodles, picking up her dry cleaning, and making coffee runs."

"Not exactly what I pictured."

"There's a level of practicality," he said. "If I'm out doing the busy-work, it means the client is safe at home and not exposing herself to potential trouble. Besides, those were some damn cute dogs. You got a dog?"

Charlie lifted an eyebrow. It was the first time Beckett had asked her anything about her personal life. Apparently she was passing muster with him. So far.

"No. Had one, when I was a kid. He passed a few years back."

"You ought to get one."

"For security work?" she asked. "I mean, does that help?"

"It might, might not. I just think everybody ought to have a dog."

Their post, once the first guests began to arrive, was right out front; they were part of the six-operative detail assigned to the non-VIP traffic. Charlie and Beckett stood beside a gap in a blue velvet cordon, just inside the lobby doors.

"Basic as basic gets," Beckett had told her. He'd handed her a clipboard and a pen. "You look over each arrival's invitation and a photo ID. If everything checks out, you slash their name off the list and let 'em through."

"And if not?"

He'd given her a faint, enigmatic smile and taken two steps back. Standing off to the side and out of the action. "If not, you do what you think is right. You'll be handling this checkpoint all by yourself. Pretend I'm not here."

Easier said than done, Charlie had thought, but once the arrivals started pouring through the revolving doors, she didn't have time to worry about Beckett looming over her. Each of the three gaps in the cordon sprouted a line of waiting guests, dressed to the nines and wearing their impatience on their tailored sleeves. The other two had a pair of operatives to share the work: she was all alone and struggling to keep up.

She fought the temptation to rush. She gave each newcomer a polite smile, checked the invitation against the sample proof clipped to one corner of her clipboard, and gave their ID a quick read through.

Beckett had walked her through the basics of spotting a fake driver's license, and though he couldn't make her a pro in one afternoon, she was now competent enough, in his estimation, "to bounce at your average dive bar." She handed back the ID and invitation, checked off a name, and stood aside to let the guest in.

Charlie eased into a rhythm, but she knew not to let the rhythm override her senses. She called on old skills for a new battlefield: she held one constant eye on the crowd, judged each guest by their body language and voice as much as their photo ID, and kept a steady read on the temperature of the room. Smooth as silk, for now.

She waved another couple of party guests inside and took a quick look at the line ahead of her. Her stomach clenched.

The situation was no longer smooth.

TWELVE

The guest in Charlie's sights stood four steps back in her line. Nobody was giving him a second glance. No reason they would: He was a stocky fifty-something dressed in a black suit and tie, clutching his invitation and driver's license in a weathered hand, clean shaven and professional. Just another Deep Country employee here to endure some executive speeches in exchange for a free dinner and an open bar.

Charlie had spent the better part of a decade in a land where attention to detail meant the difference between life and death. Where one slip, just one, could send you home for a flag-draped closed-casket funeral. And in her eyes, trained month after month by her mentors and her enemies alike, he stood out like a burning beacon.

He was clean shaven, but he wasn't used to it. Tiny nicks and cuts, fresh ones, decorated his cheeks. She followed his cheekbones up to his eyes, small and darting in every direction at once. She cleared the guest in front of her, the line advanced, and he moved in an anxious shuffle step. The suit wasn't his, or he'd bought it piecemeal and poorly; the black of his slacks was a slightly lighter shade than his jacket, and the jacket was too long, too big on his shoulders. His tie had less slack than a hangman's noose and turned a puff of skin around his collar raspberry red. No man who had to wear a tie for a living—like all of Deep Country's office staff—would knot it that tightly.

She patted him down with her eyes. No suspicious bulges under his jacket, not that she could make out, but his left hand never strayed more than an inch away from his belt. He clenched at the flap of his coat, pulling it forward, like a man trying way too hard to conceal a holster. Or a bomb.

Charlie waved the next guest through. Now he was second in line, almost close enough to touch. Time lurched into slow motion. The din of the crowd became muffled, faded, like the lobby had plunged a hundred feet underwater. Down into the black, where all Charlie could hear was the slow and steady thud of her heart.

She glanced over her shoulder, caught Beckett's eye, and flicked her gaze at the man. He gave the tiniest nod and took a step forward. Behind her clipboard, she held up her hand. Beckett stopped in his tracks. Giving her room to work.

She'd manned a checkpoint before. Sometimes people tried to come through with contraband. Sometimes with weapons. Sometimes they wanted to go home to their families. Sometimes they didn't. Charlie had five seconds to choose her next move. She thought fast as she waved the last guest through, and the man with the darting eyes and razor-nicked cheeks stood before her.

He offered her the license and invitation. She didn't take them. He squinted at her, equal parts confused and nervous, not sure what he was doing wrong. He pushed the papers at her, like she was a malfunctioning machine and it might work if he tried again.

"Listen to me," she said in a voice as smooth and even as shaved ice.

He froze. She held his gaze, and he wavered on unsteady legs like a deer caught in the headlights.

"Listen to me," she said again, "very carefully."

"Okay," he said. Too short a word to catch any trace of an accent, for certain, but he didn't sound like a local.

"My name is Charlene," she said. "I grew up in Owensboro. You ever go out that way?"

It was as big a lie as the hint of a Kentucky twang she carefully injected into her voice. He nodded. His throat bulged as he swallowed hard.

"Y'know, the people who work here," she said, "they don't get to pick and choose what companies rent out the ballroom. The caterers, the security folks, they're just good, hardworking people. They don't make a lot of money, but they work their fingers to the bone."

He held up his invitation and his driver's license. One corner of the license was already peeling, the telltale sign of a half-assed laminate job. His photo sat skewed at an angle in the corner.

"I've . . . I've got my papers," he told her, trying to get back on the script. She didn't let him.

"I'm a good judge of character." She gave a little, self-deprecating chuckle. "Guess that's why they hired me. I just look in someone's eyes, and I *know*, you know? And when I look at you . . . I know a good man when I see one. You don't really want to hurt anybody, do you? You're not the kind of man who hurts people. You're not like *them*."

His jaw clenched. He stammered, fumbling for words, as his eyes took on a wet sheen.

"It's not right," he whispered. "What they did . . . it's not right. Somebody has to pay for it."

"I know."

She reached out and gently took hold of his arm. His left arm, the one with a death grip on his coat and whatever he had stashed underneath. He didn't pull away.

"Just like I know that if I let you through, there's a good chance some innocent person is gonna get hurt. Not on purpose. You wouldn't do that on purpose, I know. But accidents happen. Mistakes get made, the kind of mistakes you can never, ever take back."

His right hand rubbed at his face. He mashed his knuckles against one damp eye.

"There's a time and a place for everything," Charlie told him. "And this isn't it. You don't want any innocent people to get hurt. And you haven't done anything wrong, not yet. So turn around, and walk away. It's the best choice for you, best choice for everybody."

He stared at her. His jaw clenched, hard enough Charlie could see it trembling, as he made his choice.

Then he turned his back on her and waded through the waiting crowd, back out through the revolving doors.

Charlie let out a breath she hadn't known she'd been holding. Pent-up tension gushed from her muscles like water from a sponge.

Behind her, Beckett put his sleeve to his mouth and spoke in low tones. "Dom, Louie, you've got a guy coming your way out the front entrance. Five feet eleven, sandy-blond hair, big shaving cut on his left cheek. He's armed. Follow at a distance; do not engage. If he gets into a car, pull the license plate number. Document anything you can so we can pass it on to the cops."

He lowered his sleeve and shot Charlie a faint, almost imperceptible nod. She returned the gesture and got back to work. Guests were still pouring in, milling in front of the velvet runners, and the job wasn't going to wait for her to catch her breath. She rode out the rush of adrenaline with a smile on her face.

Eventually the last guest was vetted and waved through. The lobby emptied out. Up a hallway paneled in vintage cherry-toned wood, Charlie heard the muffled sounds of a party in full swing.

"And now?" she asked Beckett.

"And now," he said, "we stand our post."

They stood their post. Waiting, watching nothing in particular, the silence leaden. It felt like old times. Those endless, crawling hours on watch, knowing anything could happen but probably nothing would.

Charlie shifted her weight from foot to foot, staying limber. She tried to keep her brain sharp by studying the cavernous lobby and taking in every detail. She memorized the number of light fixtures, clocked the angles on the geometric carpet design. Nothing useful, just mind games to stay awake.

"Little Duck," Beckett said.

She looked back at him over her shoulder. He hooked his thumbs in his belt.

"You did good," he said.

"Thanks."

"While you were taking invitations, I got a call from the detail out front. Guy left in a ride with Kentucky plates, lotta road dust, and dead bugs on the grille. You picked a winner."

"So what now?" she asked.

"They pass the plate number over to Boston PD. Not our problem to deal with. If he's dumb enough to stay in town, they'll find him and pick him up. After the scare you put into him, he's probably halfway back to Skeeter Hollow by now."

"Wasn't trying to scare him," Charlie said. "Just wanted to defuse the situation."

"All kinds of ways to scare a man. You made him take a look in the mirror, and he didn't like what he saw. Situation defused." Beckett cracked a thin smile. "This *is* going on your permanent record."

"Yeah? I passed the audition?"

"Far as I'm concerned. And Jake gave me the final word. So assuming you don't stumble over your own feet in the next"—he checked his watch—"hour and twenty minutes or thereabouts, you've got the job."

A gust of relief washed over her, like a stray cool breeze on a hot summer night. The money was okay—enough to live on, not enough to dig her father out of his hole—but the job meant more than that. She'd returned to the States adrift and without a foothold, feeling like a ghost. Now she had a place to be. A foundation to build on.

"Thanks," she told him. "This means a lot to me."

Beckett snorted and looked up the hall, toward the banquet-hall doors.

"Thank me when you've pulled a twelve-hour shift working parking lot duty in hundred-degree heat. Our jobs aren't *all* glamorous and action-packed escapades like this one."

Charlie waved a hand, taking in the empty lobby. "Well, that's good. I don't think I can handle this much excitement on a regular basis."

Voices up the hall drifted ahead of a slow stampede, the party breaking up at long last. This part was easy; all they had to do was clear the velvet ropes, stand to one side, smile, and keep their eyes open as the guests queued up and the valets scrambled to bring an endless convoy of cars around the building. The VIPs were being escorted out the way they'd come in, safe in the hands of veteran operatives and blissfully unaware that they were ever in danger.

Good patrol, Charlie thought, feeling satisfied.

"Yeah," Beckett said into his sleeve. He wore a bulky plastic earpiece, the ivory white standing out against his dark skin, and a tight spiral cord ran down into the neck of his jacket. "Yeah, the kid checked out. Sure. Right behind you."

He looked to Charlie and nodded to the door. "C'mon. Jake rode back to Deep Country HQ with the client. He wants to see both of us, and the client wants a debriefing, so we're going to meet him there and kill two birds with one stone. Standard client-meeting protocol: mouth shut, eyes open, let Jake do the talking. Easiest part of your entire night. The hard work is officially over."

Deep Country took up the top three floors of a modest office tower in the financial district. This late, security was a single tired-looking desk clerk who signed them in and unlocked the elevator. They met Jake up on twenty-two, where he was glad-handing the client.

Sean Ellis might have been in his sixties, but it was hard to tell: His Ken-doll features had the rigid sheen of a Botox addict, and either his teeth were too-perfect dentures, or he gargled with whitening treatment. His hair was a wispy chestnut helmet, as motionless as his forehead. Charlie and Beckett trailed behind him, down sterile beige hallways lined with powder-blue carpet, on the way to his office.

"Jake was telling me we had a problem out front," Sean said. "He also said that problem went away quietly."

"Both true," Beckett said.

"Thanks for that. The nuts are bad enough; last thing I needed tonight was a big scene. I have to tell you, I *almost* went with Eriksson Security, but it's looking like I made the right call."

"We won't let you down," Jake said. "And did I mention you're getting a significant discount with our comprehensive protection package? Eriksson can't beat that."

Sean's office was roomy, one wall lined with built-in bookshelves and the other adorned with framed photography. Vintage mines, the backwoods of the Deep South, snapshots of history captured in black and white. A crisp map traced the spread of Deep Country's holdings, each mine a blossom of scarlet on creamy white like droplets of blood. Wounds in the earth. On the opposite wall, a recessed display of glass shelves glittered with crystal, award after industry award lined up under tiny LED spotlights.

"You were pretty darn comprehensive tonight," Sean said. He pulled back his chair, plush black leather with a high, winged back. "Honestly, for the first time since this mess started, I actually feel safe."

He dropped into his chair with a sigh of relief.

The chair went click.

Thirteen

Charlie held up one hand. "Don't move."

The room froze. Sean, his Plasticine brows struggling to knit, wriggled in his seat. "What was—"

"Do not *fucking* move."

He stopped squirming. Beckett and Jake had already gotten the picture. They stood like statues. *Or those petrified people in the wake of Pompeii*, Charlie thought. *Frozen where they died when the volcano hit.*

She willed her frozen limbs into action and crossed the office floor with light, ginger steps. She crouched down on one knee beside Sean's chair and looked up at him, raising one finger.

"Hold perfectly still. Don't wriggle. Don't shift your weight. Don't breathe any harder than you have to."

He didn't argue. The light bulb still hadn't clicked on, but he was smart enough to read her tone of voice. Charlie ducked low. She craned her neck, head an inch from the powder-blue carpet, and checked under his seat.

A coil of wires stretched from a digital timer to a trio of slabs, like gold bricks, wrapped in glossy black Mylar. Adhesive glue clamped the slabs firmly to the underbelly of Sean's chair.

"Mr. Ellis," Charlie said, "it's very important that you remain calm right now. And whatever you do, *do not stand up.* Do you understand?"

His voice was a strained squeak. "Someone want to tell me what's going on here?"

Charlie knelt up so she could look him in the eye.

"That click was a pressure-release trigger in the padding of your chair. That trigger is wired to an M112 demolition block. About a pound and a quarter of C-4 plastic explosive hooked to a detonator. You stand up, we all die. That's problem number one."

Jake was already fishing his phone out. "I'll call the police—"

"That's problem number two," Charlie said. "Activating the pressure switch started a timer. He's got nine minutes and change before the package goes boom. The bomb squad will never get here in time. Whoever built this wanted to make sure they got the job done."

The facts of the situation, cold and razor edged, settled in a leaden silence between them.

"What . . ." Sean swallowed, his face going fish-belly pale. "What do we do?"

"I do my job," Charlie said. She peered over the desk at Jake and Beckett. "You two, clear the floor. Make sure nobody's working late. Then clear *out*."

Beckett's lips pursed in a hard line. "Jake, clear the floor and call it in."

Jake squinted at him. "What about you?"

Beckett folded his arms, silent.

Charlie studied the bomb. She didn't look at the timer; the luminous green countdown was stress she didn't need right now, an obstacle in the way. Every bomb was a puzzle. Every bomb builder, like a poker player, had signatures and tells. Quirks unique to their art. Quirks that could be exploited.

You and me, she thought, talking to the bomber in her mind as she cracked her knuckles. *One on one. Your skills against mine. Let's go.*

When Charlie had left the service, she'd thought she'd never dance this dance again. Part of her, buried deep in her reptilian hindbrain, rose eager for the challenge. Her fingers probed the side of the chair and ran lightly along the supple black leather. She felt resistance here and there, hard edges buried in the padding.

"Can't you just . . . cut the wires?" Sean stammered.

"No. We can't just 'cut the wires.'" Charlie looked over the desk. Jake was already gone, running up the hall and hunting for stray civilians. Beckett stood, impassive, arms folded.

"I mean it," she told Beckett. "Clear out. I can't guarantee this is going to end well for anybody."

"Jake said we were partnered up. He hasn't changed that order yet. So we're partnered up."

Charlie sighed. He wasn't going to budge. Fine, she could use a hand, and the timer wasn't waiting. She looked to Sean. "Tell me you've got a decently stocked supply room."

"Sure." His head bounced like an out-of-control spring. "Up—up the hall, on the right. Third door."

"Beckett, I need a decent pair of scissors: fabric shears would be great, but I'll take anything sharp. A knife from the break room will work if that's all we've got. Also some tape. Duct tape is ideal, but packing tape should do it if you find a whole roll. Also need a screwdriver. Phillips head."

"On it," he said. The office door swung in his sudden wake.

"Tell me you know what you're doing," Sean said.

Charlie squinted at the Mylar bricks and the detonator prongs. Straightforward assembly. Almost too straightforward. She glanced up at Sean and tried to put on a reassuring smile for him.

"Eight years as an EOD technician. You're in good hands."

She didn't tell him the truth: that in the field, she wouldn't have gone near something like this without putting on an eighty-pound bomb suit first. In the field, nine-tenths of the time she worked with a remote-controlled robot called a Wheelbarrow, supervising the job from behind a wall of sandbags with a containment unit on standby. Most

EOD jobs didn't end with a snipped wire and a frozen countdown timer like in the movies. They ended with the bomb going off, on purpose. The point of the job was to safely *control* the demolition and make sure no civilians were in range of the blast.

She glanced to a closed door, left of the desk. "Where's that go?"

"M-my private bathroom."

"Don't suppose you've got a bathtub in there?"

He shook his head, mute. She got up and poked her head inside. Five by five, porcelain tile floor, nice fixtures, no windows. If she had to contain the blast, it'd do in a pinch, minimizing the damage. That was step two of the job. Step one, getting Sean off that chair in one piece, was the hard part.

"Have you ever done this before?" Sean asked her. "I mean, one . . . one like this?"

"Once," she told him. "A village chief told the Taliban to go pound sand. They didn't like that, so they wired a bomb on a pressure trigger under his ceremonial chair. Pretty much like this one. I told him not to fidget and went to grab my tools."

"What . . . what happened?"

Charlie gave him a humorless smile.

"He fidgeted. So don't, okay?"

Sean squeezed his eyes shut. His lips moved in a silent prayer.

Beckett ran in. He tossed the screwdriver underhand, and Charlie snatched it from the air. She dropped down on one knee, getting to work while he sat the rest of his finds on the desk: a pair of office scissors and a fat, sturdy roll of packing tape.

"What else?" he asked her.

Charlie found the threads of the screws holding Sean's right armrest in place. She needed access and room to work, so the bulky black plastic had to go. She twisted the screwdriver like a mechanic working a pit stop, switching a race car's wheels while the timer ran down.

"Nothing," she said.

"I'll be right here, just in case."

She didn't have the time or the breath to argue with him. One fat screw dropped onto the blue carpet, then another. She gently tugged on the armrest. It slid from its mountings, pulled back, and then came loose.

The digital timer ticked down. Six minutes left.

A bead of sweat tickled Charlie's eyebrow, dripping into her eye and stinging. She brushed it away and gathered up the edge of the soft leather in her hand, bringing it to a tiny point. The scissors snipped through it, making an opening. Then she slowly sliced her way along the cushion, lengthwise, drawing a long and ragged line. Yellow stuffing poked out through the hole in fat rolls, like a wounded patient's guts.

Time to get surgical. She snipped at the stuffing, here and there, pulling it away as much as she dared and angling for a better look inside. There it was: the edge of the pressure trigger, a pair of steel strips with a spring and a circuit connection sandwiched in between, bare teeth on one end and a swinging hasp on the other. When Sean had sat down on the spring, connecting the strips and forming an electrical circuit, he'd started the countdown to his execution.

Four minutes left.

"Mr. Ellis," she said, "I need you to wriggle very, *very* slowly a quarter inch to your left."

Cold sweat drenched his button-down shirt. "I thought wriggling was bad."

Charlie grabbed the packing tape. She took the loose end between her teeth, yanked it free, and shoved her sleeves back.

"I'm giving you permission," she said. "Very slowly, and just a quarter of an inch. Now, please."

She held her breath as he squirmed, easing away from her. The clenched teeth of the pressure switch stood exposed now, three inches from her face. She felt the psychic weight of the demolition block. If it went off now, with her kneeling next to the chair, there wouldn't be enough left of either of them to fill a single casket.

"Good. Now freeze. Just like that."

She held the steel teeth and coiled tape around the exposed tips, pulling it as tight as she could. The roll wrapped around again and again and again, coating the steel in glossy plastic. She couldn't tell how strong the spring between the metal strips was. It was made to give easily under Sean's weight; he looked like he weighed 150, maybe 160. She gave the roll eight more turns around the steel, layering the tape on thick, weighing the risk against the ticking clock.

Three minutes on the clock. With no guarantee she could disarm the bomb, it was now or never.

"Get up," she told Sean.

"Up? You . . . you mean, out of the chair?"

"Now."

Time froze. Charlie's stomach lurched sideways, dizzy and sick.

Sean stood up.

The tape on the pressure switch held. The bomb didn't go off. The timer kept counting down.

"Out," she told him.

She didn't watch him go. No time. She stood over the now-empty seat cushion and cut along the sides, peeling back the leather and the yellow padding beneath. She gazed down at the guts of the bomb. Her eyes followed the lime-green cords running from the pressure trigger, spooling through the seat. There was the power source, nestled snug in a bed of yellow foam. She hunted for backup wires, trick fuses, all the little snares and stumbling blocks a smart bomb builder could throw in her path. This was the most dangerous part of the game. EOD techs kept finding new ways to make ordnance safe, and the bombers kept finding new and deadly games to play.

Not this bomber, though. The device had looked crudely simple at first blush, and the exposed wiring didn't change her mind. She summed it up in three words: *efficient, tight, basic*. The builder knew what he was doing, but his technique was a good three decades behind the cutting edge. Modern bomb makers had moved on, benefiting from advanced materials and techniques. By comparison this was Terrorism 101.

She didn't let her guard down. A simple bomb could kill you just as dead as a complicated one.

She pulled away more bits of foam, exposing the power source, and studied the circuit. No visible countermeasures, no backup batteries. One quick slice stood between her and the moment of truth.

"You got this?" Beckett asked her.

She snipped the cord running from the pressure switch to the battery.

"Maybe," she said.

The timer was still counting down. Thirty-two seconds on the clock. Charlie jumped up, grabbed the back of the chair, and shoved it across the powder-blue carpet, wheeling it into Sean's bathroom. The plastic wheels thumped on the porcelain tile. She slammed the door shut and broke into a run.

Charlie and Beckett burst through the office door and sprinted down the corridor side by side. They hit the emergency stairwell, thundering down the steps. Charlie kept a silent count in her head, seconds draining away as her feet pounded against the bare concrete stairs, and she braced for the sound of detonation.

Silence.

All the same, they didn't stop until they hit the lobby, twenty-two floors below. They staggered through the brushed-metal door together, drenched in cold sweat and breathless.

Fourteen

"No police," Sean told them for the fifth time.

Jake's eyebrows tried to climb into his hair. "*Excuse* me?"

They were back upstairs. Charlie listened from the other side of the open bathroom door. She knelt on the hard ivory porcelain as she stripped the chair and the bomb down into parts, like doing a jigsaw puzzle in reverse. Strips of wire, screws, washers, and metal rods sat in neat rows beside her, each stored in an individual plastic baggie, and she added to the pile with every twist of the screwdriver. Beckett stood at Jake's shoulder, arms crossed and eyes hard.

"Look," Sean said, flustered, "we don't want to embolden these people."

"But we do want to *catch* 'these people,' yes?" Jake demanded. "Mr. Ellis, our job is asset protection. We aren't investigators; we don't have police resources. We can't go out there and—"

"I'm not asking you to. Okay? That's not even on the table. I just need you to keep on doing what you're already doing."

The Mylar coating over the bricks of C-4 slowly peeled from the base of the chair, now detached and flipped onto its belly before her. Charlie worked the bricks back slowly. Her fingers massaged the adhesive, easing it away from the plastic base a fraction at a time. No tension in her tired muscles now, only eager curiosity. With the detonator safely removed, the explosives were about as dangerous as a newborn kitten.

About as useless when it came to obvious clues too. After photographing the entire assembly—twenty shots, capturing the bomb rig from every angle before she started breaking it down and bagging the parts—she did a cursory check for fingerprints. The attackers had worn gloves and wiped their handiwork clean, just like she'd expected they would.

She still would have left the rig intact and untouched, ready for the real detectives to come along and do their thing, but she understood Sean's tone even if she couldn't understand his reasoning. His heels were dug in, deep, and nobody in authority was going to take a closer look at this bomb if he had anything to say about it.

Nobody but her. So she organized, and she bagged, and she documented every step along the way.

"Mr. Ellis," Jake said, "someone infiltrated your building and planted explosives in your office."

"And you stopped them. So . . . good job!" Sean paced the carpet, bottom lip trapped between his teeth.

Charlie glanced up and caught a glimpse as he passed the bathroom doorway. She frowned. Something was wrong here, more wrong than the bomb.

"And if my operatives hadn't been here, things wouldn't have worked out so good," Jake told him. "We can't guarantee what'll happen next time."

"Next time? Who says there'll be a next time? Maybe they'll give up. Maybe they'll go away."

Jake and Beckett shared a look. Beckett had his poker face on. Jake took a deep breath, rallied, and tried again.

"In our experience, sir, assassins, and that's exactly the type of personality we're dealing with here, don't just 'go away.' This attack took planning, skill, and dedication—"

Charlie had found a big brown paper sack in the office supply room. She carefully stashed the bagged evidence, scrap by scrap, packaging it all up nice and neat.

"Just keep doing what you're doing," Sean said. "I don't think that's unreasonable. I'm not an unreasonable man."

Jake held up his hands. He took a deep breath. Charlie watched his lips move as he silently counted to five.

"Okay, okay, we've all had a long night; maybe we'll all see a little clearer after some sleep, huh? Mr. Ellis, I strongly advise you to reconsider. Sleep on it, okay? I'll call you in the morning."

"Good. Fine." Sean's eyes darted to the bathroom door. "Can you, um . . . get rid of that thing for me?"

Charlie emerged, toting the paper bag in one hand and the Mylar-wrapped demolition block in the other. Jake's eyes bulged at her. "Is that . . . is it safe to hold on to it like that?"

Charlie shrugged. "It's C-4. You can stomp on it, shoot it, light it on fire. Still won't go off without an electrical det charge. Want to see?"

Jake ran a finger along his buttoned collar. "I'll take your word for it."

They left Sean standing in his office, the remnants of his chair scattered across the bathroom floor.

Beckett gave her the side-eye as the three of them stepped onto the elevator. "You know, if he changes his mind about calling the cops, you just tampered with the evidence in the worst way."

"You heard him same as I did," Charlie said. "You think there's one chance in a million he's going to change his mind?"

"Wouldn't even give it lottery odds."

Jake stood in front of them, his back turned, facing the elevator doors as their cage glided downward.

"Doesn't make any damn sense," he muttered.

Beckett and Charlie exchanged a glance and a nod. They shared a silent wavelength.

"Cut him loose," Beckett said.

Jake looked back at him. "Huh?"

"As a client. Do yourself and all of us a favor. Cut him loose; cancel his contract; give him a refund if you have to. Do it tonight." Beckett pointed up at the bank of numbers over the elevator door, glowing lights shifting to track their downward glide. "Man's got problems."

"*All* our clients have problems. That's why they hire us. This is hardly the first issue we've shoved under the rug at a customer's request."

Beckett didn't have an answer for that. He tilted his head at Charlie.

"Little Duck did good tonight."

"Damn right she did." Jake looked over at her. "Talk about nailing your tryout and then some. You've definitely got the qualities we're looking for in an operative: skills, instincts, initiative, *and* guts. That said, wouldn't blame you if you walked out of here and never came back."

"You see me walking?" Charlie asked him.

"Nope." He rubbed his chin, studying her. "Guess I don't. Let's make this official, then."

He held out his hand. They shook on it.

"Welcome aboard," Jake said. "You are officially an employee of Boston Asset Protection."

"I won't let you down," Charlie said.

"After tonight? I'm not worried. Normally I like to take new hires out for drinks, but—" Jake gave a vague, tired wave to the night sky.

"It's been a long night," Charlie said.

"It's been a long night. Go home. Get some shut-eye. You earned it."

Jake left them at the curb outside the corporate tower, hopping into a waiting Lyft. Beckett nodded up the street.

"C'mon," he said, "I'll walk you to your truck."

Normally Charlie might have rankled at that. It was a relatively safe neighborhood, a well-lit path to her father's pickup, and she was hardly a wilting flower needing an escort. That said, she could read between the lines. He fell into step alongside her and waited until they were far out of anyone's earshot before he opened his mouth again.

"Only one reason," he said. He didn't need to elaborate.

"Sean Ellis has some skeletons in his closet," Charlie replied.

"Kind he can't afford uniforms sniffing at. Above and beyond the ones that already made front-page news."

"So what do we do about it?"

"We? Nothing. I go talk to Jake again in the morning, one on one, and try to get him to cancel the contract. We can't help a client who won't help himself, and I don't feel like getting blown up because some aspiring vigilante doesn't care about collateral damage."

"Think it was our guy? From the party?"

Beckett squinted up at the lamplight. It painted a pallid glow across the rust-spotted hood of Charlie's ride.

"Timetable works. He could have gotten turned away, driven to Deep Country, broken in, and rigged the chair before the party let out. No problem." He turned, scrutinizing her. "Now what's wrong with this picture?"

Charlie thought back, picturing the man in her mind. His razor-nicked cheeks, the fear in his eyes.

"I told him he didn't want to hurt anyone," she said. "I wasn't wrong. He wanted to be heard. He might have been planning on doing some damage, maybe even taking a shot at Sean Ellis, but he wasn't a killer, not really. If he managed to slip past me, good chance he would have lost his nerve and left on his own."

"As opposed to," Beckett said, leading her onward.

"The bomber . . . he didn't care. There wasn't any note, no message taking responsibility, no signature. The explosive device was simple. Utilitarian. It was built for one purpose and one purpose only: to murder Sean Ellis, with no regard for anyone else who might have been in the room with him."

"We got crazies coming out of the woodwork." Beckett gazed to the night sky and rubbed the back of his neck. "I'll talk to Jake. See if we can wriggle out of this, make it somebody else's problem. You did good today, Little Duck."

Charlie wrestled with the pickup's door. It chunked open, drizzling flakes of rust onto the pavement at her feet. She set her paper bag on the passenger seat. The edge of the demolition block's glossy wrapper poked out between the flaps.

"Yeah? So you're gonna stop calling me that?"

Beckett chuckled and turned his back on her, strolling down the sidewalk.

"I said you did good, not that you were done learning the ropes. See you tomorrow."

Charlie drove home.

She let herself into her father's house, stepping lightly across the living room to turn off the television set. The sounds of the Home Shopping Network faded, and a gulf of silence flooded in. Her father slept in his reclining chair, slumped back, one corner of his mouth sticky with drool. His black eye had faded to an ugly purple splotch, like a birthmark splashed across half his face. Empty beer cans littered his side table.

She clicked off the lamp and let him sleep.

She couldn't look at him without seeing the ticking clock. His deadline—ten days, now nine and counting—before Jimmy Lassiter stopped pretending to be a gentleman and came looking for his money. She wasn't any closer to finding a way out. Her father, as far as she could tell, wasn't even looking for one. The invisible hourglass strapped to Charlie's shoulders weighed her down as she trudged into her bedroom, stashed the bag with the disassembled bomb in the closet, and fell onto the bed. Her feet and her knees were having a contest, seeing who could ache harder.

Charlie's body lay leaden while her brain tossed and turned. She thought about her father. She thought about Jimmy Lassiter. She thought about the bag in the closet.

It wouldn't be hard.

She knew what booth the bookie sat in, his personal "office." It wouldn't be hard to slip in after closing hours and recreate the bomber's handiwork, rigging his seat to blow. She was trained to dismantle explosive devices; that meant she could build them too. Part of her realized how far from normal this was—that she was lying awake in the dark and contemplating a cold-blooded murder—but all alone, in the dark, she could be honest with herself.

It wouldn't be the first time she'd killed a man. She knew it was different, pulling the trigger with a uniform on. War wasn't murder; at least that was what polite society had agreed to believe. And both times she'd fired her gun in Afghanistan and connected with a target, it had been a kill-or-be-killed situation. No one in the world could point a finger of shame at her for defending herself. She was blameless. This was different.

Was it, though? Over there, she'd been fighting to stay alive. Here, she'd be protecting her father from being crippled, or worse. Protecting her family. Wasn't that justified?

Too messy. Too much risk. Charlie was pretty sure she could bury Jimmy Lassiter without losing too much sleep, but he wouldn't be the only man in that bar. The bartender, delivery people, early-morning drinkers looking to get a head start on killing their livers—they'd all be in range of the blast. That, she couldn't live with. Of course, she didn't have to use his chair. She could find out what he drove, attach the demolition block to the undercarriage and rig up a radio trigger. Charlie had spent nearly a decade learning every dirty trick of the bomber's trade. She'd just never thought she'd *use* them.

Then she thought about the blowback. Men like Jimmy were connected with a capital *C*—you couldn't do that kind of business in Boston without powerful friends—and those friends would come looking for answers. Anyone in the red in Jimmy's books would be a top suspect. It wouldn't take long to spot her father's name on that list, number one with a bullet, and even less time to find out his daughter was a freshly returned EOD specialist. A rookie cop could make that case.

Dead end. The idea of taking Lassiter out was a fantasy. Simple and reassuring, but it would only make things worse in the long run. She had to find a better way.

She wouldn't get any answers tonight. She eventually fell into a fitful sleep, with a new day hot on her aching heels.

FIFTEEN

The sunrise found Charlie back on her feet. Her hoodie dripped with icy sweat as she took her morning run. Forcing her aching feet into trainers and hitting the pavement was masochism bordering on self-destruction, she knew, but there was no better cure for a clogged-up brain. Pounding up the hill, racing between a ribbon of backwoods road and the fog-drenched forest, her heart jackhammered in a strong and strident rhythm. All her worries faded, scrubbed clean by the endorphins and the pain.

She doubled back and had just enough time for a brisk shower before heading out again. Her father was awake, back in his chair and his tattered bathrobe, eating microwaved pancakes soggy with cheap syrup.

"I'm off to work," she told him.

"Mm-hmm," he said.

"Yesterday was my first day on the job," she said. "It went good. They seem to like me. I think I like the job."

"That's good."

She stood by the door, waiting to see if he had anything else to say. He reached for the remote, changed the channel, and filled the awkward silence with the replay from a Bruins game.

"All right." Charlie nodded, to herself as much as to him. "I'm out."

"Stop off on the way home, pick up some Bud for me?"

"Sure, Dad."

She drove to Cambridge, to the big industrial box at the edge of the corporate park. The receptionist was on a call, but she pressed her palm against the receiver as Charlie walked into the stripped-down lobby. "Oh, *hey*," she chirped, "you're Charlene, right? I'm Francesca. Beckett had to go off site with Mr. Esposito. He said you should go see Dom; she's expecting you."

"Great," Charlie said. "Where's Dom?"

"Last I checked, firing range. Up the hall, hook a right, second door. I'd say you can't miss it, but . . ." She shrugged, waving a helpless hand at the office around her.

"But nothing here is labeled, there aren't any signs, and the place is built like a maze."

The receptionist gave her a perky thumbs-up. Charlie let her get back to her phone call. She went hunting.

A plain white door opened onto a narrow vestibule. A plywood rack hung on one wall, a relic salvaged from a garage and lined with utility hooks. A half dozen pairs of hearing protectors dangled from the hooks. Charlie picked up a pair; the orange plastic bubbles nestled over her head like bulky earmuffs. On the opposite wall, a range-reservation schedule had been scribbled in a rainbow of erasable markers across a scuffed whiteboard. Furious, jagged lines drew Charlie's eye to a note scrawled in the bottom left corner.

Police your brass. All of it. Every time you use the range. Without exception. THIS MEANS YOU, ASSHOLE.

Love, Dom.

Charlie pressed through the next doorway. It opened up onto an alley of water-stained concrete, where three beige plywood booths stood at the far ends of firing lanes. Opposite the booths, steel lockers with wire-grille covers dominated the wall from floor to ceiling. Just like everything else around here, Jake had spent money for effect, not looks; acoustic tiles layered every inch of open space, muffling the sound of gunfire. Downrange, where a trio of fresh paper targets were humming backward on motorized tracks, each of the three lanes ended in reinforced, commercial-grade bullet traps.

Dom stood alone on the range, perched in the center booth as she cradled her weapon of choice: a storm-gray Remington 700 rifle fitted with a long-range scope. She worked the bolt action, loading a fresh round, and nodded over at Charlie.

"Damn, just when I was getting warmed up. Looks like I have to do some actual work today."

"Don't let me stop you," Charlie said.

Dom turned back to the range and shouldered her rifle. She smiled, tight lipped, as she sighted down the scope.

"This'll just take a second," she said.

Dom took a half breath and held it. Her finger caressed the trigger.

The rifle cracked like steel thunder, and she was already working the bolt, slamming a fresh round home as her shoulders swiveled two inches to the left. Her finger never left the trigger, squeezing off a second shot, layering thunder upon thunder. Then she swung right and slapped the bolt action, snapping off a third round before the echoes of her first bullet had faded.

The steel storm settled, reverberating into the stone at their feet. The echo drifted into silence.

Dom lowered the rifle and punched the three target-return buttons, one after another. The paper targets hummed toward them on a softly buzzing track. A trio of human silhouettes, each with a perfect hole punched through its forehead.

"That's . . . impressive," Charlie said.

Dom took her rifle to a workbench by the lockers. She looked back at Charlie over her shoulder.

"I'm a strong believer in sending bad news via long-distance courier. How about you? Jake says you're ex-military."

"I'm capable with the M4," Charlie said. "Never claimed to be Annie Oakley, but I know which end of the weapon goes bang. Technically I can handle a fifty."

Dom's eyes lit up. "Yeah? You got hands on with a fifty caliber? Damn, I'd love one of those babies for my collection."

"*Technically.*" Charlie ducked her head and smiled. "See, it's officially an option for ordnance disposal. Go long range, clear the immediate area, and terminate the suspect package with one very nasty, very expensive round of ammunition. Never actually did it in the field, but it's an option. So once a year we had to go in for certification and retraining, which basically boiled down to screwing around on the range all day and playing with the big guns."

"You," Dom said, turning to face her, "just described my dream vacation. Okay. You have earned my official blessing to use this range. There are rules. Rules which must never be violated."

"I'm all ears."

"Rule number one: Anything in the cage is company property. Use whatever you like, but you either supply your own ammo or log what you take from the communal stash and kick some money into the kitty when I go to restock at month's end. If you use community ammo and fail to pay it forward, you will accrue Negative Bullet Karma."

"And that's bad?"

"That's terrible. Rule number two: You will clean anything you use. You will put anything you use—weapon, tool, anything you touch—back *exactly* where you found it. Otherwise you will accrue Negative Bullet Karma."

"I think I follow you," Charlie said.

Dom held up three fingers. "Rule three. Charlie, this . . . I cannot tell you, I cannot stress enough, how vital it is that you understand and follow this rule. When you are finished shooting, you will always—*always*—police your brass and clean up after yourself. It's neighborly.

It's courteous. It's the right thing to do. And if you fail to follow this simple rule—"

"Let me guess," Charlie said. "Negative Bullet Karma."

"Obey these rules, and the Goddess of Superior Firepower will shower you with her blessings. You will shoot straight, you will land on target, and you will reap a reward of unreported cash income as part of our monthly target-shooting competition. You will also *not* piss me off."

Dom practiced what she preached. She tugged down the perforated targets, cleaning up after herself, and Charlie pitched in. She gathered up the fallen shell casings and tossed the brass into a wastebasket marked **SCRAP RECYCLING**.

"For today's agenda," Dom told her, "we're taking a ride over to Deep Country HQ. Jake wants me to run a security-risk assessment— that's my main thing, for the record—and he wants you to see how the job gets done."

"Wait, we're keeping the contract?"

"Expanding it. After last night, Deep Country is contracting us for twenty-four-seven security at their corporate office, plus an armed escort for Sean Ellis."

"Beckett was trying to convince Jake to walk away," Charlie said.

"And I agree with Beckett; these people are more trouble than they're worth, but money has a way of smoothing rough edges. Sounds like Ellis rolled a wheelbarrow of cash up to Jake's doorstep and groveled like a champ."

Charlie weighed her words, not sure how much she was allowed to share. "Did Jake . . . tell you anything about last night?"

"Oh yeah. Chair bomb. Heard you earned your keep, and then some." She patted Charlie's shoulder and led the way to the door. "For the record? No hero shit on my watch."

"Excuse me?"

Dom's tone was light, conversational, but her easy smile didn't reach her eyes. She and Charlie walked side by side through the tight, faceless corridors, navigating back toward the lobby.

"I've got a little girl," Dom said. "At the end of the day, I plan to pick her up from day care. Nothing matters more to me than that. And to do it, I need to be alive and breathing. Thing to remember, Charlie: We aren't the Secret Service. We didn't give a sacred oath to take a bullet for our clients. Do we *want* to keep them safe? Absolutely. That's what they pay us for. Will we take risks, even big ones, to make that happen? Sure. But there's an art to this job. You've got to find the balance between protecting the primary and protecting *yourself.*"

"I'm starting to understand why you like rifles."

Dom laughed as she pushed open the lobby doors, stepping out into the summer sun. Charlie felt a wave of heat wash over her, the air humid and sucking her breath away. She fumbled for her sunglasses.

"And when you're in charge of moving the primary through dangerous territory, you'll be damn glad I'm on overwatch. I'm not a sniper, Charlie; I'm your personal guardian angel. A missionary of the Goddess of Superior Firepower. So where's your ride? As the newbie, you get the privilege of chauffeuring me around today."

Charlie led the way to her father's pickup. Dom stopped short in her tracks, staring at the wreck as it broiled silently in the sun.

"Change of plans," Dom said. "I'm driving; you can pay for lunch."

All things considered, Charlie was pretty sure she was getting the better end of that deal. She followed Dom across the parking lot. The doors of a sleek white Lincoln Continental squawked as they approached. They opened the car up to air it out, letting some summer heat boil free, and Charlie gazed in at the buttery tan leather seats and a dash the color of cherrywood.

"Damn," she said. "This job pays better than I thought."

Dom gave the car a rueful smile. "Don't get your hopes up. This baby's six years old, and I bought her before I started working asset protection. Now I'm just trying to keep her running as long as possible."

She slipped behind the wheel. Charlie eased into the passenger seat, sinking into the leather, and shouldered her seat belt.

"What'd you do before this?" she asked.

The engine purred like a kitten. Dom threw it into reverse, one eye on the rearview as she pulled out of her spot and ignored the question. Charlie recalled Beckett's words on her first morning, comparing this outfit to the French Foreign Legion; people around here weren't big on talking about their pasts.

"Let's talk about risk assessment," Dom said. "Number one rule of risk mitigation is that there is always risk. A dedicated-enough assassin, if they don't care about their own life, can get at anyone. *Anyone.* Our job isn't to eliminate risk but to minimize it and make our client as hard a target as possible, in the hopes of encouraging would-be threats to go elsewhere."

"At least Sean Ellis's assassin doesn't seem suicidal," Charlie said.

"Yet. Let's see what happens once we lock his offices down and make it harder to take a second shot at him. If we're lucky, the opportunity cost will make our mad bomber give up and go home."

"And if we're not?"

"If we're not, he'll get desperate. And desperate men do very stupid, very dangerous things." Dom glanced into the rearview mirror. "Like I said. Anyone can be assassinated. You just have to want it badly enough."

Sixteen

Dom toured the halls of Deep Country with a clipboard in her hand and absolute authority in her voice. Charlie stayed right at her side, eyes open, mouth closed, studying her every move.

"I need to get in here," Dom said to a harried-looking file clerk, pointing to an unmarked doorway. The brushed-aluminum handle jiggled in her grip.

"That's just a storage closet," he told her. "We haven't used it since we moved into this building."

"So you don't even know what's in there."

"Boxes?"

"Are you asking me," Dom said, "or telling me?"

"Pretty sure it's just empty boxes."

Dom took a deep breath and made a notation on her clipboard.

"I need to get in here," she repeated, and she stared him down until he scurried off to find a key.

"What are we looking for?" Charlie asked.

"Right now? Just taking the lay of the land. Probing for any cracks in the armor. Honestly, the security here is adequate, for most companies. Everyone has to get signed in at the lobby, elevators are key-card locked, and each of Deep Country's three floors has a vestibule with an additional key-card door to reach the offices. Employees' cards only work on the specific floor they're assigned to, further cutting down the risk of theft and misuse."

"But," Charlie said, catching the tone of Dom's voice. It sounded like she was damning them with faint praise.

"But at the moment, until the media feeding frenzy subsides, they're the most hated company in America. What's good enough for Mom and Pop's oatmeal factory is *not* good enough for Deep Country, not this month. So we need to find temporary ways of shoring up their security without hitting their pain point."

"Pain point?" Charlie asked.

Dom rubbed her thumb against her fingertips. "Money. Technically, we could surround the building with a cordon of several hundred armed security officers, put a checkpoint with bomb-sniffing dogs on every elevator and stairwell, and plate the entire tower in sheets of bulletproof ceramic. They'd be safe. They'd also be bankrupt by the end of the week. The ideal security solution lowers risk just far enough, without costing too much money. Problem is it's the client who makes that decision, and they don't always lean in the right direction."

Charlie glanced over her shoulder. She didn't want any of Sean's employees overhearing what she had to say.

"Last night," she told Dom, pitching her voice low, "his reactions . . . they weren't right. Beckett and I both think he's got something going on, beyond the scandal we know about. Something he's trying to keep hushed up. Any normal person would have called the cops last night—"

"We don't do protection for 'normal people,' Charlie. Get used to it. Goes with the territory. We do our jobs, we keep our clients' confidence, and we don't ask any questions that don't need answers. Nosy security companies don't get referrals. There's a lot of competition in this business and not enough work to go around."

"Just saying . . . seems contrary to what you said back at HQ."

Dom's eyes narrowed. She stared at Charlie like a book written in a foreign language. "Meaning?"

"We're not dealing with a nut with a gun," Charlie told her. "This person, people, whoever . . . they got access to the building, they got their hands on illegal explosives, and they used some fairly solid technical know-how to booby-trap Sean Ellis's office. If that bomb had gone off, it would have killed anyone within fifty feet of him. Employees, *us*, anyone. The assassin knew that. They didn't care."

"You're thinking about what they're going to do for an encore," Dom said.

"Can we agree that there's definitely going to be one? Nobody goes to that much trouble to kill somebody and gives up when their first shot misses. Next time their little surprise might be wired to the elevators, hidden in the engine of the car we use to drive him around, right under our feet . . . there's a thousand ways to kill somebody with a bomb, and most of 'em are dirt simple. Trust me. I know. You want to go home alive at the end of the day? So do I."

She had Dom's full attention. The woman leaned in, her deep amber eyes narrow and sharp. "What are you proposing, exactly?"

"Ellis doesn't want the cops around? Fine. But we do a little digging on our own. Just a little. Not enough to step on any toes, not enough that he's going to complain or pull the contract. But if there's any way we can find out who and what we're up against, it improves the odds for all of us."

The clerk came back. He pressed a chunky ring of keys into Dom's hand, mumbled something about not being the building's janitor, and made himself scarce before she could give him any more work to do. Dom tried the keys one at a time until the knob clicked and the closet yawned open. They gazed with dismay into a closet piled high with empty, moldering cardboard boxes, building a haphazard mountain under a burned-out bulb.

Dom nudged a box with the squared tip of her shoe. A trio of silverfish went skittering across the soggy cardboard to escape. "Now that's just unsanitary. Okay, Nancy Drew. I'm with you on principle. How about specifics? You got a plan to go with that goal?"

Charlie had been thinking about that since they'd arrived. Her forebrain was on high alert, checking every nook and cranny like she was doing a patrol sweep—*Because I am*, she realized—so she attacked it like she'd handle any other intel problem out in the field: make nice with the locals.

"I've got two advantages," she told Dom. "First, I saved Ellis's life last night. So that should buy me a little credit."

Dom snorted. "You might be surprised. Most of our clients think it's our job to die for 'em with a smile on our faces."

"Even so, he seemed pretty grateful last night, albeit understandably shaken up. Second, he knows I'm new on the job. Meaning I might ask questions a veteran operative wouldn't."

"Questions that could get you in trouble?" Dom arched an eyebrow.

"Maybe. But if I happen to overstep my bounds, it's a good thing you're here to reprimand me and apologize on behalf of the company, isn't it? No harm, no foul—I'm the only one who gets in trouble, hopefully minimal, and the contract is safe."

Dom shut the closet door.

"If this goes sideways," she told Charlie, "it's all on you. I'm not sticking my neck out."

"Not asking you to."

She looked Charlie up and down, taking her measure, silently weighing her options. Then she nodded.

"Go fish," Dom said.

One floor up, Charlie—flying solo now, toting a clipboard of her own with a few scribbled notes just for show—found Sean Ellis in his office. He sat cross-legged on the powder-blue carpet, surrounded by plastic parts and the skeletal aluminum guts of a mutant chair. He looked up, greeted Charlie with a perplexed smile, and ruffled the IKEA instruction sheet on his lap like a blanket.

"I know it's not your job," he told her, "but I don't suppose you could lend an old man a hand? This is really a two-person challenge, and my juggling days are long behind me."

She would have said yes anyway; even if Charlie wasn't helpful by habit, the army had taught her that *not my job* was a fatal phrase that inevitably led to a dressing-down and even *worse* jobs. That said, she couldn't have asked for a better opening. She cleared a space, gently shoving aside a leather arm with a backward-mounted bracket, and reached for a screwdriver.

"I think I see the problem," she said. "At least one problem. So . . . you doing okay? Had a little excitement last night."

Sean patted the breast of his jacket with a shaky hand. "More excitement than I need, but fine, thanks to you."

"Mr. Ellis," she said, walking carefully as she angled toward the subject, "if I hadn't been there, in the right place at the right time . . ."

He fumbled with a washer. A screw rattled into another length of aluminum frame. "Things have a way of working out. I've always believed that. I started this company from nothing, you know. Just dirty hands and grit. They don't talk about that in the news. Everything I did to build Deep Country up from scratch. They *used* to call me an American success story."

He pointed at the glass shelves set into an alcove, the rows upon rows of industry awards in crystal and gold. Sean looked at them like they were magic talismans, proof of his glory and shields against harm, that had somehow been drained of their enchantment.

Charlie swallowed down a flash of anger. *Maybe because thirty dead miners is bigger news*, she wanted to say. Sean was clueless. He came off affable, almost grandfatherly, assembling his new chair like a kid playing with Tinkertoys. And his biggest complaint, after a would-be attacker at his banquet and a bomb under his seat cushion, was that he wasn't getting enough applause.

"That's how fast the media will turn on you," he warned her. "Oh, they'll say they're your friend, when everything's going your way, but that's just to get their hooks in."

"But . . . yesterday," Charlie said. "Someone really went out of their way to try and hurt you. Do you have any idea who might have the motive and the skills to—"

He cut her off, charging over her words like a rhino. "No. No idea. Someone who blames me for . . . for what happened in Kentucky, no doubt. Some crazy."

"They used an M112 demolition block. You can't just buy those at the hardware store. Without the right licenses and permits, you can't get one at all."

Sean wagged a hex wrench at her. "Proves my point. We use demolitions for mining, fracking . . . I've got my people conducting a full inventory of company assets, as we speak. I'm sure we'll find some explosives 'wandered off the job' around the same time one of my employees did. We'll go to the police once we have concrete evidence to show them. Any sooner, and they'll just trample all over the evidence *and* my business. No need for it."

Charlie thought again about the man she'd turned away from the banquet. Beckett was right; this bomber had a profile, and the agitated, righteous intruder didn't fit it one bit. All the same, she had to admit Sean might have a point. His own company was the most likely source of the explosives.

Before she could answer, his phone buzzed. He slid it from his breast pocket and gave the screen a look, and the blood drained from his cheeks.

"Excuse me." His Botox-locked forehead struggled to crease as he clambered to his feet. "I have to take this."

He stepped into his private bathroom and shut the door. The lock softly clicked. Charlie took a deep breath, got to her feet, and padded across the office in his wake. She leaned close to the door. With her ear a quarter inch from the wood, she could just barely make out his strained voice.

"Made your *point?*" he whispered. "Yes, you made your goddamn point; now why won't you listen to *mine?* I'm telling you, I don't have it. How do you think I got where I—no, you do the math. I can't give you what I don't have."

Charlie shot a glance behind her, to the closed office door. If anyone came in and saw her spying on the boss's private phone call, even being a new hire wouldn't be enough to save the contract . . . or her job, for that matter.

"I wasn't with her," Sean hissed. "If I had been, I'd be buried right next to her. What, you think I didn't look? I spent the better part of a decade before I realized I was throwing good money after bad. Why can't you figure that out? You're digging for a treasure that doesn't exist."

Charlie held her breath as the conversation—Sean's end of it, anyway—went silent. She braced herself and got ready to move the second she heard his footsteps on the ceramic bathroom tile.

"Do what you want," Sean sighed. "*I don't have it.* Killing me won't change that. And stop calling me. You're wasting your time."

That sounded like a coda. Charlie tiptoed back across the office and dropped down onto the thin carpet. She snatched up her screwdriver and the chair bracket she'd been working on just as the bathroom door swung wide.

Sean looked like he'd aged five years since his phone had rung. He shoved it into his pocket, hands visibly shaking, and drummed his fingers on his desk. He didn't look at her. "I, uh . . . thanks for the help. With the chair. I . . . need to prepare for a presentation, if you don't mind?"

He showed her the door with a flick of his heavy eyes. Charlie saw herself out.

Sean's administrative assistant, a prim and quiet woman named Allison, sat at a curved desk just outside his office. Charlie had spoken to her only briefly, helping Dom to coordinate details when they'd first arrived. On an impulse, she drifted over to the desk and waited to catch the woman's eye.

"Hi," Charlie said. "Just wanted to make sure we stay in the loop. Once word comes back on the inventory audit, can you make sure either myself or Dominica Da Costa gets a copy of the results?"

Allison peered at her like she'd asked for a unicycle. "Inventory . . . audit? I'm sorry, what audit is this?"

Charlie nodded to Sean's closed office door. "The mining explosives. Seeing if anything's gone missing from the company stocks."

"First I've heard of it."

An ugly suspicion swelled in the back of Charlie's mind. All the same, maybe Sean had gone through back channels to get the job done. Sean didn't want anyone, including his employees, to know about last night's attempted murder.

"Is there anyone else Mr. Ellis might have called about it, without getting you involved?" she asked.

Allison shook her head and let out a tired chuckle.

"Mr. Ellis," she said, "doesn't even have a company phone directory. Trust me, I'm his eyes, ears, hands, and feet. If I don't know about an audit, there isn't one."

SEVENTEEN

"So he knows," Dom said. She and Charlie were parked in a back booth at a greasy spoon down the street, with plastic baskets of steak fries and cheeseburgers on greasy, soggy buns. A fresh-cut onion crunched between Charlie's teeth, slathered with mustard the same garish yellow as the vinyl seats.

"He knows," Charlie said.

She'd recounted the whole story: what she'd heard on Sean's side of the phone call, and how he'd lied to her about taking an inventory of the company stocks.

"No reason not to audit the explosives."

"Unless," Charlie said, "he knows exactly who's trying to kill him, and he knows they don't work for Deep Country."

"It sounded like they wanted something from him?"

Charlie poked her straw deeper into her cardboard cup, stirring ice in a tiny pond of black cherry Polar soda.

"Treasure, he called it. And he said he didn't have it."

"You believe him?" Dom asked.

Charlie thought about it. She sipped her soda and breathed deep, the air thick with the aroma of grilled meat patties and salt.

"I don't think Sean Ellis is a very good liar," Charlie said. "When he gets flustered—and he flusters easy—he changes subjects, he deflects, anything to squirm out of a corner. So yeah, going with my gut here, but I believe him. Whatever these people want, he can't give it to them."

"Meaning they're going to keep coming until they figure it out. If they figure it out. And Ellis would rather get himself blown straight to hell, and us right along with him, than help us solve the problem." Dom slumped back in her booth, rolling her gaze to the ceiling. "We need to get out of this contract."

"That's what Beckett said."

"He's rarely wrong. Okay, we're just about done here for today anyway. I'm going to take all of this, bundle it up in a nice report, and drop it on Jake's desk. I'll compare notes with Beckett, and we'll tag team him if we have to."

"Hold off," Charlie said.

Dom paused in midbite, dangling a steak fry between her teeth. "Mm?"

Charlie wasn't even sure why she'd said it. It was an impulse. A compulsive need to unravel this mystery and find the truth. If they walked away now, she'd never know the real story.

No. That wasn't true. She knew exactly how this would go down. Sean Ellis would be murdered. If they were very lucky, it'd *only* be him. If not, any number of innocent bystanders would go right along with him. The cops would investigate. They'd find the killers. The killers would talk. Charlie would learn the whole story on the nightly news, just like everybody else in America. All she had to do, if she wanted to get the facts, was walk away and wait for the inevitable.

Maybe it was the collateral damage. The idea of innocents dying because she walked away was hard to stomach. That was a nice, safe motivation. Made her the good guy. Nothing wrong with that, right?

At the core of it all, though, one word reeled Charlie in like a fish chasing a golden lure.

Treasure.

Whether he had it or not, the people stalking Sean Ellis believed that there was a treasure out there, waiting to be claimed. A treasure with enough trouble attached that Sean wouldn't—*couldn't*—get the police involved.

Maybe she was chasing phantoms, but all Charlie could see was her father's hourglass running down. Chasing phantoms was better than sitting on her hands and doing nothing.

"I might have a lead," she told Dom. "I'll check it out tonight."

"Wasting your time. We'll have a new assignment come tomorrow anyway."

Charlie rubbed a paper napkin across her greasy fingertips. "Just . . . give me one night, okay?"

Dom sipped her soda. She stared at Charlie over the rim of her cardboard cup.

"What are you doing, Charlie?"

"Told you. I've got one last lead. Just seems right to look into it."

"No," Dom said. "What are you really doing?"

She wasn't sure how to answer that. Dom didn't offer to elaborate. The question hung between them, suspended like a dangling sword, as they finished their cheeseburgers.

Pushing through the swinging door of the Crab Walk, the carnival smell of cheap beer and salted peanuts felt like a warm welcome home. Van Halen was rocking out on the jukebox, and Dutch was behind the bar, serving up the brew. He gave Charlie a nod as she took a stool on the far end. Eventually he got out from under the rush of customers and made his way over, sliding her a freshly opened bottle before she could ask for one. The bottle was clammy and warm against her palm, but the ale, some local blend flavored with a hint of roasted chestnuts, went down smoother than imported champagne.

"Needed that," she said. "Cheers."

"Long day at the office?"

"What do you hear?"

Dutch set a fresh lime on the rubber mat behind the bar and chopped into it, restocking the garnishes of his trade.

"Heard you impressed Beckett," he said. "Nobody impresses Beckett."

"What do you know about him?"

"Same as everybody. Nothing. Jake trusts him with his life, though, and I trust Jake." Dutch held up his thin-bladed knife and squinted as he ran his thumb across the blade. "Not one damn sharp knife in this entire bar."

"Pretty sure you have to sharpen them yourself, now and then."

"Reckon so. Problem with being your own boss: you've got nobody else to blame when things go pear shaped."

"Blaming other people's never been your style," she said.

"Mm-hmm. Isn't Jake's style either. Or his sister's."

"You heard about the bomb?"

"Heard somebody played the hero." Dutch pulled a pint from the tap for a barfly two stools down, tilting the water-spotted mug to cut down on the foamy head.

"I did my job," Charlie told him.

He gave her a noncommittal grunt and swept a couple of crumpled bills from the bar.

"So how much trouble are Jake and Sofia in, anyway?" she asked.

Dutch's left eyebrow rose almost imperceptibly. "Who said anything about trouble?"

"You did. There's some blame on the table, not about the bomb, and neither one of them is the kind of boss who passes the buck."

"Cash flow problems," Dutch told her. "The most basic kind there is. More money going out than coming in."

Charlie nodded and sipped her beer. Exactly what she'd suspected, but it was good to know for sure. Just like overseas, intel was the coin of the realm. Sometimes it was the only coin that bought anything worth having.

"That's why Jake isn't telling Sean Ellis and his mining buddies to go jump in a hole," she said. "He *needs* this contract, to keep the company solvent, doesn't he?"

"Until he lines up something better. Drums up a client or two who aren't on a mad bomber's hit list."

"I can't help with that," Charlie said.

"So what can you help with?"

She made a sound like a chuckle. Then she leaned back and took a long pull from the bottle. The ale swirled in her tummy and left a faint tingle in her brain, not enough to dull her wits, just enough to make her a little cocky.

"I don't know, Dutch. *Do* I have any experience hunting for mad bombers?"

He snorted. "Don't go buying trouble. Already starting to regret putting you onto this gig."

"Nothing to regret, unless this guy takes another shot at Ellis and I get caught in the blast. Best way to prevent that is to get proactive. Go on the attack."

"You didn't come here to shoot the shit tonight," Dutch told her. "You're playing bloodhound."

"Remember the night I came home, when we talked about your connections? You've still got a few. You said as much."

"No bombers on my Rolodex," he said. "I know a couple of people who trade money for blood, but they're more into silenced twenty-twos and such. Nobody pays for collateral damage."

Charlie finished her bottle. She set it down on the bar, the glass rattling under the music as the first chords of Rush's "Tom Sawyer" blared on the jukebox behind her. Dutch reached under the bar and gave her bottle a twin brother.

"Every hitter," she said, "no matter how they do the hitting, gets their tools from somewhere. I've got an M112 demo block in my bedroom closet. I find out where it came from, maybe I find my man before he can hurt anybody. We got lucky last night. I don't think we'll get lucky twice."

"Mining company. Sounds like an inside job to me."

Charlie shook her head. "Ruled it out. Ellis knows exactly who's trying to kill him; the reasons, whatever they are, have nothing to do with those thirty dead miners in Kentucky, and the explosives audit he supposedly ordered is a sham. The block didn't come from Deep Country's arsenal. So if I was a bomber hunting for a bomb with no paper trail and no questions asked, where would I go?"

"Hold on a sec," Dutch said.

He worked the bar, slinging bottles and refilling mugs, pausing midway down to mix an inky-dark drink in a highball glass. Charlie watched him work. Nobody had been clamoring for his attention while they talked; he was just buying time. She sipped from her second bottle of ale, slowing down now. She couldn't get sloppy tonight.

"Could find a legal demolition company with loose morals," he finally said as he made his way back. "Bribe a foreman to sell you a block under the table."

"Except every demo block is tracked and tagged," Charlie said. "Hell of a risk. Sell to the wrong person, next thing you know the ATF is hammering your door down, and you're up on charges as an accessory to terrorism. And everybody with access knows that. Stealing it outright is a better bet, lots easier than finding somebody willing to take that risk. That's what I'd do."

"Maybe so," he said. He followed her road map as if he didn't already have a destination in mind.

"Any civilian firm trusted with handling C-4, generally speaking, keeps that stuff locked down tighter than Fort Knox. Between the legal liability, insurance premiums, and the threat of getting your license pulled for a minor screwup, they don't play around. So that's no heist for amateurs."

"Sounds to me," Dutch said, "like you're stepping beyond the lines of the hypothetical at this point."

"I did some homework. McCullen Construction was a Boston firm specializing in demolitions. They got hit last winter. Cleaned out, and while the papers were light on specifics, reading between the lines tells me a certain quantity of C-4 went AWOL. Now, we haven't had any big booms since, so I'm betting the thieves didn't steal it for personal use; they wanted to sell it."

"You said every block is tagged. ATF could tell you if your block came from the McCullen heist."

"Sure," Charlie said. "And not only would they confiscate it, I'd have to tell them where I got it. I betray Sean Ellis's request not to talk to the cops, he yanks the protection contract in retaliation, and Jake and Sofia get screwed. Not looking to play it that way, so that's off the table."

"I'm hearing a question."

"Sure you are," Charlie said.

"I'm an old guy; my hearing ain't what it used to be." Dutch dug a finger in one ear and twisted it around, scratching an itch. "Maybe ask it straight, so I'm sure it's what you really want."

Charlie set her bottle down. Her fingertips rested on the sticky laminate wood of the bar as she looked him in the eye.

"The explosives from the McCullen heist hit the black market. Somebody is selling it off, piecemeal, and there's a very good chance *my* demo block is from that stolen batch. The black market isn't that big, and these guys all know each other, or they know somebody who knows. All I need is an intro to one established, reliable contact who sells firepower under the table. I can take it from there."

He stared at her for a long, hard moment. Taking her measure without a word. She held his gaze, not blinking once.

"Market's small, but it's not a kiddie pool," he told her. "Ain't the kind of crowd you run with, Charlie. You don't know the lay of that land."

"I didn't know the lay of the land in Afghanistan either. I'm a quick study. Walked into some hairy places over there and walked out again just fine. Besides, I even speak the language here."

Dutch curled his lip. He shook his head, turning his back on her, and ambled to the back of the bar. He came back with a scrap of paper in his fist and scribbled down an address with no name attached.

"Don't be too sure," he said. "Every culture has its own language. Its own way of doing things. But I imagine those same skills you picked up . . . they might just help you out here too."

He slid the paper across to her. Charlie took a furtive glance, folded it in half, and made it disappear.

"You want to talk to a man calls himself Saint," Dutch said. "He ain't one, so don't go getting your hopes up. Don't drop my name if you don't have to. Not sure how much credit it still carries. And Charlie?"

She was already off the stool, running shoes touching down on the sticky wooden floorboards. "Yeah?" she asked.

"You're walking into a war zone," he told her. "Act like it."

Eighteen

War zones were no place for a lone wolf. Even snipers worked in two-soldier teams. Charlie took Dutch's warning to heart; she went home, lingering in the driveway, watching the television's light flicker behind tugged-down dusty blinds, and made a phone call.

Half an hour later, a dull-gunmetal car glided down the hill, headlights the color of yellowed bone. It rolled to a rumbling stop in the gravel driveway. The headlights died. Up close, Charlie got a better look: it was a nineties-era Buick Skylark, a family sedan with amber-tinted windows, spotted with freckles of rust but still clinging to life. A big car for a big man. The door swung open, and Beckett, still wearing his black suit and tie, stepped out to meet her.

"Dark waters, Little Duck."

"I can swim," she told him. "That's what ducks do, right?"

"That, and get shot by hunters."

"You came anyway."

"Sure," he said. He didn't care to elaborate.

Charlie nodded at his car. "Didn't see you in a ride like this."

An eyebrow lifted. "Oh? What did you think I'd drive?"

Charlie studied him, taking him in, his smooth scalp and sculpted goatee, his broad shoulders under his tailored suit. Not one out-of-place hair or a wrinkle.

"Something stylish. Maybe something fast. Classic Detroit steel, or a modern SUV. A big one, with a big engine."

Beckett's chuckle was a rumbling tiger purr. He walked around to the driver's side, leaned in, and popped the hood. He lifted it up and waved her close. She stepped up to stand beside him. Her eyes went wide. "Beckett . . . what am I looking at?"

He beamed with contented pride.

"That, Little Duck, is an eight-point-four liter, five hundred and thirteen cubic inch V10 engine." He gestured to the black foam lining the hood and engine compartment, keeping the massive engine and coil of parts snug as a rifle in a gun case. "Damping mats and marine-grade insulation to hide the rumble. Had to widen and deepen the entire engine compartment to make it work . . . but we made it work."

"You turned a nineties Buick into a street machine," Charlie breathed. "It's kind of beautiful."

"Turned it into a street *shark*," Beckett replied. "She's got a six-speed manual transmission, run-flat tires, bullet-resistant glass, and Flex-Pro armor paneling behind the doors, sidewalls, and front and rear hoods. The engine isn't just for speed; I needed the extra power to pull the added weight. Oh, and the rust spots are all fake, painted on by a guy who does special effects for horror flicks. He owed me a favor."

"I take it back," she said. "This is exactly the kind of ride I'd see you in."

He flashed a grin and let the hood drop.

"I'm not done tweaking the build yet. My weekend hobby. So . . . you really want to go downtown?"

"The C-4 is the best lead we've got. The *only* lead we've got, really. I figure it's either that or we throw a bag over Sean Ellis's head and expose him to the wonders of enhanced interrogation. Which would get us fired and arrested, so . . ."

Beckett walked past her and opened the trunk. "You ever do that kind of work, in your old job?"

"Interrogation?" Charlie shook her head. "Not the hard way. Got a lot more mileage out of buying my sources a Coke and giving 'em a shoulder to lean on. A little understanding and empathy does wonders to get intel. Game of kickball saved my life once."

He rummaged in the trunk. "Yeah? How's that?"

"Off duty, ended up playing with these Pashtun kids. Ragged little things, but they could play some mean ball. After, I passed out some gum from the base commissary, and they taught me a few new phrases in Pashto, few of which I can say in mixed company. Anyway, next day, one of those kids runs out and flags down my convoy. He spotted an insurgent wiring an IED on the very next corner and hiding it under a trash pile. I *wouldn't* have spotted it. He remembered the nice lady with the gum, so he didn't want me to get hurt."

Beckett slammed the trunk lid. "Going to need more than gum tonight."

"I've got my winning smile," she told him.

"In other words, you're not carrying."

"Thing about the army is," she said, "you're not allowed to take your guns home with you. Government property. They're oddly touchy about that stuff. I've reapplied for my LTC, but I can't legally carry until the paperwork goes through."

"Because what we're doing tonight is *legal*. Anyway, I brought you a present. It was supposed to be your welcome-to-the-company present once this Deep Country mess was over with, but under the circumstances I figure it shouldn't wait."

He pressed a long, thin cardboard box into her hands. She pried up the lid. Inside, on a bed of white, rumpled paper, was a key chain of sorts. It was a thin black steel tube, about six inches long with a textured grip, topped by a big round brass loop. Beside it, resting in the paper, were a pair of smaller tubes, one with a blue plastic tip, the other red. Charlie picked up the black tube, feeling its weight in her hand. The textured grip felt sandpaper rough against her palm.

"ASP Key Defender," Beckett said. "Meet your new partner. When I'm not around, anyway. A compact, multitactical personal defense solution."

She eyed him. "Multitactical?"

He held out his big hand, and she passed him the tube.

"You grip it by the baton, like so," he said, demonstrating. "Right at the base of the key ring, there's your safety. Flip it with your thumb, turn, and depress the switch."

The Defender twirled in his fingers. He paused for a heartbeat, judging the wind, and pointed the baton away from their faces. A thin mist hissed from the base, spraying out and settling on the glistening grass.

"OC spray, with an effective range of five feet," Beckett explained. "You know what a Scoville heat unit is?"

"That's how they judge how spicy a hot sauce is, right?"

"Right. A jalapeño pepper is about five thousand SHU. Ghost pepper, one of the hottest peppers in the world, is rated at one million SHU. This spray is *two* million SHU. Much like your average angry wasp, this baby has a hell of a sting, and its only purpose in life is to ruin somebody's day."

He spun his fist, tailored sleeve rustling as he threw a precision punch at the air.

"If quarters are too close or the wind's against you—because you do not want this blowing back in your face, I promise—you can use the baton to augment your strikes. Alternately"—he lashed the empty key ring toward her, keeping a safe distance but close enough that she could feel the warm air buffet her face—"get medieval. You can use your keys as a flail. Go for the eyes, and you'll do some serious damage, maybe permanent."

He passed the Defender back to her. She turned it in her hand, staring down at the tool with newfound appreciation. "I think I like it."

"I think you will too. Those inserts in the box are extras. The one with the red cap is a replacement capsule of CS spray, and the blue is inert, just plain water under pressure. That's a training insert so you won't hurt yourself if you manage to eat a blast in the face while you're practicing. For hopefully obvious reasons, I strongly recommend you take advantage of it."

"Duly noted," Charlie said. "Don't really have time to train tonight, though."

"I'm armed up for both of us, if it comes to it. And if things go that sideways, we're probably good as dead anyhow. You've got an in with this Saint guy?"

"Only a name of a mutual associate, and I've been asked not to drop it if I don't have to."

"Even better." Beckett let out a deep-voiced sigh and bobbed his head at the car. "C'mon, let's do this before I smarten up and change my mind."

"Can I drive?"

He blurted out a laugh and opened the driver's side door.

"Little Duck, I like you. But I don't like anybody *that* much. Let's go."

"He lives in Murderpan," Beckett muttered. "Even better."

They cruised through the streets of Mattapan, just south of Dorchester, pale headlights strobing off shuttered storefronts and graffiti-strewn walls. The neighborhood had a heavy Caribbean vibe, faded green-and-gold signs shouting ads for Jamaican cuisine and jerk chicken. Now Charlie understood why Beckett had called his ride a shark car; the Skylark didn't roll so much as prowl, muffled engine hiding its secret power under the hood, the rust-spotted body forgettable and anonymous. The console glowed soft in the dark, and Marvin Gaye crooned on the radio.

"Left up here," Charlie said.

Left was a street lined with grand old Victorians. They would have been something to see back in their heyday. Now they'd gone to seed, sporting sagging eaves and windows with spiderweb cracks and tacked-up bedsheet curtains. They made Charlie think of old silent-film stars, aging, forgotten, still desperately clinging to the last remnants of their glory days.

The address on Dutch's scrap of paper was halfway up the block. Beckett pulled to the curb and killed the engine.

"Last chance to get some sense and turn around," he told her.

"So, what, we go back to work tomorrow and wait for the next bomb to show up?" She clicked her seat belt and sent it sliding off her shoulder. "I'm not good at playing defense. I want to go on the attack before we *get* attacked."

Beckett's lips curled in a thin smile.

"'Playing defense' is literally our job description," he said, "but you aren't wrong."

A local welcoming committee—three men with knit caps and prison-yard eyes—hung out on the front steps. They were passing around a bottle in a brown paper bag and trying to look casual, like they hadn't been keeping watch over the street from corner to corner. And keeping watch over Charlie and Beckett, nudging each other as the new arrivals got out of the Skylark.

"You lost?" one called over.

Charlie stepped up, keeping her hands open and easy at her sides. "Looking for Saint," she said.

"Don't know who it is that you're referring to, *Officer*."

That got the man in charge a backslap and a snicker from his buddies. Charlie took a deep breath and let it out slow.

"We look like cops to you?" she asked.

The man with the paper bag took a pull from his bottle, then looked her up and down before checking out Beckett.

"Yep."

"Huh," Charlie said. She took an exaggerated look at her partner and nodded. "Guess we do. Then again, that'd make us pretty stupid cops, wouldn't it? Coming down here looking like undercover rookies, asking to see a man with a houseful of weapons?"

The man with the bottle narrowed his eyes, not following. "So?"

Charlie jerked her head to the left. "Street we just turned on, Saint's got a kid watching the intersection. Should tell him to be less obvious about it. Means he must have another one a block to the west. He's got both approaches locked down, so if a raid is coming, he'll have time to book it."

"So?" he echoed.

"So," Charlie said, "call 'em and ask if they see five-oh. They don't and they won't. My man here and me are all alone, no backup. That'd make us dumb and *dead* cops. If we were cops, and if we were here looking for trouble. No way we could march Saint out of here in cuffs and live to talk about it. You know it and we know it."

He took that in, along with another swig of whatever he had in the paper bag. Something behind his eyes seemed to spark, following her logic.

"Whatchu want, then?"

"Told you. Saint. We want to talk some business."

He looked convinced. One of the other men on the stoop folded his arms. "Still think you might be cops."

"Maybe we're dirty cops," Beckett rumbled.

"In which case," Charlie added, "we're still here to talk business."

The man with the paper bag shoved himself to his feet. He passed the bottle to one of his buddies and dusted off his jeans.

"Be right back. Watch 'em until I do."

A minute passed. The two on the stoop wanted a stare-down contest. Charlie didn't oblige. She felt the heat of their gaze on her cheek as she studied the block. A quiet night in Mattapan. Every once in a while, a curtain would shiver, and she'd catch a flash of a face at the edge, someone checking the temperature of the street.

The door to the Victorian opened. The sentry poked his head out. "He says you got five minutes. Make 'em count."

Nineteen

The summer heat had cooled a little with the sunset, but sealed-up windows and no air-conditioning turned the Victorian into a pressure cooker. Charlie felt a cold bead of sweat trickle down her spine as she stood in the foyer on a dusty rug, arms out in a T pose. Saint's minder patted her down. Somebody was cooking dinner; the stifling air was thick with the mingled scents of coriander, garlic, and some kind of blistering-hot seasoning, strong enough to taste it in the back of her throat.

The guy patting her down was an amateur. He wasn't comfortable searching a woman, and it showed: his hesitant palm missed Beckett's gift entirely, the Defender's tube snug in her cargo pants pocket, and he didn't even check her inner thighs. He did better with Beckett, tugging a matte black .45 revolver from a shoulder holster under his jacket.

"You got anything else?" he asked Beckett.

"Your job to find out," Beckett answered him.

The sentry ended up plucking a .22 from a holster on Beckett's ankle, concealed under the tailored leg of his slacks, before waving them toward a rickety staircase with a floral-print runner. Just out of earshot, Charlie murmured, "Did he find it all?"

"Got one last holdout piece," Beckett said, "and it's just about big enough to scare a chihuahua. Between that and your CS spray, we're not holding a winning hand at the moment. You do know you put the idea of killing us into their heads, right? If Saint gives the word, we're not walking out of here."

"You really think they wouldn't have come up with it on their own? Doubt these people need encouragement to shoot somebody."

"Doesn't mean you need to give it to 'em either."

She couldn't argue that. She knocked on the door at the top of the stairs.

"Enter," called a muffled voice.

Saint's lair was an attic room, white paint flaking on the low-slung rafters, windows draped tight in black and the floor coated under mismatched rugs with swirling, vaguely Persian designs. Bohemian chic by way of a garage sale. The man they were looking for sat back on a fat black leather beanbag chair, knees and arms spread wide, utterly at ease. The odor of a freshly snuffed joint drifted from an ashtray on the table at his left, stronger than the food smells from the kitchen below, and a scattering of empty Red Stripe bottles clustered around a lava lamp. The lamp sent shifting orange and yellow shadows across the angular room, painting it in Halloween shades.

Saint's hands flexed. He had prison tats on his hands, jet-black ink on rich brown skin, a pair of blocky crosses that ran along the inner curves of his index fingers. He gazed between Charlie and Beckett with heavy-lidded eyes and shook his head, tossing his dreadlocks.

"You aren't cops," he said. He tossed the verbal ball in their court and fell silent.

Charlie's nerves faded as her training kicked in. She sliced the room into cross-sections, her mind like a computer sifting through data. She measured angles and distances, checked for threats, and took the measure of the man before her. She felt at home. She'd stood before village chieftains and local strongmen, sometimes with guns in her face, and this was just a different fiefdom in a different land.

Saint was laying his bona fides on the table. Letting them know that he had sharper eyes, more experience and street smarts, than his buddies downstairs. His body language, open and relaxed, was a message, too; it read, *If you're here to do me harm, I'm not worried about it, because you won't succeed.*

He'd given his credentials. Time for Charlie to present hers. She held up one open hand.

"I'm going to reach into my pocket," she said.

She held still like that until he gave her a subtle nod. A gesture of respect for his position. She dipped her fingers into her hip pocket and tugged out her laminated ID card from Boston Asset Protection. He reached out, took it from her, and gave it a sleepy-eyed once-over. There was a musical lilt in his voice as he spoke, a hint of the Caribbean.

"Charlie McCabe. Rent-a-cop. I was only half-right." He passed the card back to her. "Shouldn't give strangers your civilian name, Charlie McCabe. Didn't anybody ever teach you that names have power?"

"Is that why you go by Saint?"

The beanbag chair rustled under him as he shifted his weight. He reached for a cigarette—a straight cigarette from a tattered pack of Camels, not a blunt—and lit up with a red plastic Bic.

"Back in the day, men believed that if you knew a demon's true name, you could conjure and bind him." He exhaled a plume of gray smoke. "Best not to take chances."

"You don't look like a demon," Charlie told him.

"You haven't given me any reason to." His gaze swung to Beckett. "What do you go by?"

Beckett didn't respond. He stood at Charlie's shoulder, stone faced and motionless. Saint nodded his head, accepting that as his answer, and looked back at Charlie.

"So you work private security. Pay good?"

"Pays all right."

"Ain't what you've always done, though." Saint bobbed his cigarette at them. "Nah. You and your brick here, you've got combat moves.

Battle tested. Saw it on you the second you came in. 'S why I'm not worried."

"No?"

He put the cigarette to his lips, tasting it like a fine wine.

"Nah," he said. "Moves like yours, if you were here to rip me off or kill me, you would've done it already. Only amateurs talk first."

"Truth," Beckett said, breaking his silence.

"Which makes me all kinds of curious," Saint said.

"Last year," Charlie told him, "a stash of plastic explosives went missing from a site owned by McCullen Construction. C-4, arranged in M112 detonation blocks. My best guess is they were stolen to sell. Word is you're a man who knows how to move weapons."

She caught it. That telltale flare of his nostrils as she named McCullen Construction. Even before she got to the C-4, she knew he had the answers they needed.

"You're looking to buy some explosives?" Saint asked her.

"No. I think they've already been sold. We want the person who bought them."

A smile lingered at the edge of his voice. "And you're asking me, why?"

"Like I said, word is firepower is your business. I hoped that if you didn't know about the McCullen heist, you might be able to point us in the right direction." She paused. "But you do."

Saint contemplated his cigarette.

"I don't normally do that kind of business," he said. "Explosives. I'm more of a small-arms aficionado. Glocks, Hi-Points, the ever-popular and evergreen MAC-10. The boys around here, that suits 'em just fine, and they don't have the cash for anything with a bigger punch anyway. Every once in a while I get a customer asking for a Desert Eagle. Comes from playing too many video games, y'know? They want that big *kaplow*, makes 'em feel like they've got elephant balls."

"But," Charlie said.

"But come last winter, I get a call from a Southie crew I've got a hookup with. They've got C-4. Do I *want* C-4? No. That's a level of trouble I don't need. ATF is interested in guns, but they come down like God's thunder on bombs."

"So you turned 'em down," Beckett said.

"At first. Thing is this crew had eyes bigger than their stomachs. They took the score before they had a buyer lined up—never a smart move—and word on the grapevine said they were desperate to unload before Homeland Security kicked their doors in. According to people that knew things, they were casting a line in troubled waters. Talking to men of . . . let's say, Middle Eastern descent?"

"What?" Charlie asked. "Like, Al-Qaeda? ISIS?"

Saint shrugged. "Never found out the specifics. Point is I'm nobody's idea of a model citizen, but Boston's my home. I *live* here. Didn't like the idea that every time I went to Fenway Park, I was gonna spend the whole game worried about getting my ass blown off by the explosives I *could* have bought. So I bought 'em. Not to resell so much as to keep them out of the wrong hands."

"You're being generous with intel," Beckett said.

"Words. Words are free. I know you didn't come here to rip me off, and you're not dumb enough to try to muscle me. Only leaves one reasonable possibility: You're here to do business. This chitchat is just the prelude to a deal. You're looking for explosives? I might have some."

"Some," Charlie said. "But you already sold the rest."

Saint snuffed his cigarette. The crosses on his fingers flexed as he steepled his fingers.

"And how do you know that?"

"Because someone used them last night, trying to blow up our client and anyone standing within twenty feet of him."

Saint lifted an eyebrow. "How many bricks did they use?"

"How many bricks did your customer buy?" Charlie replied.

"And so we dance," Saint told her with a faint and tired smile. "Indulge me. Why is it you on my doorstep and not the authorities?"

"Client asked us to keep it under wraps," Beckett said.

"So you find this person, my customer . . . and you're going to do what, exactly?"

Beckett held his silence while Charlie fumbled for an answer. *Hand them over to the police* was an obvious retort, but Ellis didn't want the cops involved in the first place, and nothing in this conversation would hold up in court. Take them out permanently? No. Charlie had fought in self-defense . . . she'd killed in self-defense . . . but she wasn't a murderer.

The truth was she had no idea what they were going to do when they caught Sean Ellis's attacker or what her options were beyond giving them a stern talking-to.

The truth was she just wanted to know why they were after him.

And about the treasure they were hunting for, the one they were willing to kill to get their hands on. Ellis had said on the phone that it didn't exist. But Charlie wasn't entirely sure he was right. Or maybe she just needed it to be real.

"We're hoping to settle this quietly and peacefully," she said. It was the best she could come up with.

Saint favored her with an almost pitying look, looking right through her. "You a woman of peace, Charlie McCabe?"

"I try to be."

"I bet you almost believe that." Saint wagged a finger at her. "You know, I'm not in the habit of ratting out my clientele. Makes for a bad reputation in my line of work, and a short life expectancy."

"We'd keep your name out of it," she said.

"We can make it worth your time," Beckett added. His voice was level, calculatedly uneager, like he didn't care if Saint helped them or not.

"Sure you can. But I'm not looking for a payoff. I can help you out. Hell, I can give you a face, tell you the way they paid me, and you *do* want to know how they paid me, trust me. That information is officially on sale, here and now. It's just too valuable to let it go as a cash transaction."

Charlie put her hands on her hips. "What do you want, then?"

"Just like the stories of old," Saint replied with a smile. "You can't buy wisdom with money, but you *can* pay for it with blood."

TWENTY

"Blood," Charlie echoed.

Saint leaned back. The black leather beanbag chair rustled and curled around him, conforming to his body.

"I'm having a little . . . market issue. Fresh competition, goes by Renaudin. This *mamaguevo* setting up shop on my patch, undercutting me, saying he's got the blessing of the Patriarca family." Saint's lips curled in a sneer. "Imagine that. A pissant Haitian, getting the nod."

"Aren't you Haitian?" Charlie asked.

It was the wrong question. Saint's anger hit her like the heat from a thousand-watt bulb.

"I'm *Dominican.*"

"Sorry." She held her open hands up. "Forget I said anything."

"Not the same thing. Learn the difference." Saint inhaled and waved it off with an irritated puff of breath. "Anyway. Anyway, I think he's lying; no way the Providence crew does business with anyone darker than a well-tanned white boy, but he's good at spreading rumors and making smoke. Bottom line is I want him gone. But just in case he really is connected, I can't use my own people. Need somebody discreet. Somebody deniable, with no connection to me or mine."

Charlie flicked her gaze to Beckett. The big man stood silent, his expression unreadable. She looked back at Saint.

"You want us to . . . what, kill him?"

"You tell me you ain't done it before," Saint replied, "I'm gonna forget my manners and call you a dirty liar."

Charlie didn't know about Beckett, but the gun dealer had her pegged. She'd gotten her hands wet in Afghanistan, more than once. She'd always been told that the act of killing changed a person; she wasn't sure about that. It was war. You did what you had to do. Sometimes she thought about it. Every once in a while she woke up in the still of the night, suddenly lost in the confusion, the muzzle flash, the sharp, shrill scream of a man catching a bullet—more a cry of surprise than of pain—smelling the gunfire like the battle was raging right next to her bunk.

Usually, she didn't.

She'd done her job. Then she'd come home.

Now she was being offered another job, and if she said yes, Saint would give her the keys to the kingdom. Everything she needed to know to track down Sean Ellis's would-be killer. And maybe the way to find this "treasure" they were looking for.

With her father's clock running down and his bookie circling, smelling blood in the water, she needed a treasure more than anything in the world.

Would it be that bad? she asked herself. *A gunrunner, a mobster . . . I've killed better men than that.*

She looked at Beckett again. He met her gaze but answered the question in her eyes with stony, poker-faced silence. She'd have to look elsewhere for a moral compass.

"No," she said.

Saint squinted at her. "No, you haven't, or no, you won't?"

"This isn't my battlefield. We'll pay you for the information we need. In cash, not bullets."

He looked past her. "How about you, tall, dark, and silent?"

Beckett bobbed his head at Charlie. "She's my partner."

He let that hang in the air, not bothering to elaborate. Saint leaned back on the beanbag chair and shrugged.

"Suit yourself. If and when you change your mind, come on back. Until then, that's all we've got to talk about."

Charlie and Beckett turned their backs and made for the door.

"Hey," Saint said. "Charlie McCabe."

She stopped and glanced back at him, over her shoulder.

"Know what they call a soldier without a nation to fight for?"

She shook her head.

"A mercenary," Saint said.

"What's your point?" she asked him.

"Point is you are one. Denying it, that's just a waste of time."

"Maybe I'm just picky," she said.

He broke into a smile and lit another cigarette. "Maybe you are. And maybe I'll see you again soon. I'll be waiting."

She wanted to say, *Don't count on it.* She wanted to slam the door on his offer and nail it shut, banish any hope of temptation.

She didn't say a word. She left in dead silence, Beckett at her back. The watchers on the stoop stared at them as they got into the Skylark and the engine purred. The stereo flickered to life and filled the air with soft Motown.

"What?" she asked him.

Beckett turned the wheel. The Skylark rumbled away from the curb, leaving the row of faded Victorians to fade in the rearview mirror.

"I didn't say anything."

"No," Charlie said, "you didn't."

"So what's the question?"

"Feels like you're judging me," she said.

He kept his eyes on the road. "I judge everything and nothing at all."

"Very Zen."

"Spent a year at a monastery in Tibet," he said. "Didn't suit my temperament, in the end, but I learned a thing or two."

Anyone else, she would have assumed they were joking.

"Question," Charlie said.

"Shoot."

"What would you have done if I said yes? If I took the offer?"

Beckett stayed casual, like they were talking about the weather. "I suppose we'd be on our way to kill a man."

"Just like that?"

"If you were looking for a debate on the subject, my first question would be 'Why did you say yes?' But you didn't. So we're not. You know, Saint was right about two things."

"Which two things?"

The Skylark glided to a stop at a traffic light. A mild summer rain pattered down, misting the windshield, turning the light into a bloody neon smear against the black night sky. Beckett flipped the wipers on. The blades slapped back and forth in a slow metronome dance. He held up one finger.

"One, we are soldiers with no nation. Private security *is* mercenary work. Now, that doesn't mean you can't pick and choose. Doesn't mean you can't weigh your morals against a paycheck and decide which one is heavier on the scales. Doesn't mean you shouldn't. Life is nothing but one long string of decisions and consequences. You make your choices; you take your ride."

Charlie frowned, dubious. "And the other thing he was right about?"

"That only amateurs talk before they pull the trigger."

The blurry light strobed from red to wintergreen. Beckett eased his foot down on the gas pedal.

They rode without talking for a while, just listening to the brassy strains of a Shirley Bassey song on the stereo. Charlie was back in the Victorian's attic, walking through the conversation with Saint forward and backward. Hunting for clues in every word he'd chosen.

"They're not locals."

"Hmm?" Beckett flicked a glance at her.

"They're not locals, and they're not regular customers of his. To be honest, I figured he'd turn us down flat when we offered to buy information from him. It was kind of a Hail Mary pass. Code of the streets and all that."

"Snitches get stitches."

"Exactly," Charlie said. "Except when there's no blowback to worry about. Saint wouldn't rat on one of his regular customers. We know he's afraid of the Boston mob. He's looking for secondhand killers to take care of someone he thinks possibly might be but probably isn't connected, just on the chance it *might* come back on him. If he's that worried about crossing the Patriarcas and their pals, we can also conclude that whoever bought the C-4 doesn't have any organized crime connections."

"A lone wolf from out of town." Beckett drummed his fingers on the steering wheel. "Sounds like we're back to the original theory. That it's someone related to those dead Deep Country miners, up from Kentucky and looking for payback."

"It doesn't jibe with the phone call I overheard, though. They want something from him. Some kind of treasure." Charlie frowned. "Which has been bothering me since square one."

"Extortion? Not an uncommon crime. Not with the kind of people we protect."

She shook her head. "No. It was their opening move. If I hadn't been there, if everything hadn't worked out just right, the bomb in Sean Ellis's chair would have killed him that night. Period, end of discussion. It even had a backup timer. The person who rigged that bomb fully intended to see him dead."

Beckett's eyes narrowed, just a bit, as he followed her train of thought. He flicked the turn signal and pulled a slow, easy left turn as the cold summer rain pattered down. "Why try to murder a man, *then* ask him for money?"

"Either we're looking at some spectacular incompetence," Charlie said, "or we've got more than one perp. One trying to kill him, one trying to squeeze him."

"I'd say again we have to get out of this contract," he replied, "but saying it the last ten times didn't do us any good."

Charlie didn't like repeating rumors, but she had a feeling she wasn't about to say anything Beckett didn't already know. "Friend of a friend says the company is having cash flow problems."

"Your friend of a friend speaks true," he said, "but keep that on the down low. This ship hasn't sunk yet, and we've already had three rats jump off in the last month. Rival firm made offers to some of our best veteran assets; they had to choose between loyalty and steady cash, and they took the cash. On the bright side, that freed up the resources to bring you on board."

"I did wonder why the company was hiring new people, if they're having income problems."

"Person," Beckett said. "Just you. You didn't hear this from me, but that was mostly a favor from Jake to the guy who suggested you for the job. Owed him for something, from way back, and giving you a tryout was part of the repayment plan. Anyway, you're not wrong. Jake and Sofia need this contract. Meaning we need Mr. Sean Ellis happy, in one piece, and breathing for the duration. He dies on our watch, we might as well lock up the shop for good."

Something about the way Beckett worded it, how he took it from the impersonal to the personal—talking about *Jake and Sofia*, not *Boston Asset Protection*—sparked an insight. Charlie tilted her head, contemplating him. "You would have done it for them, wouldn't you?"

"Done what?"

"Killed that dealer Saint wants dead, to get the intel we need."

"Didn't say I would do it at all," Beckett replied.

"You didn't say you wouldn't."

He didn't answer right away.

"Material things come and go. You can be fat on Tuesday, thin on Wednesday. When it comes right down to it, there's only one form of currency in the whole wide world that matters."

"Information?"

"Loyalty," he said. "Information is the *second* most important. And we're not wealthy at the moment."

"I might have an idea." Charlie hesitated. "It's not exactly legal."

He gave her the side-eye. "As compared to dropping in for a chat with a black market arms dealer?"

"I'm just saying. We know Ellis has been getting calls from the . . . well, from *a* viable threat. They'll probably call back. If we could get ears on that conversation, it might give us a clue as to who we're after."

"You want to tap the man's phone," Beckett said. His voice was flat. She wasn't sure if he was on board or chastising her.

"I do," Charlie said. "Unless you've got a better plan."

He thought that over as he drove. The rain kept coming down, running down the windshield in long rivulets and smearing the streetlights.

"I do not," he replied. "But this is a three-person job. Any objections to turning this partnership into a conspiracy?"

"Who did you have in mind?"

"Only other person I trust around here. Also, only person who has the tech know-how to get it done." He nodded to himself, setting a course. "We need Dom for this."

TWENTY-ONE

"Oh, *hell* no," Dom said. Her breath puffed a plume of steam from the cardboard cup of coffee in her hand. "Screw you *both*."

The rains had cleared overnight, leaving wet sidewalks, a muddy sky, and hot, muggy air in between. The three of them camped in a far booth at the Dunkin' Donuts down the street from Deep Country's corporate tower. A glazed cruller sat in front of Charlie on a paper napkin, untouched. She had been hungry when she'd ordered it, but she'd lost her appetite fast.

"Just floating the idea, that's all," Beckett told her. His voice carried a soothing rumble, like a zookeeper trying to calm an agitated lion before it took someone's head off.

"Last time you 'just floated an idea,' we ended up in *Juárez*."

"That wasn't my fault."

"Wait," Charlie said, her gaze darting between them like a ping-pong ball. "What happened in Juárez?"

"We don't talk about Juárez," Beckett told her.

Dom jabbed a finger at his chest. "You should know better. Charlie's more green than the bananas on my kitchen counter, but *you* should know better."

"Don't be mad at Beckett," Charlie said. "It was my idea."

"And he should have told you to keep it to yourself."

"Look, I understand if it's impossible—"

Dom glared at her. She slapped her coffee down hard enough to slosh a few droplets onto the plastic table between them. "It's not impossible. It's dirt simple. I'm in charge of the security assessments, including electronic security. I can get my hands on Sean Ellis's phone as easy as asking him for it. It's not a question of 'can you,' it's a question of 'should you.'"

"It's not ethical; I know that." Charlie shot a quick look over her shoulder, making sure none of the other customers were in earshot. She dropped her voice to a near whisper. "But it's our only lead right now. Somebody, maybe *two* somebodies are coming for Ellis. He knows who they are, but he's refusing to tell us, and he's sticking his head in the sand like this'll all go away by itself. And you know as well as we do that it won't."

"Ethical," Dom repeated. She looked to Beckett. "Seriously? She thinks my issue with this plan is *ethics*?"

"Then what is it?" Charlie asked her.

Dom's gaze dropped to the table. She picked up her coffee, took a sip, set it down again. Her anger wilted like the air leaking from a pinpricked balloon.

"Sofia and Jake . . . took a big chance, hiring me. I didn't exactly come with a letter of recommendation from my previous place of employment. They were told that having me on their staff might hurt their chances of getting clients. Hell, for all I know it did. You know I know, right?"

Charlie didn't follow. She looked to Beckett.

"Word's getting around," he said.

"I didn't need to hear it from the grapevine," Dom said. "I'm in charge of opening security assessments. Know how many I've done in the last month? One. Deep Country. And there's no way they're keeping this company afloat with one client's money. This ship's taking on water, fast."

"Nothing to do with you," Beckett told her.

"I can get a tap on Ellis's phone," Dom said to Charlie, "but it's not zero risk. And if I get caught, we'll lose the client, we'll probably lose the company, and I'll be lucky to keep my ass out of prison. That, and I'm in the middle of a divorce, and not the 'me and my ex are best friends' kind. My scumbag sperm donor is dragging every skeleton out of every closet he can find and throwing it in my face, and it's taking every penny I've got to keep fighting him. Steady employment is my best weapon right now. I lose my job, that's it. I'll lose custody of my kid. I'm not risking that for anybody."

"I'm sorry," Charlie said. "I didn't know."

"I know you didn't," she replied, sounding tired. "Now you do."

"All respect," Beckett said, "but you need to look at the big picture. We already would have lost this client if it hadn't been for Little Duck here."

"We were lucky," Charlie said, sidestepping the compliment.

"We won't be that lucky twice. If we don't dig up the truth, sooner or later Sean Ellis is gonna get *got*. Company's already on shaky ground, and a client dies on our watch? Time to turn out the lights and lock the door. In which case we're all out of a job—"

"And my ex-husband's going to pounce on how I'm unemployed and incapable of supporting a family." Dom slumped in her booth. "Different lousy ending, same lousy result."

"You know I'm right, *tigrotta*."

Dom waved a halfhearted finger at him and sighed. "Uh-uh. You don't get to *tigrotta* me today, Beckett, not when you're trying to talk me into some half-baked gangster shit. Save the pet names. I'm still mad at you."

Charlie felt like she was piling on—she hated feeling like a salesperson, doing the hard sell routine—but she needed to throw her two cents in.

"There's something else," she said. "This person, people, whoever we're dealing with, they don't care about collateral damage. They used a block of C-4, and according to Saint, there's more plastic explosive where that came from. A *lot* more. You told me that nothing matters more than going home to your little girl at the end of the day. Well, if we don't get the intel we need and track this psycho down, there's a real good chance that you, me, all of us, could get caught in the blast next time."

"I don't want you to be right," Dom said. "And yet . . ."

"And yet," Charlie agreed.

"We're backed into a corner, and nobody's going to get us out of it *but* us." Dom looked at Beckett. "I'm still mad at you."

"If it makes you happy," he said.

"What'd make me happy is not being in this situation. Okay, so I can inject a trojan into Ellis's phone that'll give us remote access: we'll be able to read his texts, listen in on his voice mails, you name it. Easiest way is under the guise of a security audit. Thing is I'll have one and exactly one chance to get the job done. Once I've 'audited' his phone the first time, I won't have any reasonable excuse for needing it twice. If he gets suspicious, he might run a malware scan himself, and if he does that and catches my little addition, I'm screwed. We're all screwed, but mostly me."

"Have you done this before?" Charlie asked.

Dom gave her a look that answered her more eloquently than words ever could.

"*Anyway*," Dom said, "the code injection, that's the easy part. Should take me thirty seconds, tops, once I've got access to his unlocked phone."

"What's the hard part?" Charlie asked.

"You and Beckett keeping him distracted while I get the job done. Don't worry; nothing's at stake except our jobs and possibly our freedom. Zero pressure."

◆　◆　◆

Zero pressure. Dom's words resonated in Charlie's ears as she stood in Sean Ellis's office, hands clamped to her sides so she wouldn't start fidgeting. Dom sat in Sean's new chair, and the CEO loomed over her shoulder as she tapped away on his computer's keyboard.

"We're basically bringing your entire network up to the latest security specs," she told him. "Firmware, antivirus software, an upgraded firewall package, the works."

Beckett was just outside, doing the same routine with Allison. Dom had written up a checklist for him, mostly busywork, guaranteed to take a half hour or so. His real job was to act as their outside eyes and ears and send up an early-warning signal if anyone was about to walk into Ellis's office. Considering they were about to commit a crime—a felony, Charlie was pretty sure, but she didn't want to find out—the extra precautions seemed like a good idea.

"I'm going to need one solid minute of unsupervised access to his phone," Dom had told them on the elevator ride up. "If we're lucky, he'll just hand it over and walk away. Some folks are blasé about their phones, some people freak out if they're more than an arm's length away, and we'll just have to find out what kind of guy Sean Ellis is."

"You can hack his phone in one minute?" Charlie had asked.

"No. I can load the malware that'll let me in. The rest I can do remotely. Your job is to run interference. Whatever happens, keep him off my back until I give you the nod."

"This is kind of a lateral move, isn't it?" Sean asked Dom now as he leaned in to point at the screen. "I mean, with our virus scanner, we were already running update four point four seven five on the company server, and this is barely an incremental upgrade."

The look on Dom's face confirmed the slow, churning anxiety in Charlie's gut. They'd both hoped Sean was a hands-off manager and, like most older executives, willing to leave technical details to their IT experts. As it turned out, the mining tycoon was a computer buff. He'd also been glued to Dom's side since the moment she'd sat down to work.

He questioned every move she made, challenging her decisions, quizzing her credentials. Dom held her ground, politely dancing around every question and keeping him pacified, while Charlie—in her role as a new trainee, learning the ropes by shadowing Dom—mostly just tried to turn invisible.

She felt like a kid bringing a bad report card home to her parents. The minutes stretched out into an hour, but eventually, like she knew it would, the moment of truth came around. Dom pushed the chair back, stretching as she stood, and offered the seat back to Sean.

"You're all set," she said. "Now, if I could have a couple of minutes to update your phone, we'll get out of your hair."

He didn't budge, beyond lifting a single white-flecked eyebrow. "My phone?"

"It's another point of potential intrusion. These days, phone security is arguably more important than network security, at least with the specific kinds of threats our clients tend to face. Attackers mining for personal information, blackmail material, that sort of thing. No worries, we're here to keep you safe."

Dom held out her open palm, not taking no for an answer.

"It'll just take a minute," she added.

He didn't move. Neither did her open hand. Finally, he relented. He tugged his phone from his pocket, wrapped in a bulky beige shockproof case, and tilted it his way while he keyed in his unlock code. He handed the mobile to Dom and then, promptly, moved to stand at her shoulder again, watching the screen like a hawk.

"You can get back to what you were doing," she said with a nod at the empty chair. "I'm sure you're busy."

"That's fine," he replied. He stayed right where he was.

Dom shot Charlie a flicker-fast look with an SOS written in her eyes. She needed a solid minute of uninterrupted access. Charlie needed a distraction.

What did she know? People loved talking about themselves, and Sean Ellis was no exception. He also had an elephant-size ego; Charlie remembered her first face-to-face with him, when he'd whined about his press coverage and how the dead miners in Kentucky were detracting from his legacy as a self-made success story.

Charlie drifted to the map on the office wall, showing Deep Country's holdings as blood-drop splotches on clean white parchment, and raised her voice.

"Mr. Ellis? If you have a second, I was wondering about the timeline on this map. I'm really curious about how you started all of this from a single mining operation."

"Hmm?" he said. He glanced at Charlie, then right back at the phone in Dom's hands. "Oh, sure, in a minute, all right? Be happy to walk you through it, just need to focus on this."

"Sure," Charlie said, "but, um, is this correct? It looks like you have three separate facilities in Birmingham, but the marks are really close together—"

Dom shot Charlie another look, more frustrated, as Ellis ignored her and poked his finger at the screen.

"I already upgraded to the latest OS," he told her. "You don't need to waste time with that."

This wasn't working. Charlie had to make a choice and make it now: give up, let Dom finish her pointless "upgrade," and walk out empty handed—or do something drastic. Walking out empty handed was the safe choice. Arguably the smart choice.

Smart, until the bomber struck again. Sean knew who his attacker was, but he'd rather die than talk. Walking away wasn't an option.

Charlie studied the office fast, calculating, breaking every sight line into discrete wedges of information just like she'd been trained to do. Hunting for vulnerabilities, places to hit Sean Ellis at his weakest points and guarantee a distraction that would stick.

She saw her opportunity. She made her move.

TWENTY-TWO

Charlie's heart pounded as she crossed the powder-blue carpet, making a beeline for Sean Ellis's pride and joy: the recessed alcove with built-in glass shelves and tiny LED spotlights, casting a shine upon row after row of industry awards. Decades of accolades and glory, enshrined in crystal and gold.

Then, with all the grace of a six-year-old at her first ballet class, she tripped over her own feet.

She fell forward, praying she'd judged the distance right, and grabbed at the edge of the top shelf. It pivoted on its moorings and tumbled loose. She turned, trying to take the impact on her shoulder and keep her face clear as glass cracked against glass, awards tumbling down, a rain of prized possessions and broken shelves clattering to the office floor.

Charlie was right behind them. She landed hard, twisting her hip as a lance of muscle pain shot up her side and along her left shoulder. Her arm seared, and she felt wetness spreading under her sleeve, a fresh cut where jagged glass had scored a white-hot line on her skin. Dazed, she squinted as she looked up.

She had Sean Ellis's complete and undivided attention. His jaw hung open, gaping wider than his horrified eyes, as the blood drained from his face.

"Again," Jake said, standing on the opposite side of the client's desk, "I can't tell you how sorry I am."

The glass had been swept up, a couple of shelves still salvageable and already lined with the awards that had survived the crash. A trio of victims stood lined up on the desk: a cracked crystal globe, a posing and faceless man with a snapped-off arm, and a glass tower that . . . well, Charlie wasn't sure what was wrong with that one, as it looked perfectly fine to her, but Sean had been apoplectic about it.

She stood at Jake's side, head bowed in anxious contrition and a fresh bandage—courtesy of the admin, Allison, who'd rushed for a first aid kit while Sean had howled about the damage to his trophy collection—wound around her injured arm. The cut had been shallow, thankfully, and the pain had already faded to a dull throb. The pulled muscle in her hip had settled in for a nice long stay; every step she took brought a fresh twinge.

She didn't care. At this point, all she wanted to do was to get out of Sean's office.

Sean snatched up the cracked crystal globe. "This? Got this in 1984 from the American Coal Federation. The ACF literally does not exist anymore. This literally cannot be replaced. It is literally irreplaceable."

"I am literally . . ." Jake paused, catching himself. "Very, very sorry. Of course, we'll pay for any and all damages."

"Damn right you will. This is inexcusable."

Charlie bit down on her tongue. She was aching to remind Sean of how she'd *literally* saved his life in this very room. From the cracks around his apologetic mask, Jake was feeling the same way. He eased a step back, and she followed his lead.

"Please, send me an itemized bill, directly to me, not the company, and I'll personally take care of it right away."

Sean didn't answer. He picked up the tower trophy—Charlie still couldn't figure out what was broken—and mourned over it in silence. She took that as their cue to leave. She followed at Jake's shoulder like a shadow. Out in the corridor, Jake took one look over his shoulder and let out a held breath.

"What. An. *Asshole*."

"I really am sorry," she told him. "The last thing I wanted to do was make any trouble for you or the company. Especially on my first assignment."

Hopefully not my last, she thought. If her brilliant distraction led to her getting fired, she wasn't sure how she'd live with herself.

Jake just waved a casual hand and wrinkled his nose. "Forget him. You spotted a possible shooter and, y'know, defused a freaking bomb your first night on the job. He can get as butt hurt as he wants about his toy collection. Far as I'm concerned, you're still in my good books."

"Glad to hear that," she said.

"You know, some bosses would take the damages out of your first paycheck."

Charlie winced. "If . . . you need to, I understand."

"Nah. I'm just saying. Some would. So maybe, in the future, remember this gesture of largesse and try extra hard to make my life easier?"

"Understood."

"Do me one favor," he said. "For the next few days, unless I need you on his direct detail, just kinda . . . be wherever Ellis isn't. Give him some time to forget your face. We work with clients like this all the time, the high-strung CEO type. They calm down just as fast as they blow up, as long as you don't keep poking the sore spot. Speaking of sore, how's your arm?"

"Sore," she said.

"Then I consider you appropriately punished for your literally inexcusable mistake. That will be all." He glanced at his watch, a cheap

Timex, as they walked. "I have to go attend to more high-level boss stuff, such as picking up a roast for dinner tonight. My mother is coming over, which means this afternoon was really just a warm-up for me."

They rode the elevator down and went their separate ways in the lobby. Dom met her halfway to the revolving doors, her flats echoing off the span of white marble floor. Charlie quizzed her with her eyes, almost afraid to ask. In response, Dom held up her phone and flashed a lopsided smile.

"We got it?" Charlie asked.

"We did indeed. I asked for one minute, and you gave me five." She shot a look toward the security desk as they passed by. "C'mon, talk more in the parking garage."

Down in the concrete labyrinth, in a gallery of silent cars under yellow sodium lights, Dom slapped her on the shoulder. Charlie tried not to wince.

"You didn't tell me you were crazy," Dom said, laughing. "Seriously, *that* was your distraction? Throwing yourself into his trophy collection?"

"I knew it would get his attention. As far as being crazy goes . . . you do know I used to dispose of explosives for a living, right?"

"I wasn't sure about you at first, but I think I like your style." Dom paused. Her smile faded. "I mean it, though. You had my back in there. You were there when I needed you, and you didn't leave me twisting in the wind. That means a lot to me."

"Forget about it," Charlie said. "So what happens now?"

"Now we wait. The malware's in place, I carved out a nice little back door, and everything that comes to Ellis's phone is getting copied and shunted to my system. Well, *a* system that doesn't have anything to identify its owner by. Because we never did this, and we're not having this conversation. I'll keep an eye on it, and the second anything interesting pops up, I'll give you and Beckett a call."

They didn't have to wait long. Charlie heard back from Dom an hour later, while she sat in the thick of rush hour traffic. Charlie eased across lanes, angling for an exit ramp. She'd been looking forward to going home, soaking in a hot bath, and giving her aching hip a rest, but her day wasn't over just yet.

They didn't meet up at company headquarters. Too many ears, too little privacy. Dom suggested a place she knew, an Italian restaurant called DiMaggio's. It took Charlie's eyes a second to adjust once she stepped inside. They were all in on the romance angle, the room cast in the glow of flickering tea lights in glass globes. Violin music played softly on speakers concealed behind rustic wooden trellises and plastic grapevines. The aroma of fresh-baked bread and marinara sauce drew Charlie across the room like an invisible tether, her stomach growling.

She was the last to arrive. Dom had reserved a table in a cozy side room. It was sized for a small party, but only she and Beckett sat at the broad, candlelit table. A bottle of chardonnay sat out, three glasses waiting, and a wicker basket lined in burgundy cloth offered a bounty of breadsticks. Dom had cleared extra room for her laptop; it was a Toughbook model, its rugged black shell specially engineered for outdoor conditions and fieldwork.

"You made it," Dom said.

Charlie pulled back a chair, and Beckett passed her a glass of wine. "You sound surprised."

"I've seen that piece of shit you drive," Dom said. "*You* should be surprised you made it."

"True," Charlie said.

Beckett lifted his glass in a toast. "To a successful mission. Wasn't easy, but we got it done."

The three of them clinked their glasses together, but Dom shot him a dubious look.

"I risked going to prison, and Charlie threw herself into a glass shelving unit," she said. "You just had to stand guard outside the door and flirt with the man's assistant."

"And that is why I'm picking up the tab tonight, to show my deep appreciation. Besides, it wasn't a total cakewalk on my end. I had to look at cat pictures."

"Poor baby," Dom said.

"Twenty minutes of cat pictures. The same cat. She makes it wear costumes." Beckett sipped his wine and nodded at the laptop. "So. We got something?"

Dom snatched a breadstick from the basket and chewed on it while she fired up the laptop. It dangled from the corner of her mouth like an oversize cigar. Charlie followed her lead. The bread, soft as a marshmallow and fresh from the oven, was buttery sweet on her tongue. She leaned closer to Dom, scooting her chair over, and watched windows and waterfalls of green type scroll across the screen.

"Not as useful as I hoped, but it's something," Dom told them. "Someone called and left a message on Ellis's phone at 5:12. Not sure if he missed the call or just didn't feel like picking up. Anyway, the incoming number is blocked, so we've got no easy way of tracing it back."

"Can't you, you know, hack it?" Charlie asked.

"Me?" Dom glanced her way, a little surprised. "Oh God, no. I'm not a hacker; I've just got surveillance training. The malware I used, this intrusion suite, it's all total off-the-shelf software, brewed up by people who are way better at it than me. Plug and play."

"So what'd our anonymous caller have to say?" Beckett asked.

Dom rattled off a few quick keystrokes, and the answer, soft, filtered through faint static, crackled over the laptop's speakers. The voice belonged to an older man, breaking at the edges and carrying a furious hiss.

"Answer your phone, you son of a bitch. We are *done* playing around with you. Do you think this is a joke? We want what's ours. And we're not going away until we get it."

"Knew that much," Beckett muttered.

"You like the little present we left you?" the man's voice asked. "Just a reminder. We can get at you anywhere we want, anytime we want. So stop dicking around and tell us what you did with Kimberly's share. All we want is what's rightfully ours. We paid for it. You didn't. *Be. Fair.*"

Charlie listened intently with her eyes closed. Marking the name, listening to the stresses in the man's voice.

"This is your last chance to do the right thing," the recording warned. "If you don't, we might just take everything you've got. The surprise under your chair was a wake-up call. Next time, that bomb's going to be *real*."

The recording ended with a dull click.

"That doesn't make any sense," Charlie said. "The bomb *was* real."

Dom eyed her over her glass of chardonnay. "I don't want to second-guess you; I wasn't there, and bombs aren't my bag, but . . . is there any chance it was a dud? Like, maybe it wouldn't have really gone off?"

"None. Trust me; this was my MOS for the last eight years. If there's one thing I know about, it's explosives, and that one was built to succeed. The pressure trigger was rigged to splatter Ellis all over his trophy collection if he stood up. And on top of that, the bomber built a timer in as a backup, just to make absolutely sure."

"It jibes with what we noticed earlier," Beckett pointed out. "Trying to kill the man and *then* extort him didn't figure. He said *we* an awful lot too."

"Think the left hand doesn't know what the right hand's doing?" Dom asked him.

"The assassin and the extortionist aren't two different threats," Beckett mused. He sat back and contemplated his wine. "They're on the same team. At least, the extortionist *thinks* they're on the same team."

Charlie walked back through her memory. "That thing he said about 'Kimberly's share' lines up with what I heard Ellis say, last time he was on the phone with this guy. He said, 'Did you think I didn't look?' and mentioned a 'treasure that doesn't exist.'"

"So he claims," Dom replied, "but the voice on the recording sounds pretty convinced. And as I recall, you didn't entirely buy Ellis's act either."

Charlie shook her head, slowly, and sipped her wine.

"Whatever it's about, it's bad news." She gestured with her glass at the laptop screen. "Look, we know Ellis is freaked out about the very idea of cops digging into his life . . . freaked enough that he'd rather risk being blown up than invite a detective into his office. Then there's this guy. He scrambled his number, but beyond that . . . no attempt to disguise his voice, and naming names on tape? Either he's insanely overconfident, or he *knows* Ellis won't go to the police. I'm betting on door number two."

"So we need to dig deeper into the man himself." Beckett picked up his menu and rapped it on the table. "Find out where he's been and what he's been into, before our angry caller takes his next shot. But first, dinner. Can't invade a client's privacy on an empty stomach."

TWENTY-THREE

The next morning, Charlie's phone lit up while she was halfway ready for work. With her wet hair bound up in a towel and a fresh bandage wrapped around the cut on her arm, she leaned over the bathroom sink and spat a mouthful of toothpaste. Her image was a ghost in the steam-fogged mirror as she scooped the phone off the sink's rim and held it to her ear. The pulled muscle in her hip twinged with a dull ache.

"Morning," Jake told her. "Got an important assignment for you today."

"Not being anywhere near Sean Ellis?"

He chuckled. "That's a given, until he forgets he's pissed at you. But no, got a special request. I need you to go down to the District A-7 police station, over on Paris Street, and talk to a detective named Riley Glass. They picked up that guy you turned away at the banquet, you know, the one you thought might be carrying a piece? Well, they think it's him, anyway, and they need you to make an identification."

Best news she'd heard in days. Her gut told her the guy wasn't their primary threat—he was driven by moral outrage, not money, and Charlie had been able to talk him into walking away—but it'd be good to rule him out for certain. Now that they knew the person threatening Ellis on the phone was connected to the bomber, and that something between the two suspects had apparently gotten lost in translation, anything to clear these muddy waters might help.

Next time, that bomb's gonna be real. Those words had bounced around in her head all night, wrenching her brain awake. She felt like she'd spent the last six hours standing outside a club offering slumber and peaceful oblivion, just on the other side of a velvet rope, and the recording was a beefy-fisted bouncer keeping her out.

In the end, she only saw two possibilities. Either the bomber had misunderstood the caller's instructions, planting a real explosive device when a fake one was required—and that was one hell of a mistake—or the people conspiring against Sean Ellis had opposing agendas, and at least one of them didn't even know it. There had to be a way to capitalize on that. She just wasn't seeing how. Not yet, anyway.

"Will do, boss," she said to Jake. "And after I'm done?"

"Eh, give me a call, but don't expect you'll get out of there anytime soon. They didn't want Deep Country holding that banquet in the first place, and Sofia's calls with the station have not been, shall we say, mutually respectful."

"You think they're going to take it out on me? Keep me sitting on a bench for a few hours while they play solitaire?"

"Do me a favor," Jake said. "Don't break their trophy collection."

"No promises."

He snickered and hung up on her.

The district house was all business, the entrance steps flanked by dour Ionic columns like a temple to some stone-faced god of justice. She asked the desk sergeant for Detective Glass, was unceremoniously waved to a hard wooden bench, and sat. And waited. And kept waiting. She watched the slow, steady stream of humanity passing in and out through the double doors. People looking for help, some of them just needing someone to listen to them. The desk sergeant was gruff, terse, but Charlie could tell he cared. He lived here. These were his people.

She had considered going into police work after her discharge. There were always recruiters at the job fairs on her base, looking for vets; she figured it was easier to train someone who already had the assertiveness and discipline elements of the job down. The dangerous, dirty parts of the policing life didn't scare her off—after Afghanistan, she couldn't imagine much else they could throw at her—and she liked the idea of helping people. Being a positive part of a community. Setting down roots she could be proud of.

And yet, she thought. And yet here she was, gravitating to private security like a moth to an open flame. In the last two days she'd had a sit-down with an illegal arms dealer and helped to plant spyware on her own client's cell phone, all in the name of getting the job done. She'd done everything *but* follow the rules. And after eight years of having every aspect of her daily life governed by rules and regulations from sunrise to sunset, she was strangely okay with this.

Maybe I just like being a mercenary, she thought. Something to ponder, later, when people weren't trying to blow her client up and she had the luxury of being able to relax.

A man crossed the scuffed-up tile floor and held out his hand. She rose to greet him.

"Ms. McCabe?" he said. "Detective Glass. Sorry to keep you waiting."

Despite Jake's predictions of being snubbed, he seemed genuinely apologetic. Riley Glass made her think of foxes, with a sharp, angular face and a shock of unruly ginger hair. He was young for a detective. He wore a yellow button-down shirt and a black tie that dangled a little loose, crooked at the collar.

"It's fine," she said. "Happy to help. My boss says you found the guy who we turned away at the hotel?"

"Technically, I can only say that we found a vehicle with Kentucky plates and a number matching the one your colleagues wrote down, and we've taken the registered owner of said vehicle into custody."

"So . . . you found the guy."

Riley nodded for her to follow, leading the way up a dusty side hall. An overstuffed corkboard hung on the wall, accumulating layers of tacked-up bulletins. Faded and yellowed papers poked out from beneath like the strata of an archeologist's dig.

"Normally I'd sit him in an interview room, walk you up to the mirror, ask for an ID, and send you on your way," he told her, pitching his voice low. "Unfortunately, he drew Mason for a public defender, and Mason thinks his first name is Perry. So I have to run a full-on lineup and waste all our time. 'Cause, y'know, I didn't have any real work to do today."

"Public defender?" Charlie asked. "So he is being charged with something."

"Technically I can't tell you that he was pulled over for driving under the influence, the morning after you folks reported him trying to crash the party. I also can't tell you that the arresting officer found an unlicensed thirty-two revolver in his glove compartment and a fistful of newspaper clippings about Deep Country, along with pictures of the board of directors."

"Just a gun?"

He tilted his head at her. His fox nose twitched, just a little, catching a scent.

"You were expecting more than that?"

Charlie watched her footsteps, deciding how much to give away. "We had some bomb threats, but we weren't sure how credible they were. I was concerned a former employee might steal some mining explosives and make a go at it."

"Nah, not this guy. Just the gun, and it's kind of a sad gun—looks like he bought the thing at a flea market and never learned how to clean or oil it."

"I didn't think he really wanted to hurt anyone," Charlie said. "*He* thought he did, but even if he'd gotten past me, I'm not sure he would have pulled the trigger."

"That's my take, after talking to the guy. Between you and me, he got pulled over on I-93 South, trucking toward the interstate."

Charlie drew a map in her head. "He was going home. Back to Kentucky."

"That's what he says, and I believe him. It's our collective bad luck that he downed half a six-pack first. Anyway, right in here."

He ushered her into a claustrophobic booth, swimming in shadow. The station's anemic air-conditioning didn't quite reach this far; the box was sweltering hot and stank of dry sweat. They had company, a tall and balding man with bushy eyebrows that formed improbable, inverted-V arches. *Perry Mason*, she thought.

On the other side of a pane of one-way glass, a line of tired, slump-shouldered men shuffled in before a white wall marked with height lines. She spotted her guy the second he came into view. He'd stopped shaving after his poor attempt at a corporate disguise, whiskers already growing out over the nicks and cuts that marred his face, but his blood-shot eyes hadn't changed one bit.

"Number three," she said.

Perry Mason glared daggers at her. "Please wait until *everyone* has lined up."

She looked at Riley. Riley gave her a helpless shrug. She waited. Eventually, six men stood in the lineup, facing the glass.

"It's still number three."

"Take your time," Mason told her. "Don't identify anyone unless you're absolutely certain."

Charlie leaned closer to the glass. Her eyes widened in sudden shock, and her mouth hung open.

"Oh, wait, I see it now, *wait*—" she gasped. Then her voice suddenly became deadpan. "Nope, sorry, it's still number three."

Perry Mason was not amused by her antics. The detective, on the other hand, squeezed his lips together to keep a smile off his face as he led her out of the booth.

"Okay, that was almost worth the pain in the ass," Riley told her once they were alone. "Thanks again for coming out."

"No problem. What happens now?"

"Now?" He pointed his thumb back toward the door. "Depends on whether we're really going to go after this hump for 'terroristic threats' and whatnot, or just charge him on the unlicensed gun and the DUI and call it a day. Seeing as he didn't actually do anything illegal at the hotel, and your boss tells me you didn't see a weapon on him, I don't imagine anybody's going to make a big production out of this. I generally run across two kinds of criminals: bad and stupid. This guy's not bad; he's just stupid."

"Pretty much what I thought," Charlie said. "Do you want my phone number, just in case you need to follow up?"

"I would love to have your phone number," he said.

She caught a rakish twinkle in his eye. Charlie felt like she had just managed to stumble a step, while standing perfectly still.

"Are you—I mean, do you mean—"

"For follow-ups," he said. "I mean, we can reach you through your employer if something official comes down; it's completely voluntary. But you know, it'd be good to have in case something unofficial comes up that I need to see you about."

She narrowed her eyes at him, trying to get a read on his intentions. "Like . . . dinner?"

"Like dinner," he said, snapping his fingers. "That's an excellent idea. I mean, I might need to follow up on the facts of the case. Just you and me. Very informal."

She gave him her phone number. He jotted it down on a spiral pad, gave her his card, and thanked her for her service to the community. Charlie left the station house with a curious smile on her face. A hot summer breeze ruffled its fingers in her hair.

She called Jake on her way back to the parking lot and gave him a recap, leaving out the bit about trading phone numbers with the ginger-haired detective. "Good," he said, "one less problem to deal with. Tell ya what—Sofia's out of the office, which means I'm in paperwork hell at the moment, and I don't really have anything for you today. Why don't you take the afternoon off? Meet me at HQ tomorrow morning, around seven, and I'll set you up with another training assignment."

She wasn't going to say no to a little off-the-books time. If nothing else, she could hit the public archives and dig up anything she could on Sean Ellis. He had a giant skeleton in his closet, a skeleton connected to someone named Kimberly; it was a thin lead, but better than nothing.

"Hey, McCabe."

She paused, gripping the pickup's door handle, as a gruff voice sounded at her back. She looked over her shoulder. Malloy, the tow-headed bodyguard who'd picked a fight with Dom at their first briefing, was standing in the parking lot behind her.

"Tell me something," he said. "Did you really think you'd get away with it?"

TWENTY-FOUR

A flood of reactions hit her at once, taking her on an adrenaline-fueled roller-coaster ride. Should she deny, argue, misdirect? Malloy just stood there with a borderline smirk on his face, waiting in expectant silence. Finally—it had only been a second or two, but it felt like a lifetime—she chose her retort.

"Are you following me, Malloy?"

He nodded at the looming stone face of the district house. "Nah, it's my day off. Dropping by to chat with some buddies of mine. Just happened to see you across the parking lot and figured I'd say something." He jabbed a finger at her, the smirk blooming. "Gotcha good, though. For a second, you looked like you got caught with your hand in the cookie jar."

The tension drained from her shoulders. *He doesn't know anything,* she thought. *He's just a jerk who thinks he's funny. Good.*

"You do that a lot?" she asked him.

"To everybody I meet. See, everybody's guilty about something. You got no idea how many confessions I've gotten just by hinting around the edges. This one time, I used that very line on a guy we were sweating . . . *Did you really think you'd get away with it?* . . . and he led us straight to his stash of kiddie porn. Thing is we only liked him for a minor hit-and-run; we had no idea he was a closet pedo. He talked himself straight from a fender bender to the state pen. Shoulda seen the look on his face when I told him so."

"You were a cop?"

"Used to be," he said. He kept his eyes fixed on hers, studying her like he could read her life's history on her face. "So I've got this theory. Everybody's guilty, and they carry that guilt around all day, every day. Dragging it like chains. And in their heart of hearts, people want nothing more than to drop that weight. Give 'em an opportunity, and they'll do it, even if it means looking at hard time. Lot of people would rather rot behind bars than drag those chains around one second longer."

Charlie rested a hand on her hip. "So what are you guilty about?"

"Me?" His smirk went lopsided. "Nothing. I sleep like a baby. I'm the one honest man in this godforsaken city."

"Sounds unlikely."

"But it's true. On that note, are you the kind of girl who listens to good advice?"

"No," Charlie said, "but I'm the kind of woman who keeps an open mind."

"Touché. Saw you've been palling around with Da Costa."

She didn't like where this was going, especially after Malloy had called Dom out at the briefing, but she kept her breath steady and her face guarded.

"I've been assigned to train with her, if that's what you mean."

"Maybe," he said. Playing the cop again, hinting he knew more than he did. He was so good Charlie almost fell for it, but he'd already blown his ace card.

"You don't like her very much, do you?"

Malloy's smug smile faded, and his eyes went hard.

"There's not a whole lot to like. Oh, she seems nice at first. Solid, reliable. That's how she reels you in."

"I'm training with her," Charlie said, "not dating her. Is this what this is, Malloy? Is she your ex? Because I'm not looking for any office drama. Just leave me out of it."

"I'm trying to *help* you," he told her. "And no, she's not my damn ex. Dominica Da Costa is a rattlesnake in a woman's body. And if you think she's your friend, just wait: there's nobody she loves stabbing in the back more than her so-called friends."

Charlie wrenched open the pickup's door. Rust flakes scattered onto the pavement at her feet.

"Yeah," she said, "we're done here. Whatever your damage is, leave me out of it."

She slammed the door shut, penning herself in the sweltering heat of the cab. He said something, raising his voice on the other side of the glass, but she cranked the ignition and drowned him out. She didn't look his way, and she didn't roll the window down until she was out of the parking lot, heading for the open road and leaving that bit of unpleasant weirdness behind.

Malloy might have been an ex-cop, and he might have had buddies in the station house, but she didn't believe for one second that he "just happened" to arrive at the same moment she was leaving and had spotted her by random chance. Simple logic told her the odds were astronomical.

The odds that he was following her, stalking her, were a lot closer to reality.

He clearly had an ax to grind with Dom, and that grudge extended to anyone in her orbit. And just because he didn't know anything about their off-the-record activities didn't mean he wasn't sniffing. So how good of a bloodhound was he? Charlie needed to find out, fast, before Malloy escalated from a nuisance to a genuine threat.

Thinking about Riley Glass made for a nice distraction. She wondered if he'd ask her out. She wondered if she'd say yes. She hadn't seriously dated anyone since college; military life and romance didn't go hand in hand, especially once you earned a sergeant's stripes. She knew folks who had made it work, somehow, but she'd never learned that trick.

She liked the detective's style, and he seemed nice enough, but she found herself hoping he wasn't one of the old buddies Malloy was stopping in to chat with. That was a complication she didn't need.

Charlie didn't agree with Riley's take on criminals, that simple divide between bad and stupid. *Too easy,* she thought. *You can be both at the same time. Or bad and smart, or, like our wayward miner with a gun, basically good at heart but worked up into making bad choices.*

She hoped the people coming for Sean Ellis were in that category . . . basically decent, the kind of criminals you could reason with. It fit her general philosophy. Charlie had been a lot of places, and her biggest takeaway was that wherever you went, people were pretty much good at heart.

Naturally, it wasn't long before someone came around to play the exception to that rule.

Charlie figured she'd stop off at her dad's house before going to the library for research. The kitchen was low on everything but beer, and asking her father what he wanted from the grocery store was the closest thing she could find to a conversational icebreaker. Not that she'd found a way to break that ice. It coated everything in his house, from the pictures of her mother on the mantel to the dusty decor that never changed, a life frozen in time.

She wasn't alone. She approached the house from the west, and a black Mercedes E-Class was coming east. She rumbled onto the gravel driveway, and the car followed her in, blocking the only escape route.

She knew the car. She reached over, opened the glove compartment, and grabbed the ASP Key Defender. She'd stowed the slim steel weapon away before her visit to the police station—she wasn't sure if they were legal for civilian ownership in Massachusetts, and she didn't want to find out the hard way—but right now, she was thankful for Beckett's welcome-aboard gift.

She hoped she wouldn't have to use it. She palmed the Defender and jumped down from the pickup, sneakers crunching on gravel. The front doors of the Mercedes swung wide. Grillo and Reyburn, Jimmy Lassiter's professional leg breakers, clambered out and headed her way. Reyburn, towering over his barrel-chested partner, sported a blotchy shiner from when she'd coldcocked him at Jimmy's bar.

Charlie stopped dead, standing between them and the front door. Her stance drew an invisible line, and her body language dared them to try and cross it.

"You're on private property," she said, "and you're not welcome here. Leave."

They stopped in front of her, side by side. Grillo pulled his jacket back just far enough to show her the holster on his hip. She recognized the janky .38 revolver; it was the same one he'd pressed to the back of her head. Only Jimmy Lassiter's command had stopped him from pulling the trigger, that time. Jimmy wasn't here now.

"Your old man needs to pay up," Reyburn said.

"In ten days," Charlie said. "Your boss gave us ten days."

"Clock's ticking," Grillo said. "We just dropped by to deliver a friendly reminder."

"I'll pass on the message," Charlie said.

"All the same," Grillo told her, "we'd rather deliver it in person. Want to make sure he understands how firm this deadline is."

Charlie held his gaze, locking eyes with the shorter man, while her brain raced through all the variables. The Defender sat nestled against her palm, fingers slightly cupped, hand turned to keep it out of sight.

The last thing she wanted right now was an escalation. Her best bet was to try and simmer things down, get them to leave peacefully.

The odds of that happening weren't looking so hot. She had to try anyway.

"C'mon, guys." She spread her empty hand, keeping the Defender close to her hip. "You know that money isn't going to be coming from him. It's coming from me. You don't need to talk to him about anything."

The bruised skin around Reyburn's eye glistened as he squinted at her.

"So maybe we need to talk to you," he said.

"We are talking."

"Maybe we need to do more than talk," he said.

"To make sure you get the message," Grillo added.

One of his hands curled into a fist. A shock of adrenaline hit Charlie's veins, coursing in like white-water rapids, urging her to fight or run. She declined both options—for now—but braced herself and squared her footing.

"So you're going to, what, beat me up for no good reason?"

"I got a reason," Reyburn told her.

"You got a reason to piss your boss off?" she asked. "Like I said, I'm out getting the money my dad owes. You tune me up, maybe put me in the hospital, then I can't get the money, meaning *Jimmy* doesn't get the money."

Reyburn moved a little closer. One of his dusty, chunky-toed shoes dug a divot in the gravel.

"Maybe you didn't give us a choice. Maybe we just came around, all peaceful, and you jumped us like a crazy bitch. We were just defending ourselves."

She wanted to tell him he was taking this too personally. Then again, she'd given him that black eye he was sporting in the first place because *she'd* taken this mess personally. His motivation was easy to read: he wanted payback.

Grillo was a little harder to figure. He didn't come across quite as bloodthirsty, but he was clearly down to roll along with whatever his partner wanted.

Drop Reyburn first, then go for his partner, she told herself. Her grip tightened on the cool steel tube of the Defender.

"Jimmy thinks you might actually come through with the twenty grand," Grillo said. "Me, I don't see it."

Neither did Charlie, but she wasn't going to tell them that.

"I've got my ways," she said.

Grillo flicked a casual hand at the house behind her. "How? Don't see a 'for sale' sign on the lawn here, and no chance you can turn this shit hole into ready cash in ten days. That pickup's worth maybe a few hundred if you sold it for scrap metal. Maybe. You've got nothing to sell but your tits and your ass, and frankly, I don't see you coming up with twenty g's that way either."

"Gee," Charlie said, her voice flat, "not sure if I should take that as an insult or not."

"Take it how you want. All I know is you're supposed to be out finding that dough, and here you are, not doing a damn thing."

"Get off my dad's property and let me get to work, then."

"Oh, we tried," Reyburn told her. "Then we turned to go, and you jumped my poor buddy here from behind. That's the story we're going to tell, anyway."

"Don't do this," Charlie said.

Both of his hands became eager fists. The adrenaline roller coaster in Charlie's veins pushed her to the top of a hill. She felt herself teetering at the summit, leaning forward, about to take a one-way plunge at terminal velocity.

"You shouldn't have taken a swing at me," Reyburn seethed. "Not at all, and not in front of my boss. You made me look like a punk."

Charlie was long past hoping to resolve this without a fight. That door was closed, locked, and welded shut. She slid her left foot half an inch to one side and turned her shoulders in.

"Last chance," she said. "Walk away."

For a heartbeat, one flicker-fast heartbeat of hope, she thought he was going to listen. Reyburn turned, relenting . . . and then he dropped the feint and lunged at her.

TWENTY-FIVE

Reyburn threw everything he had into a killer right hook, the weight of his entire body dragged in the wake of his fist. Charlie leaned back, dipping under the swing, and squeezed the Defender's trigger. A blast of concentrated CS spray hit Reyburn in the face. He shrieked, staggering, and Grillo went for his gun. The .38 cleared his holster, but Charlie was already on him. She'd anticipated the move, and she'd planned her response: her left hand chopped down on his wrist, breaking his aim, and her right lashed out with the Defender. The edge of the steel tube slashed across his forehead, cutting a vicious gash.

The Defender fell from her grip as Reyburn got behind her and swept her up in a bear hug. His face was beet red, eyes screwed shut and leaking tears, but the pain didn't blunt his brute strength. His arms squeezed the breath out of her and lifted her off the ground. A misty cloud of pepper spray still hung in the air, dissipating fast, and it hit her in the face as he whipped her around like a rag doll. She felt like she'd been chopping onions and had leaned in to take a long, deep breath; her eyes stung, sharp, blurring her vision, and her breath turned to fire in her throat.

Her training kicked in, and she moved on instinct. She lifted one leg and brought her heel down hard on Reyburn's kneecap, hearing it connect with a satisfying snap. He let go, howling, dropping her. She landed in a crouch just in time to see Grillo's revolver swinging toward her face. Charlie darted left, lunged in, and grabbed the barrel of the gun. Her other hand lashed out with a precision strike to Grillo's elbow. She'd been aiming to break bone, but all she managed to draw was a yelp of pain as his arm twisted out of joint. It was good enough to loosen his fingers. She snatched the revolver and spun it in her grip.

She pressed the barrel to his forehead. Grillo and Reyburn froze like statues. Her eyes stung like hornets and a hot wind blew the burning pepper spray mist around, sending tears streaming down her cheeks. Charlie thumbed back the hammer on the gun. It was a purely TV cop-show move. She knew the revolver would fire just fine with a simple pull of the trigger, but the gesture got her point across. Her voice came out in a raspy whisper.

"I'm an honorably discharged army veteran with a pristine record," she said. "You're a couple of leg breakers for a shitty little Boston bookie, and I'm betting you've been in and out of the system since you were teenagers. You're trespassing, you outnumber me, and you came armed. You know what that means?"

Grillo gave a tiny shake of his head. As much as he dared, with the muzzle pressed to his skull.

"It means I could kill you both, right here and now, and I won't spend one *hour* behind bars. Textbook self-defense."

Charlie took a deep breath and wished she hadn't. The pepper spray scorched her lungs.

"Get off my father's property. Leave. And don't come back. Next time, I *will* pull the trigger."

Grillo staggered backward. His shoulders flexed like he might suddenly run up on her, but they both knew he wouldn't. He just had to show some kind of defiance on his way out. Reyburn, blind and limping, put an arm around his partner's shoulder and leaned on him. Somehow, they managed to get back in their Mercedes. Charlie stood her ground, watching them go through her blurry, stinging vision, and then crouched down to scoop up the fallen Defender. With the tube in one hand and Grillo's revolver in the other, she stumbled to the front door of her father's house.

Her father was on the recliner, watching television. He grunted hello in her general direction, not even turning his head. That was fine, she figured. She didn't need to explain why her face was tomato red or her hair was a disheveled mess, nor why she was clutching a stolen handgun. She patted her way along the wall, making her way into the kitchen, and yanked open the refrigerator. Charlie had undergone a couple of days of chemical weapons instruction back in Basic, and she remembered just enough to know her first instinct—wash her eyes out with water—would only make the spray's effects worse.

What she needed was on the top shelf. Milk. She grabbed the plastic jug and gave it a shake, listening to a cupful slosh around inside— her father hadn't put it back empty for once, thank God—and leaned over the sink. The cold liquid hit her face and her open eyes, washing her tear-stained cheeks under a torrent of milky white.

The burning faded. The deeper, poisonous ache, like a wasp had plunged its stinger into her heart and snapped it off inside of her, lingered. Charlie washed her face off and stood there for a while, frozen, lost. Grillo's words resonated with her. He was right. She didn't have the money, and she didn't have any way to get it. The grace period she'd bought for her father was halfway up, and she hadn't come one inch closer to finding a solution.

Jake had left a message on her phone, sometime during the fight, asking her to drop by the company HQ in a couple of hours. Briefing for a new assignment. She found herself out in the cab of the pickup truck, heat battering down through the dusty, cracked windshield, just sitting perfectly still. She couldn't will her limbs to move. Didn't seem to be any point.

Forcing herself, fighting through the inertia, she took a better look at Grillo's revolver. It was a cheap little gun, but someone had kitted it out with custom walnut grips and a monogrammed *RT* under the barrel in faded gold leaf. She tossed it in the glove compartment. Then she unscrewed the cap on the Defender, tugged out the red-capped canister of pepper spray, and replaced it with the blue-capped training insert. Until she learned how to use the thing without getting a face full of her own weapon, it seemed like a smarter choice.

It was busywork. Giving her hands something mechanical to do. The job done, she was back to staring at the ramshackle house, the drawn curtains, the sagging eaves. She squeezed her eyes shut. Fresh tears threatened to fall, nothing to do with the pepper spray this time, and she fought them off with everything she had inside of her.

She took a deep breath, steadied herself, and turned the key in the ignition. The pickup wheezed, rattled, and died.

"No," she said, "come on—"

The engine kicked and rattled again. Then it fell silent, not even a spark as Charlie cranked the ignition. Her fear and her rage boiled over all at once, and she exploded, slamming her fist against the plastic dashboard, stomping the useless pedals, shouting and cursing at the dead truck until her breath ran out.

Spent, she sagged back on the vinyl seat.

One thing at a time. One foot forward, then the other. She took out her phone and tried to call Beckett, but he wasn't picking up. Then she tried Dom.

"Hey," Charlie said, "long shot, but I'm trying to get to HQ for the briefing, and my dad's truck finally kicked the bucket. You aren't anywhere near Spencer, are you?"

"What's wrong?" Dom asked her.

"Told you, the truck—"

"No. What's really wrong?"

"Nothing," Charlie said. "I'm fine."

"I'll be there in twenty."

Dom hung up. Charlie looked in the rearview and tried to do something with her hair. She still felt like a mess. Eventually she got out and walked up and down the driveway, keeping herself in motion, until Dom's Lincoln Continental purred up to the house.

Charlie got in. Dom glanced over at her, peering over the rims of her dark glasses. "Hmm."

"What?" Charlie asked. "What's 'hmm'?"

She didn't answer. They hit the highway, cruising in silence for a while, and then Dom flicked her turn signal and slid across three lanes to hit an exit ramp.

"It's faster if you stay on the road for another three exits or so," Charlie said.

"Briefing isn't for a while yet. We've got time. I haven't had lunch. How about you?"

Charlie hadn't even thought about food. Her whole plan had been to make a quick stop at home, then head out again and grab lunch before hitting the library for research. An entire afternoon's worth of plans in the trash. Her stomach growled.

"I could eat," she said.

Fifteen minutes later they were sitting across from each other in a blue vinyl booth, listening to 1950s bubblegum pop on a reproduction Wurlitzer jukebox. Dom's haunt of choice was a retro-themed café, bright and cheerful and covered in chrome. A perfect reproduction of an era that had never existed outside TV and movies.

"You like french fries, Charlie?"

"Probably more than I should," Charlie said.

"Me too." Dom flagged down a waitress in a poodle skirt. "We'll have the fries."

Charlie lifted an eyebrow. "Just fries?"

"You haven't seen the way they do 'em here."

The fries arrived heaped in a wire basket lined with greasy paper, a mountain of them, perfectly browned and steaming and glittering with salt. They'd been cut four different ways, from slender sticks to rounded waffles, and the waitress served them alongside a platter of twelve different dipping sauces.

"*The* fries," Dom said.

They dug in. Good old-fashioned comfort food took the edge off every heartache. Something told Charlie that Dom hadn't brought her here by coincidence, and the veiled glances Dom was giving her just confirmed the feeling.

"So I went to District A-7 this morning to make an ID," Charlie said. "They nabbed that guy who tried to sneak into the banquet. He's clear. I mean, he had a gun, but he's not the person . . . people . . . we're looking for."

"Nice to rule him out, anyway."

"That was my thought." Charlie paused, not sure if she wanted to broach this subject or not. "Ran into Malloy in the parking lot."

Dom's lips pursed like she'd bitten into a lemon. "Did you, now?"

"He said he was there to visit some old cop buddies of his. That he just happened to see me and came over to say hi. Total coincidence. So he said."

"Malloy says a lot of things."

"He doesn't like you very much," Charlie said.

Dom's pursed lips curled into a bitter little smile. She plucked a fry from the basket and dipped it into a cup of hot mustard sauce. "Warned you to stay away from me, right?"

"I'm not the first person he's done that to, I assume."

"Did he tell you I'm a brown recluse spider in the shape of a woman?"

"Actually," Charlie said, "a rattlesnake. But yeah, same spiel otherwise."

"That's a shame. I prefer spiders."

"Dom, do I need to worry about this guy?"

She thought it over, munching on her french fry.

"Normally, no, he's just an asshole. Given our recent little crime spree . . ." She trailed off. Her gaze flicked to one side as she considered the angles. "No. Let me worry about Malloy. I'm the one he's digging for dirt on, and he isn't going to find any."

"So what is it between you two, anyway? What'd you do, run over his dog?"

"I'll answer your question if you answer mine," Dom said. "Dish. You sounded wrecked on the phone, and don't tell me you're all broken up over your truck's engine dying. What's going on with you?"

"Nothing you need to worry about. I promise, it won't affect my work—"

Dom reached across the table and put her hand over Charlie's. Firm. She gave it a squeeze and locked eyes with her.

"This isn't a performance review. I'm asking as a friend, because I think everybody but you can see how badly you need one right now. So tell me what's going on."

Twenty-Six

Charlie told her the whole story. Slowly at first, in fits and starts, working through her shame by proxy, her father's debt, her visit to Lassiter—

"*Jimmy* Lassiter?" Dom asked.

"You know him?"

"Keep going."

She kept going, all the way to the showdown on her father's lawn and the stolen .38 in her dead truck's glove compartment.

"You should wipe that down and ditch it," Dom advised, pointing the tip of a french fry at her. "Gun like that's probably got weight on it."

"Yeah, well, I wasn't going to be nice and give it back, considering he was sticking it in my face."

"Also, you're smart not to take a shot at Lassiter. You're absolutely right; he's connected up to the eyeballs. Killing him would make your dad's problem go away for a little while, but a whole lineup of guys even nastier than Jimmy would come sniffing around for payback before his body hit room temperature."

"How do you know about Jimmy Lassiter?" Charlie asked.

Now it was Dom's turn to hedge. She trailed a waffle fry in a tiny pool of barbecue sauce, drawing a slow scarlet wake.

"You don't seem like the judgmental type, Charlie. Am I right about that?"

"I try not to be."

The waitress in the poodle skirt came by, bringing a pair of fountain vanilla Cokes in big vintage glasses. Dom leaned a little closer to the table and tore the paper wrapping from a fat plastic straw.

"Malloy isn't the only ex-cop on the company payroll."

"You retired?"

"Not as such."

"Don't tell me," Charlie said. "You and Malloy were partners."

Dom snorted a laugh. "Oh God, no. But we knew each other, all right. See, I was working a regular patrol shift, trying to make my neck of Boston a little safer for Joe and Jane Taxpayer, while Malloy, due to being spectacularly incompetent at everything else he'd ever tried, was relegated to the rat squad."

"Internal affairs?"

"Bingo. Now, Malloy had a major hard-on for me, largely because he'd gotten blind drunk at a holiday party. He tried to pin me to the wall and give me his *real* hard-on in a coat closet. I not-so-politely declined and delivered the message on the end of my knee."

"Jesus," Charlie breathed. "Did you report him?"

"No, I didn't want to make waves. I probably should have. In hindsight I wish I had, but like they say, hindsight is always twenty-twenty." Dom stirred her straw in her glass, bumping ice around. "But I've always had this thing about handling my own problems. So I did my job, and he made me *his* job. Chasing a lot of nothing, because I'd kept my nose clean, but he was always digging into my business. Then he found the one thing he needed to tank me for good."

"How could he tank you if you weren't doing anything wrong?"

Dom's straw turned slow circles. Ice clinked against the sides of her fluted glass. She stared down at the table, then lifted her eyes to meet Charlie's.

"It wasn't what I was doing; it was where I came from. I misrepresented myself on my original application forms to pass my background check. See, Da Costa is actually my mother's maiden name. I didn't want anybody poking into my father's side of the family."

"How could your family name keep you out of the police academy?"

"My uncle on my father's side is Giuseppe Accardo."

Charlie knew that name. She weighed a question, wondering if she should ask, then gave it voice. "As in the Accardo crime family?"

Dom chuckled and nodded. "Surprise, I'm a Mafia princess. Yay. Truth is I never got involved with that side of my family. I mean, I *know* all those guys; I've known them all my life. Don't think I've ever been to a holiday dinner where half the men in the room weren't packing heat. My dad, he did five years in Suffolk County for a cigarette-resale racket while running ten other scams he never got caught for. Stuff like that, growing up . . . it was normal."

"But you wanted to be a cop."

"With my uncle's full blessing and support. For starters, joining the family business was out of the question. They're very old country, you know? No women allowed."

"Would you have?" Charlie asked. "If you could."

Dom shrugged. "Like I said, growing up, that life seemed normal. Moot point. Anyway, if I'd wanted to become a fed, or a prosecutor, *that* would have raised some eyebrows. But even the bad guys, my family's kind of bad guys, appreciate a good uniform on the beat. Keeps things peaceful and orderly in the neighborhood, you know? Plus they figured I might be useful later down the line."

"I guess," Charlie said. "So Malloy found out who you really were?"

"Oh boy, did he ever. Next day I'm standing on the carpet in front of my captain's desk, and he's standing right next to me, wearing the most punchable smirk I've ever seen. Well, at that point, didn't even matter who I was related to: just the act of lying on my application was a call for immediate termination. Bye-bye, badge. Jake and Sofia gave me a second chance, and I've been paying them back ever since."

Charlie reached for the basket between them. Grains of salt rubbed against her fingertips as she scooped out a thick-cut fry and debated over the dwindling sauces.

"Sounds like he's a sore winner."

"Oh, that," Dom said. "Well, funny story. About a month after I was terminated, an assistant DA got an anonymous package in the mail. Ironically, I wasn't dirty, but Malloy was. Somebody caught him taking a bribe, on audio *and* video, plus plenty of candid snapshots."

"Somebody," Charlie echoed.

Dom stretched like a cat and flashed a preening smile.

"Like I said, I've always had this thing about handling my own problems. And when someone screws with me, I tend to screw right back, twice as hard. Not that I'm admitting to setting him up or anything. That'd be entrapment, and extremely ethically dubious."

Charlie opted for the barbecue sauce. She dipped her fry and took a bite, savoring the sweet, salty taste.

"Extremely," she said in mock-solemn agreement. "So how'd he end up *here*?"

"Same way I did," Dom told her. "Floated around looking for work suited to an ex-cop's talents, and Jake and Sofia—bless their hearts— gave him a job before I even knew he'd applied. I walk in one day, and there he is, the brand-new hire. I told 'em I'd do my part and keep the peace, out of respect for them and the company, so long as they never tried to make me partner up with him. They didn't have an issue with that."

"He's still got an issue with you, though."

"He's very good at stepping right up to the line," Dom said. "Pushing me just far enough, then backing off before Jake can call him on it."

"He wants to do worse," Charlie said. "If he finds out what we've been up to—"

"And I'll make sure he doesn't. You let me worry about that."

She waved the waitress over and asked for the check. Charlie dug for her wallet, and Dom waved her off, brandishing an ocean-blue Visa card.

"On me," Dom said. "You can buy next time. Besides, I think we both needed to unburden a little. We cool?"

The idea that they wouldn't be jarred her. It wouldn't have even occurred to Charlie to judge a new friend on who her family was or where she came from. The idea that Dom had even worried about it, meaning she'd faced guilt by association more than once in the past, got her hackles up. At the same time, a question occurred to her. One she really didn't want to ask, but it felt like an obligation.

"Of course we're cool. So, um . . . about Jimmy Lassiter . . ."

Charlie fell silent. She knew what to say, just like she knew the imposition she was about to put on Dom's shoulders. Dom sensed her meaning. She shook her head.

"Sorry," Dom told her. "Lassiter is *Irish* mob. Not the same capital-*F* Family, and my folks and their folks are just barely on speaking terms at the moment. I'd ask my uncle, you know, about getting him off your dad's back, but he's not in a position to get that done."

"Hey, thank you. I mean, just that you would ask if you could. That means a lot."

"Forget about it."

The waitress brought over their check. Dom eyed the slip of paper, nodded, and handed over her credit card. The poodle skirt flared as the waitress spun away from the table.

"So," Dom said, "what are you going to do about the cash? I mean, you're not even going to see your first paycheck for another couple of weeks, and that's going to be a long, long way from twenty grand."

Charlie slumped back against the cool, slick vinyl of the booth.

"Don't know," she said. "I keep thinking I'm going to find an answer out of the blue, like there has to be something I can do . . . but some problems don't have answers."

"Some problems don't have *good* answers." Dom slid to one side, rising from the booth. "Or palatable ones. But they all have answers. Speaking of problems, let's get over to HQ. If we're lucky, Sean Ellis finally got scared enough to wise up and come clean about the people stalking him. Either that or Jake found another client, and we can kick Ellis and his garbage to the curb where it belongs."

In retrospect, Charlie figured it had been foolish to hope. There was no new client, and the afternoon briefing, conducted in the drywall confines of the company's conference room, was all about their expanded duties when it came to protecting Sean Ellis and his interests. But mostly Ellis himself. Malloy was already there, drinking instant coffee from a paper cup and hovering on the edges of a conversation. He shot Charlie a questioning glance when she walked into the room. Dom took a seat in the last row, and Charlie made a point of holding Malloy's gaze as she sat down right beside her.

Malloy let out a barely audible snort and turned his back on them. *Good*, Charlie thought. At the front of the room, while Sofia rigged up an office-surplus slide projector, Jake held his hands up.

"If everybody could grab a seat, that'd be good. Anytime now, guys. It's cool, keep talking over me; I'm just the boss."

Mismatched chairs scraped across the bare concrete floor as the company's operatives found their seats and simmered down, forming uneven aisles. The hot, stagnant air smelled like fresh paint and sawdust.

"Our client at Deep Country signed off on a new contract today, authorizing us to expand our security coverage. There will be overtime." Jake held up his palms to wave down a chorus of groans. "There will be *paid* overtime. Also, mandatory, so keep your dance tickets open and don't even think about putting in for vacation days. We're going to need all hands on deck to get this done."

"Gonna need more than that," Dom murmured. "Your research on Ellis turn up anything good?"

"Didn't get the chance yet," Charlie replied under her breath. "Got in a fight. Ate french fries with you. That's basically been my afternoon so far."

Sofia clicked the projector. A hazy map flashed on the lopsided screen, blocks of Technicolor marking streets and directions. Jake gestured to the image.

"Starting tomorrow morning, we will have one team on call to escort the primary from his condominium to his office at Deep Country, and a second team scheduled to bring him back at the end of the workday. First up, the breakfast buddies." Jake glanced down at a clipboard. "Beckett, you're taking lead."

"I'm taking Charlie and Dom," Beckett replied.

Beckett was sitting in back, too, on the far side of the ragged line of chairs. Charlie blinked. She hadn't seen the big man come in, let alone take a seat ten feet away from her.

Jake glanced between Beckett and his clipboard. "I . . . already had people picked for teams."

"And I'm supposed to be training Little Duck over here." Beckett folded his arms. "Proper escort technique is eighty percent of this job. I'm not having somebody else teach her the wrong way. Then I've got to take twice as long to show her how to do it right. I want Charlie, and Dom backing me up."

Jake tried to stare him down from across the room. He gave up fast. With a sigh, he grabbed a Sharpie and scribbled a few quick changes to the roster.

"I think Sean Ellis might kinda hate me now," Charlie said. "That could be a problem."

Beckett favored her with an inscrutable smile.

"He'll get over it," he told her.

Twenty-Seven

The next morning, Charlie called a Lyft and rode to work in the back seat of a stranger's beat-up Camry. She winced at the fare on her phone as she tapped a five-star rating and added a tip. Car service wasn't cheap, and like Dom had pointed out, she wasn't going to see her first paycheck for another two weeks. Then again, repairing a dead truck engine wasn't cheap, either, if it could even be repaired. She suspected the old beater had breathed its last, at the worst possible time.

A storm of butterfly wings in her stomach battened those little anxieties down, making room for a deluge of fresh ones. Beckett waved to her from the edge of the industrial park's lot. Time for another round of education and hours of standing right next to a client targeted by a mad bomber. One who didn't care about collateral damage.

"Thought about the situation," Beckett told her as he crouched down, grabbing hold of a garage door. "Then I talked to Jake, and he gave up the keys to his company ride."

The door, bare aluminum tinged with spots of rust, rattled upward as Beckett gave it a heave. A small garage bay waited just beyond, and a single vehicle: a jet-black Ford Explorer with tinted windows, polished and ready to roll.

"We use our vehicle, one that's locked up all night long, out of enemy hands, instead of letting Ellis use his. We'll call it chauffeur service. Bottom line, that's one less place his fan club can plant another bomb."

Charlie circled the truck. Motes of dust danced on the light streaming in from the open bay door. She watched where they fell on the oil-stained pavement, shifting across the Explorer's glossy front bumper.

"All the same," she said, "are we in a hurry?"

"Technically, but Dom's not here yet, and we can't leave without her. Why?"

She rapped her knuckles lightly on the hood. "I don't trust any vehicle I haven't examined myself, locked up or not. Back in Afghanistan, we caught insurgents trying to sneak into our base garage with IEDs *way* too many times for that. They never got lucky, not while I was there, but . . . I just don't trust that easy."

He lit up the shadowy bay with a smile. "Damn, I'm glad you said that."

"What, was that some kind of test?"

"Nope." He fished out a ring of car keys and tossed them over the hood to her. "I just like knowing everyone around me is as paranoid as I am. Makes me feel right at home. So I heard you and Dom had a chat yesterday."

Charlie unlocked the side door, leaned in, and popped the hood.

"Yeah?" She glanced around the door. "She tell you . . . anything about my situation?"

"Your situation is your business until you feel like making it my business, just like her situation is her business."

At that moment, Dom's business was with her lawyer. She'd tossed her phone onto the passenger seat of her Lincoln, and his voice echoed over the tinny speaker like he was riding to work alongside her.

"But we do need at least one-third payment of your outstanding bill by the fifteenth, in order to continue with your case."

"Explain something to me," Dom said. "Three calls this week. Two and a half of those calls have been about my outstanding bill. Five minutes of those calls have been about what you're doing to earn the money."

"These things move slowly," he said. "Your husband is making a very strong push for sole custody, and he has a lot of resources to throw into the fight."

Dom gunned the gas, speeding through an amber light just before it flickered red, and punched the steering wheel. "He's trying to wear me down. *Fuck* him."

"Ms. Da Costa, this really isn't productive—"

"I will *get* you your money. Do your job. I'm not losing my kid. Period."

She hung up. They were billing her in fifteen-minute chunks, and they'd probably charged her another fifteen just to talk about her bill.

When Dom finally swept into the garage, Charlie was crouched on the concrete, leaning low and strobing a light from her phone across the Ford's undercarriage.

"Sorry, sorry," Dom said. "Damn lawyer kept me on the phone for twenty minutes; then I had to let the people at day care bitch at me for picking Natalie up late last night. Pretty sure I'm paying them enough to show a little understanding now and then, but they don't see it my way."

Beckett nodded down at Charlie. "It's fine. We're checking for bombs."

"Probably a good idea. Find any?"

Charlie stood up and dusted her hands off on her slacks. "Clean as a whistle and good to go."

"All right," Beckett said. "Let's roll. Charlie, you just graduated to Asset Protection 102: Escorting the Primary. Pay close attention, because the final will be graded."

Dom walked past and gave her a pat on the shoulder.

"I'll give you a hint," Dom said. "The class is strictly pass-fail. If the client ends up dead? You failed."

Sean Ellis rested his head in a penthouse at the Grandview, a tower overlooking the rolling greens of Boston Common. Sitting in the front passenger seat while Charlie drove, Beckett cast a narrow eye at the big, glassy front entrance.

"Circle around," he told her. "See if we can find a back route, service entrance, maybe."

"Primary's going to squawk if we march him out through a delivery door," Dom said from the back seat.

"Let him squawk. Took me ten minutes on the internet to get this joker's home address, just to see if I could do it. That means everybody with a grudge against the man has it too. This is way too open for my liking."

Charlie agreed in silence. The park on the other side of Tremont Street was a spot of paradise in the heart of the city, in full bloom and packed with summer visitors—and that was exactly the problem. Too big, too open, too many strange faces, and too many angles. She found an access alley and brought the Ford around back.

"Entry and exit points," Beckett told Charlie, "are pretty much just like how we ran 'em at the hotel banquet. Check your angles and watch for avenues of attack."

"Ask yourself how you'd kill him," Dom said.

Beckett turned, glancing around his seat at her.

"It's how I do it," she said with a nonchalant shrug. "Think like a bad guy. If you can do that, you've got ninety percent of this job handled."

They pulled into a cul-de-sac behind the building just big enough for a delivery truck, with a pair of steel double doors shielded by a curving six-foot brick wall. A grimy sign screwed into the concrete, left of the doors, listed delivery hours and contact numbers for the building's management company.

Charlie was thinking like a bad guy.

If the opposition had access to Sean Ellis's home address, they could scope out the back as easily as the front. The cul-de-sac offered reduced lines of sight and fewer ways to approach, but it was also quieter. Fewer witnesses. If she were going to kill someone and hope to get away clean, she'd do it right here. Her practiced eyes scouted for debris, stray trash bags, anything that could conceal an explosive device. The pavement was clean, save for a scattering of cigarette butts, and the only hiding place she could spot was a dumpster parked about fifty feet up the alley.

She pulled to a stop, close to the doors. They weren't alone. A scruffy kid in a concert T-shirt was leaning against the wall and having a smoke. A fixed-gear bike stood propped up next to him, and he wore a heavy canvas messenger bag slung across his chest. A courier, or somebody who wanted to look like one. The perfect disguise if you needed to lurk in plain sight, waiting for your shot. Beckett followed her gaze.

"You like that?" he asked her.

She killed the engine. "I do not."

"Then handle it, Little Duck."

Charlie hopped out of the SUV. Her credentials, laminated and dangling from her neck on a lanyard, swung as she approached the courier. She remembered Beckett's little trick from the hotel banquet, and now it was her turn to try it out. The kid looked her way, casually curious, and she brandished her ID card.

"Sorry, sir. Building security. I'm going to need you to clear the alley."

She didn't make up a reason. A reason would invite an argument. All the same, he gave her a bleary-eyed look, nursing a hangover, she guessed, and said, "Can I just finish this?"

"Sorry, sir. Need you to clear out. Now."

He tossed his half-smoked cigarette at her feet, hopped on his bike, and wheeled out. She watched him until he disappeared around the corner.

"Not bad," Beckett said, standing behind her. "Okay, doing a transfer, we always keep at least one person with the vehicle. Eyes on, so nobody can rush in and tamper with it. This morning, that's you. Keep the alley secure and clear while me and Dom go up and fetch the primary."

They buzzed themselves in through the delivery doors. Charlie stood alone.

The alley took on an eerie, removed quality. She listened to the sounds of the street, heavy traffic on Tremont filtered through a skyscraper valley, echoing distantly but still a stone's throw away. She glanced up, checking windows as she walked, slowly circling the SUV.

Seven stories up, a curtain ruffled in a window.

Charlie's feet jolted to a dead stop. In a heartbeat, she ran a dozen mental calculations: distance, trajectory, cover. Contingencies and reactions.

Nothing moved behind the glass. False alarm. She went back on patrol.

Back on her tour, she'd experience two dozen moments a day just like that one. Snapshot beats with deadly potential. It was funny how fast that kind of life became normal, like she couldn't remember a time when she hadn't been on high alert at all times. She had thought, once, that she wanted nothing more than to get back to the States and live like a normal person again.

Alone in the alley with her thoughts and her mission, she had to admit the truth. Part of her, deep down inside, wanted no part of a "normal" life. She missed the danger. It was addictive.

And people die from addictions, she warned herself.

The service door rattled open. Beckett led Sean Ellis out, Dom taking the rear. Charlie moved around the SUV, fast and smooth, opening the back door.

Beckett had told Charlie the statistics on the average assassination attempt. Five seconds, from start to finish. If it was going to happen here, it was going to happen right now.

They bundled Sean into the back seat, Dom followed, and Charlie hopped behind the wheel while Beckett rode shotgun. She didn't like the looks of the dumpster up the alley. She made a snap decision, hit the gas hard enough to push everyone back in their seats, and hauled the SUV around back toward Tremont, the way they'd come in.

From the sour look on the old man's face, Sean hadn't forgiven her for wounding his trophy collection. All the same, he didn't complain about her being there. She pushed her concern aside. She wasn't there to be his friend; she was there to protect him, and that had to take priority over everything else.

"Here's how this is going to work," Beckett said. "Charlie, you're going to pull us into the parking garage and proceed directly to the loading bay at the far end of the first floor. We've got the freight elevator on lockdown; I radioed ahead, and Garcia and Brooks are covering it. They've got eyes on the garage entrance, and one of 'em is riding inside. This will be our morning routine, going forward."

"Good place to plant a bomb," Charlie said. Thinking like a bad guy.

"Already covered," Beckett told her. "They ran a check on the maintenance hatch and surveyed the cage and cables, top to bottom, an hour ago."

That satisfied her for now, but she didn't like the long-term prospects. Charlie knew from experience that regular routines were the biggest danger to base security. Not just because the enemy could learn your schedule and adapt their tactics but because doing the same thing day in and day out made people lazy. She was sure they'd done a great job of searching for explosives this morning. Maybe they'd even do a great job next week. After a month, two months, of the same exercise every single day? She wasn't so confident their eyes would be as sharp.

Assuming Sean Ellis is still alive a month from now, she thought. *Not betting any money on that, if we don't figure out who's after him.*

"Dom," Beckett said, "this time you're going to stay with the car. Me and Charlie will escort Mr. Ellis to his office, hand off responsibility with the guards stationed on twenty-two, and come back to rendezvous. Any questions?"

"Yeah." Dom leaned forward, pointing between the front seats. "What the hell is *that*?"

Charlie stared dead ahead, squinting as a spot of sun glare kissed the windshield.

"Trouble," she said.

TWENTY-EIGHT

A short line of cars backed up onto the street, traffic swiveling into the left lane to get around as an angry horn blared. The entrance to the parking garage, nestled at the foot of Deep Country's corporate tower, was blocked.

"Don't wait in line," Beckett told Charlie. "Ease up and around, nice and slow. Let's see what the problem is."

The problem was a vintage Volkswagen Jetta, broken down right next to the ticket dispenser and effectively sealing off the only way in. Plumes of smoke boiled from under the propped-up hood, and the hazard lights strobed a steady heartbeat rhythm.

"Pull up to the corner and bring him in through the lobby?" Dom asked.

"No," Charlie said. Her grip tightened on the steering wheel as a flash of memory dragged her half a world away and kicked her senses into overdrive.

Ellis hunched forward, leaning so close over the seat she could feel the hot puff of his breath on her neck. "What is it? What's going on?"

A textbook Taliban play. They'd get word of a convoy coming through and block key streets with broken-down trucks, staging a traffic jam and funneling American forces down a corridor of death. The detour *was* the trap.

"You think it's a setup?" Beckett asked her.

"Don't know," Charlie said, "but if it is, bringing him through the lobby is exactly what they want us to do."

He nodded, sharp, and took his sunglasses off.

"Pull over. We stick to the plan. We'll walk in through the garage. Charlie, think you can run up ahead of us, check that wreck out? We won't advance unless you give us the sign."

She heard him, crystal clear. The odds were it was just a random breakdown. Some poor driver had stopped to take their ticket, only for their engine to die. The same had nearly happened to her, twice, driving her father's pickup. But if it had been placed here on purpose, there were two possibilities: either it was meant to divert them to the tower's lobby, getting Ellis out in the open for an easier shot, or they were hoping to lure them closer to the broken-down car.

Tight funnel, only one approach . . . perfect place to hide a bomb.

And bombs were her field of expertise. Beckett was counting on her to scope it out, scout for danger, make a life-or-death judgment call. Fast.

"Someone tell me what's happening," Ellis demanded. "Am I in danger?"

Charlie left comforting the client to her partners. She pulled the SUV to the curb, jumped out, and hit the ground running. She jogged to the edge of the garage entrance. The exit lane was wide open, but bent-spike bumps lined the mouth of the concrete tunnel, promising punctured tires to anyone trying to get inside the wrong way. Then came a raised center curb, the yellow box of a ticket-dispensing machine and wooden swing arm, and the stalled VW.

She slowed down, assessing, mentally chopping the scene into slices of information. She saw movement on the far side of the Jetta. A tall, thin man in a panama hat bent over the exposed engine, cursing under his breath. He took his hat off, baring a bald, liver-spotted scalp, and whisked it at the plumes of white smoke.

"Sir?" Charlie said.

He jumped, startled, and looked her way. She guessed he was in his late seventies, but his eyes were sharp and clear.

"Oh, sorry, miss, didn't hear you coming." His eyes flicked to her lanyard and the ID card around her neck. "I really am dreadfully sorry about this; the old girl picked the worst place to give up the ghost."

"Do you need me to call a tow truck for you?"

He held up his cell, an old flip-phone model with a clamshell, and gave it an awkward wave. "Already done. Triple A is sending someone for me, but thank you so much for asking. Again, I truly am sorry. Didn't mean to be a bother."

She could call and verify his claim, but every second she spent here was another second Sean Ellis was out on the curb, partially exposed in the back seat of the SUV. It was time to choose, the garage or the lobby.

She jogged back to the mouth of the garage and gave Beckett a wave.

The wreck could still be a distraction, but she ruled out a concealed explosive. The people hounding their client showed signs of being disorganized, not suicidal; if the elderly man in the panama hat was in on this, and she had her doubts, he wouldn't want to be anywhere near the Jetta when the bomb went off. Still no guarantee of safety, but like Beckett had taught her, their job was about minimizing risk. Compared to risking a move through the lobby, the garage was the smart-money play.

She kept watch over the driver—he wasn't even glancing their way, back to huddling over his engine and fussing—while Beckett and Dom hustled Sean into the garage. Charlie waited until they were about twenty feet ahead. Then she broke away and jogged after them, catching up fast.

"Legit?" Dom asked her.

Charlie nodded. "I think so. Bad luck, bad timing."

The cavernous garage blotted out the summer sun and trapped the heat. It turned the air stale and muggy, smelling of spilled gasoline. They walked the middle of the silent gallery, eyes sweeping in all directions. The rows of parked cars on either side, silently gathering dust, were a

360-degree threat. Every one of them could be holding a lethal surprise, from a bomb on the undercarriage to a shooter hunched down in the back seat.

Charlie's pulse kept time with her footsteps, fast and steady. The plain brushed-steel door of the service elevator, extra wide to bring in furniture and big deliveries, waited fifty feet ahead and off to the right.

They made it to the doors. No sound but their own shoes slapping on concrete. Beckett punched the call button, and it lit up pale amber.

"One of our people will be on the elevator," Beckett told Sean. "You're in good hands."

Sean ran a finger along the collar of his neck and loosened his floral silk tie. "I'm not worried."

His tone made a liar out of him. Charlie wrestled with the sudden urge to grab him by the necktie, jerk it tighter than a noose, and pull until he coughed up a name. He knew exactly who was trying to kill him, and the longer this went on, the more likely it was they'd get their wish. She swallowed her frustration and waited, shifting her weight from foot to foot as the freight elevator continued its slug-slow descent.

Her ears perked at a sound in the distance. An engine.

"Coming or going?" she said.

Dom tilted her head, eyes squinting. "Coming. Must have cleared the entrance."

Back the way they'd come, headlights strobed around the bend. It was a white, battered Ford panel van, built for hauling cargo, puttering slow as if the driver were looking for an open parking space.

The Jetta's driver had said he'd called for help. Not unreasonable to believe AAA had showed up right after Charlie had left. Still. The timing didn't work. It had only been a few minutes, and the tow truck would have to reverse on a busy street, line up with the car, get it hitched up and loaded . . .

Another possibility fit the timing just fine. A perfectly functional VW with a device under the hood, built to emit a harmless plume of smoke. And when they'd declined the detour, refusing to bring Sean Ellis out into the open, it would only have taken a matter of seconds to shut the hood, clear the way, and call for a change of plans.

The van kept coming. And sped up. It turned, and the headlights hit Charlie right in the eyes.

"It's a setup!" she shouted. "Get Ellis out of here! *Now!*"

The van roared up, lurched hard to one side, and screeched to a stop. The panel door rattled open. Three attackers boiled out like ants from a kicked-over hive, two men and a woman, their faces concealed under black knit ski masks. The woman had a rifle in her hands.

"Everybody get on the—" one of the men roared. He didn't have time to finish the sentence. A slim nine-millimeter pistol appeared in Beckett's hand like a magic trick and roared with a cannon crack of thunder as he opened fire. The man fell back, yowling like he'd been hit, but Charlie didn't see a mark on him.

The rifle erupted, muzzle flash cutting the shadows, drawing white supernovas in Charlie's vision. Dom threw herself onto Sean and hauled him to the dirty concrete as a three-round burst cut the air where they were standing. Bullets chewed into stone and sparked off the elevator door. Beckett darted behind a pillar; Charlie wasn't sure if he'd been hit or not. She had her own problems. The second man came at her, faster than he looked, brandishing the slim black-and-hornet-yellow box of a stun gun in his beefy grip. He was a giant, even bigger than Beckett, glaring down at her with tiny, piggish eyes.

He lunged, stun gun sparking. She crossed her arms at the wrists and drove them upward, hitting his forearm and shoving the weapon over her head. He staggered to one side, momentum off, but he rallied fast. He swung his other fist in a haymaker punch. It caught her across the temple and felt like she'd just been slammed in the head with a brick. Charlie kept her focus, her mind in the fight, and dropped low. She hurled a knuckle punch straight between the big man's legs. He wheezed, almost dropping the stun gun, and grabbed his wounded groin as he listed back.

Beckett stuck his gun hand around the pillar and pulled the trigger like he'd just won a lifetime supply of free bullets. Shots rained down on the van, blasting out a side window, blowing craters in the white paint. The freight-elevator door chimed, rattling open, and the backup man inside the cage didn't hesitate to join in the fight. Charlie heard him open fire, using the elevator door for cover.

"Jesus, *abort!*" screamed the wounded attacker. He fell onto his back inside the van, and the giant jumped in after him. *"Go, go, go!"*

The van lurched around, tires squealing. The woman with the rifle clung one-handed to the edge of the open door, squeezing off wild bursts, trying to keep everyone's heads down as they made their escape. Charlie dove for cover. She hit the floor hard and rolled behind a parked car, out of breath. Beckett stepped from cover, sighted down the barrel of his gun, and squeezed the trigger until his hammer snapped dry on an empty magazine. His last bullet gouged a rent in the van's back bumper. It rounded the bend too hard and too fast, rocking on its tires, and vanished from sight.

TWENTY-NINE

"Anybody hit?" Charlie shouted. The aftermath of the gunfire still reverberated in her ears, the world around her sounding swimmy and distant. She shoved herself up on wobbly, adrenaline-shocked legs, clinging to the hood of the car.

"Clear," Dom shouted back.

"Clear," Beckett said. He pointed to Ellis. "Dom, get him on board. I'm calling 911. Charlie, you get a plate number on the van?"

Charlie tapped her temple, still aching from the big man's fist, with a wobbly finger.

"Every digit," she said.

Beckett holstered his gun and tugged a slim phone from his breast pocket. "Good girl."

"No cops," Sean gasped. He was on his knees, shaking, as Dom half helped and half pulled him to his feet.

"Sir," Beckett said, "at this point we have a legal obligation—"

"Your obligation is doing what I *tell* you to do. You work for *me*." Sean got to his feet, pale and shaking like a leaf as Dom eased him toward the open elevator door. "Don't worry about the damage here. You know how much we pay in rent? I'll make a few calls; the building owners will clean this up for us. They won't say a word."

"Sir, the damage isn't the point. We wounded at least one of them. The police have access to information we don't: if someone shows up at a hospital with a gunshot injury, the doctors are legally bound to notify them about it. If we pass on the intel, they can use that to find your attackers."

Ellis staggered into the elevator. He pointed a shaky finger at Beckett. "I swear to God, you make that call, and I terminate our contract on the spot. Not only that, and not only will I sue you and your company into oblivion, I'll make sure nobody in this town touches Boston Asset Protection with a twenty-foot pole ever again."

Charlie watched the war raging behind Beckett's steel-hard eyes. He had a duty to report the gunfight. He also had a duty, in his eyes, to Jake and Sofia and the company that had given him a home. She knew which one would win, even before he answered Sean with a gruff nod and put the phone back in his pocket. He looked to the bodyguard on the elevator.

"Please," Beckett said, every word bound behind a wall of barely restrained fury, "see that Mr. Ellis is taken safely to his office on twenty-two. We'll discuss this later."

The elevator door rumbled shut. The garage fell silent. Dom, Charlie, and Beckett looked to one another, alone in the aftermath.

"Y'all okay?" Beckett asked.

Dom leaned forward as she stood, legs apart, shoulders hunched, poised like a lioness on the prowl.

"No," she said. "I'm pretty damn far from okay."

"Same," Charlie said.

Beckett turned to stare at the bullet craters in the elevator door, buckling the brushed steel.

"Man's going to get us killed," he said.

"Unless we do something about it," Charlie replied.

He touched a finger to his chin and nodded, slow.

"The three of us, we're taking the afternoon off. I'll clear it with Jake." He nodded toward the exit. "Saw a coffee shop, just up the street. Looked cozy."

Charlie wanted something stronger than coffee. They all did. What they needed more, at the moment, were clear heads and a solid plan. They camped in the back-corner table of an indie coffee house, the Magic Bean, and tried to find their footing over three white porcelain mugs of dark roast. Charlie ripped open a single-serve tub of half-and-half, watching the cream spiral into the depths of her mug. She felt like she could follow it down. Just dive on in and let the steaming darkness swallow her whole.

It wasn't her first gunfight. The aftermath was always the same. Muscles fueled by a surge of adrenaline became twitchy, achy, like rubber shot through with sewing needles. Her stomach was a knotted fist. She could tell Beckett and Dom were feeling the same way. The truth was in the eyes, but they both tried to mask it. Beckett was hard, stoic. Dom was seething.

"We could jump his ass," Dom hissed. "Get our own ski masks, corner Ellis, and go to work on him with a sack of oranges. He'll tell us who these people are. Give me fifteen minutes; I *guarantee* he'll tell us."

"Considering our own company is providing him with round-the-clock protection," Beckett said, eyeing her over his mug, "that'd be a little hard to orchestrate."

Dom jabbed her finger at him. "I am *not* letting this asshole turn my kid into an orphan."

"We won't let that happen. As it stands, though, keeping his secrets secret is more important to the man than living. And normally I'd respect that, except it's us and ours in the cross fire right next to him. No. If Ellis wouldn't talk after what just happened, he's not going to talk at all. How about the tap on his phone? He get any follow-up calls?"

"I just checked, and no. Looks like they're done negotiating."

Charlie stirred her coffee. It gave her hand something to do while her thoughts bounced around in a jumble, trying to sort themselves into order.

"It doesn't make any sense," she said.

"Sure it does," Dom said. "He's a reckless, rich idiot who thinks he can just keep throwing money around until his problems go away."

"No. Look. They weren't there to kill him."

Dom lifted an eyebrow at her. "You think that rifle was firing blanks? One of those shots almost parted my hair."

"Yeah, she opened fire, *after* Beckett did. But I think the guy was shouting for us to get on the ground. The other man, the big one, he only had a stun gun on him. And they kept their faces covered; if they were planning to kill us all, why bother? There weren't any witnesses around."

Beckett followed her train of thought. He steepled his fingers. "It was an abduction attempt."

"Which holds with the phone call. They want something from him. 'Kimberly's share.'"

"Since he won't hand it over," Dom mused, "they want to snatch him and make him give it up. But that brings us right back to the part that doesn't fit."

"The bomb," Charlie said. "We've got three kidnappers, plus whoever was driving the van—"

"Plus the old man with the VW, if that wasn't the same person," Beckett added. "Given the timing, the breakdown had to be a decoy, trying to force us out into the open. The van was probably waiting right by the lobby doors to snatch Ellis up. When we didn't change course, they came in after us."

Charlie sipped her coffee. The caffeine kicked her brain into gear, chasing off the postbattle lethargy. "At least one of these people wants Ellis dead," she said. "And the others, or at least the person who made that phone call, have no idea. They want him kidnapped instead. So we've got two different angles of attack to watch for."

The three of them fell into a contemplative silence. They drank their coffee and worked the problem from three directions, each walking their own psychic maze. For Charlie, it was a maze with no exits, a blind wall behind every turn in the labyrinth. She kept doubling back and finding her own footprints in the dust, marking ideas tried and thrown away.

They had one avenue of information left. The gunrunner, Saint, and his open offer to trade a favor for a favor. They'd just have to murder his competition to get it. The last couple of days had pushed Charlie to the breaking point, but she still wasn't going to kill a man in cold blood, a criminal or not, to get what she needed. That wasn't who she was. Beckett and Dom might be less reluctant—she wasn't sure and didn't want to ask, didn't even want to step onto that path—but she still couldn't be a party to murder.

Maybe I don't have to, she thought. An idea sparked in the back of her mind.

"Dom," she said, "question about your family."

"I reserve the right not to incriminate myself or others," Dom replied with a practiced blandness suggesting she'd said those words plenty of times before.

"Are the Accardos on good terms with the Patriarca family?"

She answered with her hand, resting it on the table while Charlie watched. Her index and middle fingers curled together, snug and tight.

"Another question," Charlie said, "at the risk of being racially insensitive."

Dom pursed her lips in a tight smile as she lifted her mug. "Oh, lay it on me."

"Would these people ever recruit Haitians?"

She almost spat out her coffee. "Say *what* now?"

"When we found the man who sold the C-4 for that bomb in Ellis's office," Beckett told her, "he mentioned trouble with a new competitor. A Haitian claiming to be tight with the Patriarcas. Tight enough that Saint, our gunrunning friend, was afraid to move on him."

"Bull. Shit." Dom snorted. "That's not how things are done. Old-school families, old-school rules, and ethnicity is something they have very firm opinions about; my relatives won't even do business with the *Irish* if they don't have to."

"So if they found out this guy was working the black market in Boston and claiming to be under their banner, what would happen to him?" Charlie asked. "Would they kill him?"

"Depends on who found out and what they thought they could get out of the guy. I mean, there'd be one vicious ass kicking, that's for certain. Most of the guys I know would put the squeeze on him instead of killing him; after all, he's been claiming protection from on high." Dom rubbed her thumb against her fingertips. "That kind of protection doesn't come for free. He'd have to pay up if he wanted to stay aboveground. Retroactively, in full, and with excessive damages attached. Why?"

"Saint's terrified of the Patriarcas." Beckett's voice was an amused rumble. "He knows he's a small fish in a big pond. He was pretty sure his competition was lying about their alleged family ties, but he still didn't want to chance making a move, just to be safe. Tried to get us to do it for him."

"And he can tell us who bought the C-4," Charlie added.

Dom rapped her fingernails on the table. They were short and shiny and red as blood. The tiny smile on her lips grew wider. She eased her chair back a few inches.

"Drink your coffee," she told them. "I'll be right back. Need to make a couple of phone calls."

Thirty

Sunset fell across a Mattapan backstreet, casting broken concrete and a stray, overturned shopping cart in shades of russet and tarnished brass. Traffic was backed up, rush hour hitting the city like a key twisting in a lock, jamming everything to a sudden halt. A row of cars, battered sedans and SUVs wearing skirts of dried mud, slowly inched its way toward the intersection on the corner.

Charlie stood behind the smudged plate glass window of a jerk-chicken joint and watched and waited. The air was thick with the mingled aromas of charred meat and burning spices. The last rays of the sun slipped behind the Boston skyline, leaving the starless azure sky streaked in long shadows. The traffic eased up, moving faster, growing sparse. Charlie's eyes were on the sidewalk.

"There he is, right on time," Saint said. He peered out from under the cowl of a long white hoodie, draping him like a trench coat. Charlie followed his gaze to the man casually sauntering up the street, moving like he owned the pavement.

On her other side, Dom tapped a speed dial button and said a few quick words into her cell phone. "Eastbound. Cornrows, olive jacket, jeans, looks like he's packing a sidearm in a shoulder holster on his left side."

Saint looked her way. He nodded, appreciative. "Good eye."

"It's what we do," Beckett said, looming behind them.

"He thinks he's coming to see me about a buyout. I leave town; he stays; nobody gets hurt."

"Slight change in plans," Dom said.

Her eyes twinkled as she cradled her phone against her chest and watched. A sedan with tinted windows purred up the block. It pulled curbside a few feet behind the Haitian man. Two bruisers, with bar bouncers' builds and low-slung hats, jumped out and converged on him. He didn't even know they were there, not before one clamped down on his arm and the other, turning his body to keep anyone from noticing, snaked the pistol from under his jacket. They wheeled him around, talking in soft voices, and marched him toward the waiting car.

Charlie flicked a glance at Dom. "They're not going to kill him, right?"

"Nah. Cousin Lou is just going to have a nice long talk with him about why lying is bad. Basic Goofus-and-Gallant-type stuff he should have learned in kindergarten. I told them to go easy on him."

Charlie winced as they bounced the man's head off the roof of the car, then shoved him in back.

"Not *that* easy," Dom said. "Anyway, they'll slap him around a little, take every last penny he's got plus his entire stock of contraband, and put him on a train out of town. He's lost his Boston privileges. Cousin Lou makes some fast cash; our problem is resolved; everybody's happy."

Saint folded his arms. His mood shifted, growing taciturn. Charlie could read him like a book: he'd just been handed everything he wanted, and now he was thinking he might get out of his end of the bargain.

"I wanted him dead."

"You wanted him *gone*," Charlie told him. She rounded on him, going toe to toe and fixing him with a hard glare. "He's gone. You're a smart guy, Saint. You're not bloodthirsty. You might sell the tools of the trade, but you know that murder brings heat. We didn't just solve your problem; we solved it the best possible way for you. No cops, no commotion, nobody looking for payback, and your name never came into play."

He took a step back, smiling now, holding up his open palms.

"Okay, okay, Charlie McCabe." He was still using her full name like a talisman, ever since she'd shown him her ID card. "Point taken. You held up your end; I'll hold up mine."

"Let's start with a name," she said.

"Don't have one." He took another step back, three glares hitting him like heat lamps on full blast now. "Hey, everything but! I've got everything you need, swear it. C'mon, my feet hurt, and I'm starving. Supper's on me."

Considering they'd picked a chicken joint as their stakeout spot—everybody behind the counter knew Saint, greeting him with a shout as he came in, and Charlie suspected he might own a piece of the place—they only had to go as far as the front counter. The four conspirators camped out in a side booth with a feast spread out on greasy plastic plates: smoked chicken, crispy and black, smothered in rich spices, along with buckets of sweet plantains, mac and cheese, coconut rice and beans, and "island slaw"—coleslaw made from green and purple cabbage, tossed in cool dijon vinaigrette instead of mayo.

"You got yourself a posse now," Saint said to Charlie.

"A posse that landed on the wrong end of a rifle this morning," she replied. "Did you *only* sell the C-4 to these people, or did you forget to mention throwing some guns into the mix?"

"Person." He speared a chunk of blackened chicken on his white plastic fork. "I only had contact with one person. But he did mention not being alone. And yeah, might have let go of a few extra goodies."

"Be very specific," Dom said.

He chewed, talking with his mouth full as he thought back to the sale. "Just some treats from a shipment that walked off Fort Dawes about a month ago. One M4 carbine—"

"An M4, or an M4A1?" Dom asked.

He quirked a smile. "You single?"

She stared at him in stony silence until he answered the question.

"M4," he said. "Army's phasing 'em out for the new models; they're easier to lay hands on right now. Gave the buyers one of those, a couple of Beretta M9 pistols. They wanted Tasers too. Like, four if I could get 'em. Surprisingly tricky. They're illegal in Massachusetts, but my regular clientele want more permanent solutions to their problems, so I don't normally keep that kind of thing in stock. Best I could do on short notice was round up a couple of Vipertek stun guns. You gotta press them right against the target's skin to work; they don't shoot barbs out like actual Tasers. On the plus side, you can't miss."

Charlie remembered the giant coming after her, black plastic box clutched in his beefy fist. If they'd wanted four of the things, it just confirmed that they were out to kidnap Ellis, not kill him, and that had been the plan from the very start.

All except the one person in their crew who had built that chair bomb.

"Anything else?" she asked.

"That's the whole goody bag." Saint paused. He nodded at his chest. "I'm gonna reach into my hoodie right now, pull out something to show you. Cool?"

As he sat in the booth next to him, Beckett's eyes were hard as flint.

"Cool," Beckett said.

Saint slid out his cell phone and laid it on the table, shoving aside the basket of plantains to make room.

"I've got a webcam set up in my office, up in the rafters. I don't record audio or video . . . don't want anything that'd incriminate *me*, if the wrong people got hold of it . . . but I like to take glamour shots of the folks who grace my doorstep."

He tapped the phone and called up a photograph. Saint was smart: the hidden camera was angled high and back, perfectly poised to give a full-face shot of his visitors while keeping him, so long as he stayed on his beanbag throne, just outside of the black-and-white image.

"Son of a bitch," Dom breathed, leaning close. Charlie nodded in grim agreement.

It was the driver of the broken-down Jetta. The elderly man sat, placid, eyes earnest, his panama hat perched on his lap.

"You know him?" Saint asked.

"Not by name," Charlie said. "Tell us about him."

"We met twice, once to set up the deal, once to make the handoff. His accent was local, but I'd never seen the man before. I asked him for a reference, how he knew about me. He gave me a name: Seth MacIntyre, who *used* to be a regular of mine."

"Used to be?" Beckett asked.

"Liquor-store holdup went bad. Seth's doing a twenty-year stretch at Souza-Baranowski."

"So this guy"—Charlie tapped the photo on the screen—"he was incarcerated with him?"

"Or he works there, guard or an admin or something. Kind of hard to have a candid conversation with my former client at the moment. I did manage to smuggle word in and out, grapevine kind of thing, but it just boiled down to a vague thumbs-up. Guy checked out, as much as anybody in this trade checks out."

Charlie frowned. She stared at the photograph and matched it up with her memory. "Did he say what he wanted this stuff for?"

"Hey, I operate on a strict don't-ask-don't-tell basis with my clientele. None of my business, don't want it to be my business. I can tell you this, though: man wasn't looking to start a war. He specifically asked for guns for crowd control."

"Like for an armed robbery," Dom said.

"Right. In, out, and bloodless. Also, he wanted his crew to carry concealed. See, I tried selling him on shotguns. You want somebody to hit the floor and stay there, sticking a shotgun barrel in their face gets the job done every time. We waffled back and forth, I showed him all his options, and he ended up going for the brace of M9s and the one rifle."

Beckett leaned back in the booth. Dark lines creased across his brow as he thought it over.

"It fits this morning," he said to Charlie and Dom. "Detour us toward the building's front entrance, nice and open, wave guns around to get everybody down, stun Ellis, and grab him. If it went right, they'd have been in and out in less than a minute."

"I've seen worse attempts," Dom said.

"One last detail," Saint said. "You might find this interesting. He didn't pay cash."

"I doubt you take IOUs," Charlie replied.

He chuckled and shook his head. "Not even from my own mother."

He put the phone back in his hoodie. His hand came back out with his fingers curled over his palm. He held his hand out over the table, turned it upward, and opened it.

A tiny stone glinted in the middle of his palm, catching the light and scattering it, dazzling in Charlie's eyes.

"Man paid me in diamonds," Saint said. "Tiny ones, like this. Ranging from zero-point-zero-three carat weight to point twenty-five, which is about four millimeters diameter. Not going to pretend I knew any of that; I had to bring in a specialty fence and get myself an education. Already turned 'em into ready cash. This one, I saved as a souvenir. Might get an earring made."

"Did he say why?" Charlie asked.

"Said it was all he had to barter with. Not only that, he asked if I knew anybody who might convert the rest of his stash into spendable green. He didn't say how many rocks he had, and I didn't press him."

Saint made the diamond disappear. This time, his hand came out with a scrap of paper. He set it on the table and shoved it an inch toward Charlie.

"I gave him a list of locals who might be willing to make a deal. This list. Follow up, find the fence he ended up doing business with—you might find the man himself." Saint paused, meeting Charlie's gaze. "That's all I've got. Every last bit of info on your mystery man in the panama hat. So. We good?"

"If he shows up again," Charlie said, "you'll let us know?"

"If he shows up again, I'll have my boys sit on him until you get there."

Beckett didn't budge from his seat, keeping Saint penned in without a word. Charlie looked his way. She gave him a tiny nod.

Beckett rose. He stepped aside, and Saint slid out, his overlong hoodie ruffling behind him. He flashed a smile at her.

"See you around, Charlie McCabe."

Beckett sat down again as Saint pushed through the chicken joint's doors and out into the bustling dark. The trio fell into a contemplative silence.

"You're all thinking what I'm thinking," Dom said.

"He met Saint's former client in prison," Charlie said, her voice slow and careful as she put the pieces together. "He looks like he's in his seventies, maybe ten years older than Sean Ellis. Gets out of the joint and immediately goes looking for guns. He doesn't have cash, but he does have diamonds stashed away. He's angry at Ellis about a past injustice, and he wants 'Kimberly's share.'"

"Mr. Ellis has been a very naughty boy," Beckett said.

Charlie swirled her plastic fork in the last remnants of her mac and cheese, dragging trails of cold sauce around the plate.

"Sure sounds like he screwed the wrong person, back in the day," she said, "and now that skeleton buried at the back of his closet is clawing its way out. We need to dig into his past. *Way* past, like, before he was the head honcho of Deep Country."

"I've got a friend at my old precinct who doesn't mind slipping me the occasional low-key favor," Dom said. "Give me the number you took off that van's plate, and I'll have him run it through LexisNexis. I'm positive the van was stolen—they couldn't be dumb enough to bring their own wheels to a kidnapping—but it's worth making sure."

Beckett reached over and plucked Saint's scrap of paper off the table. "While you're doing that, I'll run down the list of fences who handle loose diamonds."

"By yourself?" Charlie asked. "Could get dangerous."

He favored her with a thin, eager smile.

"It's been a long day," he said. "Maybe I need to blow off a little steam."

THIRTY-ONE

Charlie's father was sound asleep, in his bed for once, not the recliner, by the time she made her way back home. Part of her wanted a chance to talk to him, another stab at détente. Part of her was just exhausted and relieved to be done with the day. She trudged into her bedroom and collapsed onto the stiff mattress. For the first time since her homecoming, despite the oppressive silence of the countryside, she drifted off in no time.

She woke with the dawn, took a shower, changed into her gray sweats and running shoes, and hit the open road on foot. Her destination was a little over a mile away: the Richard Sugden Library, in the heart of Spencer. The big redbrick building was nestled on a quiet residential street in the town's historic district, and the sight of it greeted her with memories of childhood. She jogged up the front steps, catching her breath, and stepped inside.

More memories were waiting for her amid the crisp, clean air and warm scent of old books. Charlie had been a library rat from the time she was old enough to read, spending hours wandering the tight aisles and exploring the stacks, discovering the big wide world outside her tiny town through the pages all around her. Familiar as this place was, she needed a guide in the wilderness. She made her way to the reference desk.

The woman behind the desk, reviewing library records through steel-rimmed bifocals, was an unexpected sight. "Mrs. Frinkle?" Charlie asked.

The elderly woman looked up, blinked, squinted at her . . . then her eyes went wide. "Oh, my stars. *Charlene?*"

She gave her an awkward smile. "In the flesh."

Mrs. Frinkle rose up, skirting the desk's edge, and pulled her into a frail hug. She stepped back, clutching Charlie's forearms, and looked her up and down.

"Well, isn't this a lovely surprise. I haven't seen you since the week you shipped out. Are you home on leave?"

"Home to stay," she said. "Why are you working here, though? I thought you'd be teaching history class until . . . well, forever."

"Oh, the school offered me an 'early retirement' package—early, my left foot—and I know a good deal when I see one. Still, you know me, never been a homebody, have to stay busy. So here I am. And what brings my favorite student to the library?"

"I need to do some research," Charlie told her. "Problem is I don't know where to start."

She gave her former history teacher a quick rundown of what she was looking for, omitting the bloody details. Frinkle was curious, still sharp eyed, and a bloodhound to the core, but she graciously allowed Charlie to dance around her more probing questions. Twenty minutes later Charlie sat ensconced in front of a reference computer, with a low stack of reference books on finance at her left-hand side. The monitor lit up, the long rectangle of the screen flickering to life and displaying a twenty-year-old issue of the *Boston Globe*, digitized from the library archives. As Charlie's search got underway, Frinkle regularly walked by and added fresh handpicked books to the growing stack.

Charlie went on the hunt. She had brought a legal pad and a pen, and she jotted notes as she cross-referenced names and dates. She pursued Sean Ellis back through time, a silent predator on his trail. The trail led her back to Deep Country's inception back in 1971 and to the gaping mystery of Sean Ellis's past.

A mystery she slowly pieced together, dragging the bones out of his closet one by one and building a skeleton.

Someone pulled a chair up beside her. Not Mrs. Frinkle. Dom leaned in and squinted at the computer screen.

"You've been staring at this all morning?" she whispered. "God, the eyestrain. Could they have made the print any smaller?"

"Worth it," Charlie whispered back. "Check this out: Sean Ellis dropped out of college at Boston University back in 1970. In '71, he started Deep Country with a single coal mine. Still, beaucoup cash to get it up and running."

Dom frowned at her. "Who gave start-up capital to a dropout?"

"According to his official bio, an anonymous angel investor. Any luck running the van plates?"

"Nada. As expected, it was reported stolen from a parking lot about three blocks from Deep Country's corporate HQ. Police found it dumped curbside around two this morning. Nothing left behind, no prints, no leads. So, this 'anonymous' angel investor . . ."

Charlie hooked her fingers in the air, drawing quotes. "'Anonymous,' right. Ellis never took the company public. Still hasn't, to this day, even though he could make crazy retirement money off a stock offering."

"Public companies have to file public financial reports," Dom said.

"Bingo. He'd still have to square things with the government, but there're loopholes inside loopholes on that end. Important thing is he's never allowed his records or his past to come under serious scrutiny. His official bio is nothing but vague hand waving and PR talk."

"Then the man in the panama hat comes around, after being locked away for who knows how long," Dom said. "With a stash of diamonds and wanting a missing share. You connecting those dots?"

Charlie nodded. "There was no angel investor."

"Our client is a jewel thief," Dom said.

"He ripped off his partner, walked on the crime, and laundered the loot. Then he turned it into start-up capital."

Mrs. Frinkle set Dom up with a second reference computer, in the booth next to Charlie's, and they took a new tack. Moving from the financial section to the front page news, they probed through the annals of Boston starting in 1971 and waded their way backward, week by week, month by month. The hours stretched on. Charlie felt like she was inches from cracking the case, mouth watering as she closed in on their quarry. Then . . .

"Gotcha," she breathed.

Dom scooted her chair over. Charlie pointed to a grainy headline from February of 1969. **Diamond-Exchange Robbery Leaves Four Dead, More Missing.**

"We got our guy?" Dom asked her.

Charlie scrolled the page down, and a black-and-white photograph slid up on the monitor. He was over forty years younger, but the man being frog-marched in handcuffs down a snowy flight of granite stairs had the same face, the same eyes. They'd found the man in the panama hat.

Professor Gordon Kinzman, the caption read, **arrested Tuesday evening in connection with the violent robbery.**

"I'm gonna call Beckett," Dom told her. She patted Charlie's shoulder as she got up. "See if you can make some copies of this stuff. Print *everything.*"

Beckett rode into town in his shark car. The muscle-bound Skylark prowled into the parking lot across the street from the library. He kept the engine and the air-conditioning on as Dom and Charlie—Charlie clutching a manila folder stuffed with fresh printouts to her chest—bundled into the car.

"Check it out," Charlie said. She passed a couple of key news clippings across to the front seat. "Kinzman was an economics professor at Boston University—"

"Same school Sean Ellis attended," Dom said, "and dropped out of."

"The professor also headed up an unofficial student union, the SPD—Students for Peace and Democracy. It was the late sixties, and they were heavy into protesting the Vietnam War. Kinzman had a reputation as a Svengali. The SPD only had a few members, but the parents, after . . . well, after what happened that February . . . said none of their kids had a history of being political radicals until they fell into the professor's orbit. After the Manson murders in the early seventies, more than a couple of news outlets compared Kinzman to Charles Manson himself."

"I take it they didn't stick to the 'peace' part of their name," Beckett said.

Charlie passed him another clipping. "They did not. They needed operating capital to fight the power, and campus bake sales weren't cutting it. In 1969, Kinzman organized a heist. They knew a winter storm was coming in, a bad one, and he figured they'd raid the Washington Street Diamond Exchange using the weather as a cover. The plan was to hit early in the morning just as the storms were coming in, rob the place blind, and slip out under snow cover before the authorities—who would be swamped with emergency calls—could catch up with them."

"Great plan, except they screwed up," Dom said. "One of their members was a janitor at the exchange; he said he could get them in, and that's why they chose the exchange in the first place. They didn't figure a manager would show up early, or that a pair of cops were getting their morning coffee right next door."

"They also didn't figure that the 'bad weather' in question would later be known as the Great Boston Blizzard of '69," Charlie said.

Dom nodded. "One of the worst storms in the city's history. They bargained for a storm; what they got was six-foot drifts, zero visibility, and a completely paralyzed city. That was outside; inside, things went bad from the jump. The guns came out, and the janitor, the manager, and two cops ended up dead on the showroom floor. The SPD had a six-person crew, including the janitor. Well, six *known*. Those were the ones who got caught, but the authorities never figured out if they had any other help."

Beckett studied the press clippings. "Help like Sean Ellis."

"You got it," Charlie said. "His name never comes up, but here's a familiar one."

She handed him another clipping, with one line marked in yellow highlighter.

"Kimberly Hutchens," Charlie said. "Fellow student. After they set off the alarm and caused a bloodbath, the thieves split up, presumably hoping the cops couldn't chase them all down. Kimberly, they didn't have to chase. She got lost in the blinding snow, on foot and under-dressed for the weather. She was found five days later when the storms started to clear."

"Dead in a snowbank." Dom poked her finger at the highlighted part. "Hypothermia. Bet I don't have to tell you the curious part."

"The curious part," Beckett echoed. "That'd be how the authorities failed to find any of the stolen diamonds on her, I assume."

"According to Kinzman's testimony, they split the loot and split the team up when they ran, hoping to get away with as much as they could."

Charlie sat back. She held the folder open on her lap, cool air-conditioning washing over her face as she wandered through fragments of the past.

"If you want my guess," Charlie said, "Sean Ellis was the one that got away. He was there, and he and Kimberly ran together. She started to slow down as the hypothermia set in—she was only wearing a wind-breaker, in no condition to be out in a blizzard—and Ellis took the loot. He left her to die out there."

"Wouldn't she have tried to take shelter?" Dom asked.

"Maybe she did. Locked doors, no way in, nothing to break glass with. Or maybe she thought she could make it to safety if she just kept moving. She was probably more afraid of the cops than she was afraid of the weather."

Beckett touched his fingertips to his lips as he nodded. "It scans. Kinzman and the others wouldn't rat on him, because if they did, the cops would snatch him *and* the missing diamonds. Besides, looks like the professor stashed at least some of his portion before going behind bars. Better to stay patient. Serve that revenge up nice and cold."

"He got out of prison two months ago," Dom said.

"Giving him operating capital—the stash he was able to hide—and one hell of a motive for payback," Charlie added. "But now we know why Sean said the treasure he's looking for doesn't exist. He sold the diamonds, laundered the money somehow, and used it to launch his career in capitalism. Deep Country *is* the missing loot."

THIRTY-TWO

Charlie leaned forward and passed the rest of her folder up to Beckett in the driver's seat. His stereo was on but turned down low, so only the soft, disconnected strains of a saxophone drifted over the hum of the air-conditioning. Like the faint reminder of a once-loved song, hovering on the edge of memory.

"Here's what we've got on the rest of the SPD," she said. "Professor Kinzman was arrested with two of his students, Leon Guster and Sally Weinstein. Guster was a rich kid playing at being a socialist revolutionary; his parents got him the best lawyers money could buy, they severed his trial from the others, and he almost walked. In the end, he did ten years in minimum security. These days he's a real estate agent in New Bedford. Sally, on the other hand, was a true believer and then some. She had to be removed from the courtroom for standing up and singing 'The Internationale' at the top of her lungs. She got out a while back and vanished off the grid."

"Stayed in touch with her good old professor, I'm guessing." Beckett leafed through faded mug shots. The last in the stack filled the frame, glaring at the camera with tiny, piggish eyes and uneven bristle on his cheeks. "Who's this guy?"

"Brock 'the Brick' Kozlowski," Charlie said. "All-star Boston University Terriers running back. His best friend, Guster, got the best lawyers; he got the worst. They convinced him to cop an insanity plea.

Landed him in a state institution, where he received a decade or so of regular electroshock treatment and a regimen of antipsychotic drugs."

Beckett glanced over the folder at her. "I'm guessing he wasn't actually crazy."

"Not before he went in, he wasn't." Charlie nodded at the mug shot. "Given his size, I'm guessing that was the one who came at me with the stun gun."

"These people were all students? They'd have to be in their late sixties now, just like Ellis."

"A sixty-year-old can still pull a trigger," Dom said.

"And Kozlowski can still hit like a sledgehammer," Charlie said, rubbing the side of her head. "Trust me, he's been keeping in shape. So that's where we're at: The professor's spent the last forty years waiting to catch up with our client and get those missing diamonds back. Diamonds the client *spent* and turned into a corporate empire while his student union buddies were rotting behind bars."

"He's a lousy socialist," Beckett said.

"A lousy human being all around," Dom said, "but we don't get to pick our clients. Not in this market, anyway."

"One of 'em doesn't care about the money. Which one do you peg as our bomber?"

"Can't say," Charlie replied. "Could be any of them. None of the gang showed any past proclivities for explosives; they didn't use them on their heist, and the worst thing any of them had been arrested for before that was trespassing and vandalism. That's the kind of knowledge they could have picked up since, though, either behind bars or once they got out."

"How did the canvass go?" Dom asked Beckett. "Those fences have anything good to say?"

"Came up empty. Sounds like Kinzman hasn't made his move to divest just yet. Probably waiting until he gets the rest of the diamonds from Ellis."

"The diamonds he doesn't have," Charlie said. "Okay, so we know the who and the why. The million-dollar question is, What are we going to *do* about it? If we can find out where Kinzman and his gang are holing up, we could make an anonymous phone call and sic the cops on 'em. I mean, wherever they are, they're sitting on enough illegal guns and plastic explosive to send them all right back behind bars."

"True, true," Beckett mused, "but you've got to consider the siren song of self-righteous payback. If Kinzman goes back inside for the long count, well . . . the only reason he's stayed silent about Sean Ellis for the last four decades is because he wants those diamonds."

"Forty years," Charlie said. "He's got to know there's a good chance Ellis spent the money a long time ago."

"When a man goes inside," Beckett said, "he needs something to cling to, to keep himself sane. Maybe it's family waiting on the outside, or a woman. For Kinzman, it was the loot. But once he realizes he's never going to get his hands on those diamonds, nothing's stopping him from dropping a dime on his former compadre. A civilian and two cops died in that heist, and there's no statute of limitations on murder."

Dom narrowed her eyes at him. "I'm not seeing a downside. Sean Ellis abandoned a classmate to freeze to death in a blizzard so he could cover his own ass. He's a prick—screw him."

"The downside is that Deep Country is Boston Asset Protection's sole client at the moment, and sole source of income. We need this job to end smooth, clean, and with glowing references, or Sofia and Jake are looking at closing up shop once the next round of bills comes due."

"I appreciate that," Charlie argued, "and your loyalty to them, but we can't take risks. We aren't the only operatives handling security. There are two dozen people—*our* people, including Jake himself—out at Deep Country right this minute, and they have no idea what kind of danger they're in. Not to mention the innocent people working for Ellis himself. The longer we wait to fix this, the more time we give

Kinzman and his gang to launch another attack. They won't make the same mistakes twice."

"Well, they're not giving up and going home, not without those diamonds," Dom said.

Something occurred to Charlie. It was a nasty little voice, cold and reptilian, whispering from the back of her brain. An idea she would normally never contemplate. That said, she'd taken a few brisk steps over the line of the law since coming home.

One big leap didn't feel like such a transgression anymore.

"There is something we can do," she said.

Beckett and Dom turned in the front seats, giving her their undivided attention.

"We walk into Ellis's office," Charlie said, "we shut the door, and we tell him what we know."

Dom tilted her head. "To what end?"

"He's got something better than stolen diamonds: he's got the corporation he turned them into, with a ready cash flow."

"You want to blackmail him?"

"Yes," Charlie said. "But not for us. We tell him that he has to make a deal with Kinzman and his former classmates. He'll come to an agreement on exactly how much money he owes them, pay up, and end this before someone gets killed. If he does, it's all settled. No harm, no foul. And if he doesn't . . . well, if he doesn't, we'll tell him that we'll drop a dime on him ourselves."

"You think he'll go for that?" Dom asked.

"A little pain in the wallet is better than disgrace and prison. He's not afraid of the bombs or the kidnapping attempts, because we're there to protect him. So we make it clear that his free ride is over. He needs to worry about *us* now."

"He's not exactly going to give us a five-star performance review after that," Beckett said.

"Sure he is," Charlie replied.

She startled herself when she spoke. Her voice was colder, harder, than it needed to be, as the stress of the last few days found an outlet. Her reptile mind woke up and wrapped her brain in leathery dragon's wings.

"One anonymous call to the right person will trigger an investigation," she said. "That investigation will end in Sean Ellis's arrest, his trial, his incarceration, and the destruction of everything he's ever loved or cared about. We have a weapon we can hold over his head for the rest of his natural life, and after all the shit he's pulled, he is *damn* lucky that all we want is what's fair. As it stands, he'll do what we tell him to do, when we tell him to do it."

Dom looked to Beckett, silently following his lead. He met her gaze with an inscrutable expression. Something wordless passed between them.

"Let's do it," Beckett said.

Before Charlie could say a word, he held a hand up.

"But," he said, "not at his office. Not where he feels like he's in control. If you're going to put the screws to a man, you need to do it right. Have to put him on the defense from the jump, and keep him there."

"Where, then?" she asked him.

"Where he's most vulnerable. Where he sleeps. We do it tonight, after hours. And once we lay down how things are going to be, we keep him locked down tight until he holds up his end. He's going to call Kinzman right in front of us, on speaker, and we'll supervise every aspect of the deal. We'll even play the middle and deliver the cash for him."

"You're both forgetting something," Dom said. "One member of the professor's gang wants Ellis dead. They aren't going to go away for a payoff."

"Which is *why* we'll handle the transfer. That's our chance to get a good look at these people up close and ferret out which one's the mad bomber."

"And then?" Charlie asked.

"And then Professor Kinzman can clean up his own backyard, or we'll have to do it for him. We've got options."

He didn't go into detail. Charlie didn't ask him to. One problem at a time.

"Be in the lobby of the Grandview at eight sharp," he told them. "Wear your ID cards; the staff won't give you any hassle. I'll go up first and smooth things with whoever's working the door, then call you up. But wait for my call, just in case. Never know with this kind of deal."

"How many 'this kind of deals' have you done?" Charlie asked him.

He sidestepped the question. "I'll tell the operatives on door duty that Jake sent us around to ask the client some follow-up questions about next week's security detail."

"What if they call Jake?" Charlie asked.

"They won't. They'll take my word for it. And that's our ticket for as much alone time in the man's penthouse as we require. We'll make our case; then the ball's in his court."

Charlie strode through the doors of the Grandview with a purpose. Despite all the turmoil in her life since she had come home from the service, all the danger, she felt buoyant. They were about to lay a major problem to rest, once and for all, and that would give her the breathing room she needed to focus on getting her father out of trouble.

One problem at a time, she told herself.

Dom was already there, sitting on a sofa in the lobby with her legs crossed and a newspaper unfurled in her lap. She glanced up, nodded Charlie over, and patted the empty seat next to her.

"Beckett just went up to clear the way for us," Dom said. "He's going to see if he can get the guards on the door to take a smoke break. Once they're out of sight, we move in."

"Not sure why. We work for the same outfit, and his story about needing to follow up with the client is airtight. Why the extra trouble?"

"Deniability," Dom told her. "In the remote chance that this plan goes sideways and Ellis flips his lid, nobody needs to know we were ever here. We are about to blackmail him. Not sure if you're aware of this, but that's kind of illegal."

That didn't bother Charlie. And it bothered her that it didn't bother her. She felt like she should have some moral gag reflex, some natural aversion to what they were about to do.

What she had, instead, was clarity of vision. This was a mission. She'd do what she had to, to make sure she and her people survived. At the end of the day, coming home safe was all that mattered.

"But they'll know Beckett was here," Charlie said.

"And he's got big, broad shoulders, and he doesn't mind loading trouble on 'em. It's you and me he's trying to keep—"

Her phone chimed. She put it to her ear. Then she snapped it off and jumped to her feet, letting the newspaper flutter to the floor. "C'mon. Upstairs. *Now.*"

Charlie followed her in a sprint to the lobby elevator doors. Her ID card flapped on its lanyard, trailing behind her.

"What's going on?" Charlie asked, tight on her heels.

Dom punched the call button and looked back over her shoulder.

"They didn't wait to make their next move. We just lost our client."

THIRTY-THREE

Dom and Charlie burst from the elevator on the penthouse floor and raced down a corridor of ivory lined with brass-numbered doors and pristine crown molding. Beckett wasn't alone. One man was flat on his back on the freshly vacuumed carpet, out cold. Another sat propped up with his back against the wall. He kept his eyes squeezed shut and the heel of his hand pressed to his forehead, like he was fighting off a migraine.

"She was, like, somebody's *grandmother*," groaned the sitting man. "Can't believe we got jacked like that. We're getting fired over this for sure."

"Nobody's getting fired," Beckett said. He lightly slapped the other man's cheeks until he started to stir.

Charlie crouched down beside the conscious one. To his left, the door to Ellis's penthouse hung lazily ajar. Not kicked in: they'd either picked the lock or just knocked, posing as his minders, and gotten Ellis to open up.

"What happened?" she asked.

"Stupid distraction. This old lady comes over, starts making small talk; she was . . . I don't know, nice. Suddenly somebody grabs me from behind, and there's this wet towel over my mouth and nose, cutting off my air. Next thing I know I'm waking up on the floor with a jackhammer inside my skull."

"Chloroform," Dom said. "You'll live. The client?"

"Gone."

Dom pushed through the open door to see for herself. Charlie followed. Ellis's penthouse was a gorgeous span of polished oak and antiques, floor-to-ceiling windows offering an elite view of the Boston skyline. Nothing was broken, no signs of a struggle.

"They probably stuck a gun in his ribs and walked him right out of here," Dom said. She threw her hands in the air. *"Fuck."*

"There's a security camera in the lobby," Charlie said.

"Sure, we can pull the footage, and it can tell us what we already know."

"We know who took him," Charlie said, "but the footage will tell us what they look like now. Except for Professor Kinzman, all of our photos are forty years old. It's a lead."

"A lead to what?" Dom shot a glance over Charlie's shoulder, toward the open penthouse door, and dropped her voice. "We can't call the cops. We call the cops, at best they rescue Ellis, and he fires us. Or they rescue Ellis, figure out the connection between him and the kidnappers, and he goes to prison. Same outcome: we're screwed."

"We can't *not* call the police, Dom. It's one thing to keep quiet about an assassination attempt. When Ellis stops showing up for work, his own people are going to file a missing persons on him, at which point we're a party to the kidnapping if we don't report it."

"I know. I know." She paced the floor in front of the windows, an angry shadow backlit by the city lights. "I know. Damn it. We're out of options."

"We did what we could," Beckett said. He filled the doorway at Charlie's side. "Want you two out of here. Fewer people on the scene, the easier dealing with the police is going to be."

"You going to make the call?" Dom asked him.

"I'm calling *Jake*. I'll brief him, and he can call the shots from there."

Dom stopped pacing. She turned and folded her arms. "Brief him on what, exactly?"

Beckett encompassed the empty penthouse with a slow wave of his hand. "Only what happened here tonight. Everything we've done the last couple of days, everything we planned . . . well, it's a moot point now. No reason Jake needs to know anything about it. That stays between us."

All the time they'd spent, the risks they'd taken, the secrets they'd unearthed. Charlie clenched her fists at her sides. Nothing. It had all been for nothing. If Sean Ellis wasn't already dead, he would be soon enough. Her new employer was about to be out of business. And there she was, broke, unemployed, and her father was days away from being crippled or worse over $20,000 she couldn't find a way to earn. She'd done everything perfectly wrong.

Dom was talking to her. She shook her head, the words slipping past.

"I said, did you need a lift?"

Charlie shook her head.

"Think I'm going to go for a walk," she said. "Clear my head a little."

She rode the elevator down alone.

She took off her lanyard as she trudged through the lobby and stuffed her laminated ID in a pocket of her cargo pants. Then she pushed through the doors and out into the hot summer-night air. She drifted across the street at the intersection, cast in headlights. She wandered the outskirts of Boston Common for a while, following the wrought iron fencing nowhere in particular. She didn't want to be here, didn't want to go back to her father's house.

The last time she'd felt like she belonged anywhere was in Afghanistan. Everyone told her she was "home" now, but she was a puzzle piece that just didn't fit.

Her phone rang. Call from a blocked number, but it was too late for telemarketers. Out of curiosity, she picked up.

"Hello?"

She recognized the voice on the other end in a heartbeat. She'd heard it for the first time yesterday morning, in the parking garage.

"Ms. McCabe? My name is Gordon Kinzman. Please don't hang up. This is extremely important."

The breath caught in her throat. She kept walking, inertia pushing her down the sidewalk.

"I know who you are, Professor Kinzman."

"I thought you might by now," he said. "I apologize for what happened yesterday. We didn't intend to use our firearms. Just for show, you understand? But when your colleague opened fire, well, my people panicked. We're a peaceful organization; we truly are."

"Those two police officers and the diamond-exchange manager you killed back in '69 might say otherwise."

"An accident which I deeply regretted. And if you know about that, you also know I paid my debt to society for it. We all did. Except for one of us."

"And here you are," Charlie said, "going right back to a life of crime. How'd you find out about me?"

"The same way you found out about me," he said with a faint, dry chuckle. "I admire your dogged perseverance, Ms. McCabe, but you did hand your full name and place of employment to an arms dealer. You weren't difficult to track down."

Charlie cursed under her breath. So much for having his boys sit on him and calling her right away if Kinzman showed his face at Saint's place again. He'd stabbed her in the back with a smile.

"Please," he added, "don't be cross with our mutual friend. You were simply outbid. And he only surrendered your information after I assured him I meant you no harm. You see, we need help, and given the . . . messy nature of our present situation, you're in a unique position to render it."

"Sure. Give our client back, and I'll be happy to help. You know the police are about to get involved, right? People are going to notice when he doesn't show up for work tomorrow morning."

"They will," Kinzman said, "and the police will mobilize in, oh, forty-eight hours or so after that, the bare minimum for accepting a missing persons complaint. That gives us a very tight window to work in. You could speed things up by telling the authorities about us, and all you've doubtlessly learned about Mr. Ellis, but then we'd be left with no alternative but to kill him. I'd like to avoid that."

"So would I. What do you want?"

"Your services as, well, a mediator, you could call it."

"You mean a hostage negotiator?"

"If you like," Kinzman replied. "In any case, we need a bit of help to ensure everyone gets what they deserve. I'd like to resolve this situation without bloodshed, and as I said, we have a tight window of opportunity."

Charlie's mind raced, gears turning as she put together a plan. She could use this. Find out where they're keeping Ellis, call up Dom and Beckett, swoop in, and save the day. One way or another, they could have this handled by sunrise.

"Deal," she said. "Tell me where to meet you."

"Saint also told me about your intrepid friends. No, Ms. McCabe, three is definitely a crowd, and I can't have you inviting guests along. Just keep walking along Tremont Street, exactly as you're doing now."

"How did you know—"

"My people have been following you since you left the Grandview. I could have simply had them swoop in, but I wanted to talk to you first. To show my good faith and avoid any risk of gunplay, like in the parking garage."

"I'm not carrying a gun," Charlie said.

The muzzle of a pistol jabbed against the small of her back.

"I am," said the woman behind her. She nudged Charlie forward with the barrel. "Keep walking. Don't look behind you. Don't make a scene. Do exactly what I tell you, and you get to live through this."

"It sounds like you just met Sally," Kinzman said, his voice mild. "I'll see you directly, then. Looking forward to it."

He hung up the phone. Charlie held it, useless in her hand, as she walked.

"Gonna put this in my pocket," she said. "That okay with you?"

"As long as your hand comes out empty," Sally Weinstein told her. She gave her another nudge with the gun. "Up here. The green SUV idling at the curb. Get in the back seat."

As Charlie clambered into the vehicle, she got her first clear look at her captors. Leon Guster sat behind the wheel, his pretty-boy looks gone to seed, wearing a polo shirt tugged over a beer gut. Sally got in back, close, holding her pistol—one of the stolen army Berettas they'd bought off Saint—tight against Charlie's ribs. Her hair had gone silver gray, aging with feline grace, and her eyes were every bit as fervent as they were in her 1969 mug shot.

Fervent felt like a safer word than *crazy*.

She reached down with her free hand, scooped a burlap sack off the floor, and handed it to Charlie. "Put it on."

Charlie lifted an eyebrow at her. "I already know who you are and what you look like."

"Maybe we don't want you knowing where we rest our heads and leading the pigs back to us later. So unless you want this to be a one-way ride, put the damn hood on."

Made sense, even if her "hood" was a repurposed grocery sack. Charlie tugged it over her head, blocking out the world in a scratchy burlap haze. The inside of the fabric smelled like raw potatoes.

Sally and Leon weren't inclined to make small talk, and that was fine with Charlie. It let her concentrate on what was really important:

focusing on all her senses but sight and trying to draw a mental map. The SUV took a left, then a right. They idled at a stoplight, then turned, and Charlie realized Leon was doubling back. He'd anticipated she'd do exactly what she was doing, and he was muddying the trail. She listened for unfamiliar sounds, anything that might give the game away, but all she could hear was the grinding din of city traffic all around them.

She took slow, deep breaths. She knew she needed to keep her wits sharp and be ready for anything. Professor Kinzman had said he didn't mean her any harm, and she believed him. But Kinzman didn't know one of his own people was a killer.

THIRTY-FOUR

The traffic sounds faded as the SUV rolled on. The wheels rumbled, going from paved road to gravel, and Charlie's ears perked under the burlap hood. Eventually they stopped. Sally holstered her gun and tugged Charlie's arm, easing her out of the back seat. Loose stones crunched under her running shoes.

"This way," Sally said, giving her arm a tug. Charlie walked along with her, careful of her footing. Fresh smells drifted under the hood: something moldering, like compost or old garbage. Metal clanged just up ahead, maybe a steel door swinging open.

The air suddenly went humid, stagnant, and the ground under her feet turned flat and hard. *Maybe linoleum*, she thought, *too much give to be tile, but it's not groaning like wood*. Sally turned her by the arm, and they made a hard left. Another door rattled open on loose hinges.

Rough hands shoved her down. Charlie's heart jumped into her throat for a dizzying second as she free-fell, and then she landed in a hard-backed chair. The sack was ripped from her head. She squinted against sudden hard light shining in her eyes.

The glare from the overhead lamp, a single bulb dangling under a bare aluminum hood, slowly faded, and her vision swam into clear focus. She sat at a folding card table in a spare room with rusting sheet-metal walls. The only decor was a dead clock under a dusty plastic bubble, the hands stuck at five minutes to midnight, and a tacked-up calendar advertising motor oil. The calendar's pages hadn't turned since May of 1996.

Maps littered the table, foldout atlases of Boston's streets, festooned with splashes of red ink and angry arrows. A couple of ashtrays collected dead cigarettes, and the air was stale with faded smoke.

Sean Ellis sat on her right. He was tied to his chair, arms behind his back, and his sweaty face sported fresh bruises on his eye and chin. Dried blood clung to a split lip. On her left, Brock "the Brick" Kozlowski hunched against the table and stared daggers at her with his tiny hateful eyes. She guessed the big man remembered how she'd punched him between the legs, back at the parking garage, and he was hoping for some payback.

Charlie stared straight ahead. Professor Gordon Kinzman looked exactly as he had in the parking garage, waving his panama hat at the fake steam spewing from his car. The hat sat to his left, a gun to his right. Too far for Charlie to grab. As if reading her thoughts, he pulled the weapon a little closer to his edge of the table.

"I'm sorry for the circumstances," he told her. "Funny way to word it, hmm? 'Circumstances.'"

"Giant mess is what it is," Sally said. She pulled over a folding chair and dropped down next to Charlie, keeping her own pistol loosely pointed at her. Leon dragged over a second chair and sat close to Sean.

"A mess we're hoping you can help fix," Kinzman said to Charlie. "You know who we are, and you mentioned the unfortunate incident back in 1969. Is it safe to assume, then, that you know exactly why we've abducted your client?"

Charlie turned her head and locked eyes with Sean. She felt a twinge of empathy for him, bound and beaten . . . and then she remembered what he'd done to earn it.

"Sean was another member of the Students for Peace and Democracy," she said. "And he was in on your heist. The only one who got away clean. When the alarm went off at the diamond exchange and the shooting started, he ran with another one of your students, a woman named Kimberly Hutchens. Sean lived. Kimberly didn't."

Sean didn't say a word. He didn't need to. He flinched like Charlie had just slapped him across the face. The man wore his guilt like a cattle brand, scarred deep and permanent.

"You should have been the one who died," Sally told him. His gaze dropped to the table.

"Regardless," the professor said, "if he'd merely escaped justice, I'd have been happy for him. The problem is that he took the lion's share of proceeds from our . . . political action. Over four decades, Mr. Ellis. Four decades, and you've done nothing to offer reparations. Nothing to contact any of us, to aid us in our times of need, to make things right."

Charlie couldn't believe she was arguing on Sean's behalf, but just like a defense lawyer with a guilty client, somebody had to do the job. Besides, she was still his bodyguard. Protecting him, whether he deserved it or not, was still her job.

"He can't change the past," she said. "I'm not defending what he did. I don't think anybody can. But you have to decide what you want more: Do you want revenge or the money?"

"We want *justice*," Sally snapped. Leon nodded in grim agreement. Brock just kept staring at Charlie like he was imagining her head on a stick.

"The money," Kinzman said, "will be sufficient."

Just like that, Charlie saw the invisible lines dividing the room. Everything teetered on an axis between Sally and her former professor. Once you stripped him of his political trappings, Kinzman was nothing but a thief and an extortionist. He was only here for the cash.

Sally was out for blood. And she couldn't prove it yet, but Charlie strongly suspected she was the one who had put that bomb in Sean's office chair.

"None of us want this to get out of control," Charlie said. She tried to keep her voice steady, soft, simmering down the tension before it could reach a boiling point. "Not any more than it already has, anyway. As it stands, Sean isn't even officially a missing person yet. We can find a solution and put him back, safe and sound, before the police get involved. We can all win here."

"Mr. Ellis has unfortunately been recalcitrant about revealing the location of our missing goods," Kinzman told her.

"Those diamonds are gone, Professor. I know that's not what you want to hear, but it's true. Look at the timing: the heist was in '69. Sean dropped out of college and started Deep Country in '71. He fenced the loot and used it for start-up capital. There's no other explanation."

Sean shook his head and slumped against his ropes. His voice was weak. "No, I didn't. I told you—"

"Shut up," Sally snapped.

Charlie held up a finger. "The good news is, well, today he runs a pretty big corporation with closed books. He doesn't have diamonds, but he does have cash, and there's a hundred ways we can disguise those reparations you want. He can probably hire you all as 'consultants' and just cut a paycheck, legal and everything. So let's try this: We'll settle on a dollar amount. You keep Sean here while I go and get the money, however we decide to make it work. You can even send Leon or Sally with me to make sure I don't call the police. Then we'll meet up again at a neutral location to make a trade. Everybody walks away happy."

"That," Kinzman said with a smile, "is *exactly* why I brought you here. You see, Mr. Ellis? Cooperation doesn't have to be so difficult."

"There's no *dollar amount* that can bring Kimberly back," Sally said. "And it's not just about money. She was a soldier. She died trying to deliver those diamonds to the revolutionary cause."

"The revolutionary cause," the professor said, "can benefit from ready cash much more easily than it can from illegal, difficult-to-fence diamonds. I suggest we graciously allow Mr. Ellis to get his checkbook out and make things right, while we still have time."

"Doesn't matter," Sean said. He let out a faint, bitter laugh. "I don't have cash *or* the diamonds."

Every face at the table swung his way.

"Do you people even understand how screwed I am?" he said. "Thirty miners died when that gas line ruptured. That's thirty families bringing civil suits against Deep Country. And I've got an eight-hundred-dollar-an-hour lawyer telling me that with the evidence on hand, there's no way they can lose. The Kentucky licensing board is tearing into my business, and the feds are right behind them. I'm ruined."

"That's not our problem," Leon said. It was the first time he'd spoken up, and Charlie recognized him as the angry voice on Sean's intercepted phone message.

"Yeah, it is. Because you're looking for liquid assets, and I don't *have* any. What do you think, I've got a big safe in my office stacked with hundred-dollar bills? That's not how corporations work. All of my operating capital is tied up in this legal fight. And when the fight's over, I'm not going to have any capital, period."

"The diamonds, then," Sally said.

Sean threw his head back and let out an exasperated groan.

"There. Are. No. Diamonds. Charlie's half-right. I took the ones I pocketed on my way out of the exchange and fenced them a year later, once the heat died down. Kimberly was carrying the lion's share. I never laid hands on them."

"You were with her," Leon said.

"No. I wasn't. We got separated a block outside the exchange. Don't you remember what it was *like* out there? The snow was coming down like a monsoon. You couldn't see three feet in front of your face; every step sucked you deeper as it piled up around you. I lost her."

Sean's eyes squeezed shut. A single tear blossomed and rolled down his cheek, glistening against the bruise on his chin.

"I lost her," he whispered. "She was my friend, too, you know. And I lost her."

Leon leaned toward him, sitting on the edge of his chair. "You lying sack. I saw the pictures they took, when the rescuers hauled her body out of that snowbank. I read the reports. She didn't have the diamonds on her."

"Then she stashed them before she died."

"*No.*" Leon jumped up and slammed his fist down on the table. The ashtrays rattled and jumped. He swept his hand across the marker-littered maps. "I've spent years on this. I've gone over every possible route she could have taken between the diamond exchange and the spot where she died. There's no place she could have hidden them that I haven't checked."

"It was over forty years ago, Leon—"

He jabbed his finger at Sean's chest. "You're holding out on us."

"It *doesn't matter*," Sally said. "Why are we wasting our time? This isn't about money; it's about getting justice for Kimberly. We all had to pay for what happened that morning. All of us except *him*."

Kinzman sighed. He pinched the bridge of his nose like he was fighting off a headache. "And we agreed, Ms. Weinstein, that payment in the form of financial reparations would be acceptable in lieu of his life. That was the plan, and we all agreed on it. Which is why we've so generously, so patiently encouraged him to cooperate up until now. Alas, it seems his reluctance demands that we take more severe measures."

The room was slipping out of control, fast. Charlie had to make a move. Time to set off a bomb of her own.

"If the plan was to rip him off," she asked, "then why did you try to kill him?"

THIRTY-FIVE

It was Charlie's turn to be the center of attention. The table fell silent.

"Excuse me?" Kinzman asked. "I told you, the gunfire at the parking garage—"

"Not that. The bomb in his chair."

The professor waved a dismissive hand. "It was a warning, a feint. The explosives were real, but it never would have gone off."

"Yes," Charlie said, "it would have."

He snorted at her, incredulous. "And you know that how?"

Charlie locked eyes with Kinzman. She squared her shoulders and laid her palms flat on the table.

"Because my name is *Sergeant* Charlene McCabe, United States Army. My military occupational specialty was explosive ordnance disposal. I spent eight years in Afghanistan handling everything from scrap-metal IEDs to sophisticated terrorist threats. I know my job. I'm pretty good at it. And I just came home last week, so I haven't had time to get rusty yet."

She took a slow look around the room. Reading their faces, weighing their reactions. Slicing the data into bite-size pieces. Brock was impossible to read—he had one expression, mute and furious—but the others were open books. Kinzman was shocked. Leon didn't believe her. And Sally looked like a kid who'd just been caught stealing gum from the corner store.

"I was the person who disarmed the device in Sean's chair," Charlie said. "Not only was it a live bomb, it had a backup timer attached to the pressure switch, to make absolutely certain it would go off."

The professor gaped. *"Sally?"*

"What?" she snapped. "Leon's obsessed with those damn diamonds, you kept talking about his corporate assets, and it feels like nobody but me and Brock gives a damn about *Kimberly.*"

"Kimberly," Brock grunted in agreement.

"This bastard murdered her," Sally said. She brandished her gun and jammed it in Sean's face. "He has to pay for it. I'm sick of waiting."

Sean cringed, pulling away as far as the ropes would let him. He tucked his chin against his chest and turned his face from the gun. Charlie tensed up, arms tight at her sides. She weighed her chances. She was close enough to jump Sally, not close enough to keep her from pulling that trigger.

Kinzman got to his feet fast enough to knock his chair back. It fell to the dirty linoleum with a clatter.

"I trusted you," Kinzman said. "I brought you in on this. We had a *plan.* You agreed to it, same as the rest of us."

Sally shook her head wildly. The gun wavered in her hand.

"You forgot where you came from, Professor. You forgot what you used to stand for. The revolution, remember? A new day, an equal and just society. A day when leeches like this"—she ground the gun's muzzle against Sean's cheekbone hard enough to make him yelp—"would be lined up against the wall and *shot!*"

"Sally," Charlie said, "he's a bad guy, okay? Nobody's denying that. But you spent decades, the prime of your life, behind bars. You don't want to go back to prison. Nobody here does. There's a better way. Let me help you find it. Let's work this out before anybody gets hurt."

She punctuated her words with a look to Leon and Kinzman, driving the point home. And from the looks on their faces, she'd scored a direct hit. Charlie had divided the gang by bringing up the bomb, just as she'd hoped. Now she needed them working against each other.

"She's right," Leon said. "C'mon, Sally, I'm not going back to prison. Not for this slug, not for anybody. We were just supposed to scare him a little and get the money, that's all. Nobody was going to die."

Sally turned her glare on him, a spotlight of malice. "The professor, I know *he's* a sellout. But you disappoint me, Leon. You used to be just like me."

"The sixties are over, Sally. The revolution is over. We lost—deal with it."

"*No,*" she spat. "Revolution is not something fixed in ideology, nor is it something fashioned to a particular decade. It is a perpetual process embedded in the human spirit."

Kinzman shook his head. His voice was dry as a desert. "So you can quote Abbie Hoffman. The devil can quote scripture, too, I'm told."

The pistol swung around in her hand. "You sanctimonious piece of—"

Kinzman lunged for his gun. He snatched it up from the card table—and Sally pulled her trigger first. And again, and again, driving the professor backward as three shots peppered his chest and tore out a chunk of his throat, spattering scarlet and flesh across the wall behind him. He pitched over and hit the floor, stone dead, eyes wide open in eternal shock.

Everyone froze, like a roomful of statues, as the sounds of gunfire faded into reverberating echoes. Then silence.

"Jesus, Sally," Leon breathed.

"He went for his gun," she said.

Brock's perpetually furious expression twisted into odd confusion. "Didn't have to do that."

"He was going to shoot me."

"You pointed your pistol at him; what did you *think* he was going to do?" Leon said.

"I was just trying to . . . I mean, I wasn't really going to . . ." She shook her head. "He shouldn't have gone for his gun."

Leon got out of his chair. He crouched next to the professor's body and pressed two fingers to his neck, feeling for a pulse.

"Well," Leon said, "he's pretty dead."

Sally stepped backward until her shoulders bumped the wall. The blood drained from her face, and she clutched her weapon in a white-knuckle grip.

"I didn't mean to," she said.

"You didn't shoot harsh language at him, Sal. You can't exactly take it back." Still crouched, Leon waved a hand at Sean and Charlie. "What now?"

"They're witnesses." A little of Sally's fear faded, her bloodthirstiness flooding back in to fill the empty space it left behind. "They need to die. Both of them. We bury all three bodies and get out of here. Out of Boston. No one will ever know."

Charlie's chest tightened. Brock wasn't going to argue with her, and Leon might be looking to cut his losses; he'd been on Kinzman's side, out for a payday, but Sean's revelation that he didn't have any money to offer the gang might have written a death sentence for him and Charlie both.

Leon rose, dusting his hands off on his jeans. "I'm not looking to kill anybody," he said. "I *thought* you weren't either."

"You heard her," Sally said. Charlie tried not to flinch as the barrel of Sally's gun swung her way. "Do you want to go back to prison?"

Charlie hated it when people threw her words back at her. Especially when they were heavily armed. Sally couldn't be reasoned with. She needed to focus on Leon, to find something she could offer him that would outweigh the risk he'd be taking by letting her and Sean live.

She thought back, focusing on his words, his deeds, everything she knew about the man. She knew from his voice that he'd been the one making the phone calls to Sean; he was all about the money, just like the dead man on the floor. He'd also spent a decade behind bars, and from the way he tensed up at the very mention of the subject, he'd die before he ever went back again. Getting past that fear would take the kind of treasure Charlie didn't—

Treasure. Before either of them could say another word, she blurted her offer.

"I'll find the diamonds."

Leon and Sally both stared at her. "Bull," Sally said.

"Give me two days. Keep Sean here as collateral—*alive*—and let me go. I'll find the diamonds for you."

"Leon's been looking for years," Sally said, waving the muzzle of her gun at the maps on the table. "Years. And you think you can do it in two days?"

"You've been looking alone, and I'm guessing on a shoestring budget. I have no-questions access to an entire modern security company. We've got scanners, infrared scopes, topographic imaging. The best and most advanced technology on the market."

None of that was true, and Charlie wasn't even sure how infrared scopes would help her find diamonds, but it sounded good in the heat of the moment. Right now, all that mattered was keeping them talking and staying alive long enough to come up with a better plan. Leon and Sally looked to one another. Sally stood her ground, but Charlie could see Leon starting to slide her way.

"If there's a chance we could still get what we came for—" Leon said.

"She's just trying to save her own hide."

"Of course I am," Charlie said. "And if saving my own hide means we all get what we want, what's the problem? Calling the police won't do me any good: I came in here with a bag over my head, and I assume I'll leave the same way, so there's nothing useful I can tell them."

"She's got a point," Leon said.

Charlie talked fast, not giving Sally a chance to rebut. "You went to so much trouble setting this up. You spent so much time and money. Why walk away empty handed if you don't have to? And then there's me. You're not bad people. I know this. You know I didn't do anything to you, and you've got no good reason to kill me."

She directed that entirely at Leon, watching his face soften. Charlie knew perfectly well that Sally had absolutely no problem with collateral damage, given her stunt with the chair bomb, and Brock was an attack dog on her leash. Leon was the only path to survival now.

"Let me help you get what you deserve," Charlie said. "Forty-eight hours. If I fail, you've still got Sean, and you can do whatever you want to him. If I succeed, we trade Sean for the diamonds. No matter what happens, *you win*. How often do you get a deal like that?"

Even Sally nodded, just a little bit. They shared another glance.

"One other thing," Charlie added. She pointed to the body on the floor. "Let's face it: you're going to have to deal with this. That means covering it up, or it means running, or both. So ask yourself this: Do you want to run with nothing but the shirt on your back, or with diamonds in your pocket?"

Sally folded in on herself. The gun drooped in her hand, giving away her defeat. Charlie's logic was an iron wall; she couldn't batter it down with slogans and ideology. Couldn't shoot it, either, as much as she clearly still wanted to.

"Sal?" Leon asked.

She waved the pistol's barrel at the table.

"Gather up the maps and notes," she said. "You've got two days. We'll give you a throwaway Skype address to contact us with. Don't bother taking it to the cops; they won't be able to find us with it."

"I'm not going to the cops," Charlie said. "My job is keeping Sean Ellis alive. I won't do anything to jeopardize that."

Sally gave her a long, hard look.

"I hope you're right. I really do. Because if I don't have those diamonds in my hand in forty-eight hours, you can go pick him up at the bottom of the Charles River."

They dropped Charlie off with a burlap potato sack over her head and a stack of maps and notepads in her arms. She took the sack off, saw she was on a street corner in a neighborhood she didn't recognize, and called for a ride.

It was past one in the morning by the time the cab dropped her off at her father's house. Too late to do anything but sleep, and her exhausted legs trudged up to the stoop by sheer momentum. With an hourglass dangling over her client's head, sleep felt like a betrayal, but she knew she'd be useless without it. *Six hours*, she thought. *Six hours and a cold shower, and I'll be back in fighting shape.*

Her key rattled in the lock. She opened the door slowly, trying not to wake her father up.

His body was a lump on the living room floor, silhouetted in the skewed light of a fallen lamp.

THIRTY-SIX

Charlie raced to her father's side. The living room looked like a whirlwind had hit it. Or his body had, bounced off every wall and every piece of broken furniture. He lay, limbs skewed and unmoving, in a clutter of shattered wood and glass. She fell to her knees, gently rolled him over, and put her fingers to his throat. A pulse beat under the skin, weak and slow. His head lolled in the fallen lamplight and showed her a face pounded to raw hamburger. One of his eyes was too swollen to open, the other locked in a razor-thin squint.

"Charlie," he croaked.

"Stay still." She already had her phone out, dialing 911. "I'm calling for help. It's going to be okay. You're going to be okay."

"Charlie—"

"Don't try to talk. It's going to be okay."

"Why did you come home?" he breathed.

Her lips tightened. She stared down at him.

"You should have stayed away," he told her. "You made everything worse."

The ambulance came and went, carrying out their delicate cargo on a stretcher, leaving the debris behind. Charlie sat out on the front stoop.

A county sheriff came over to talk. Most of his words washed over her, around her, like numbness had become an invisible shield in the air between them.

"So you don't have any idea who might have wanted to hurt your father?"

"No," she said.

Of course she did. She even knew their names. Grillo and Reyburn. Jimmy Lassiter's debt collectors had mean streaks a mile wide and egos made of spun glass. She'd scared them off her father's land last time, but she'd also humiliated them, the thugs scurrying off more angry than afraid.

They couldn't get at her, so they'd taken out their anger on the next best target. Charlie's father was on his way to the ER, strapped to a stretcher with an oxygen mask over his face, and it was her fault.

"Sometimes," the sheriff was saying, "local feuds tend to . . . escalate. That's something we don't want to see, you understand?"

Grillo's pistol was still sitting in the glove compartment of her father's dead truck. Charlie thought about heading over to Lassiter's bar. Three men, three bullets. She wouldn't say a word before she pulled the trigger. After all, like Saint and Beckett had told her, only amateurs talked first.

"I don't know who did it," she told the sheriff.

Her voice rang as hollow as she felt. There was nothing inside of her now, nothing but a slow and simmering core of molten anger, and it took everything she had to keep it under control.

The sheriff didn't believe her, so he asked her the same question four more times, four more ways. She bounced his words off her shield until he gave up and went away. The last car pulled out and left her sitting alone on her father's porch with nothing but an upset stomach and a broken heart.

She'd gone past the border of being too tired to think. She trudged through the wreckage of the living room and up the hall and fell onto her mattress with her clothes on. She barely remembered to kick off her shoes before sleep took her, roaring up to grab hold and drag her down into a dreamless abyss.

◆　◆　◆

Come sunrise, Charlie ran. A quick sprint up the hill and back again, just far enough to flood her aching body with endorphins and coat her skin in a sheen of cold sweat. She scrubbed it off under the shower's harsh spray, changed into a T-shirt and cargo pants, and laced up her boots. She made two phone calls and headed into town.

Over at the library, Mrs. Frinkle guided Charlie to a study room off the first floor. Just a little nook with a wooden table and a scattering of low chairs, a place for her to lay out the notes and maps she'd taken from the kidnappers. She read Kimberly Hutchens's final epitaph, the grainy black-and-white copy of the police report, for the fifth time. It didn't yield any fresh clues. She only saw the stark facts, just like Leon had: Kimberly had been found dead of hypothermia, buried in a snowbank, wearing nothing but a light windbreaker over her thin blouse and jeans. Not even a pair of gloves. And while everyone agreed she'd fled the heist with a big share of the diamonds, there had been nothing in her pockets but a wallet, twenty bucks in rumpled, small bills, and a knife intended for cutting drywall. She hadn't even carried a gun.

Beckett arrived first, with Dom close on his heels.

"Jake was up all night doing some soul-searching," Beckett told them. "Decided not to call the cops. Hard choice, but I don't blame him."

"So he's just going to pretend Ellis didn't get jacked last night?" Dom asked.

"He's going to pretend we don't know what happened to him, and those ops guarding his front door were never there. It's a lose-lose situation. We file a formal report and the cops find the client dead, the company loses everything. The cops find him alive, Ellis fires us *because* we called the cops, and the company loses everything. Right now, Boston Asset Protection has one chance to survive this mess: we find Ellis ourselves and get him back, safe and sound, without anybody on the outside knowing about it."

"I've got good news and bad news," Charlie said.

She started with the call from Kinzman and the gun against her spine. She ended it with Kinzman's dead body on the floor and the deal that kept her from joining him.

"She *shot* him?" Dom said, clearly trying to lower her voice. "Jesus."

"Leon wasn't happy about it, for what it's worth."

"So Sally's our bomber," Beckett said.

"And a head case," Charlie said. She pointed to her temple. "Brock is worse. Whatever they did to that guy in the loony bin, there's nothing going on upstairs. He does what Sally tells him."

"Meaning Leon's the only one we can negotiate with. You think he'll keep his word if we deliver the goods?"

"I think he knows he's in over his head. If we give him a lifeline, he'll grab it."

"Why are we just hearing about this now?" Beckett asked. "You should have called as soon as they cut you loose. We could have already been moving on this."

Under the table, Charlie's hands squeezed her knees tight.

"I've been at the hospital."

She tripped over her words, fumbled, dropped them all at her feet. She gathered them up and started over again.

"My dad. Jimmy's people, they, uh . . ." Charlie's jaw clenched. "They couldn't get at me, so . . ."

Beckett sat up and pushed his shoulders back. Dom reached over. Her hand rested, firm, on Charlie's shoulder.

"He'll live," Charlie said. "He's just . . . yeah."

Beckett held his silence, unknowable gears turning behind the walls of his eyes.

"I can only imagine how much it's burning you up," Dom told her, "but what I said before stands. You don't want to go after these guys."

"No, I really, really do."

"You know what I mean. Look, Charlie . . . you take out Lassiter's leg breakers, and no one on earth would blame you—I mean, they've got it coming—but Lassiter's going to come around asking questions. You take out Lassiter, and some men from New York are going to come around asking questions. You do *not* want that."

"I had another idea," Charlie told them. "I was thinking, this morning, on my run. Putting it all together, you know?"

"We're listening," Beckett said. He tilted his head, like he was catching a scent in the air.

She spoke slowly, feeling the weight of her words, knowing she couldn't take them back once she'd given them voice.

"Sally and her crew can't go to the police, obviously," Charlie said. "And neither can Sean Ellis. If his connection to the diamond-exchange theft is ever exposed, he's ruined for life."

"Sure," Dom said. "Where are you going with this?"

Charlie's fingers played across the stack of notes and maps. Slow, like a piano player warming up.

"What if we found the diamonds and used them as leverage to get Sean Ellis back safe and sound?"

She hesitated, took a deep breath, and finished the thought.

"And what if," Charlie said, "once we took care of Ellis, we kept the diamonds for ourselves?"

Neither Dom or Beckett replied, not at first. They shared an unreadable glance.

"You want to rob the robbers," Beckett said. Not judging. Just confirming.

"My dad is in a hospital bed right now, and it's my fault. When Jimmy Lassiter's deadline runs out, I don't know what they're going to do for an encore. Cripple him. Maybe kill him. My only way out right now, my father's only way out, is to get the money to pay Lassiter back."

Dom drummed her lacquered nails on the table.

"I've got bills piling up like you wouldn't believe," she said. "My scumbag ex is dragging the divorce out as long as he can, trying to break me. And he's winning. I lose this case, I'll be lucky to see my little girl once a year at Christmas."

She locked eyes with Charlie.

"I'm in. Let's do this."

They both looked to Beckett. His gaze was distant, contemplating, calculating.

"You realize this could get messy," he said. "The kind of messy you have to dig six-foot holes to clean up."

Charlie knew. "I've seen that kind of messy before."

"This isn't a battlefield, and you aren't a soldier anymore. It's not the same thing."

"That's where you're wrong," Charlie said. "As far as I'm concerned, this is *absolutely* a battlefield. Right now, it's the only battle worth fighting."

Beckett leaned back in his chair. His gaze fell upon the table, to the scattering of maps and notebooks. He weighed his verdict in silence.

"Then we've got a lot of work ahead of us," he said. "Let's dig in."

They divvied up the pile of research and plunged in, following Leon Guster's tangled trail. He'd tried to recapture his own history, rebuilding the night of the diamond-exchange heist from memory and padding it out with newspaper clippings and police reports. Grids on graph paper traced each one of the robbers' movements down to the minute.

7:22 a.m., manager gets loose, opens front door for cops. 7:23 a.m., Michael, left of door, opens fire. One cop and manager go down. Second cop retaliates, kills Michael. Sally, standing behind west-facing counter, shoots second officer.

Less than five minutes of chaos given a clean, clinical breakdown, right up until the moment when Professor Kinzman had split up the loot and sent everyone in opposite directions, out into the storm.

That's when the carefully annotated time column became a string of increasingly fevered question marks, jotted in a shaky hand.

He'd traced Sean and Kimberly's doomed route through the snow fifteen different possible ways, using the exchange as a starting point and the recovery site of Kimberly's body—a five-foot snowdrift in a dead-end alley—as the final destination. He'd checked every storefront along the way, though the whole city had been locked up tight that morning due to the incoming blizzard. He'd even, at one point, finagled his way into the junction tunnels under the street in case she'd stashed her share of the diamonds under a manhole cover. Years of work, and nothing to show for it but question marks and *X*s marked in red highlighter showing all the places the diamonds *weren't*. He'd meticulously constructed the exact opposite of a treasure map.

"This is useless," Dom said. Nobody had spoken a word in maybe an hour.

"Her share went *somewhere*," Charlie said. "She left the exchange with the diamonds. They weren't on her body. Something happened to them between point A and point B."

Beckett furrowed his brow at the map before him, tracing highlighter trails with his fingertip. "Two possibilities we need to consider. Number one, Sean's lying. He really did take her share when he ran."

"They're going to kill him," Dom replied. "If that's true, he'd be stupid not to give it up."

"Sure. But never underestimate how money, or the fear of losing it, can make a man do stupid things," he said. "Number two, the diamonds *were* on the body."

"You think someone stole them?" Charlie asked. "An EMT, maybe, or a cop?"

"Wouldn't rule it out. And if they did, that trail's ice cold. We'll never find them now. Time to start thinking about a plan B."

Plan B. There might be a plan B for saving Sean Ellis. There wasn't one for saving her father. Charlie pushed her chair back.

"I need to stretch my legs," she said. "Be right back."

The stacks held a little comfort. That empty nostalgia glow, taking her back to when she was a kid, when the stakes had been so much lower. She knew she couldn't stay. That kind of reminiscing was a poison, a distraction from the mission at hand. On her way to the bathroom, she crossed paths with Mrs. Frinkle.

"I found some more material in the archives for you," her former teacher said, lighting up at the chance to be helpful. "Some newspaper articles, all about the Blizzard of '69, mostly the emergency response and the cleanup timing. Would love to know what you're researching it for . . ."

Her voice trailed off, leaving her bait on the hook. Charlie didn't bite. "Thanks, Mrs. Frinkle. I appreciate that. Every little bit helps."

"Talk about bringing back memories." The elderly woman chuckled. "I thought the snow would never end."

"You were there?"

"Oh yes, I grew up in Boston. Started my teaching career there. Don't tell anyone, but teachers enjoy the occasional snow day too. Of course, *that* was a bit much." Her gaze went distant, thinking back. "The city was so different then. The tumult in the seventies, the development boom in the eighties . . . oh, I'm not complaining; I still love going into town now and again, but it doesn't look anything like my memories. Goodness, when the blizzard hit, they hadn't even finished work on One Boston Place. I lived right by there; I remember the snow clinging to the shell, glistening like crystal on those brand-new windows."

Intel. Every mission Charlie had ever run in uniform had come down to field-intelligence reports. Good intel meant you had a shot at coming home alive. Bad intel left you chasing your tail while the locals got some free target practice. She held up a finger.

"I'll be right back," she said.

She darted into the study room and grabbed the nearest map, spinning it around, hunting for the small print on one corner of the rumpled paper.

"Leon made a mistake," she said. "One very big mistake, and everything he did, everything, was built on one critical error. He didn't see it. But I do. No wonder he never got anywhere."

Beckett eyed her, curious. "What do you see, Little Duck?"

"His maps. He based all of his research, his timeline, Kimberly's trail . . . all of it, he based off these maps."

She rapped her short-cropped fingernail on the copyright print at the corner of the rumpled paper.

"*Modern* maps. He's trying to trace Kimberly's trail, all the way back in 1969, on maps that were printed five years ago. He's looking at the wrong Boston."

THIRTY-SEVEN

Paper maps of Boston showing the streets of 1969 were hard to come by. But with Mrs. Frinkle's help and a couple of library computers, half an hour of research struck gold. Charlie printed out a vintage set of maps in big, bulky blocks and assembled them on the study-room table like puzzle pieces.

She circled the diamond exchange and Kimberly's death site in cherry-red highlighter. Then they huddled around, comparing the vintage map to Leon's, combing the grid one quarter inch at a time.

"Here." Dom jabbed at the printout. "This little side street. Barely bigger than an alley, but it doesn't even exist today."

Charlie leaned closer and squinted. "She could have run through there, yeah."

"Better hope she didn't toss the stash in a trash can, thinking she was going to come back for it later," Beckett said. "She did that, game over."

Charlie drew a highlighter trail, marking Kimberly's possible route through the alley. The hot-yellow line of ink sparked a fresh explosion of possibilities, streets, and hiding places Leon hadn't even glanced at. The vintage map had a key, numbered circles highlighting points of interest. One bubble along the most direct route to Kimberly's final destination caught Charlie's eye.

"McCormack Building?" She pointed to a purple square, one block off Water Street. "That ring a bell with either of you?"

Dom took her phone out. "Not offhand. I don't know that area super well, though. Let me see if it changed names at some point."

It had changed more than names. A quick dive into the building's history told a tale of broken promises and broken investors. The McCormack had been slated as competition for the city's fast-rising skyline, only to run out of money less than half a year into the project. The site had sat abandoned, a skeleton with its steel bones on the verge of rust, until the bank had swooped in and sold it off for pennies on the dollar. Today, the McCormack was Emerald Springs, a midrange condo tower catering to the young-urban-professional crowd.

In February of 1969, construction on the McCormack had already stalled. Only the foundations had been finished. The foundations, the rudiments of a parking garage, and the skeleton of the HVAC system.

"I'm running along the street," Charlie murmured. She traced the line of highlighter ink past the McCormick's purple block. "I left the exchange maybe . . . five minutes ago, tops, judging by the distance. The snow's coming in fast, faster than we anticipated. It's cold as hell, and I'm only wearing a windbreaker. I can barely see five feet in front of my face. And I can hear police sirens."

Dom leaned over the map. "They'd sound like they were coming from everywhere. All around her. She'd have to get off the street and find a place to stash the diamonds so she wouldn't get caught with them."

"And then get some distance," Charlie said. "The cops were bound to catch up with her; she would have known that much. She just didn't imagine hypothermia would catch up with her first. So she ducked into the first empty, open place she saw, dumped the loot, and then kept running."

She drew a highlighter circle to mark her best guess. "Right here, I'm thinking. And considering the new owners used the guts of the unfinished McCormack to build their condo—"

"Good chance the diamonds are still there," Beckett said. "So what are we waiting for?"

They needed more. "Somewhere in the foundations" wasn't good enough; it was still a needle in a haystack. Still, they could narrow their search down with a few key facts. Given the timing, Kimberly would have had less than ten minutes to stash her share. When she'd ducked into the construction site, only the unfinished garage level and the utility rooms had been complete, along with the skeletal shell of the lobby.

"She would have picked a place that was out of sight but easy to get to," Dom said. "Both because she didn't have long to find a hiding spot, and because, as far as *she* knew, she'd be coming back for the diamonds as soon as the heat had simmered down."

Mrs. Frinkle came to the rescue. With her help and another couple of hours on the hunt, they found a guide in the historical wilderness. The clue was buried in an issue of *Modern Architect* from September of 1969, titled "The Tragedy of Grand Designs." The piece offered a detailed breakdown of the McCormack's troubles, complete with lavish sketches of the corporate palace it had been intended to become. The photographs—black-and-white snaps presenting the final, sorry state of the building alongside sketches of the architect's dream—showed them exactly what Kimberly would have seen on her desperate, doomed run.

They were halfway to Water Street, cruising down the boulevard in Beckett's shark car, when Dom looked to the rearview mirror and swore under her breath. Charlie sat in the back seat. The nylon belt tugged on her shoulder as she leaned forward.

"What is it?"

"Don't look back," Dom said. "Malloy's tailing us."

She almost looked back on instinct. As it was, she had to tense up her shoulders to keep her body rigid, staring straight ahead. She shot a glance at the mirror and caught a glimpse of the car behind them, a minivan with a harried-looking soccer mom at the wheel.

"You sure about that?"

"*Behind* the Caravan," Dom said. "He's good. Just not as good as me. Beckett, hang a left up here; let's see what he does."

They slid into the turn lane, and the minivan kept going straight. The car behind, a white Ford with a bug-spattered grille and windows tinted amber, had no choice but to fall in on the shark car's tail. Chunky plastic sunglasses and a watch cap weren't enough of a disguise to keep Charlie from recognizing Malloy's reflection. Dom's former fellow officer and full-time nemesis was stalking them.

"I believe in coincidences," Beckett said, "but only small ones."

"How did he find us?" Charlie asked.

"How'd he 'just happen' to cross paths with you at the police station?" Dom said. "Dirty tricks are the only tricks he's got."

"Better question is why," Beckett said.

Dom shifted in her seat. She crossed her arms and glared at the mirror, sharp enough to slice the glass. "He's a bloodhound. Always has been. Jake may have clamped down on what happened to Sean Ellis last night and told the ops who got jumped to keep their mouths shut, but *something* leaked."

"And if he asked around Sean's condo, and someone remembered seeing us there—" Charlie said.

"Seeing *me*," Dom said. "I doubt Malloy has any idea what he's even looking for; he just knows something is up and I'm in the mix. That's all the incentive he needs to start digging."

"Going to be digging his teeth out of his throat, he keeps this up," Beckett growled. He drummed his fingers on the steering wheel as they waited for the light to change. "But this is a problem we've got to deal with here and now. What's the call? Scrub it until we figure out how he's tracking us?"

Charlie's stomach was as tight as their deadline. They'd been given forty-eight hours to find the diamonds and trade them for their client's life. Over twelve hours were already gone, and Charlie had no doubt that Sally would pull the trigger on her traitorous classmate the second the last grain of sand ran out.

If she hadn't done it already.

"No chance," she said. "No time."

"Seconded." Dom looked to Beckett. "Can you lose this clown?"

His answer was a tight-lipped smile.

The left-turn light flickered green. Beckett eased into the turn, then stomped on the gas and swung the wheel right, swinging across two lanes of traffic and shooting straight through the intersection. Horns blared behind them, tires squealing. Charlie chanced a quick look over her shoulder. She saw Malloy stalled out and helpless, straddling two lanes and blocked by the near collision. His bug-flecked Ford faded into the distance as Beckett torpedoed up the boulevard.

Emerald Springs was a midprice condo with midlevel security. A single uniformed guard sat in a booth beside the entrance to the parking garage, but the movie playing on his tablet PC had his undivided attention. He didn't even glance up as they cruised on by, down a short, steep ramp and into the gallery below the tower. Beckett pulled into the first open spot and killed the engine.

"I need to give my baby a pat down," he said, "try and figure out how Malloy found us."

Charlie was already halfway out of the back seat, with a beige folder filled with printouts from the library tucked tight under her arm. "We'll get started on the hunt," she replied.

"Sure," Dom said. "Still a needle in a haystack, though."

Charlie tugged out the photos they'd copied from the *Modern Architect* article. She held one up and to the side, comparing the black-and-white image of the abandoned, half-finished garage with the real thing, and tried to put herself in Kimberly's shoes. The college student would have been running from the storm, half-frozen, in a mad panic and hearing police sirens closing in from every direction. She imagined her heart pounding as her wet shoes slapped across the fresh concrete, looking for a quick place to stash her share of the loot. Someplace secure but simple, where it could linger for a few days, a couple of weeks, until the heat died down and she could come back for the treasure.

She walked along the half-empty parking rows, under hot white light bars, and drifted like a ghost between stout square pillars decorated with eggshell-white stucco paint.

"Probably a lost cause," Dom said, "but I'm going to see if I can get into the boiler room."

Dead end, Charlie thought. The skeleton of the HVAC system had been built by February of '69, but the whole thing would have been gutted and replaced by now. Maybe two or three times over, the building adapting to changing times and growing needs as the condo flourished. If Kimberly had tossed the diamonds under the boiler or into the ductwork, they would have been found years ago.

She looked back to the photographs. Workmen's tools littered the empty gallery, the yellow parking lines only half–filled in, the shot ending in a span of open space and a pair of skeletal pillars shelled in white-spotted drywall.

"What did you see?" she murmured to the silent cars, the ramp stained with old oil and time. "Show me."

Behind her, Beckett was on his back, halfway under the belly of the Skylark. The sounds of rustling and metallic clanking faded as she slipped into detail mode. The black-and-white photographs, locked in her memory, superimposed themselves onto her vision. She sliced the room into pie wedges and came at them one controlled and calculated step at a time.

Where an SUV now parked, she saw a sawhorse and some dusty bags of concrete mix. In a pair of empty stalls, her gaze lingered over buckets of paint captured in black and white, a brush dangling precariously off one metal lid.

"It's a no-go," Dom was saying, walking past her. "They've got a Selex lock on the utility room door. I'm good, but I'm not that good."

"Son of a—" Beckett said, his voice muffled by the underbelly of his car.

He squirmed out from under the chassis and brandished his discovery. It was a tiny gadget cased in glossy black plastic, about the size of his thumb.

"What am I looking at?" Dom asked him.

"Found it under the wheel well. My guess?" He shoved himself to his feet, glaring daggers at the plastic box. "GPS tracker. That's how he's been tailing us. Probably got one on your daddy's pickup, too, Little Duck. Explains how he 'just happened' to cross your path at the police station."

Charlie didn't answer. She was lost in 1969, following a dead woman's footsteps through a black-and-white world.

"He slipped one under my ride, too, no doubt," Dom said. "And good luck proving he put 'em there. Sneaky bastard. You want to do the honors, or can I?"

Beckett shook his head. "I'd love to take a tire iron to this thing right here and now, but it might be better if he doesn't know we're onto him. Let's keep it in play a little while longer, in case we need to lead him off our trail."

Charlie stood in the heart of the aisle. Part of her mind kept pulling her toward the police report. The discovery of Kimberly's body. What they hadn't found in her pockets, and what they had.

"Tire iron," she breathed. She looked back over her shoulder. "You have one?"

"Sure." Beckett nodded toward his trunk.

Charlie bit her bottom lip. For the first time since they'd set out, she felt something new: a glimmer of hope. A tiny, crackling flame in the pit of her heart, aching to surge and blossom bright.

"Grab it," she said. "I know where Kimberly hid the diamonds."

THIRTY-EIGHT

Dom put her hands on her hips, skepticism warring with hunger behind her eyes.

"Don't keep us in suspense," she said.

Charlie waved the folder in her hand. "Kimberly was a pacifist. We know, both from the police reports and from Leon's write-up, that she didn't carry a gun on the heist. She didn't want anything to do with weapons."

"Sure," Beckett said. He glanced over his shoulder as he reached into the front seat of his car. The trunk popped with a dull clunk.

"But when they found her body," Charlie said, "she had a knife in her pocket."

"Self-defense?" Dom asked. "I've always got a knife on me."

Beckett gave her a sidelong glance. "You've always got a gun on you too."

"At least one. But point taken, I'm not exactly the poster child for peace, love, and hugging trees. So . . . what's a knife got to do with the diamonds?"

Charlie took out the spread of photos from *Modern Architect* and fanned them out like a winning poker hand. She darted across the aisle and rapped her knuckles against a stucco pillar. They rang solid against the stone under the swirling, textured paint.

"Okay, by the time construction stalled out in '69, they were half-way done. Look at these photographs. Here, here, here, bare concrete and rebar. These are load-bearing pillars."

"With you so far," Beckett said.

She sprinted across the gallery and held up the final photograph.

"The ones in the middle? These *aren't*. They're drywall shells. Decorative."

Her knuckles rapped against the stucco with a deep thumping sound.

"Hollow," Charlie said.

"But the knife . . . ," Dom started to ask.

"According to the police report, it was a knife for cutting drywall. It wasn't meant to be a weapon, and she didn't have it on the heist. She took it from *here*. After she cut a hole in one of these pillars, stashed the diamonds, and sealed it up again."

Beckett swung his tire iron with both fists, putting his back and his shoulders into it. The rod smashed against a pillar and powdered the stucco. A cloud of white particles flooded the air as the drywall beneath crumbled. From her guard post at the far end of the parking gallery, Charlie's shoulders tensed at the gun crack sound of impact. Just like they had for the last three he'd cracked open. Dom covered the opposite end, shouting back warnings every time footsteps echoed along the gallery or a car's engine purred to life.

Three pillars, and nothing inside but dust. She felt like a kid on an Easter egg hunt that had turned into a cruel practical joke. The pillars were a mad gamble, her last chance. Last chance to save the client, the company, and their jobs. Last chance to save her father's life. If she was wrong, if she'd wasted an entire day on a wild-goose chase while Sean Ellis's hourglass was running down—

"Think we've got something," Beckett said.

She was at his shoulder in a shot. Dom, too, brandishing her cell phone and flipping on the light app. She strobed a beam into the dusty depths of the cracked pillar. There was something inside, nestled low, a shapeless lump in the dark.

"Do the honors," Beckett told Charlie.

She got down on one knee, shoved her sleeve up, and gritted her teeth as she reached into the darkness. Her fingers stretched out, straining . . . and brushed faded leather. She shoved herself closer against the pillar. The jagged drywall scraped against her shoulder as she made a grab, snatched the prize, and hauled it out into the light.

It was a pouch in golden-brown calfskin, sealed with a black drawstring thread. She tugged it open, her fingers trembling, heart hammering a staccato beat. The pouch was almost weightless. Thick but light, airy, about as fat as a couple of walnuts.

She didn't dare to hope, didn't dare to think or do anything but breathe, as she tipped the pouch over.

A cascade of pinpoint diamonds spilled into the palm of her hand.

It was a waterfall of dreams, catching the overhead lights and blazing like dozens upon dozens of tiny suns. A supernova explosion glimmering in Charlie's open palm. Dom and Beckett leaned in close at her shoulders.

"Sweet Jesus," Dom said. "They're beautiful. How much do you think they're worth?"

"Enough." Charlie barely even breathed now, whispering like the diamonds had swallowed her voice in their white-hot glow. "Enough for all of us."

Enough to save her father. Enough to fix Dom's divorce. Enough to save their jobs and the client's life, if they made all the right moves.

If.

"We need to go." Beckett rested his tire iron against his shoulder like a batter heading to the dugout. "That tracker is still live. Only a matter of time before Malloy traces us here, and I don't want this to be the end of the road. That'll just make him wonder why. Figure we'll drive around, park at a few more random spots, see if we can't confuse him a little."

They rolled out of the parking garage and into a Boston sunset. Traffic thickened in the streets like molasses as the sky shifted to azure blue. While Beckett drove, taking a random rat-maze wander down side roads to throw Malloy off the trail, Charlie and Dom sat side by side in the back seat. Dom had her laptop out; she powered it up and opened Skype, while Charlie read off the throwaway address Sally had given her. The speakers let out a watery electronic *bloop* as they connected.

We have the diamonds, Dom typed.

The response barely took five seconds: Bullshit.

Charlie poured the mound of pinpoint stars into her hand and snapped a photograph. This time, they got nothing but silence for a good ten minutes. She imagined Sally and Leon arguing, debating their next move, while the mammoth Brock Kozlowski sat there and stared with his quietly furious, piggish eyes.

You give us the diamonds, we tell you where to find Ellis. Deal?

"Uh-uh," Charlie said. Dom was a step ahead of her, eyes narrowed to gunport slits as she typed.

Same time or no deal. And we want proof of life before we go one step further.

They sent over a photograph. Sean, still cuffed to his chair, sporting a black eye but otherwise not looking much worse for wear.

"They could have taken that five minutes after I left," Charlie said. "And shot him six minutes after."

You can do better than that, Dom typed.

The kidnappers went silent. Beckett turned at an intersection, the shark car humming along the streets of Boston's Back Bay with no particular destination in mind, as they waited for a reply.

The response came in the form of a video attachment. The camera focused on Sean Ellis, with a man's hand—Leon's, Charlie assumed—holding the front page of today's newspaper next to his face with the date on full display.

"Charlie," Sean said, sounding weak, "this is the proof of life you asked for. It's me, okay? I'm fine. For now, I'm fine. Just . . . do whatever they tell you. Give them what they want, and nobody will get hurt."

She wished she could believe that, but Sally had already tried to murder him once. Leon wanted the money. Sally only wanted blood.

Which meant, at the end of this dance, Sally was going to have to be dealt with. Charlie had been trying not to think about that part too hard. But the closer they got to their final stand, the less she could pretend it wasn't a problem that needed a permanent fix.

"How do you want to play it?" Dom asked her. The kidnappers were waiting.

The ideal solution, the only one that scanned, was to take off with Sean Ellis and the diamonds. They could strong-arm Sally and her gang, ambush them at the meeting point and force them to walk away empty handed, but that still left Sally—and to a lesser extent, Brock, her mad-dog buddy—free and able to come after their client again and again.

"You remember what I said." Beckett caught her gaze in the rear-view mirror. "This could get messy."

Six-foot-deep-holes kind of messy. The fastest, easiest way to get rid of the problem was to get rid of Sally Weinstein. Charlie even had the revolver she'd stolen off Lassiter's leg breakers. An unlicensed gun with someone else's crimes attached to the ballistics.

It wasn't a question of *could* she pull the trigger. Charlie knew she could. She'd done it before. Never in cold blood, but hot and cold didn't feel like too much of a difference from where she was standing. All the same, she didn't want to spend the rest of her life with a murder rap chasing her heels, making her keep one eye over her shoulder while she waited for the hammer to come down. She didn't want to live like Sally Weinstein.

That was it. The solution she'd been looking for, right under her nose.

"Sally," Charlie said. "When we do the handoff, she's going to come armed."

Dom shrugged. "Figure all three of them will. They'd be stupid not to."

"It'd be natural for us to want to make the exchange in a public place. Safer for us. Safer for them too. Nothing suspicious about that."

"Where are you going with this?" Dom asked.

"What if," Charlie said, "a well-timed anonymous call alerted the police to some suspicious activity in the area?"

Dom's lips curled into a mean little smile. "Like three ex-cons, who legally can't carry firearms, walking around in a busy public place with concealed and *extremely* stolen guns."

"Bingo," Charlie said. "All we have to do is stall and keep them occupied until the cops show up. The police swarm in, they grab Sally and her crew—grab 'em red handed with illegal weapons, and that's a felony beef. They go right back to prison, and by the time they get out, Sean Ellis probably won't be our problem anymore. At the very least it buys him a few years of peace and quiet."

"And the diamonds?" Beckett asked.

"We never hand them over. Oh, we'll show them off, just to buy a little time and make sure we have eyes on Sean before the fireworks start, but they stay in our hands. Who's going to say a word to the police? Sally and company will already be facing gun charges; what are they going to say? 'Oh, we were actually here to get those stolen diamonds in exchange for our hostage?' *Last* thing they'll want is a kidnapping rap on top of everything else. And we know the client's going to keep his mouth shut."

"Especially once we take him aside and teach him the facts of life," Dom said. "He keeps his mouth shut, so do we, and nobody ever has to know that he was once a budding jewel thief. Then we hit up Saint's list of friendly under-the-table fences, find one to turn those diamonds into cash money, and it is *payday*. I don't know about you two, but I'm feeling pretty good right now."

Beckett gave a tiny shake of his head. He flicked his turn signal.

"Don't feel too good just yet. Lot can go wrong between here and the finish line."

"Then let's keep running." Charlie nodded to the laptop screen. A cursor flashed in quiet anticipation. "Set up the meet."

Thirty-Nine

After some back and forth, tiny arguments over when and where as both sides jockeyed for a better position, the meet was set. Tomorrow morning, one hour after sunrise. Nothing to do now but try to get a few hours' sleep and brace for the dawn.

Almost nothing to do. Charlie argued with herself over whether or not to go to the hospital and see her father. She argued all the way to the admissions desk, and all the way to the elevator at the end of the sterile beige hallway. She argued on the ride up to the second floor, the cage smelling like someone had spilled an entire bottle of mouthwash on the spotless flecked-tile floor, and right up to the door of his room.

Then she took a deep breath and let herself in.

Two beds, separated by a paper curtain, lay as silent as the twin television sets mounted to opposite corners on steel brackets. The lamps were doused, the only light coming from the soft neon glow of the monitors flanking her father's bed. He was out cold, flat on his back, half his face wrapped in gauze. The half that wasn't wrapped looked like he'd gone ten rounds with a heavyweight boxer. He breathed in and out through cracked, puffy lips. One leg was elevated, wrapped in a cast.

Charlie sat in the chair beside his bed and stared at him. At the ruin of his body, at the slow rise and fall of his chest under the paper-thin sheet. She listened to the steady, faint beep of the monitors and the bustle of nurses in the corridor outside, on the move at all hours of the night.

Grillo and Reyburn couldn't get revenge on her, so they'd settled for the next best thing. He wouldn't be here if it weren't for her. He was right. She'd come home, where nobody wanted her, and only managed to make things worse.

No, she thought.

A slow coil of anger unspooled inside her chest, where it had been wound up all this time. Sleeping, cold and dormant, like a rattlesnake. Now, waking, it shook its tail in warning and glowed white hot.

Sure, some of the blame was on her shoulders. She'd started a fight, and she hadn't finished it. But her fists hadn't done the beating. And Grillo and Reyburn wouldn't have been around in the first place if her father had gotten his demons under control.

Which brought the spotlight of guilt full circle back onto her. Because she hadn't been there when he'd needed her most.

"Charlie," he croaked.

She wasn't sure how long he'd been awake. Lost in the maze of her thoughts, she hadn't noticed his good eye opening up, his head tilting on the pillow.

"Yeah, Dad. I'm here."

He took a deep breath and let it out in a wheezing sigh. "What I said, when you found me—"

"Don't worry about it."

"It wasn't true," he told her. "I'm . . . I'm not good at showing it. But I'm glad you're home. You're a good kid, Charlie."

She pushed herself to her feet. She needed to move, to pace, as if her footsteps could push the cogs of her brain into gear. "No," she said. "I'm not."

She stood at his bedside.

"You were right. When Mom was dying, after she passed, I could have come home. I could have taken compassionate leave. I just . . ."

She lifted her open hands, then let them fall. "I *couldn't*. I bailed. To be honest, fighting a war was easier than dealing with losing her. And that's bad enough, but I bailed on you too. That's the part I can't forgive myself for."

"Everybody," he breathed, "everybody grieves their own way."

"But we're a family. And family is supposed to be there for each other."

She turned away. She looked up to the corner, to the ghosts of their reflections in the dead television screen.

"I found a way to get the money. To take care of your debt to Jimmy Lassiter."

"The . . . Charlie, that's . . . twenty thousand dollars. How? What are you—"

"Don't ask," she said. "You don't want to know."

He didn't have a response to that. The implications of her words seemed to press his battered body down into the mattress. She steeled herself, then turned to look him in the eye.

"But this is the last time."

"Charlie—"

"No. You listen to me." Her voice was tight, strained with the weight of time. "I remember when I was a kid. How the power would sometimes go out, because you 'forgot to pay the bill.' Or Mom scraping together change from the sofa cushions to get me something to eat. I didn't understand until I was older."

"I got it under control."

"No, Dad. You didn't. You stopped for a week here, a week there, maybe a month. Usually when Mom threatened to walk out. Somewhere along the line, I think you figured out she was never going to. Somewhere along the line, so did I. She was strong enough to watch you kill yourself. I wasn't. So I left."

Charlie jabbed her finger at him, talking faster now, the words she'd kept bottled up for years bursting free.

"But the things you've done, the choices you made, that is *not* on me. I won't take the blame for your failures. So this is what's going to happen. I'm going to bail you out with Jimmy Lassiter. And you are going to get your shit together. I'll help. I'll help you find a therapist, drive you to meetings, whatever kind of support you need to kick the habit for good. But you are *going* to get your shit together."

She leaned over the bedside rail and dropped her voice to a deadly whisper.

"Because if this ever happens again, I won't be there to bail you out. I love you, Dad. I love you so damn much. But I won't be there. I'm not going to put my life and my freedom on the line to pay for your mistakes. Not after tomorrow, anyway."

"Charlie . . . what are you going to do?"

"Told you," she said, "you don't want to know. It's just going to be handled, okay? And when it's done, I'll take you home, and we can try to get back to something like normal. Like a family again. If you want that."

He lifted one shaky arm. His hand closed over hers, feather light. He shut his good eye.

"I want that," he said.

She leaned in and kissed him on the cheek. Then she let him sleep.

Charlie caught a few hours' fleeting sleep in her father's empty house. She washed away the night under the spray of an icy-cold shower and had her boots laced up by dawn. No time for a morning run. That was fine. Her heart was already pumping, strong and clear and ready to fight.

They'd agreed on a public site for the trade: the Boston Public Market, on the ground floor of Haymarket Station. It was an indoor marketplace, a roomy supermarket with over forty different vendors, sporting clean, spacious aisles under open ductwork and hooded lights. The Public Market showcased the best of New England; everything was locally sourced, from fresh produce to prime cuts of meat and artisanal cheeses to flower stalls and wine displays.

Most importantly, it opened at eight in the morning and always drew a crowd. A crowd meant cover for the handoff, and a threat the police wouldn't ignore once the anonymous call went out. A warning about three potential shooters running loose on the market floor would bring a heavy response in a heartbeat.

For the kidnappers' part, Charlie assumed they liked the number of exits. The market connected to the street, to the Haymarket mass transit station, and to a parking garage, offering plenty of ways to slip away with the loot.

Not that they were ever going to touch those diamonds. Charlie almost felt bad, until she remembered who they were dealing with. Then all she felt was a sense of wary resolve. They were about to go up against three armed killers with nothing to lose; no matter how good the trap, that meant Sally and her crew still held the balance of power. And she was just crazy enough to start shooting if she felt cornered, no matter who was in the path of her bullets. From this moment forward, every move they made, every split-second decision, had to be the exact right one.

At five minutes to eight, Charlie stood in a growing and eager crowd outside the market's doors. Dom and Beckett hung on opposite edges of the fray, eyes sharp behind their dark sunglasses, checking the street in both directions. They'd laid out their roles ahead of time, and everyone knew their job.

Charlie held the diamonds. That and the .38 revolver she'd stolen from Grillo, snug under a battered olive jacket. Ideally she wouldn't have to draw it, but if things went south, she didn't want to be caught without a weapon. As grateful as she was for Beckett's gift of the ASP

Key Defender, after her last experience, she wasn't about to unleash military-grade pepper spray in the heart of a crowded market. It sat snug in her hip pocket, still fitted with the harmless blue training insert.

Dom was her backup. She slid close as the doors unlocked and the crowd surged inside, staying tight at Charlie's shoulder. Armed and ready for a fight if the situation came down to it, but it was Charlie's job to make sure that didn't happen. If they were going to save Sean Ellis's life, they'd have to do so with words and wits, not bullets. Beckett hung back and kept a low profile. His job was overwatch, spotting the kidnappers from a distance if he could and making the crucial phone call to the police.

Perfect plan. The only problem with perfect plans, as Charlie knew from experience, was how fast they fell apart under the cold, hard light of reality.

They passed a baker's stall, the air warm and laden with the buttery, mouthwatering scent of fresh-baked bread. Charlie's stomach rumbled as she eyed a tray of flaky croissants. Then she locked onto a glimmer of movement up the aisle. Fifty feet ahead, passing a produce display, Sally and Leon were on the move and closing in fast.

"Left, behind the florist's stall," Dom muttered. Charlie flicked her glance to one side. Farther back, Sean Ellis's face looked pale and strained as he stood motionless behind a spray of bright wildflowers. Brock just loomed behind him, squinting, his double chin tucked low like his broad shoulders were trying to swallow his head. One brick-size hand clamped down on Sean's shoulder. The other was out of sight behind his back.

In the middle of the aisle, Sally and Leon came to a dead stop. Charlie and Dom squared off five feet away, like gunfighters preparing for a showdown.

"Where're our diamonds?" Leon asked.

"Where's our client?" Charlie replied, as if she hadn't already seen him.

Sally nodded back over her shoulder in Sean and Brock's general direction. "There. Safe. Hand them over, we let him go."

Beckett, Charlie knew, had already ducked into a quiet stall to make his phone call. He'd bought a prepaid burner last night just for the job, and once he was done, he'd toss it in the nearest trash can.

The timer was ticking. Her job was to keep the kidnappers talking and keep Sean alive until the police showed up. If she could get Sean closer and away from Brock so they could defend him in a standoff, all the better. There were no guaranteed victories, not now; all Charlie could do was what Dom had taught her. Minimize the risk.

One wrong move, one stray bullet, and her entire plan would go down in flames.

FORTY

The market bustled around them. Shoppers, tourists, innocent people going about their daily lives, unaware of the vipers in their midst.

"Bring him over," Charlie said, locking eyes with Sean from across the crowded market stalls.

"You see him," Leon said. "He's alive and he's safe. What else do you want?"

"She doesn't have the diamonds," Sally said. Her lips twitched at the corners. "This is a setup, I *told* you this was a setup—"

Sally was getting agitated, and that was the last thing they wanted. The last time she'd gotten agitated, she'd put three bullets into her former professor without blinking. Charlie held up one open hand.

"I'll show you. I'm going to reach into my pocket, all right? Is that okay?"

Sally's nose twitched in time with her lips, like her face was trying to crawl off her skull. She looked to Leon. His hand edged closer to his own unseasonably heavy jacket and to the bulge just underneath.

"Yeah," he said. "Slow, all right?"

"Okay."

Slow was fine with Charlie. She was playing for time.

The leather pouch slithered from her pocket, nestling in the palm of her hand. She tugged the drawstring like the wires of a bomb. The leather folds slowly parted, overhead lights snaking inside to dazzle off the mound of precious stones within. Leon's eyes went wide as saucers, and his fingers twitched at his sides. Sally swallowed hard, torn between the promise of treasure and her hunger for revenge.

"Give us Sean," Charlie said, "and it's all yours."

She tugged the drawstring once, hard, and sealed the gate to paradise.

Leon held out his hand. "Diamonds first."

"Uh-uh," Dom said. "You, we can *maybe* trust. Your psycho pal here, not so much. Wouldn't put it past her to pump a couple of bullets into our client on her way out the door."

"She won't." Leon looked sidelong at Sally. "You *won't*."

"Wouldn't dream of it," Sally said. If there were an award for least convincing lie, she would have taken home the trophy.

But she wouldn't be taking the diamonds. Charlie kept a tight hold on the pouch and chanced a quick glance at the milling crowd behind the kidnappers, hoping to see uniforms closing in. *Can't be long now,* she told herself. *Just keep them talking, keep them distracted.*

"What guarantee do we have that this little feud of yours is over?" she demanded. "For all we know, you'll be back to take another shot at our client next week."

Leon spoke fast, before Sally could get a word out.

"Because she'll be with me. Somewhere far, far away from here, in a country with no extradition agreement. Trust me, the farther away from here we can get, the happier we'll be."

Sally gave him a "Speak for yourself" glare, but she held her silence. Something caught Charlie's eye: a flicker of movement behind Sally and Leon's shoulders, off to the right.

Beckett was low, the big man crouched behind a glass butcher's display case. His eyes were wide, and as they locked with Charlie's, he made a frantic slashing motion across his throat.

Something was wrong. Beckett could see something they couldn't farther up the aisle, something bad enough that he wanted to abort their best and only shot at getting their client back alive. Charlie's mind raced. No time to figure it out. She had to trust him and break this off, fast. That meant getting some distance.

"Okay," she said, taking a step back. "You have a deal. Wait right here; I'll get the rest of the diamonds."

"The *rest*?" Leon said, boggling at her.

Charlie eased back. She tried not to be obvious as her gaze flicked over Leon's shoulder, heartbeat quick. Crowds, shoppers, tourists, nothing out of the ordinary. She forced a disappointed smile.

"You didn't know? Damn, Dom, we could have walked away with half the loot, and they never would have guessed."

There was an edge in Dom's voice and a sharp glint in her wary eyes. She'd seen Beckett's warning too. "Oh well. Fair's fair. Go grab the rest of the loot. I'll stay here with our new friends until you get back."

She knew what Dom was doing. Sacrificing herself to whatever trouble was coming their way and covering Charlie's retreat. Noble, but Charlie didn't leave people behind. She stepped along the aisle, hands at her sides, nice and easy, while she scrambled to come up with a plan.

She looked back and saw what Beckett had seen. A swarm of uniforms cutting through the crowd like sharks on a blood trail, just like they wanted.

And Malloy, smirking like a cat who'd just found his way into a birdcage, was with them.

No time to figure out how or why, no time for questions. Charlie had ten seconds, tops, before the cops made their move, and they'd all be leaving in handcuffs. She was acutely aware of two things—the illegal, unlicensed .38 in her waistband, and the pouch of stolen diamonds in her fist—and she'd have just enough time to deal with one of them.

"We stashed it over here," she said to Leon and Sally, stepping just out of sight behind a produce display.

Charlie made her choice. She tugged the drawstring, yanked the pouch open, and crouched down. She hiked up one leg of her cargo pants as the lead officer's shout cracked over the market air like a bull-whip: *"Everybody! On the ground! Show me your hands!"*

The pinpoint diamonds poured into her boot in a shimmering cascade. She wriggled her foot around, working them down under her heel and toes, her bottom lip trapped between her teeth as she prayed for just a few more seconds.

She tossed the empty pouch behind a head of lettuce and stood up. She was reaching under her jacket, hoping to ditch the gun, when rough hands clamped down on her arms and wrenched them behind her back. She hit the floor on her knees, hard enough to send jolts of electric pain up her legs. Metal bracelets clicked tight around her wrists.

Riley Glass had been a lot friendlier when Charlie had been on the right side of the law. The fox-faced detective was still cordial, but his smile didn't reach his eyes the way it had when they'd first met. His sharp nose twitched when she talked, like he could smell the lies on her from the other side of the stainless steel interview table. They'd been talking for two hours, no company in the cramped brick room but a single dangling light and a one-way mirror, and she'd repeated her story backward and forward.

Not the true story, but close enough.

They'd searched her on the spot, of course. Plucked the .38 from her waistband, the gun she didn't have a permit to carry. She was still in her street clothes, though, and her left boot was smuggling a small fortune in diamonds. They had settled, mostly, nestling under her foot. Every step felt like walking on thumbtacks.

She'd walk on thumbtacks for miles if that was the only way out of here.

"You have to understand how this looks from our perspective," Riley told her.

"I'd very much like to," she replied. "Tell me."

"Sean Ellis, your company's client, is missing. The last place he was seen was at his condominium. That same night, a reliable informant places you, Mr. Beckett, and Ms. Da Costa at the scene—"

"Considering he's our client, that seems odd to you?"

Riley held up a finger. "The morning after, despite him, yes, being your client, and despite having paid for around-the-clock security, no one from Boston Asset Protection escorted him to his workplace. Your boss can't explain the discrepancy, nor can he explain why no one filed a missing persons report on the spot."

Sean Ellis hadn't been seen, all right. Probing, asking as many questions as she could without showing her hand, Charlie had quickly learned the score: She, Beckett, and Dom had been arrested. The kidnappers had walked away free in the commotion and took their hostage with them. Sean had been standing right there, right under the cops' noses, but thanks to Malloy's interference they'd developed a case of tunnel vision.

"Our informant," Riley continued, "alleges that you and your friends have been sniffing around Mr. Ellis's personal life and finances. Right around the same time that Mr. Ellis received a number of phone calls attempting to extort him."

"Maybe I'm not too bright," Charlie said. "That's a whole lot of dots and *allegedly*s. Mind connecting them for me?"

Riley rested his palms flat on the brushed-steel table. The metal caught the gleam from the overhead light and cast a white halo around his outstretched fingertips.

"One interpretation is that this was an inside job. That you and your friends kidnapped Mr. Ellis, and your boss is either in on the scam or covering it up."

"Can I offer an alternative interpretation of the facts?" she asked.

"Please do."

"Your 'reliable informant' is a scumbag. Malloy was a dirty cop, he *is* a lying asshole, and shame on you for giving him one ounce of credence."

Direct hit. Riley glanced away, just for a second, down and to the left. A flicker of regret crossed his face before it turned back to a mask of professional stone.

"Some people," he said, with an emphasis on *some*, "think he was framed."

"Some people think the earth is flat. I don't think you're one of them, though."

That side-glance again. He took a deep breath.

"Malloy has . . . some friends on the force. High up the food chain."

"Higher than you," Charlie said.

"When you were a soldier," he asked, "you ever have to follow really dumb orders from people who never left their cushy offices?"

"Every damn day."

He turned his palms to the dangling light and spread them wide. Enough said.

"Another theory," Charlie said, "is that we're trying to recover our client quietly and safely, and that involving the police could get him killed."

"Is that what happened?"

"Given it's not just my butt on the line here, I hope you can understand that I'd rather call it a theory."

"We've got another problem," he said. "Tell me about the gun."

Charlie's stomach clenched. She'd had all the right reasons to carry that .38, but now it was standing between her and the door. If he charged her for it, she'd be processed. If she was processed, they'd take her civilian clothes. If they did that, they'd find the fistful of pinpoint diamonds currently gouging into the sole of her left foot.

If they did that, she was going to prison, and her father was a dead man. She rubbed her big toe against the needle-hard stones. The pain kept her sharp.

"If you call Spencer PD," she said, "they'll tell you my father was attacked in his home."

"Okay," Riley said. Noncommittal but willing to hear her out.

"I'm sure they've got an idea about who's responsible. Truth is my dad's up to his eyeballs in gambling debts. Overdue. That wasn't the first time his bookie's leg breakers showed up at the house. The first time, I was home."

"So the gun is . . ."

"Not mine. I took it from one of them when he threatened me with it. I've been carrying it ever since, because . . ." She trailed off and threw her hands up. Barely acting, as the frustration welled in the pit of her stomach. "I don't know what to do, okay? I'm trying to protect my family."

"You can't just steal a man's gun and—" He shook his head. "Why didn't you call the police? Or tell them what happened to your father?"

She locked eyes with him. "My father's bookie is a man named Jimmy Lassiter. Irish mob, connected up to his eyeballs. Look, it's just you and me in here; let's be straight. You *know* what happens if you rat out a guy like that. I admit it, I screwed up, but I was doing the only thing that made sense at the time. What would you have done, if you were in my shoes?"

He held her gaze for a long count to ten. Then he pushed his chair back.

"I need to make a few phone calls. Sit tight."

He left her there alone. She sat at the table, clenched and unclenched her hands, and waited for him to decide her fate.

FORTY-ONE

"All I'm saying is," Dom told Beckett, "thank God I had an LTC for my piece and left my pigsticker at home. They tossed me in a room and badgered me until my lawyer showed up, but when it was all over, they couldn't actually find any crimes to accuse me of."

"Your boy Malloy jumped the gun. Got himself hot and bothered, chasing us all over town, and called in his pals on the force before he even knew what he was looking for."

"He's not my boy."

They were camped in the private dining room at DiMaggio's, two people sharing a table for ten. Dom had her laptop open, the black brick showing a silent chat screen. A cursor strobed on an empty line, slow, like a lighthouse beacon keeping an eye out for wayward ships.

"Don't know which outcome I'm more worried about," Dom said. "Either the cops found the diamonds on Charlie when they brought her in, in which case we're screwed, or she ditched them somewhere, in which case we're screwed."

"Not the only possibilities."

"Well, yeah, maybe the diamonds have sprouted wings and are flying toward us as I speak, but it's not too likely." She stared at the blank line, the strobing cursor. Her hands clenched and unclenched. "How can you be so goddamn calm right now?"

Beckett turned his gaze to the ceiling. "A Zen monk was walking through the wilderness when he came upon a—"

Dom smacked the table with the flat of her palm. "*No.* Do not fortune cookie me right now. Do not."

Beckett clasped his hands behind his head and leaned back in his chair. "Then I shall wait in contented silence."

"It's like Juárez all over again," Dom grumbled.

"Thank God," Charlie said from the doorway. She shut the rattling wooden partition behind her and swept into the room. "I wasn't sure if I was the only one who made it out."

Dom held up one hand. "Two hours ago. Beckett was right after me. You got the *special* treatment. I shouldn't have to ask this—"

"You don't have to. Answer's no. I didn't tell them a damn thing. I got the sense they were a little embarrassed."

"Sure," Beckett said. "Rousted us on the say-so of their old buddy Malloy, he pushed them into top gear, and they came up empty handed. Fishing's no fun if you don't bring dinner home. And *if* we had anything to do with Ellis's disappearance—which we don't, but tell Malloy that—they just showed us every card they're holding."

Charlie circled the table. She pulled out the chair next to Dom, dropped into it like she had a pile of bricks on her shoulders, and gave a tired nod to the laptop screen.

"What do we know?"

"Not a word since we tried to make contact," Beckett said. "They're making us wait."

"Might not have gotten back to safe harbor yet," Dom said.

"No. They're making us wait."

It made sense to Charlie. Either the kidnappers were running scared, realizing how close they'd come to getting caught red handed and going back to prison for a long count, or they were just trying to figure out why the cops had shown up in the first place.

Or they'd already killed Sean Ellis and dumped his body and were on their way to Mexico or Canada. There were too many *ors*, too many possibilities to juggle, and nothing to do for it but sit and stare at the empty screen.

"How are Jake and Sofia doing?" Charlie asked.

"Not good," Beckett told her.

Dom leaned back in her chair and clasped her hands behind her head.

"Jake's been asked to come down to the station and have a chat with the nice detectives," she said. "He's got a lot of explaining to do, mostly centered around why he never reported the client missing."

"I assume Malloy's super fired now," Charlie said.

Dom's lips pursed, sour. "No. Because Jake's only defense right now is playing dumb. Malloy hasn't done anything illegal, and *technically* the bastard hasn't done anything wrong; he just saw some suspicious activity and reported it to the authorities, like any solid citizen would. Jake fires him, it looks crazy suspicious."

"So where's this put us?"

"Puts us right here, waiting." Beckett's eyes narrowed at the screen, like he could make it light up with sheer force of will. "But if we don't get Ellis back pronto, safe and in one piece, we're all going up against the wall."

Twelve minutes later, the laptop chimed.

What the hell was that?

Dom commandeered the keyboard. Some Good Samaritan saw a gun and called the cops. Wasn't us, we weren't carrying. You get out ok?

You worried about our well-being?

No, Dom typed. We're worried about our client. We held on to the diamonds, and we still want to trade. Same terms.

She glanced sidelong at Charlie. "Please tell me you have the diamonds."

Charlie pushed her chair back and unlaced her boot.

Sally thinks you set us up.

That meant it was Leon on the keyboard. Good. Out of the three, Sally was blood hungry, and nobody knew what was going on behind Brock's mad, squinty eyes. Leon wanted the loot, making him the voice of reason. For now.

We were ten seconds from handing over the diamonds, Dom typed. And WE walked out in handcuffs, not you. Pretty lousy setup.

All the same, we're picking the handoff site. We pick the terms. You do what we want, when we want, or Ellis gets what's coming to him.

Dom looked to Charlie and Beckett. Beckett nodded.

"Play along," he said. "We'll improvise."

When and where, Dom typed.

The cursor strobed on an empty line. Radio silence.

"They have no idea what they're doing," Dom murmured.

"Makes 'em twice as dangerous," Beckett said. "Rats don't bite if they can run. Back one into a corner, and you're bound to lose a little blood if you're not careful."

Charlie upended her boot and poured a waterfall of baby stars onto the table. They danced across the wood, glittering under the overhead lights, and she carefully scooped the diamonds into a mound.

"You were *walking* on those?" Dom asked.

By way of response, Charlie lifted her left foot and gave Dom a look at the tiny red flecks staining the heel of her sock.

"Hardcore." Dom looked back to the screen. "Respect."

On the other side, the kidnappers settled whatever argument they'd been wrestling with. They came back with their demands.

There's an out-of-business wrecking yard about seventeen miles south of Boston and five minutes off Interstate 93. Fitzsimmons & Sons. Bring the diamonds. We've got visibility for miles in every direction: if we even see a hint of a police car, Ellis dies, and we'll be long gone before they close in. If we see a gun, same deal. You bring nothing but the diamonds.

Charlie played back her visit to the kidnappers' home turf. They'd put a burlap sack over her head and driven her around in circles until she was dizzy, but a wrecker's yard would fit the details she remembered: industrial smells, a metal-walled shack, out-of-date motor oil, a calendar on the wall.

"It's their hideout," she said. "That's where they took me."

Beckett held her in his steady gaze. "Pop quiz, Little Duck: What does that tell you?"

"That they're not planning on sticking around. A safe house isn't a safe house once people know where it is. They're leaving."

When? Dom typed.

The answer came back in seconds: Sunset's in less than two hours. Be here.

"They're leaving *tonight*," Charlie said. "They might be reluctant to meet us in public again, after what happened last time, but . . ."

"But they might not be looking to play fair," Dom said. "If they're spooked, they might be thinking about killing us, killing the client, and taking the diamonds. Be a long time before anybody found our bodies out there. Plenty long enough for the three of them to get away clean. What's the play, gang? Do we risk it?"

Charlie searched for another option. All she found was a hallway lined with locked doors and ending in a brick wall.

"I think we have to," she said.

"So we go in, but we go in smart," Beckett said. "We assume it's an ambush. And we plan accordingly."

He pulled back the sleeve of his dress shirt and checked his watch.

"Just enough time. Let's head over to HQ first. Get geared up proper for this gig."

◆ ◆ ◆

Fitzsimmons and Sons was a boondocks fortress. Twelve-foot walls ringed the circular compound like a coliseum made of scrap-metal sheeting. Beyond the open gates lay a maze of rust, with wrecked cars stacked in piles three bodies high. Beckett's shark car took a long, slow lap around the outer ring, kicking up loose dirt. Beckett and Charlie sat up in front. The back seat was empty. The sun was simmering down now, orange and cold and stretching out the shadows, turning every silhouette into a gunslinger.

The light was west. Beckett parked on the east side. He nuzzled the dusty Skylark up against the compound wall, killing the engine in a patch of shadow. The gates weren't far.

"Last chance to back out," he said.

"Do I look like I'm backing out?"

He studied her. Then he shook his head.

"We tried playing it your way," he told her. "The way that wouldn't leave any bodies behind. It was a good plan. Would have worked, if Malloy hadn't poked his nose in."

"Sure."

"We are past the point of not leaving bodies behind. If it was just Leon we were dealing with, we could still end this with everybody shaking hands and walking away with various degrees of satisfaction. Sally and her attack dog, though . . . some people, you just can't reason with. So if you've got any hopes of resolving this situation with words alone, you need to leave 'em in the car. Those are the kind of hopes that get the wrong people killed."

Charlie leaned forward. She stared up at the compound wall.

"Sally can make her choices," she said. "I already made mine."

She clicked her seat belt, swung open the door, and got out of the sedan.

They walked side by side through the open scrapyard gates, eyes open and hunting for any signs of life. A cold wind rustled through the maze of dead metal and sent a couple of crows winging from their perches. One wheeled around, ruffled, flapping its way to the top of a powerless crane.

Sean Ellis's cell phone lay abandoned in the middle of a boulevard of junk. The screen lit up. It rumbled, dancing on loose dirt. Beckett scooped it up and set it on speaker mode.

"There were three of you at Haymarket Station," Leon said.

"And three of us got arrested," Charlie replied. "Me and my friend here, we got out. She didn't. She had some outstanding warrants to take care of."

"How do I know that?" Leon said.

Beckett stared at the phone, cupped in the bowl of his hand. "What difference does it make?"

He shared a glance with Charlie. They both knew the answer. It made a difference if Leon and his gang wanted to bury every last loose end.

"It doesn't," Leon lied. His voice was tight now. "Here's how this is going to work. Put the diamonds down, right where you're standing. Then you're going to get back in your car, get back on the interstate, and drive south. Keep the phone. In ten minutes, we'll give you directions where you can find Sean."

"Uh-uh." Beckett's brow furrowed. "Ten minutes away, ten minutes back, that gives you twenty to snatch the diamonds and run. That's not the deal."

"The deal is what we say it is. You aren't calling the shots here."

While they argued back and forth, Charlie scanned the battleground. The piled wrecks formed walls, barricades, avenues of fire. She couldn't see Leon anywhere, but he had to have eyes on them—which meant he probably had at least one gun pointed their way. They needed to tilt the odds before he lost his patience and used it.

"Give us one of your people," Charlie said.

"What?" Leon said.

"As a show of good faith," she said. "I don't think you'll run without Sally. I don't think Sally will run without Brock. Give us one, to ride along with us, so we know you'll hold up your end. We'll let them go once we've got our client back."

The gesture was futile. She already knew he wasn't going to hold up his end. The only question was how and when the double-cross hammer would come slamming down. The more she could keep him off balance, the better the chances he'd make a mistake.

Something was happening. She heard muffled sounds over the speaker, like he'd cupped his hand over the phone and was halfway into a heated argument with someone on the other end.

Beckett leaned close, pitching his voice low. "Right about now, Sally's arguing he ought to just kill us both."

"Leon's the smart one," Charlie murmured back. "He won't pull a trigger until he knows we've got the diamonds on us."

She hoped those same smarts had kept Sean Ellis alive for now, holding on to him just in case. Maybe they could use that.

Leon came back on the line. "Maybe we can work something out," he told them, in a tone that said *not a chance*. "First, let's see the diamonds."

"First, let's see our client," Charlie replied. "Send him out here."

Leon's response was a subsonic *crack* as a rifle slug plowed into the dirt three feet in front of them. The bullet spat dust and broken stone across Charlie's boots. She heard the bolt action working over the phone as he chambered a fresh round.

"Figure you both know where the diamonds are," Leon said, "so I only need one of you alive. Next time I pull this trigger, only one of you will *be* alive. Diamonds. Show me. *Now.*"

Beckett curled his hand under the phone, tilting it Charlie's way. He flashed three fingers. She nodded.

Three. Two. One. Beckett broke left, Charlie broke right, and two more shots rang out with peals of bitter thunder.

FORTY-TWO

They'd stopped at headquarters on the way to the scrapyard so that Dom could pick up her gear. It rode in the trunk, in a black nylon duffel bag. So did she. She curled, fetal in the stifling darkness, and listened to the doors slam as Beckett and Charlie got out. Then she counted to fifty.

By then, all eyes would be on her partners. She popped the inside trunk release and squinted in the dusky light. Her back groaned as she clambered out of the trunk, sneakers touching down on asphalt, and shouldered her bag. It rattled, heavy. Beckett had picked his parking spot just for her: close to the gates but out of sight, and right next to a pyramid of burned-out cars that stretched almost to the top of the compound wall. She scampered up the pile, light on her feet, her leather-gloved hands careful on the jagged, rusty edges. She found a perch on the wall. She lay flat on her belly and unzipped the duffel.

Less than a minute later, Dom was staring down the scope of her storm-gray Remington 700. She caressed the rifle like a lover's body, holding it steady while she went on the hunt.

Spotting Beckett and Charlie was easy. She saw them talking on the phone. Too far away to hear their voices, but she got the gist with tone and body language. Leon and his buddies wanted them to drop the loot and walk. Meant they'd probably already killed Ellis and scattered his body parts across a lonely junkyard acre, which would suck, but at least they still had the diamonds.

"C'mon, you little bitch," Dom murmured as she swung her scope across the rust barrens. "I know you're watching them from somewhere. Not too close, not too far. Give me a clue."

Her request was delivered in the form of a bullet. She watched the round plow into the dirt near Charlie's feet. The woman barely flinched, and Dom felt a surge of admiration as she tracked the echoing sound.

Across the scrapyard, up on the far end of the compound wall, a second scope glinted in the dying sunlight. Just for a second. A second was all she needed. She had him now, spotting Leon lying prone with his hunting rifle on a tripod. He was working the bolt action, lining up a fresh shot. She swiveled her sights, back to Beckett, looking for a sign.

He flashed three fingers.

Negotiations had broken down. She zeroed back in on Leon. He was aiming, finger on the trigger, and she knew she didn't have time for a perfect shot.

The Remington bucked against her shoulder, half a second before he opened fire. Her bullet went wide and sparked off the wall six inches to Leon's left. He jerked in shock, his rifle swinging off balance just as the muzzle flashed white, wasting his shot.

Dom broke into a feral grin as she cradled her rifle and rolled. She came up on one knee, pushing up and sprinting along the wall, hunting for a new perch before he could drop a bead on her. Under her breath she whispered a prayer to the Goddess of Superior Firepower.

Beckett heard the gunshots as he ran, barreling behind a tower of scrap and getting out of Leon's line of sight. On the far side of the boulevard that ran down the junkyard's heart, he watched Charlie dive to the dirt, roll, and come up dusty but not bleeding. She gave him a quick thumbs-up and darted out of sight. Good girl.

He hoped Dom had taken out Leon with her first shot, but he never put much credence in hope. The big man kept his head down and his eyes up, hunting for shooters from above. The scrapyard crane was empty, no sign of movement inside the operator's cab, but that left twenty more obvious hiding places and probably another twenty he hadn't noticed yet. That was all right. He could adapt to the battlefield.

Beckett always found a strange center of calm when the bullets started to fly. He stood square in the eye of the storm, his heartbeat steady, his breath falling into a yoga rhythm: four seconds in, four seconds out, slow and easy. He moved with purpose, fast but not rushing. The job wasn't complicated. Step one, search and destroy. Step two, rendezvous with Dom and Charlie, make sure they were all right. Step three, secure the client, or whatever was left of him.

He gave Sean Ellis fifty-fifty odds of living through this. Wasn't something he needed to think about right now, much less worry about, until the fight was over. He was alive or he wasn't. Schrödinger's client.

He rounded a corner . . . and ducked, fast, as a chrome bumper whistled through the air and crashed into a wall of junked cars. Metal slammed against metal, showering flakes of rust. He fell back, catching his balance, as Brock came for him.

Brock gripped the bumper like a caveman's club, swinging it high over his head and roaring as he charged. Beckett closed the distance, driving two jackhammer punches into the madman's stomach. The bumper fell, clattering to the dust, and Brock's fists slammed down onto Beckett's shoulders.

Brock had earned the nickname Brick for a reason in his college-football days, and age hadn't stolen the fury burning in his eyes. Beckett dropped to one knee under the onslaught, stunned for the space of a breath, and Brock locked one fat arm around his throat. He hauled, twisting Beckett around, making his spine ache as he bent him backward and cut off his air.

Beckett threw an elbow back, then another, hammering Brock's ribs. He just squeezed harder. Gray spots flooded Beckett's vision, and he scrambled to keep his footing as Brock dragged him backward. He spun around, feet twisting out from under him. Five feet away, a pile of cars stood in half collapse, buckled by weight and time. A chunk of a doorframe jutted out at chest height like a jagged spear sheathed in grime.

Brock grunted as he hauled Beckett toward the spear, closing ground fast. The last of Beckett's air ran out, and the darkness roared up to claim him.

Charlie loped between the junk piles, making her way toward the crane at the heart of the labyrinth. It stood silent now, but she knew the machine's rumble from when they'd first brought her here, blinded with a burlap sack over her head. She'd heard the sound just before they'd brought her into their hideout.

If Sean Ellis was still alive, that's where she'd find him. And with the handoff gone sour and the bullets flying, Sally wouldn't hold back any longer. Ellis would live or die depending on who got to him first. Charlie dug into the pocket of her cargo pants and gripped the ASP Key Defender like a medieval flail, bracing the metal spike in her clenched fist.

Another pair of rifle shots cracked across the cold and dusky sky. Neither was aimed at her. Somewhere, far to her left and right, Dom and Leon were dueling at long range.

She ducked as she rounded a corner, the treads of the crane in sight, and off to the left, the low-slung and dirty walls of the yardmaster's shack. The front door hung open, pale electric light burning inside.

All of Charlie's instincts and training came back in full force, as if she'd never left her tour of duty. She checked every corner, measured the approach, slicing her field of vision into chunks of data like the pieces of a poisoned pie. There was no such thing as safe harbor, out in the field, only measured risk and reward. She took a longer approach to the shack, one that kept her body in cover, weighing her safety against the client's life and deciding she could spare four extra seconds.

Only four, though. And as she eased across the threshold of the shack, Charlie froze dead in her tracks.

"Not one step," Sally told her. She brandished a slim steel box, weighing it like it was heavy in her hand, finger poised over a toggle switch.

Sean Ellis sat in a chair in the middle of the shack, hands bound with duct tape. A leash of piano wire looped around his throat, running to an eyelet in the wall behind him, then up, disappearing into a pencil-size hole. Two more leashes lassoed his upper arms, and another pair pulled taut around his knees. He sat frozen, trembling, a fly trapped in a metallic spiderweb.

"Please," Ellis breathed, "don't let her kill me."

"Not planning on it." Charlie sidestepped, slow, eyes on the older woman and steering clear of the wires.

Sally held up the box. "I mean it. I push this switch, we all die. I'll do it. You know I'll do it."

Half of Charlie's career had been spent learning about bombs. The other half had been learning about bombers. How they thought, how they worked, the difference between the kind of bomber who strapped on a suicide vest and the kind who planned to live and fight another day. She looked Sally hard in the eyes and took her measure.

"No," Charlie said, "you won't."

Sally waved the box like it was a crucifix, warding off a vampire. "I'll do it! I'll kill us all!"

Charlie took a deep breath. She was gambling her life and Sean's, putting it all on a single roll of the dice.

She stepped forward. Sally fell a foot back, but she didn't hit the switch.

"You don't want to die," Charlie said. "You want to kill Sean, you want it as bad as anything you've ever wanted, but not *that* bad. No. At the end of the day, you'd give up both Sean and the diamonds if it means you live to see another sunrise. And that's exactly what you're going to do, right here and now."

As she came closer, and as Sally's hand twitched, she got a good look at the detonator box. Charlie nodded to herself as the last details clicked into place.

"I don't have anything to live for," Sally snapped.

"I don't think that's true, but honestly, it doesn't matter if you do or not. The drive to survive is baked into the human condition. We're hardwired for it. You need a certain pathology to blow yourself up along with the man you hate. You aren't that kind of woman."

"You don't know a damn thing about me."

"Sure I do," Charlie said.

She stepped another foot closer. Sally's shoulders thumped against the shack wall. She was cornered, nowhere left to run.

"You were up on the wall, arguing with Leon," Charlie said. "You ran back here as soon as the shooting started, same as I did. I figure you were planning to finish Sean off, from a safe distance, when I interrupted you."

"Last chance. Stay back."

"Go ahead, flip the switch," Charlie told her. "I dare you. I double-dog dare you. Do it. Flip the switch."

Sean twisted his head as far as he dared, his face glistening under a sheen of sweat. "*Charlie,*" he croaked.

"It's fine," she told him. "See, that detonator was probably stolen from the same construction yard where Saint got the explosives. It's an Energex Technology D-model, pretty common gear, same kind the

Army Corps of Engineers uses sometimes. You see that little hole in the bottom of the box?"

Sean stared at the bottom of the box. Sally did too.

"That's where the electrical line is inserted," Charlie said, "at the end of a very, very long spool of det cord. In other words . . . it's not a remote control. It doesn't work if you don't plug it in."

Sally wavered on her feet, suddenly uncertain, lost. Then her nerve shattered with a scream of raw frustration, and she darted under the piano wire and lunged for Charlie's throat.

FORTY-THREE

Charlie brought up her hands, squared her stance, and braced for a fight as Sally howled toward her. Sally feinted left, her free hand snapping out a punch that only hit air; then she hurled the detonator. The corner of the heavy steel box cracked against Charlie's temple, splitting her skin and spattering the dirty floorboards with blood. She went down under Sally's weight, and they both hit the floor, rolling in a clinch.

A trickle of hot blood ran into Charlie's left eye. Sally's fist cracked across the right, leaving her fighting blind for a few spare heartbeats. She grabbed one of Sally's wrists, trying to wrench her arm back, and fished out the ASP with the other hand. She fumbled, keys rattling, and Sally snatched it out of her grip.

Sally screamed again, incoherent, her face a twisted mask of rage as she turned the metal spike and shoved down on the trigger. Spray hissed from the nozzle, blasting Charlie square in the face. She twisted, going fetal and pressing her palms over her eyes, trying to escape the spray.

"That's what you *get* . . ." Sally was half crowing, half babbling, pushing herself up to her knees and pressing the button until the ASP ran dry. "That's what you fucking *get* . . ."

She didn't even see it coming. Charlie's rabbit-jab punch pulped her nose, shattering cartilage and dropping her to the floor, out cold and bleeding. Charlie shoved herself up and plucked the ASP from her limp hand.

"Blue cap," she panted, tapping the metal spike's tip. "Training insert. Nothing but water. Actually . . . feels kinda nice, all things considered."

She turned her attention to Sean, trapped in his web of piano wire leashes. She reached for one, and his eyes bulged.

"Don't! One of them is attached to a bomb!"

Her hand froze. "One of them?"

"She said she was going to give me the same chance . . . the same chance those miners in Kentucky had, when the Rockhouse mine exploded. If I pull the right wire, it'll come loose, and I'll be able to get myself out. If I pull the wrong one, the whole place goes up."

Charlie frowned. Her fingers idly brushed a fresh trickle of blood from her water-misted face. Her scalp burned like a hornet sting, but she shoved the pain into a little box in the back of her mind marked *distractions*. She studied the wires, how they snaked along eyelets, vanishing into crudely drilled holes all along the shack walls.

Every bomber had a profile. Every bomb had a signature.

"Yeah, no," Charlie said. "She's lying."

He got a glimmer of hope in his eyes. "There's no bomb?"

"I didn't say that."

She prowled past Sally's unconscious body, edging to the walls. Her fingertips brushed old rust-caked steel.

"There's absolutely zero chance Sally would have given you a way to survive. She was just messing with you."

"They're . . . *all* attached to the bomb?"

Maybe. Maybe not. Charlie fell silent, studying the wires.

Every bomb was a puzzle. A battle of wits between her and its maker. She might have taken Sally down, but their real duel was just beginning.

A second duel was going down out in the scrapyard, mostly silent, punctuated by the occasional rippling echo of rifle fire. Dom ducked low as a shot tore into a wall of cars to her left, blasting out a drooping side-view mirror and sending silvered shards scattering across the dusty ground.

She sat with her back to a wreck and chanced a slow lean, open hand straining for a triangle-shaped shard of mirror. She snatched it up and yanked it back into cover like a fish on a line. Then she held it out at arm's length and turned it from side to side, scanning the battleground in its tarnished reflection.

There. Forty yards away, Leon hid in the shadows of the compound wall. Huddling behind a girder, he jerked from side to side like a marionette on drunken strings. Popping out of cover in one direction, then the other, as he hunted for any sign of his opponent.

"Sloppy," Dom muttered under her breath as she scooted to the opposite end of the wrecked car. "*Definitely* Negative Bullet Karma."

The sun was almost out, dead and down and painting the sky in streaks of cold violet. Dom judged the direction of the last fading rays, weighed the broken mirror in her hand, and gave it a throw. It glittered as it spun, reflecting, but she didn't see it. She was already bringing up her rifle, bracing it on a rusted-out hood and dropping a bead on Leon. The glimmer drew him like a magpie, and his barrel swung to track it.

She pulled the trigger. A quarter second later, on the other end of her scope, Leon crumpled in a puff of red mist.

Charlie darted outside the shack, following the crudely drilled holes. Sean's piano wire bonds slipped outside, strung through hammered eyelets, wrapping around the back of the building. She traced them to a twisted metal knot where all the strands wound together in a crude clump, fixed to the shack wall with a single jutting spike.

No bomb.

Which didn't mean there wasn't one. She grabbed hold of the spike with both hands and braced one boot against the shack wall.

"Sean," she called out, "you're going to feel a pull on the wires. It's me. Do *not* get out of that chair, okay?"

She wriggled the spike until it started to slide, then gave it a heave. It came loose with a grating squeal. She untwisted the strands of wire mechanically, her hands in motion while her mind was working the angles. There *was* a bomb. Sally still had explosives left over from the stash they'd bought from Saint, and there was no chance she would have left Sean alive. Charlie built a profile, working fast.

Sally was technically capable, just barely. Her wannabe-supervillain routine with the wires was a scare tactic; she hated Sean enough to torture him, but she wasn't clever enough to actually rig the contraption like she'd said she had. Back when she'd planted the first bomb in Sean's office, she'd rigged up a pressure switch with all the finesse of a first-year mechanical engineering student: solid, functional, but not fancy.

Charlie darted back inside. Sean was flexing his sore arms and wriggling out of the wire leashes. She snapped her fingers at him.

"Stay put. Don't move. Don't breathe more than you have to."

She took a knee and checked the obvious culprit, but the seat of Sean's chair was barely a quarter inch thick, and the underbelly was bare. All the same, she didn't dare move him, not until she figured out what Sally had been planning. With every breath she took, Charlie felt the hourglass running out.

There was one other piece to Sally's profile. She knew how to rig a pressure switch. She also knew how to rig a timer.

Brock Kozlowski's arm was a noose made of meat and muscle, slung tight around Beckett's throat. Beckett's air was gone, his vision flooding with spots of gray, then red, as he fought to stay conscious. The grunting hulk was dragging him toward the junk pile, toward the jutting spear of a twisted doorframe. Beckett's feet slid out from under him and stole his balance as his heels kicked up dust. He threw punch after punch, his knuckles glancing off Brock's chest. Brock didn't even seem to notice.

Panic swelled in his chest along with his bursting lungs. The roar of blood in his ears took on the world-swallowing echo of mortar fire. As he struggled on the edge of passing out, the familiar sound brought him back to another time, another place.

"Beckett. Stay with me. You hear me? Stay awake."

He tried to speak and coughed up a gout of blood for his trouble. A woman's hands, sheathed in tactical gloves, held his shoulders tight as another mortar round shook the earth.

"You're going into shock," she told him. "Your body is trying to tell you that you're dying. Your body is a dirty fucking liar, and you're going to prove it, right now, by walking out of here with me."

"There's too many of 'em," he managed to croak. "They've got every exit covered—"

"Remember what I taught you," she said. "Rule number one: Amateurs die because amateurs panic. A professional stays cool, and a professional finds a way."

He wasn't going to die here.

As Brock hauled him toward the killing spear, Beckett spent his last fleeting seconds of thought on a physics problem. He couldn't get his feet under him at this angle. He couldn't muster the force to hurt Brock, no room to throw a solid punch, and the giant didn't seem to register pain. That was his mistake; he'd been wasting his energy on a losing battle when he needed to change the terms of engagement.

He grabbed onto Brock's belt with both hands. Then he dug deep for one last burst of strength and bucked his hips, heaving his legs off the ground. As his feet rose up, pointing to the overcast sky, his center of balance shifted with them. Brock lost his grip and stumbled. He went down, crumpling to one knee. Beckett sprang backward, landing on his feet in a crouch, and took a deep gulp of air as his lungs screamed in relief.

He had time for only one breath. Brock was already lumbering to his feet with his brow furrowed in confusion and rage. Still crouched low, Beckett's fists fired like pistons, and he used the giant's left kneecap for a punching bag. Something snapped, a wet, crackling sound. Brock grunted and reeled a step backward. Beckett rose, pivoted on one foot, and lashed out with a brutal kick. A rib broke under his heel, and Brock fell, arms flailing as he lost his balance.

His shoulders hit the wall of debris. The rusted spear of metal punched through the back of his neck and ruptured his throat. Brock dangled there, eyes wide, and a raspy, clicking sound echoed from his punctured neck. The twisted steel drooled rivulets of syrupy red. The man wasn't dead, but he was dying, and Beckett didn't waste a word or another glance on him. Rule number two: only amateurs talked. He headed deeper into the scrapyard, hunting for his partners.

At least with the chair bomb, Charlie had known exactly how much time she had. Searching the shack, stepping around Sally's unconscious body, she was flying blind. There might be an hour left on the clock, or seconds. Sean was frozen in his chair, watching her, wearing a sheen of sweat on his pale, puffy face.

The stunt with the wires was a cruel joke. They weren't connected to anything but a railroad spike out behind the shack, and Sean could have squirmed himself loose anytime he wanted. Why?

You wanted to make sure he'd stay put for a while, she thought, putting herself in Sally's shoes. *Long enough to get some distance between you when the bomb went off. But that meant he'd have a chance to get away. No. You hate him too much for that.*

She knelt next to Sean's chair again and pressed her fingertips to the warped, dirt-stained floorboards. Wood creaked as she pushed down, feeling a little give. The screwheads at the end of one board caught her eye.

They were new. The wood was filthy, but the screws were brand new and clean.

"It's *under* you," she told Sean. "It's the same kind of bomb she rigged in your office, same kind of pressure switch, but she mounted it under the floorboards. You eventually would have gotten those wires off, thought you were home free, then blown yourself to hell the second you tried to leave."

He held on to the seat like he was trapped on a roller coaster. "What do we do?"

"You stay put. How much do you weigh?"

"A hundred and . . . forty, maybe?"

Charlie arched an eyebrow at him.

"A hundred and sixty," he said.

On her way out the door, she almost bumped into Dom on the threshold.

"C'mon," Charlie said, "I need a hand. Have you seen Beckett? Is he okay?"

Dom followed her into the yard. "No, but I'm sure he's fine. Leon's not a problem anymore. What are we doing?"

"Looking for something compact and heavy. Remember the opening of *Indiana Jones*, where Indy switches the gold idol with a sack of sand? We've got to do that with Sean Ellis. We want about a hundred and sixty pounds of junk. Heavier is fine, if we can manage it."

Dom jerked her thumb toward the open door of the shack. "You had at least a hundred and ten on the floor back there."

"Sally's not dead; she's just out cold."

"My point stands."

Charlie had already thought about that. Leaving the bomber in her own trap felt like poetic justice. It also felt like murder. She wouldn't have shed any tears if she'd killed Sally when they'd been grappling, earlier, and a guilty part of her wished she had. It would have made things a lot easier, cleaning up that homicidal loose end. There was still a thin line in her mind between a righteous battle and a cold-blooded kill, and she didn't want to cross it if she didn't have to.

She knew, by the end of this job, she still might.

FORTY-FOUR

Dom and Charlie worked fast, wrenching open hoods and rummaging in the guts of dead cars for whatever they could pry loose. A couple of carburetor blocks and a broken chunk of axle formed a slowly growing mound next to Sean's chair, piled up on a shredded tire. Beckett rounded the bend of a junk pile, his suit rumpled and torn at one shoulder but his skin intact.

"Grab anything you can lift," Charlie said. "We need a hundred and sixty pounds, and we need it fast. Just bring it close to the door and set it down; I'll carry it in from there."

Beckett poked his head into the shack, then looked over his shoulder at Charlie and Dom. "You've got at least a hundred and ten right there on the floor."

"See," Dom said, "that's what I told her."

"Why aren't we bringing the stuff all the way in?" he asked.

Charlie found the mother lode: a loose, cracked engine block under the hood of an old four-cylinder Honda. Her back strained as she tried to haul the block up, barely budging it.

"Because," she said, leaning against the wreck to catch her breath, "Sally's a two-trick pony when it comes to bombs. She likes pressure switches, and she likes backup timers. No idea how much more time we've got, and I'm not letting either of you risk being inside when that clock hits zero."

Beckett walked up alongside her. He shook his head and gave the cracked block an experimental tug.

"Not a choice you get to make, Little Duck. Hmm. Feels like about two hundred, right here. Dom, c'mere, the three of us should be able to lug it inside."

They wrangled the block together, easing through the doorway, and wedged it next to Sean's chair. Charlie took a step back. She studied the floorboards and the position of the debris. Without being able to see the bomb, and the exact position of the pressure switch, all their effort still came down to an educated guess.

"That's all you can do," she told Beckett and Dom. "The rest of the job is on me. Clear out, and get some distance just in case. I'll be right behind you."

"What about *me*?" Sean said.

She fought the urge to slap him. Instead, she got into his personal space, easing up against his hip. "You're next. Stand up and move over to your left, nice and slow. I'm taking your place."

"Why? I thought that's what all this junk was for."

"Theoretically," Charlie said. "Theoretically the weight distribution is perfect, and theoretically the pressure switch won't budge. Only problem is those are very real explosives under the floor, and they don't care about my theories. Scoot over."

As they traded places, he looked at Charlie as if he were seeing her for the first time. His eyes went as doe soft as his voice.

"Hey," he said, "thank you. I mean that. For every—"

Charlie pointed to the door. "We are not having a moment here. *Out.*"

She gave him five seconds to get clear. Then she shot a look at Sally, still passed out on the floor with a puddle of dried blood under her nose. The plan was simple: step away from the chair, and *if* she'd spread the weight out right and *if* the bomb didn't go off under her feet, she'd scoop Sally up in a dead lift and haul her out. Charlie took a deep breath, bracing herself, and—

Something under her feet let out a shrill electronic bleep.

A second later, a second bleep.

Time lurched into slow motion, her thoughts outracing the world.

It was probably a fail-safe, designed to scare Sean Ellis into moving. It would force him to jump out of his chair and set the bomb off if he hadn't done it already.

Or it was a fail-safe Sally had built for herself, to warn her if she was in the blast range when the backup timer ran out. In a split second, Charlie had to decide: hope there was enough time left to drag the unconscious woman clear, or save herself. She made her choice on instinct and launched herself toward the door of the shack. Her running shoe hit the threshold on the third bleep. On the fourth, she was five feet away.

On the fifth, the shack exploded.

A fist of superheated air slammed into her back and knocked her sprawling to the dirt. The sound of the blast echoed in her eardrums, ringing and reverberating, a chorus of twisted metal and flame. Tongues of fire licked at the darkened sky from the ruptured roof, spitting gouts of black smoke. Charlie lay flat, dazed, tasting ashes on her tongue and listening to the blood drumbeat of her pulse.

Firm hands pulled her up. They gave her a shoulder to lean on as she stumbled, walking away from the scene of the crime. Her eyes refused to focus, washing out the world in shifting blurs. "You're okay," somebody said, sounding a million miles away. Or maybe it was a question. She wasn't sure what the answer was. Later, when her senses returned one by one and left her with a splitting headache and a brain full of bad memories, she still wouldn't be.

But they had the client, alive and intact.

And they had the diamonds.

◆ ◆ ◆

They reconvened the next morning. Charlie carried the night's worries with her.

"We need to do something about the bodies. Sooner or later, they're going to get found, and we had to have left fingerprints all over the scene—"

"It's taken care of," Beckett told her.

"How? What did you do last night?"

"Little Duck." Beckett took off his sunglasses and looked her in the eye. "It is *taken care of*. C'mon, let's get to work."

It was time to deal with Sean Ellis. The word *blackmail* was never spoken.

That would have been unprofessional, after all, and Boston Asset Protection believed in discreet, confidential, and polite service. Charlie met with Jake and Sofia. She told them what they needed to know—maybe half the story, a little less—and then they had a sit-down with the client. By the end, everybody understood the score. Sean had never been abducted; he had gotten stir crazy and gone off on a short vacation without telling anyone, and that was the story he'd bring to the cops. Also, he would have nothing but glowing things to say about his favorite security firm. If he could manage that, Charlie and company could manage to forget that he was a former jewel thief who'd started his corporate career with blood money.

Everybody would keep smiling, with their lips squeezed tightly shut, and everybody got to come out a winner.

"They're not all like this," Jake told Charlie, in the hall outside his office.

"What, you mean, bombs, gunfights, kidnappings—"

He shook his head, giving her a tired smile, and his greased-back hair glistened under the overheads.

"Believe it or not, most of these assignments are pretty boring. We started you off with a tough one. Still . . . you did okay. We're glad to have you on board, Charlie."

"Glad to be here," she told him. She meant it. Some people might have walked away, after a ride like that one. Some would have taken off running. For the first time since coming back stateside, though, Charlie knew she was right where she needed to be.

For now, at least, this felt like home.

Jake cast a glance up the empty hallway. "So the loot these chuckleheads were all fighting over . . . nobody ever found it, huh?"

"No, sir. It was lost in the Blizzard of '69. No idea where those diamonds all ended up."

He met her eyes. His smile grew, just by a hair.

"Well," he said, "if anyone did find the loot and manage to turn it into cash, I'm sure they were smart about it. For instance, they would have sat on the money. No big purchases, nothing flashy that could draw the attention of the police. They wouldn't put it in the bank, either; banks report to the IRS. I imagine they'd just sock it away somewhere secure for a rainy day."

"That sounds like excellent advice, sir, and I imagine that if anyone did find the diamonds, they'd take that to heart."

Jake's smile became a lopsided grin, flashing a wedge of pearly teeth as Sofia shouted his name. He jerked his thumb over his shoulder at the office door.

"Sounds like she just read my expense report. Excuse me, I gotta go get yelled at a little."

Charlie's phone buzzed. She glanced down at the screen. Shooting range, it read, five minutes.

On the other side of the building, Malloy passed Charlie without saying a word. He didn't even make eye contact. She didn't either. She just moved to let him by, then turned on the ball of her foot and followed him. He walked into the company firing range, and she trailed in his wake.

Beckett and Dom were already inside, waiting for him. Charlie shut the door and flipped the lock.

Malloy turned, slow, as they closed in on him. He was a lone gazelle in the middle of a pride of lions. He still dug deep and managed a defiant sneer, focusing like a laser on Dom. "You ain't gonna do shit," he told her.

"If you mean I'm not going to give you the curb stomping you so righteously deserve," she said, "you are correct. But that doesn't mean it's off the table for later."

"This little feud you've got going with Dom," Beckett said, "it's over. As of now. You can either hand in your resignation, or you can learn to act like a professional. Those are the only two choices we're offering today."

Malloy spread his hands. "What are you going to do about it, big guy? I know the three of you are dirty. I blew my shot at proving it *this* time, but nobody stays lucky forever."

Beckett loomed over him. He leaned in and eclipsed the overhead lights like a cold and angry moon. "This company is more than a business. It's a family. My family. And we only come home at the end of the day, safe and sound, if we can trust each other. Keep breaking that trust, bad things are going to happen."

Malloy's wall of insolence sprouted cracks. He wavered on his feet, holding his ground but obviously aching to back away.

"Such as?" he said.

"Such as," Dom said, "one day, shit's going to go bad out in the field, and you're going to need backup in the worst way. And you might just find out that in your darkest hour, after you've burned every bridge you ever crossed . . . *nobody* is coming to save you."

"Think it over," Beckett told him.

As the next day faded into night, Charlie got a call from Saint. He was more than cooperative, once Charlie reminded him how he'd sold her out to Kinzman and his gang. He pointed the way to a pawnshop in Mattapan. No name above the door, just *Pawn* and three balls etched in dirty yellow neon.

Inside, the woman behind the wire cage had a smoker's cough and an eagle's eyes. She looked from Charlie to Beckett to Dom and back again and snuffed out her cigarette.

"Saint seems to think you're good people to know," she said. "Which means jack squat, coming from him, but at least it tells me you're not Johnny Law. So how about you flip that 'closed' sign around and show me what you've got?"

The fence's name was Carmen—she didn't offer a last name, and nobody asked—and five minutes later she was studying a scatter of diamonds on a bed of black velvet. Her left eye bulged, magnified behind the circular lens of a jeweler's loupe.

"Damn," was all she said after that. Time dangled like a sword as she silently moved from stone to stone, sorting them into tiny piles, an order Charlie couldn't begin to decipher. Carmen's chipped fingernail tapped one pile, then another. Her lips moved as she did the math under her breath.

"You understand," she finally said, "this isn't the kind of business where you get the official going rate. It's a buyer's market, and the reality of our little situation here—"

"Is that you're going to offer us pennies on the dollar and tell us to like it," Dom replied.

"If you want to be crass about it, sure." Carmen plucked the loupe from her eye and squinted, reaching for a bottle of Visine. "But to be fair, I'm taking all the liability here. It's going to take me two, maybe three years to get these off my hands, spreading 'em out through different buyers, and every transaction is a risk. You three get to take the money and run."

"How much money are we talking about?" Beckett asked.

She took one last look at the piled stones. Her hands wavered in front of her, palms flat, like she was piling cash on an invisible scale.

"Let's call it ninety thousand," she said. "You get a third of that right here and now. That's all I keep in the shop. Come back for the rest tomorrow night. Before anybody says one more word, this isn't an invitation to haggle: you can take the ninety, or you can take your rocks and walk. You won't get a better offer in Boston; I can promise you that."

Charlie's heart pounded. Thirty thousand dollars, free and clear, for each of them. Twenty would pay off her father's debt. The rest was a down payment on a car, a place to live, a new start. Beckett looked at her, then to Dom, taking a silent poll. He turned back to Carmen.

"It's a deal," he said.

FORTY-FIVE

Charlie strode into Deano's, right past the bar, and over to Jimmy Lassiter's booth in the back. Grillo and Reyburn pushed away from their stools and followed her like a pair of sharks who smelled blood in the water. She didn't even look at them. She dropped the brown paper sack in her hands onto the table, right next to Jimmy's half-eaten porterhouse. The bag thumped hard enough to make his steak knife jangle on the plate.

The bookie squinted at her, then the bag. He unrolled it and peeked inside.

"Remind me," he said, his Irish brogue light on his tongue, "is it Christmas or my birthday?"

"It's everything my father owes you," Charlie said. "Tear up his marker and forget his name."

He rolled the paper bag shut again. Then he picked up his napkin and dabbed a spot of grease from the corner of his mouth. When he looked back at Charlie, he had a new appreciation in his eyes.

"Don't know how you got the money, lass, but there's better ways to spend it than on bailing out your old man. Take yourself out on the town. Get yourself a manicure and a new dress, you know, one of those designer numbers with the frills and sequins and shite. Your dad, he's just going to break your heart again one way or another. Men like him always do. Remember what I told you, about the frog and the scorpion?"

"My money, my choice," she told him. "Take it. One other thing."

He sawed into his steak. "I'm all ears, my dear."

"If my father ever contacts you, you don't take his bets. Ever. You and him are done. Talk to him again, for any reason, and there will be consequences."

He looked up from his plate. He didn't say a word, searching for something in her eyes.

"It's not a threat," she told him. "Just a fact."

Whatever he was looking for, he found it. He nodded.

"Reckon you believe that," he said. He tugged the paper bag a little closer to his side of the table. "And this concludes our business. Do drive safe."

Life fell into a rhythm. Charlie spent a little of her cash on the first payment for a used car. Sturdy, cheap, nothing outside her pay grade. Jake put her onto a new assignment, working security for a local talk show host who had worked a little too hard at riling up his audience. The worst threat she'd faced so far was someone pelting his front door with rotten eggs. The gig was almost blissfully boring.

Her father came home from the hospital. She'd been apartment hunting, and she was ready to move out, but not until he was 100 percent better. She helped him as he hobbled around, moving from a cane to walking on his own feet, and went out on grocery runs while he rested up at home.

The job kept her away from the house for a couple of days when the client managed to drop a racist slur on a live microphone and suddenly needed twenty-four-hour security. "I don't think it was an accident,"

Sofia told her. "He just likes the attention. Remember what I always say about our clients—"

"They create their own worst problems," Charlie said.

When she finally got back home, a familiar black Mercedes was pulling out of the driveway.

She scrambled with her keys and raced through the front door. Her father was fine. Sitting in his armchair, slumped, red eyed and drunk next to a pyramid of empty beer cans, but unhurt. This time.

"How much?" she asked him.

"It's not your problem—"

"How much?"

"Just . . . just a couple of grand," he said. "It's fine, Charlie. I just wanted a taste, you know? I wanted to end on an upswing. I can still get ahead—I just have to place the right bets, you'll see—"

She didn't even hear him, after that. She walked into her room and threw her clothes into a duffel. She scooped up the brown paper bag from the closet floor, laced her boots, and headed out again.

"Don't leave," her father said as she put her hand on the doorknob.

She took a slow, deep breath.

"I meant what I said, when you were in the hospital," she told him. "You're sick. You know you're sick. You always knew, even when I was a kid and you were gambling away the grocery money. Now, I'll do what I can to help you get better. I'll drive you to meetings, all that twelve-step stuff or whatever kind of program you want to get into. I'll be there for you, all the way. But you have to try. It's your responsibility, not mine. And I'm done watching you kill yourself, Dad. I'm *done*. If and when you're ready to get your shit together, you can call me."

She opened the front door.

"And now I have to make a liar out of myself," she told him, "because I said I wouldn't bail you out again. But this is the last time."

The next morning, the bartender at Deano's got a call from a blocked phone number. He toted the house phone out from behind the bar, ferrying it over to Jimmy's table.

"For you," he said.

Jimmy frowned at the phone. His regulars all contacted him on his own line. He put it to his ear.

"Yeah?"

"We had a deal," Charlie said.

"The deal," Jimmy said, "was that you'd pay what your father owed me. Anything else was just you dictatin' terms. I never agreed to a thing. You forgot my little fairy tale. We all act according to our natures. Your father's a scorpion. And so am I, I reckon."

"Oh, I didn't forget," Charlie said. "That's why I'm watching you from across the street with a pair of binoculars. I had to make sure you were sitting down in your favorite booth before I called you. Tell one of your boys to crouch down and look under your seat."

From her perch in the alley across the street, lenses fixed on the bar's plate glass window, Charlie watched Grillo get down on all fours. The thug was the size of a thumbnail from here, but she could still see how the blood drained into his feet and turned his sweaty face sheet white.

"Remind me," Charlie said, "what happens at the end of that story? Oh, right. The scorpion did something self-destructive and thoughtless. Then he drowned."

Jimmy's voice trembled around the edges. "You listen to me—"

"No. You listen to me. I broke in last night and installed a pressure trigger inside your seat cushion. You stand up, that block of C-4 *goes* up, and you'll be taking bets in hell. Now that I've got your undivided attention, this is just a taste of the consequences I warned you about. I could have put a bomb in your car's engine, under your pillow where you rest your head at night, *anywhere*. Or I could have just not made this courtesy call and let nature take its course. You're only alive right now because I chose to *let* you live."

"Stupid choice," Jimmy said.

"More like mercy. There's no tricks here. It's a simple pressure switch, no funny wiring or backup fuses or anything sneaky. You probably know somebody who can come out and disarm it, or if worse comes to worst you can call 911. Now here's what you're going to do: You're going to forget my father's debt. You're going to forget about my father entirely, and about me."

Charlie held the phone tight to her ear. Her binoculars zoomed in on Jimmy's face, tight enough that it felt like they were standing eye to eye.

"Because if you don't," she said, "I will kill you. That's a promise. Oh, and once you take care of that present I left for you, you'd better think hard. Is that the *only* bomb I planted, do you think? Maybe there's more than one. Maybe they're hidden all over your little world, and I can end you anytime I want, with the push of a button. Or maybe they'll go off if I go missing for some reason, and I *don't* push the button once every twelve hours or so. You just don't know, do you? You're a bookie, Jimmy; you calculate odds for a living, so I don't need to tell you the smart-money play here: stay away from me and my family, and you get to keep breathing. It's a sure thing."

"You just made a very bad mistake," Jimmy breathed.

"I guess that's the problem these days," Charlie said. "Everybody's a goddamn scorpion."

She hung up on him.

Something else Jimmy had told her, the first time they'd met, had stayed with her. "Never fight another man's war for him," he had said. Thinking back on it, Charlie supposed she'd spent her entire life fighting other people's wars, for love or for money. As much as she'd denied it at the time, Saint was right about her. Charlie was a mercenary. Tomorrow was another mission, another battlefield, and she didn't know how to live any other way.

She was comfortable with that.

ACKNOWLEDGMENTS

While I'm mainly known as a dark fantasy writer, crime novels and thrillers were my first love as a budding reader. I was enraptured by the styles of Elmore Leonard, Lawrence Block, Richard Stark, and others, an influence that still shines through in my more occult-themed stories. When Thomas & Mercer gave me a shot at working in the same wheelhouse as those giants who inspired me, I jumped at the chance. *The Loot* was the result. Thank you so much for taking this journey with me.

No novel is the work of a single person. I'd like to thank Jessica Tribble and Carissa Bluestone at Thomas & Mercer, Clarence Angelo for his help with developmental editing, Riam and Leslie for their work on copyedits and proofreading, Morgan Blake for their assistance with Boston navigation, and the great folks at Battlefield Vegas for their firearms advice (and the range time). Last but not least, thanks to my ordnance buddy who requested not to be named (for reasons), who both checked my work and advised me on certain items that should probably be swapped with fictional counterparts (also for reasons). All of these people did an amazing job; all successes are theirs, any remaining errors are mine.

If you'd like release notifications when my books come out, I have a newsletter over at http://www.craigschaeferbooks.com/mailing-list/. If you'd like to reach out, you can find me on Facebook at http://facebook.com/CraigSchaeferBooks, on Twitter at @craig_schaefer, or just drop me an email at craig@craigschaeferbooks.com.

About the Author

Photo © 2014 Karen Forsythe

Craig Schaefer writes about witches, outlaws, and outsiders. Whether he's weaving tales of an occult-shrouded New York in *Ghosts of Gotham* or the gritty streets of Boston in the Charlie McCabe thriller series, his protagonists are damaged survivors searching for answers, redemption, or maybe just that one big score. To learn more about the author and his work, visit www.craigschaeferbooks.com.